RESNICK ON
THE LOOSE

RESNICK ON
THE LOOSE

MIKE RESNICK

WILDSIDE PRESS

To Carol, as always,

And to my favorite curmudgeons:
Eric Flint
David Gerrold
Guy H. Lillian III
Barry Malzberg
Frank M. Robinson
Bill Schafer

RESNICK ON THE LOOSE

Published by Wildside Press LLC.
www.wildsidebooks.com

CONTENTS

RESNICK ON THE LOOSE

INTRODUCTION

I met Mike Resnick long before I actually met him. This is not a tricky literary device, it's the simple truth. Here's how it happened:

Some years ago—many years now, thankfully—I was among the teeming ranks of those miserable unfortunates known by the oxymoronic term of "unpublished authors." This is a state of affairs which is sorry enough in its own right. What makes it worse—far worse—is that there is no clearly defined route, mechanism, seminar, study group, transcendental meditation or mystical rapture through which the unpublished author can figure out how to get from the aforementioned oxymoronic state to that of an actual, you know, Author. Which is to say, someone who is actually Published—and in a recognized and accepted professional venue, to boot.

The problem isn't lack of advice and counsel. Oh, no. Advice and counsel is ubiquitous. I would go so far as to say that those who advise unpublished authors on how to get published are as multitudinous as the walking, talking oxymorons themselves.

This is not surprising, since most of the people giving advice on how to get published to unpublished authors are themselves unpublished. At least 85%, at a rough guess—and if you're looking simply at the instructors of creative writing classes, that figure climbs well past 95%.

But even the remaining counselors aren't usually much help. True, they are genuine authors, in that they have indeed gotten published in one or more professional venues. The problem is that the great majority of them fall into one of two camps:

First, those who have indeed gotten published and can therefore legitimately call themselves "authors," but...

Barely. As a rule, most authors have only published a handful of stories, and those consist almost entirely of short fiction. Half the time, probably, they've only published one or at most two stories.

So how much good advice can they really give you? Not much. In fact, in many cases their advice is more damaging than what you get from unpublished authors, because their status makes their advice seem weightier than it really is.

Of the remaining counselors, we are now talking about a very small percentage of people who try their hand at writing. These people are indeed successful authors and have gotten published many times. And yet...

Nine times out of ten, the best you can say for their advice is that you need to take it with a pillar of salt. That's because the simple fact is that most successful authors don't really understand very much about publishing. They got where they are from their own talent, usually combined with the services of a good agent—and it's their agent who handles all their business.

Such was the state of affairs in which I was mired, those many years ago. Luckily for me, I subscribed to a magazine for unpublished authors called *Speculations*. (Which, sadly, is no longer being published.) At the time, the centerpiece of the magazine was a column titled *Ask Bwana*. And that's how I met Mike Resnick. Mike was the author of that column, and issue after issue he would respond to questions sent in by wannabe authors with answers that for the first time in my experience made sense, were coherent, and provided me with a guide to action.

I didn't actually meet Mike in person for another decade or so. That encounter happened in 2006 when he submitted a story to a magazine I was editing at the time, *Jim Baen's Universe*. I bought the story, which went on to get nominated for the Hugo. It wasn't long before we became friends, and about a year later I asked him to co-edit the magazine with me. Since then, Mike and I have edited an anthology together

(*The Dragon Done It*) and will soon be collaborating on a novel (*The Gods of Sagittarius*). We are also both judges in the Writers of the Future contest.

My opinion of Mike's knowledge of publishing in general and science fiction in particular hasn't changed a bit over the years. There are very few people who understand the subject as well as he does, and none who know it better. As you will find out for yourself when you read this volume.

—Eric Flint
March, 201

PART 1: THE JIM BAEN'S UNIVERSE EDITORIALS

INTRODUCTION TO PART 1

Jim Baen's Universe was a noble experiment, the highest-paying prozine in the business. It lasted for just about four years, and I was Eric Flint's co-editor for the last three of them. One of my jobs was to write an editorial for each issue, and here they all are, in order.

HOWDY

So here I am, the new Executive Editor of *Jim Baen's Universe*. And here you are, wondering who the hell I am and what I like.

Who I am is easy. I'm Mike Resnick. I sold my first science fiction novel exactly 40 years ago (don't hunt for it; it's pretty awful). I sold my first few science fiction stories even earlier (you might very well enjoy hunting for them; they were the "redeeming social value" in a trio of men's magazines, stuck in there to make all the naked women legal). I attended my first Worldcon in 1963—I was a mature 21, my child-bride was 20—and we've been going back ever since.

I started selling stories and articles when I was a teenager. Somewhere along the way to 2007 I learned how to write acceptable prose (though I'm sure there are critics who would disagree). After producing a few million lesser words in lesser fields, I've now sold over 50 science fiction novels, close to 200 stories, more than a dozen collections, even a couple of screenplays, and I've edited close to 50 anthologies. Along the way I've won a bunch of Hugos (5), lost an even bigger bunch (23), and according to *Locus* I have won more awards for my short science fiction that any writer living or dead. (I have also lost more, but you have my permission to forget or ignore this fact.)

I've edited anthologies, as I said, and I spent a couple of years this decade editing science fiction for BenBella Books, but until now I have never edited a science fiction magazine. I've wanted this freedom for a long time. By freedom, I mean that just about every time you sell an anthology, you must sell it based on a theme, and while it's interesting to edit the best Alternate Kennedy stories or the best Sherlock Holmes in the Future stories, it *is* a bit limiting for both the writer and the editor. Here at *Jim Baen's Universe* I am free to select the *best* stories regardless of theme or subject matter, to help writers produce the best stories they can write rather than the best Space Cadet or Dinosaur or Christmas Ghost story they can write.

So what do I like?

It's going to sound like a cop-out, but I like good writing. I used to write in the "adult" field, so I guarantee you can't shock me. I've sold perhaps 60 funny science fiction stories, so you're not going to get turned away because your story isn't serious enough. I've won awards at every length, so I will not react unfavorably to any length.

But give me a story that's poorly written, carelessly conceived, clumsily worded, or filled with cardboard characters, and I don't care if you've been my friend for half a century, you're not going to sell me. *Jim Baen's Universe* is not just paying the best rates in the field, but *much* the best, literally 3 times more than *Analog*, *Asimov's* and *F&SF* pay for short stories by major authors, and for that kind of money, we expect—and I demand—stories that are worth what we're paying. Simple as that.

Other than the demand for good writing, the market's wide open. I don't believe in editorial soap boxes. I learned a long time ago that trying to shoehorn a writer into a style or subject *I* liked, rather than helping him create what *he* liked, was counter-productive. I love Robert Sheckley's humor, and I loved the humor in Robert E. Howard's Breckenridge Elkins stories—and neither of them wrote the kind of humor I do. I can admire Edgar Rice Burroughs' fantastic adventures and Eric Flint's alternate historical adventures and Fred Saberhagen's futuristic adventures, and none of them read remotely like my own adventures. Indeed, when I make a list of my favorite science fiction writers—Alfred Bester, Barry Malzberg, C. L. Moore, Clifford D. Simak, Robert Sheckley, James White, a number of others—I find the one thing they have in common is that none of them writes like me. In fact, that's one of the prime reasons I admire them: because they come up with stories and styles and approaches that are fascinating to me precisely *because* what they write is so different from what I write. (Why in the world should I want to read Imitation Resnick or Watered-Down Resnick when I can read unique and original Heinlein and Zelazny and Willis? And on those occasions that I want to read a Resnick story, whose writing I immodestly admit to liking, well, I'm on pretty good terms with the source and will simply suggest that he write one.)

Over the years, I've edited a number of stories that have won or been nominated for Hugo Awards, but the editorial feat of which I am proudest is that in the decade of the 1990s I bought more first stories than any of the major magazines, indeed than all of them put together, and that 8 of "my" discoveries made the Campbell ballot (science fiction's Rookie of the Year award), and one of them—my daughter, in fact; good genes there—won it.

I am committed to editing the best science fiction around, but I am equally committed to encouraging the next generation to produce it. When Burroughs and A. Merritt and Olaf Stapleton had shot their bolts, along came Robert A. Heinlein and Isaac Asimov and Theodore Sturgeon. A decade later we had Sheckley and William Tenn and Jack Vance. Then came Robert Silverberg and Harlan Ellison, A few more years and we had Roger Zelazny and Ursula K. Le Guin and Anne McCaffrey. Then along came George R. R. Martin and Connie Willis and Orson Scott Card. A new batch of superstars makes the scene every few years. Along with presenting the best of the current ones, we owe it to the readers, and indeed to the field itself, to find and present the next generation as well.

Newcomers have a lot of stories to tell. They don't fall into the trap of telling the same story over and over again. That they leave to television, and that we'll leave to lesser magazines, which is one of the reasons I am so committed to finding the best of them.

I'm glad to be aboard. Eric is still the head honcho, and production schedules being what they are very little of my editing will show up here before the last two or three of issues of 2007. But I'm at work on those future issues right now, and I promise to do my best to please you.

Welcome to the Future

Okay, I hear you ask, how the hell can *Jim Baen's Universe* pay such phenomenal word rates? Are we just a loss leader for Baen Books?

The answer is that we're not a loss leader for anybody. We intend to make a profit, and I'll show you exactly how. But first let me tell you a little story about the sex industry. (Yeah, I could explain it just as easily without sex, but Topic Number One does tend to capture the attention.)

Move the clock back to 1965 (and how I wish we could—at least when I look in the mirror). I'm a 23-year-old kid, and I've landed my first job in Chicago's publishing industry. None of the legitimate papers or magazines had any openings, so suddenly I find myself editing *The National Insider*, which is just like *The National Enquirer* only worse. The first thing I learn is that the only number that matters in my little universe is 41. That's the break-even point. For the *Insider* to stay out of the red, we have to sell 41% of our print run… which is to say that the cost of printing, shipping, distributing, editorial, overhead, everything added together, gets covered only if we sell 41% of our print run, which was about 400,000 back then. (Don't drool; we only sold for 15 cents an issue.)

We were selling about 38% when I took over. I figured that if one naked lady was good, 6 were better; if one silly story about saucers flying off with Jackie Kennedy was good, four were better; if one Hollywood gossip column filled with innuendo was good, lots were better. And I was right. Suddenly the paper was regularly selling between 70% and 75% every week.

Okay, move the calendar ahead to 1969. I've quit my job and gone freelance. Doing what? Same damned thing. I'm packaging four monthly (and later bi-weekly) tabloids out of my house in Libertyville, Illinois. But there is a huge difference. Now my magic number is 9.

You see, now I am working for Reuben Sturman, the true kingpin of the American porn industry (though my tabloids are his one non-porn publication. We're just sexy, thank you very much.) Now, Reuben wasn't born the kingpin of porn; he was a self-made smut king. He'd been a comic-book jobber in Cleveland in the 1950s. Then one day the major distributors decided they wouldn't handle a bunch of "muscle books"—we'd call them bottom-level body-building magazines today—and Reuben volunteered to distribute them, You know how the *New York Times* prints "all the news that's fit to print" and the *National Enquirer* prints the rest? Well, the major distributors handled all the material that was fit to display on your local newsstand or in your local supermarket, and Reuben handled all the rest, especially those with (*sigh*) naked ladies.

And got rich. And started a whole chain of what were known as secondary distribution agencies. When the dust cleared in the early 1960s, there were 65 secondary agencies nationwide, and Reuben, under various corporate veils, owned 59 of them. He figured if it would work for distribution, it would work for retail outlets, and soon, of the 800 adult book stores in the country—I haven't been to one in thirty years, but they were the kind where men in raincoats paid a dollar to browse and got it back if they bought something—Reuben owned over 600. He also invested in a printing plant.

Back to the new magic number: 9. My break-even point for Reuben's tabloids was 9%. That's right; we could pulp 90% of our print run and still show a profit.

How? Simple. He got rid of the costs that others had to pay. (Remember that: we'll come back to it later). He didn't pay a printer anything but the cost of paper, because he *was* the printer. He didn't pay a national distributor because he *was* the national distributor. He didn't pay the local distributor (the equivalent of Charles Levy in Chicago, or Long Island News Agency in New York) because he *was* the local distributor. He didn't have to give the bookstore its usual percentage, because he *was* the bookstore.

9%. Simple. And then he made sure of his profit by forbidding any of the 600 bookstores, or any of the 59 secondary agencies, to sell a single copy of a rival tabloid—all of which had to use his services—before we'd sold half of our own print run.

(Sound familiar? If you're a Resnick reader it should. The protagonist of my 1984 science fiction novel, *The Branch*—which is being reprinted by Pyr in 2008, hint, hint—was based on Reuben, and his business was lifted lock stock and naked ladies from Reuben's.)

We're going to talk about science fiction magazines now. I'm inclined to say something flip, like "Back to the real world," except the point of all this is that what I just related to you *was* the real world. My first publisher went belly-up a few years after I left because the expenses whelmed him over; Reuben stayed profitably in business until the Feds finally nailed him for tax evasion. (He died in jail.)

The way I see it, the great printzines—*Asimov's, Analog, F&SF*—are my old Chicago publisher, and *Jim Baen's Universe* is Reuben Sturman.

Let's see if I can explain—and please understand, I *love* those three magazines. I've been reading two of them all my life, and the third since its inaugural issue thirty years ago. I've sold to all of them. I have won five Hugos, and each winner was from one of them. I will never refuse a request from one of their editors, and will write for them right up to the end. I will weep bitter tears when they die.—but die they will, and for much the same reason my Chicago tabloid publisher died.

And *Jim Baen's Universe*, or some as-yet-unborn *JBU* clones, will live and prosper, for the same reason Reuben Sturman's publishing empire lived and prospered.

Consider: what does it take to get a copy of *Asimov's* or one of the others into your hands?

Well, there's an office, which means an overhead.

There's an editor, a top-notcher, who has to get a salary commensurate with his or her talent.

There's paper for the magazines to be printed on.

There are color separations for the covers.

There is the cost of printing tens of thousands (formerly a couple of hundred thousand) of copies of the magazine.

There are shipping costs. The subscribers don't drive to the printing plant to pick their copies up. Neither do the distributors. Neither do the stores.

There are the distribution costs, both for the national and local distributors. They're good guys, but they don't place the magazines in the stores for free.

There are the stores themselves. If they sell a $5.00 magazine, most of them are going to want $1.50 or thereabouts for their troubles.

There are warehouse costs for those magazines that are neither sold nor pulped.

And a month later, every copy has vanished from the newsstands and bookstores, to be replaced by the next month's issue.

Now let's take a look at how these expenses effect *Jim Baen's Universe*:

There is no office expense and no overhead, because Eric, Paula, me, all of us, work out of our houses.

There are no editorial salaries for Eric, Paula or me. We're so confident that the magazine's going to make money that we each opted to get a piece of the profits.

There are no paper expenses, because the magazine doesn't appear on paper.

There are no color separations, because we simply post the artwork right on the screen.

There are no printing expenses, because the magazine is not printed.

There are no shipping costs, because the magazine is not shipped.

There are no national or local distribution costs, because *JBU* is not distributed. It's right here, and we don't have to pay anyone to put it in your physical proximity.

There is no cut for the bookstores, because we are not sold in bookstores. Or newsstands. Or supermarkets. We're right here on line. You pay us, and we give you the magazine, and there are no middle men. (You might think about that. You pay $4.95 for a digest magazine, they might wind up with about $1.85 of it; you pay us $5.00, we keep $5.00.)

There are no warehouse costs, because the magazine exists in electronic phosphors, not paper pages. We'll post another issue in a couple of months, but this one won't be through earning us money, because it will always be available for anyone who wants it. It just won't be the new issue on the website.

Do you begin to see where the print magazines are at a bit of a disadvantage?

Now, there is one expense that they and we both have, and that's content, which is to say, the stories that are our reason for existence.

The three digest magazines pay seven to eight cents a word. It seems reasonable. Hell, when you look at their expenses and their diminishing print runs and sales, it seems positively generous, almost philanthropic. How can *JBU* possibly compete with that?

Easy. By paying our major writers three times as much, and by paying every writer, even our rank beginners, at least as much as the digests.

Remember: they're paying overhead, color separations, editorial salaries, paper, printing, shipping, national distributors, local distributors, bookstores, warehouses, and authors.

And us? We're paying…authors and artists. Period. And we won't be happy until our best authors are getting 50 cents a word, and *all* of our authors are getting at least twenty cents. Give us three years; we're working on it.

Next question: is there enough of a cyber audience to keep an e-zine in business?

I didn't know until a couple of months ago. Now I do.

Let me tell you about that. There's a young man named Steve Eley who runs a podcast site called *Escape Pod*. Last year he asked me for a story. At the time I didn't pay much attention to it. I mean, who the hell listens to podcasts? Then a French producer/director who had never been able to get the magazine my story appeared in heard the podcast and optioned the story for maybe 75 times what Steve had paid for it. So of course I instantly became a huge supporter of podcasting, sent a bunch of top writers to Steve, sold him a bunch more stories, gave out podcast interviews all the hell over… and couldn't help wondering if anyone except the occasional French movie producer actually listened to these things.

So I asked Steve if he had any figures. He said yes, that "Travels With My Cats," my second *Escape Pod* story, had 22,000 hits in its first month.

22,000 hits? I couldn't believe it. It had appeared in *Asimov's*. If every single person who bought that issue read the story—and my guess is that probably a quarter of them didn't—that was still only 18,556 readers according to this month's *Locus*.

More people *heard* the story online in one month—and of course it's *still* being heard months later—than read it!

Okay, I said to myself, the story was a Hugo winner and Steve advertised it as such. For whatever reasons—its content, its awards—it touched all the right buttons. But surely not every story on this one little web page could do that.

So this month he posted another of my stories. It's a tongue-in-cheek fairy tale. It won no awards. It was written for teenagers. It has nothing in common with the other story.

I couldn't even wait for an entire month. I e-mailed Steve after two weeks to ask how many people had downloaded it. (Hold onto your hats.)

14,000!

14,000? This is *me*. Not Anne McCaffrey. Not Kevin Anderson. Not Mercedes Lackey. Not Robert Jordan.

Are the readers out there in the ether?

You betcha. In vast quantities.

Are we positioned to find them?

We think so. We hope so. And if we're wrong, then the next e-zine to come along will find them (or be found by them), or the one after that.

The one thing you can be sure of is that *JBU* and its electronic imitators will bring you the very best writers and artists money can buy.

After all, we've got nothing else to spend it on.

STRAITJACKETS

I've received some interesting comments over on Escape Pod, an audio site where they read one of my stories every now and then. To date they have read two Hugo winners and a Hugo nominee—and each time someone, or a few someones, write in to say that the stories are all well-written and moving and all that crap, but they clearly aren't real true-blue science fiction.

Which gave me my topic for this issue's editorial, because people have been trying to put science fiction in a straitjacket for close to a century now, and it just doesn't work.

The first guy to define it was Hugo Gernsback, the man who created the first all-science-fiction magazine (*Amazing Stories,* back in April, 1926). He's the guy our most prestigious award is named after, even though he had some difficulty speaking English, clearly couldn't edit it, and usually refused to pay for it except on threat of lawsuit.

Hugo declared that "scientifiction" (his first term for it) existed solely to interest young boys in science. (Young girls, presumably, were too busy playing with their dolls.) The science had to be reasonably accurate, and central to the story.

Now, at about the same time Hugo was creating science fiction, H. P. Lovecraft was perfecting a fantasy fiction that rarely involved science (although he did sell a few pieces to *Astounding* in the 1930s), and clearly wasn't meant for the impressionable young boys Hugo saw as his audience.

Okay, move the clock (the calendar?) ahead 80 years. Lovecraft is just about a household name. Eleven of his books are still in print. You'd need extra fingers and toes to count the movies adapted from or suggested by his work. Science fiction is happy to claim him as one of us, at least a close cousin if not a wandering son.

And Papa Gernsback of the rigid definition? Not a single word he wrote in his entire life—and that includes novels, editorials, non-fiction, the whole shebang—is still in print.

The first major critic to come along was Damon Knight. Damon knew that science fiction was the pure quill. It annoyed him when science fiction writers didn't know the craft of writing, and it annoyed him even more when they got their science wrong.

But what really drove him right up a tree was when they didn't even *try* to make the science accurate. When, for example, they put the key in the ignition and the spaceship started up just like a car. When, for example, they put an oxygen atmosphere on Mars.

When, for example, they were Ray Bradbury.

Damon acknowledged that what Bradbury did was Art; he knew his craft too much to argue with that. But Art or not, it sure didn't fit his notion of science fiction, and his criticisms and essays left no doubt that Ray Bradbury was a gifted imposter who should either mend his ways or stop posing as a science fiction writer.

The result? Almost every word Ray Bradbury has written for the past 60 years is still in print, and the Pulitzer committee just honored him for a lifetime devoted to science fiction. Of all the dozens of pure science fiction books Damon Knight wrote or edited, only two are in print today.

The next major critic was James Blish, not quite the writer Knight was and a hell of a lot nastier, but he knew his stuff, and that meant he knew science fiction was Important (note capital I), that no practitioner dared take it lightly, that it was just this side of sinful to be flip and flippant, and that the greatest offender was Robert Sheckley. How dare he make fun of the honored tropes and traditions of science fiction?

Okay, move the clock ahead a quick 60 years and (you saw this coming, right?) there are 11 Sheckley books in print. Of all the books, fiction and non-fiction, that James Blish wrote, only two remain available. Even his Star Trek books have gone the way of the dodo.

But more to the point, no one argues any longer that humor cannot be valid science fiction (and indeed, such humorous stories as Eric Frank Russell's "Allamagoosa" and Connie Willis's "Even the Queen" have won the Hugo). No one says that the science is more important than the emotional impact of a story, by Bradbury, by Zelazny, by anyone. And no one denies horror and supernatural fiction (perhaps excepting vampire novels that are thinly-disguised category romances and outsell science fiction ten-to-one) a place in our family tree.

Now you would think that after the originator of our field and our first two major critics all fell on their faces trying to keep science fiction within their rigid definitions, future generations of self-appointed Keepers of the Flame (or the Definition) would have slunk off into the shadows. But they didn't.

At the midpoint of the 20th Century, everyone knew that sex had no place in science fiction. Our field was like a George Bernard Shaw play, which is to say that an alien, reading (or watching) it could learn everything there was to know about human beings except that we come equipped with genitals and an urge to use them. Then along came Philip Jose Farmer with "The Lovers" and its sequels, and when God didn't strike him dead, all the writers who had been avoiding Topic Number One for years, even such traditionalists as Heinlein and Asimov, began making up for lost time…and by 1960 it was never again suggested that sex had no place in science fiction.

J. G. Ballard got a lot of grief, because clearly you couldn't fool with the actual form of the science fiction novel. But after he did it, so did dozens of others, experimenting every which way as the New Wave was born, fought for its right to exist, and was finally incorporated into the body of the literature.

So okay, they lost a lot of battles, but there was one thing the traditionalists knew would never change, and that was that science fiction took place in outer space. Then Robert Silverberg began exploring "inner space" with books like *Dying Inside*, Barry Malzberg explored it with *Herovit's World*, the Defenders of the Faith howled like stuck pigs, and a few years later everyone agreed that Outer or Inner Space were equally valid venues as long as the story worked.

Alternate history was okay for historians like McKinley Kantor and politicians like Winston Churchill, and the *very* occasional science fiction short story, but everyone knew it wasn't really science fiction—until Harry Turtledove began proving it was on a regular basis, and suddenly dozens of writers followed suit. Now there's no more controversy. Of course alternate history is science fiction.

And what's driving the purists crazy these days? Just look around you.

Connie Willis can win a Hugo with a story about a girl of the future who *wants* to have a menstrual period when women no longer have them.

David Gerrold can win a Hugo with a story about an adopted child who claims to be a Martian, and the story never tells you if he is or not.

I can win Hugos with stories about books remembered from childhood, about Africans who wish to go back to the Good Old Days, about an alien tour guide in a thinly-disguised Egypt.

The narrow-minded purists to the contrary, there is *nothing* the field of science fiction can't accommodate, no subject—even the crucifixion, as Mike Moorcock's Nebula winner, "Behold the Man," proves—that can't be science-fictionalized with taste, skill and quality.

I *expect* movie fans, making lists of their favorite science fiction films, to omit *Dr. Strangelove* and *Charly*, because they've been conditioned by Roddenbury and Lucas to look for the Roddenbury/Lucas tropes of movie science fiction—spaceships, zap guns, robots, light sabres, and so on.

But written science fiction has *never* allowed itself to be limited by any straitjacket. Which is probably what I love most about it.

About the only valid definition that I'm willing to accept is this: all of modern, mainstream, and realistic fiction is simply a branch, a category, or a subset of science fiction.

SLUSH

Everyone talks about slush, but no one does anything about it. Except read it. Very reluctantly.

But it's what keeps us going. Sooner or later just about every author you've ever heard of, or *will* ever hear of, comes out of a slush pile. Sooner or later every editor reads slush, if not all of it, then at least the slush that's passed up the line to him by the people who are paid to read nothing *but* slush.

If you go to enough conventions, sooner or later you're going to attend a panel with a title like "It Came From the Slush Pile," in which editors discuss—humorously, it is to be hoped—the most awful stories ever to appear in their slush piles. I never participate in such panels, because I think it smacks of a certain cruelty. I don't like making fun of people who are trying their best to become writers, and of course you never know if one of them is in the audience, sitting there being quietly humiliated by editors poking fun at his lack of skill.

Every now and then someone who has attended such a panel asks me if slush is *really* like that. The answer, alas, is that it's every bit that bad and nowhere near that amusing.

So let's talk about slush a bit, since I have never, in four decades in the publishing industry, seen a *small* slush pile.

Why do we have them at all?

An editor is a lot more than a purchasing agent. He has to work hand-in-glove with writers. He has to attend sales meetings. He has to sort out his budget. He has to work with his artists and his art director. He has to work with his columnists. He has to balance his issue, which becomes quite interesting when a story he was depending on—or a segment of a serial—comes in late or not at all. He has to justify what he is doing to his publisher—and when it doesn't work, he has to justify his continuing employment to his publisher. In this field, he has to attend conventions and glad-hand authors, especially authors who are writing for rival magazines and whom he would like to have writing for *his* magazine. And he has to read dozens of stories every week.

The amazing part is that he gets it all done. What he *can't* get done is reading 250 or more unsolicited stories a week. He knows that he's got to look at all the journeyman writers, all the award winners, all the agented stuff (though these days a majority of agents don't want to be bothered with short fiction)…but he simply hasn't got enough hours in the week to read 250 stories by the authors he doesn't know, the authors whose accomplishments are either nonexistent or at least unknown to him. By arbitrary definition, those stories are known as slush, and until someone reads them they reside in what is known as the slush pile.

And since he hasn't got time to read them himself, the editor—or his boss—hires slush readers, who are usually referred to by the more dignified title of first readers. They wade through the slush, always hoping they'll find the next Asimov or Lackey in the pile, and usually going home wondering if any author they read that day actually graduated grammar school.

So…that's slush, and that's where stories go until the author has developed enough of a reputation to get his work out of the slush pile.

What are the odds?

For twelve years I wrote a bi-monthly column for the Hugo-nominated semiprozine *Speculations* titled "Ask Bwana" (no, I didn't choose the name), in which I gave not artistic but career advice to hopeful science fiction writers. And one day, in the mid-1990s, someone asked me that very question: what are the odds of selling your story out of the slush pile?

I didn't know, so I asked some editors.

Gardner Dozois, who was editing *Asimov's* at the time, told me that he got about a thousand slush stories a month.

How many did he buy? Three a year. Odds against selling a slush story to *Asimov's?* 4,000-to-1 against.

Kristine Kathryn Rusch was editing *F&SF* at the same time, and I asked her the same question. Her answer differed only in degree. She got about 7,500 slush submissions a year, and bought seven or eight. So the odds against selling a slush story to *F&SF* were minimally better: 1,000-to-1 against.

But you know what? People *do* come out of the slush pile. I did. Eric Flint did. Anne McCaffrey did. Nancy Kress did. Joe Haldeman did. And so did 95% of the authors you can name, the authors you see on the Hugo and Nebula ballots and the bestseller lists every year.

You've got to be good, and you've got to be a little bit lucky, but most of all you've got to persevere.

Now…are there any tips for getting out of the slush pile?

Yeah, there are.

The first is: learn how to format a story, whether on paper or in phosphors. You wouldn't believe how many stories are left at the starting gate just over that.

Second, check your spelling and punctuation. Again, that seems awfully basic, and in truth no good story ever failed to sell because of a couple of typos…but a sloppy manuscript implies that the author had no respect for his work and his craft, and if *he* didn't then why should the reader (and in this case, the slush reader)?

Okay, any high school teacher could have told you that. Now for something they don't tell you.

Third, spend 90% of your effort working on Page 1. If you don't capture the slush reader by the bottom of that first page, the odds are hundreds to one that you've already lost the battle.

Let me tell you a depressing little truth. Back in my starving-editor days in the late 1960s, I edited a trio of men's magazines. And it was company policy to fire any first reader who couldn't reject a story every two minutes, because that's how fast they arrived. That means he had to open the envelope, pull out the story, read that opening page, attach a rejection slip, stuff and seal the envelope, and put it in the outgoing mail tray, all in 120 seconds. If you hadn't captured him by paragraph 2, he never got to all those gems that you had up ahead on pages 8 and 19 and 22.

When I joined *Jim Baen's Universe* there was a ton of slush that had been passed on by our enthusiastic but inexperienced staff. The reason I so characterize them (and they are still enthused, but no longer inexperienced) is because the slush reader, when he or she would forward a story to Eric or me, would write a brief comment…and I came to too damned many comments that said, in essence, "It starts slow, but it gets really good on Page 7." I didn't even have to read those, because that's an automatic reject. Our subscribers are not being paid to wade through all the junk to get to Page 7; if we haven't captured them in the first couple of pages, the odds are that they'll stop reading that story and go one to one by a major author (we don't lack for them), or at least a known commodity.

There are many other reasons for rejecting a slush story (beyond the fact that most of them are simply not written at a professional level). In the mystery field, it's an old and honored tradition to create a detective, and present him with one crime after another for the remainder of his (and the author's) career. Doesn't work in science fiction. We've got all time and space to play with, and twice-told tales don't cut it, not in the magazine with the highest word rates around. It is *essential* for the hopeful science fiction writer to be well-read in the field. (There used to be a rejection slip back in the 1970s, I can't remember the magazine now, where there were 8 or 10 reasons for rejection, and the editor would check the one that applied. One of them, and it was checked more often than you might think, was "Heinlein did it better. And earlier.")

A quartet of helpful tips:

1. There's no sense nagging an editor about your story. The odds are that he hasn't seen it yet (and indeed may *never* see it, if the slush reader doesn't pass it on to him)—and you have no idea who's reading his slush pile.

2. You will no doubt come up with several innovative scams for getting your story out of the slush pile. Trust me: they may be new to you, but there won't be any that the editor hasn't seen a few dozen times.

3. Don't lie about your credits. They are too easy to verify.

4. Don't brag about your amateur or semi-pro "sales". They won't impress any professional editor, and if it appears that you think otherwise it tends to scream "bush league".

Ready for one final unhappy truth? A slush story can't be as good as a story by a "name" writer; it's got to be better. It is a simple fact that if *Asimov's* puts Connie Willis's name or my name on the cover, they know from past experience that we will draw a certain number of additional readers. Same as when *F&SF* runs Harlan Ellison or Ray Bradbury on their cover, or when *Analog's* cover brags about a new Lois McMaster Bujold or Robert J. Sawyer story. If you're going to knock one of these authors, or the dozens of others you can name, out of an issue, you've got to have written one hell of a story.

The flip side to all this, of course, and what makes it all worthwhile, is that once you sell to a major magazine, like the ones I mentioned (or the one you're reading), you've beaten the odds and there is no question that you belong there. Not many triumphs in your future will be quite as satisfying or meaningful.

Okay, so much for slush. It's probably just as depressing as when you began reading this, but hopefully it's a little less mysterious.

REVEALED FALSEHOODS

Over the past century, the giants of science fiction have occasionally written a line or two that somehow survives them and their work, and is eventually viewed by most members of the field as a Revealed Truth.

Being a natural-born cynic (well, Caesarian actually, but let it pass), I'm here to tell you that Truth, revealed or otherwise, never set anyone free. It is Doubt that sets people free.

You think not? Let's examine some of these truths that science fiction readers and writers seem to think are immutable.

And let's start with one that even non-science-fiction people like to quote: Isaac Asimov's First Law of Robotics, which states that a robot cannot harm a human being, or through inaction allow harm to come to a human being.

Sounds sensible. Of course we'll build that into every robot we ever make. Everyone knows that.

Uh…well, maybe not quite everyone. Seems to me that in 1991, the entire world saw a smart bomb, which is nothing but a robot in other-than-humanoid form, find its way down an Iraqi chimney. In 2003, we saw the Navy fire a smart bomb into the air while at sea, and the bomb, using its (non-positronic) brain, found its target 450 miles away.

So much for First Law.

Then there's TANSTAAFL—the war cry of fans in the 1960s and 1970s, which was Robert A. Heinlein's acronym for "There ain't no such thing as a free lunch," a battle cry voiced in *The Moon is a Harsh Mistress*.

But of course it's ridiculous. There are free lunch programs all the hell over. Check your local school. Or look at New York, where Mayor Michael Blumberg has just proposed not only free lunches, but cash payments to poor people who don't break the law, to parents who actually read their kids' report cards, to kids who obey the law by attending school, and so on.

If there ain't no such thing as a free lunch, it's only because it's been surpassed by a couple of hundred more lucrative free things.

Okay, let's go back to one of the fathers of science fiction, H. G. Wells. Wells explained, time and again, that the proper way to write science fiction was to take one, and only one, scientific breakthrough and write a story around it, that the public couldn't possibly buy more than one a book.

Sounds logical...but it's *dumb*. It presupposes that the 1950s public couldn't deal with, say, jet planes, television, and the Salk polio vaccine at the same time, or that no 1990s story proposing space flight, cell phones, AIDS medications, and DVDs could be assimilated by the man (or reader) on the street.

And another revealed truth bites the dust.

Sir Arthur C. Clarke states that "Any sufficiently advanced technology is indistinguishable from magic." The only answer is: to whom? Not to the people who create it. Not to the people who apply it. Not to all the people who benefit from it. (I love the late George Alec Effinger's response to reading about faster-than-light drives and zap guns and all the other tropes of science fiction that some misguided authors feel they must explain, at length, in their stories: "Any sufficiently advanced technology is indistinguishable from doubletalk.")

Then there's Damon Knight's classic definition of science fiction: "Science fiction is what I'm pointing at when I say 'That's science fiction.'"

Witty as all get-out. Great line at parties. But I've been hearing it quoted as something meaningful for more than four decades now. Let's try an experiment: substitute the word "Jabberwocky" or any other nonsense word of your choice. Seems just as brilliant (and just an uninformative), doesn't it?

Then there's Robert E. Howard's classic and oft-quoted line (though of course Nietzsche said it first): "That which does not kill us makes us stronger." Sure sounds good. But maybe you should ask a quadriplegic car crash survivor, or someone who's just lost a lung and a kidney to cancer, if *they* think they're any stronger because of what didn't kill them.

Sturgeon's Law—"90% of everything is crap"—is so famous that even the *New York Times* has quoted it. I'd have no problem with it if it were limited to television, movies, and Windows Vista, but it's all-inclusive, and your brain would surely qualify for Sturgeon's 90% if you believed 90% of all medical and technological breakthroughs (or Baen books, for that matter) were crap.

Back to Isaac Asimov, whose second most famous statement is "Violence is the last resort of the incompetent." Which may very well be true, but doesn't acknowledge the far more meaningful corollary, which is that the competent don't wait that long.

I'm sure you can think of more of science fiction's Revealed Falsehoods and Half-Truths, but you get the idea. Even in a field as cerebral and forward-looking as ours, we pay lip service to a lot of lines that *sound* brilliant but hold about as much water as a sieve.

So the next time someone comes up to you and proves how brilliant we are by quoting an unquestioned statement by one of our leading lights, make sure you're within reach of the saltcellar, because you're going to have to take what they tell you with a few grains of sodium chloride.

BREEDING LIKE RABBITS—OR HUGOS

Walk up to any serious science fiction reader and name the last hundred Hugo winners. Chances are he'll know less than a quarter of them, no matter how much of the stuff he reads.

There's a reason for it.

Movies have the Oscars. Theater has the Tonys. Television has the Emmys. Mysteries have the Edgars. And we here in the field of written science fiction have the Hugos.

They're our most prestigious award. Even overseas, every science fiction writer, reader and fan knows what the Hugo is.

The problem is that it's not what it used to be. Maybe it never was.

The Hugo was first awarded in 1953. It went to Best Novel, Best Magazine, Best Cover Artist, Best Interior Artist, Excellence in Fact Articles, and Best New Author. Six awards, and only two went to writers (although everything went to professionals, a situation that would change before long.)

Move the calendar ahead to 1957, and only three Hugos were handed out. Right—just three.

1957 was an aberration. By 1963 we were back to giving out six Hugos—Novel, Short Fiction, Artist, Magazine, Drama and Fanzine. No one had a problem with that. We were thrilled that TV and movies were starting to take us seriously, and since fandom was responsible for putting on the Worldcon where the awards were handed out, it made sense that they'd want to award Best Fanzine.

It started innocently enough. But let's take a quantum leap ahead, to 2007. You know how many Hugos were awarded this year? Fourteen.

And of those fourteen, you know how many were given out for written science fiction, which is the basis for this entire field? Four. That's right. Less than 30% of the Hugos now go to written works of science fiction.

How did this come about?

Well, 1967 was a very fannish Worldcon. More panels were devoted to fandom, as opposed to written science fiction, than ever before. And since there was nothing in the rules that said you could *only* give out six Hugos, NyCon III (the 1967 Worldcon, the last to be held in New York), added Best Fan Writer and Best Fan Artist to the list. So, when you include Best Fanzine, NyCon III handed out as many Hugos to fans as to works of science fiction.

By the time of Noreascon II (the 1980 Worldcon, held in Boston), the academics had discovered us, and we them, and a new category was added: Best Non-Fiction Book—and suddenly we had seven annual Hugos that did *not* go to works of science fiction.

Now, all during the late 1970s and early 1980s, fanzine editors and publishers were grousing about the fact that *Locus* kept winning Best Fanzine every year. Which figured. It was professionally printed (almost no other fanzine was), it was supported by dozens of ads from major publishing houses (almost no other fanzines had any ads at all), and it had a circulation that was well over 6,000 and climbing (most fanzines printed and distributed less than 300 copies). Clearly there was no way a "traditional" fanzine would ever win the Best Fanzine Hugo again—but aha! The 1984 Worldcon committee came up with a brand-new category—Best Semiprozine—where *Locus* could win every year to its heart's content and traditional fanzines could once more win the Best Fanzine Hugo.

And suddenly there were four Hugos for fans and four for written science fiction. In fact, the overall tally by the time of LACon II (the 1984 Worldcon, held in Anaheim) was four fiction Hugos and eight everything-else Hugos.

And so it remained until Buffy came along on the boob tube, and Buffy fans bemoaned the fact that a short TV show couldn't compete with a $130 million movie. So Torcon 3 created a second Dramatic category for the 2003 Toronto

Worldcon: Best Short Dramatic Presentation. It was informally called the Buffy Award, just as the Semiprozine Hugo was informally known for years as the *Locus* award, the delicious irony being that although *Locus* has indeed won something like 20 Best Semiprozine Hugos, Buffy never did win the Buffy Award.

As you can see, it's become a bit of demonstrable folk wisdom that if you lose enough Hugos, sooner or later you can put together enough disenfranchised (read: Hugo-losing) friends so that you can get a new Hugo category installed and maybe have a chance to win one. (The fan awards were not proposed by professional writers, and the short dramatic award was not proposed by people who only watched or produced full-length movies.) This year's Japanese Worldcon marked the first time that Best Editor was divided into Best Magazine Editor and Best Book Editor. Some of the book editors were getting tired of losing to magazine editors every year (only two book editors ever beat the magazine editors in open competition, and both of them did it posthumously), so one of the book editors, through a fannish surrogate, proposed splitting the award—and to make sure the new one went to a true-blue novel editor, anthology editors were lumped in with magazine editors.

What's next? I don't know.

But I know this. We now give out fourteen Hugos every year, and only four go to the reason for the existence of the field, the Worldcon, and the Hugo itself—written science fiction.

Think about it.

TELEVISION HAS A LOT
TO ANSWER FOR

It was close to seven decades ago that Isaac Asimov looked around at the current state of the art, realized that except for Eando Binder's crude, pulpish hero Adam Link, almost every robot in science fiction was a malicious monstrosity, applied a little rationality, and came up with the Three Laws of Robotics.

It was a brilliant breakthrough, and forever put an end to the kind of robots that dominated the covers and interiors of the science fiction magazines of the 1930s. In fact, it seemed reasonable to assume that from that day forward every science fictional robot would be governed by the Three Laws or some variation of them.

So what happened?

Clifford D. Simak created Jenkins, the robot servant in the classic *City*, a robot who felt, empathized, and could even lie in a good cause. John Sladek created Roderick, a robot whose middle name might well have been Satire. Robert Sheckley created a robot with (very humorous) sexual accomplishments. I picked up a Hugo nomination for a story about a robot whose greatest desire was to cry.

During the same time period that Asimov developed his laws, Robert A. Heinlein created the ultimate time paradox tale in his classic novella, "By His Bootstraps." No need for anyone to ever write another.

But Heinlein himself topped it with "All You Zombies." So did David Gerrold with *The Man Who Folded Himself*. So did William Tenn with "Me, Myself and I." And none of them had anything in common with "By His Bootstraps" except that they concerned time paradoxes.

Phillip Wylie actually created the first superman in his novel, *Gladiator*. Then came Olaf Stapledon's *Odd John*, a mental rather than a physical superman. Then came a whole series of supermen created by A. E. van Vogt. And of course there was Asimov's Mule, and Henry Kuttner's Baldies, and James H. Schmitz's delightful Witches of Karres…and need I go on? The only ones who bore more than a passing resemblance to Wylie's original were the continuing pulp character Doc Savage, and the continuing comic book character Superman.

Olaf Stapledon gave us a thinking dog in *Sirius*. Which was nothing like the thinking dogs Clifford D. Simak gave us a decade later in *City*, or Fredric Brown's thinking dog, or Brown's thinking mouse, or any number of thinking cats, horses, dragons, you name it. None of which had anything in common with Sirius, except that they were animals and sentient.

Okay, move the clock ahead to the 1990s and 2000s. I can't tell you how many young people I've spoken to at lectures, workshops, and online who only want to write Star Trek books or Star Wars books (and in the 1990s you could add Beauty and the Beast books). The CompuServe network, back in the 1990s, had about 300 embryonic writers who only wanted to write Pern stories, even though the laws of copyright were explained to them and Anne McCaffrey had to land on a couple who ignored those laws.

For the longest time I didn't understand it. These aren't detective or Western stories, where you create a Sherlock Holmes or Hopalong Cassidy and tell his adventures for the rest of your career—and even in mysteries or Westerns, you created your own detective or cowboy, you didn't swipe someone else's.

We're not mysteries or Westerns. We're science fiction, which gives its writers all time and space to play with. Our galaxy has about one hundred billion stars. We've got at least a couple of billion Class G stars, just like our sun, and we're starting to find out that damned near every star we examine has planets. The possibilities, scientific and fictional, are endless. So why do so many people want only to tell second-hand stories about Kirk and Spock and Picard and Skywalker in a handful of third-hand, shopworn, thoroughly-explored and not-very-logical universes?

When they see something that interests them or impresses them, why don't they do what Simak did when he read about Asimov's robots, what van Vogt did with he read about Wylie's and Stapledon's supermen, what Gerrold did when he encountered Heinlein's time paradoxes? Why are the book and magazine slushpiles filled almost to overflowing with thinly-disguised Enterprises and Darth Vaders and the like?

And then it occurred to me. There is one major difference between most of the writers I named, and all of the hopeful ones I've been encountering for the past decade or so… and that is that most of the writers I named did not grow up watching television. Television didn't exist during their formative years, so they grew up reading. They did not watch the same unchanging characters in the same trite, interchangeable plots week in and week out. They did not spend hours every night exposed to uncreative, unthreatening mental pablum that convinces each new generation of couch potato that it is Art. And, uninfluenced by the tube, they kept science fiction lively, creative and innovative.

Conclusion: even our here in the boonies where written science fiction lives, television has a lot to answer for.

ATTENDING WORLDCON

Jim Baen's Universe has come of age. We put a story on the Hugo ballot in our first year, we just put one on the Nebula ballot for our second year. We've had a lot of stories get picked up for Best of the Year anthologies. More and more top writers are sending us their best material.

The next step is to win an award one of these years. The Hugo is the most prestigious—and along with voting for the best stories we run, don't forget that Eric Flint is also eligible for Best Short Fiction Editor.

To nominate and to vote, you must be a member of Worldcon—and if you're going to pay your dues, you might as well attend science fiction's biggest celebration of the year. One of the things I've gleaned from Baen's Bar and from a number of private e-mails is that a lot of you have not yet bitten the bullet and attended a Worldcon, so I thought it might not be a bad idea to let you know what's in store for you, and perhaps encourage you to join and attend.

PARTIES

You've probably heard endless tales about all the parties at Worldcon, and indeed, most nights there will be over 50 of them—big ones, little ones, public ones, private ones. There are all kinds of parties—the single events, the pro events, the bid parties, the hospitality suites. You'll get most of your info from various bulletin boards, and also from the twice-daily (and often thrice-daily) convention newsletter, which will be made available in most public places. Hollywood to the contrary, not all parties feature drugs, nudity, drunken behavior and wild sex, and Worldcon parties are among those that feature none of them. These are just friends visiting with old and new friends who share some of the same interests.

Every group that's bidding for a future Worldcon will have at least one party, most two, a few every night. These are "open" parties and will be posted/advertised all over the hotels and in the newsletters.

A number of regional conventions will also have open parties to interest you in attending their upcoming cons. Almost any new convention with ambitions of becoming a major feature on the convention calendar will also have an open party to announce its existence.

The winners for the next two years usually have open parties. In fact, next year's winner traditionally hosts the Hugo Losers Party. Frequently the previous year's host has an open "thank-you" party.

Then there will be open and semi-open Hospitality Suites, including the Con Suite, which will be run by the host committee and open to all.

There will be a SFWA (Science Fiction Writers of America) Suite. You'll need a SFWA member to get you in the first time. If you want to return, you can probably pick up a sticker for your badge that will get you in.

There will be an ASFA (American Science Fiction Artists) Suite, usually less crowded and easier to gain entrance to.

There will be pro parties. They're not exactly open, and not exactly closed. Basically, you'll need a pro or a well-known fan to get you in, but once inside they won't have to stay with you or vouch for you:

- Tor always has a party.

- Baen always has a party.

- Eos, DAW, Bantam, and Ace occasionally have parties.

- *Asimov's* and *Analog* will have a party, but it usually consists of renting out the SFWA suite and supplying food and drink for the writers for one evening.

Many of the semi-pro and specialty publishers will have open parties. Just check the daily newsletters for time and location (or look at the elevator walls, which are usually plastered with notices of the night's parties.)

Almost every special interest group will have a party, some private, most open.

A number of fan clubs, computer networks, and the like will have parties. First Fandom, a last-man organization consisting of anyone who can prove he was active in science fiction prior to 1938, often has a party.

Any foreign group with enough attendees from home will throw a party, usually though not always an open one. The Japanese always have one. So do the Australians. Others have them from time to time, including the British, the Slovakians, the Germans, and the Dutch.

There'll be 15 or 20 rooms where fans have brought their favorite movies or tv shows, legitimate or bootlegs, and will show them to anyone who wants to watch. This won't be advertised, but just walk up and down the hotel corridors, and when you find an open door, take a peek in—it's usually a small party or a group watching videos.

And of course, I'm barely scratching the surface. Despite the 15-to-20-track programming and the Hugos and the masquerade and the dealers room and the art show and everything else, 70% of a Worldcon takes place from 10:00 at night until 4:00 or 5:00 in the morning, once you learn your way around.

STANDING EXHIBITS

There will be a number of standing exhibits, open from 10:00 AM until 6:00 PM or thereabouts. Two are huge, most aren't; the two big ones are easy to find, while most of the others take some looking for.

- The Dealers' Room, a/k/a the Hucksters' Room. It used to sell only books and magazines, but these days it sells games, CDs, toys, clothes, jewelry, videos, medieval weapons, anything associated with sf. Probably a third of the dealers still sell books and magazines, which is a lot, since there will be about 300 tables and a number of booths.

- Autograph sessions—they'll be announced well in advance—are usually held in or near the hucksters' room. But those are just the "official" Worldcon autograph sessions. Most of the popular writers will also be signing at dealers' or publishers' tables as well, so that they put in from two to five hours signing during the convention, enough time for just about anyone to get their autographs. (And if you see a writer whose work you admire in the hallways, just walk up and ask for an autograph; that's part of what they're there for. You're paying good money to attend, so don't be shy about asking for anything at all.)

- The Art Show. Just about every major artist from Whelan to Eggleton to Giancola to Maitz to Picacio to whoever will display some paintings here, as will hundreds of minor artists. The hangings will all be in the middle of the room; sculptures and other 3-dimensional pieces will be on tables lining the walls. Almost everything will have a minimum-bid pricetag on it. The auction rules change from year to year, so ask how to bid at the entrance to the art show—but know that 90% of what you see will be sold during the con.

- Kaffeeklatsches. These are one-hour (and occasionally two-hour) periods where you sign up to meet with your favorite writer or artist. They serve coffee and sweets, and usually there are 10 or 12 to a table—the writer plus 9 or 11 fans. Sign up for the kaffeeklatsches you want to attend as soon as you get to the con. It's always first-signed first-seated.

- Fanzine room. There is always a room devoted to fanzines. Usually it's a small, unpublicized room, difficult to find, but it's worth the hunt, because it gives away dozens of fanzines. Not the perennial Hugo nominees, but enough to get you started.

- Fanhistorica room. This doesn't occur every year, but it's present more often than not, and will be a room devoted to the history of fandom—books, photos, artifacts, famous (and incredibly valuable) old fanzines, Hugos from previous years, everything you'll want to know about sf fandom from its origins in the 1930s to the present day. Often old-time pros and fans will lead docent tours of the exhibit.

- Fan lounge. Many Worldcons have a fan lounge. It'll be somewhere near the dealers and lecture rooms, and you'll find tables where you can plop down, relax, get soft drinks or coffee, read fanzines (which will be supplied), and meet other fans.

- Costume exhibit. This doesn't occur at every Worldcon, but when it shows up it's stunning. It'll be a display of the greatest masquerade costumes of the past 20 or 30 years, draped on mannequins.

- Photo exhibit. Over the years SFWA's former attorney, M. Christine Valada, who was also a photographer, took black-and-white portraits of just about every pro who attends Worldcon, and there is a standing display of all of them every year.

- Fan photo exhibit. Encouraged by Valada's traveling photo show, fandom now has its own portrait exhibit.

There will doubtless be more exhibits, but these are the ones that tend to show up every year, or at least most years. I encourage you to hunt them all up. You do yourself a disservice if you travel all the way to Worldcon, pay your money to become a member, pay even more to stay at the hotels, and then don't take advantage of all the exhibits that your money is paying for.

SPECIAL EVENTS

Along with the regular programming, every Worldcon has its share of special events.

Hugo Ceremonies. This is where the Toastmaster gets to shine (if he shines at all; alas, some don't). 15 Hugos will be presented in the pro and fan categories, but that's not all. Also presented are the Campbell Award for Best New Writer; the Big Heart Award; and the Seiun (Japanese Hugo) for the Best Translated Novel and Best Translated Short Fiction. There will be photo ops for everybody, and you can probably watch the Hugos and the Masquerade in your room on closed-circuit television.

The Masquerade: This is the biggest draw of the Worldcon, but it's a mere shadow of its former self. All during the 1970s and 1980s the Worldcon masquerade used to draw well over 100 costumes and take at least four or five hours, often longer. Now, thanks to Costume Con and the proliferation of minor costume conventions, the masquerade barely draws 35 to 40 costumes…but it's still a fun event to go to. And if you're an author, not much gives you a bigger kick than watching a fan who spent months of effort creating a costume based on one of more of your characters.

Opening Ceremonies: The Toastmaster introduces the Pro and Fan Guests of Honor, who will make brief speeches. You'll be told where to find everything, and then sent off to do just that.

Pro Guest of Honor Speech(es): There used to be just one Pro GOH, and 90% of the time it was a writer. These days there's usually a Writer GOH, an Editor GOH, and an Artist GOH, and each will have an hour in which to make a speech.

Fan GOH Speech: It probably draws a bit better than the pro speeches, which is only right and fitting. Unlike the

Nebulas, Worldcon is put on by and for fans, a fact that many pros forget or are simply unaware of. Pros are an attraction and their function is to draw more fans to the con, but never make any mistake about who the con is for.

Hugo-nominated movies: These will play free of charge sometime during the con before the winner is announced.

There may be other special events. They can be as diverse as a miniature golf tournament (1991), a pro vs. fan basketball game (1986), a trivia contest (just about every year), the world premiere of a science fiction movie ("A Boy and His Dog" in 1974; "Watership Down" in 1978) or the first peek at a new TV show ("Star Trek" in 1966).

PROGRAMMING

OK, I've mentioned 18-track programming and the like, but until you run into it, I don't think any of you can truly realize the magnitude of Worldcon programming.

A typical hour will have 3 or 4 panels on science fiction, all featuring well-known writers; a pair of panels on fantasy; a panel on horror; a panel or two on science; a couple of panels on the business end of science fiction, from writing to editing to selling to reading contracts; an item or two of children's programming; a pair of panels on various aspect of fandom, from fan history to publishing a fanzine; a publisher's editorial staff telling you what they're looking for this year; a panel of critics evaluating the year's fiction; and a couple of more panels or speeches on various subjects.

That's every hour, from 10:00 AM to 6:00 PM. It'll slow down then, but you'll still have perhaps four panels an hour from 6:00 PM to 10:00 PM, and maybe two panels an hour from 10:00 PM to maybe 2:00 AM.

While all this is going on, three or four rooms will be set aside for writers to read their most recent works, and at the same time half a dozen authors will be autographing in or near the dealers' room. And of course there will be from two to four kaffeeklatsches occurring at the same time.

And let's not forget the free, round-the-clock science fiction movies that will be showing in an auditorium.

That's it. Every hour. And while all this is happening, the dealers room, the art show, and most of the other exhibits will be open as well.

Yeah, I know, it's overwhelming. Probably the best thing to do is log onto the Worldcon's web page after the final schedule is posted—usually two or three weeks before the con—and make your decision as to what items you definitely don't want to miss. It can take a few hours, and why spend that time at the convention when there are so many interesting things to do?

WHAT TO BRING

OK, so it's you first Worldcon. What do you pack? What do you bring? What do you leave behind?

Clothing: There is no panel or party where you won't be accepted wearing a t-shirt, shorts, and sandals…so what else you bring depends to a great extent on what makes you comfortable and where you plan to go when you leave the hotel.

If you're dining out, and especially if you plan to visit some upscale restaurants, bring along the appropriate clothes. If you plan to use the hotel's pool, bring along a swimsuit. (The skinny-dipping days of the 1970s and 1980s Worldcons are long gone.) If you're entering the masquerade, make sure you pack your costume in a way that won't break or otherwise harm it. If you plan to participate in the Regency dance (yes, every Worldcon has a Regency dance, don't ask me why), you might bring the appropriate Regency costume.

If you're on any medication, bring enough to see you through the convention; it's murder trying to fill a prescription in a strange city on a weekend.

I wouldn't bother bringing a laptop. First, there's too much to do (and you're paying quite a bit to do it) to waste time with your computer—and second, most of the people you want to chat with and send e-mail to are already at the con. (And most downtown hotels in major cities will charge incredibly high connect rates, measured by the minute if not the second.)

Bring any books you want autographed. This is your one chance all year to find 80% of the major authors in the field in one place, and they're all there for your convenience. Ditto any magazines.

Bring any guide books you may have purchased. Why try committing them to memory?

If you're into photo memories, bring your camera, or camcorder, with enough film, tape, disks, and batteries that you won't have to go out to purchase any.

Bring cash and/or credit cards. No one in a strange city wants to cash your checks.

Above all, bring the one item I never do without, the most important single item you can bring (besides money, that is): a small blank notebook—paper or electronic, makes no difference—that fits easily into a pocket.

Why?

Well, to begin with, before leaving home you'll write down the titles of all the books you're looking for in the huckster's room, as well as the dates of all the magazines, to make searching through the dealers' room a little easier.

You'll want to write down the room numbers of all your friends—and that could come to a cool 100 numbers right there. Impossible to remember them all.

As you find out when and where the parties are, you'll want to write down the times and room numbers of each. That's dozens more numbers and times.

You'll want to write down those events that you absolutely don't want to miss. Still more times and places.

You might also write down the addresses and phone numbers of all the restaurants you want to visit (and on a busy summer weekend in a major city, almost all the better ones, inside and outside the hotel, will require reservations.)

If you're a hopeful writer, you'll want to write down whatever it is you have sold, or promised to send, to which editor. Even if you're not, it helps to write down anything you promise to send/sell/trade with other fans.

If you're trading addresses, either street or e-mail, with new friends, you'll want to write them down.

So be sure you bring that blank book. You'll fill it up soon enough.

SAVING AND SPENDING MONEY

Worldcon isn't cheap. There are a few ways—not many, but a few—of saving money. To wit:

- Car pool to get there. With gas prices going through the roof, and airfares ditto, the cheapest way to get to any Worldcon (at least, any Worldcon on this continent) is to car pool.

- You'll hear stories of fans sleeping ten and twelve to a room. They are not an exaggeration, but it seems a bit excessive to me. Still, if you're traveling on a budget, it makes sense to share a room with perhaps 2 or 3 others.

- The price of an attending membership goes up every few months. The initial price is about a third of the at-the-door price. If you're late buying your membership—and the lead time is two years—there's a way around this. Surf the net and find someone who has an attending membership and can't use it; it can be sold and transferred to you prior to mid-July of the year the Worldcon is held . . . after that, it has to be done at the door. (Example: someone who bought his membership early at $80 wants to sell; the price is currently $200 if you buy from the convention; you offer to split the difference, the seller agrees, you get an attending membership for $140, you save $60, the seller makes $60, and everyone's happy.)

- If you see a second-hand book or magazine you want in the hucksters' room and it's too expensive for your budget, make an offer. Half the time you'll find the huckster is willing to deal.

And now a couple of proper ways to spend money:

- The maid who makes up your room doesn't work a 7-day week, so for the best service, and just to be fair, leave a buck or two on your pillow every morning when you go out for the day, rather than leaving $10 or $15 in a lump at the end of the week.

- Most parties don't want your money. But a few hospitality suites will have a bowl out with a note asking for donations. Put a couple of bucks in, or you may never be asked back.

- Okay, that's pretty much it—a way to vote for your favorite stories, books, editors, artists, movies and fanzines, and mingle with like-minded fans and writers at our grandest annual event.

REMEMBERING GIANTS

There is a great *Secret History of Science Fiction* to be written, one that exposes all the scams, lies, dirty-dealings, illicit affairs, and the like—but while I know more than my share of it, someone else will have to write it. I prefer pleasant memories of our giants, and I thought I'd share some with you before they're all forgotten by me and others.

* * * *

The late Robert Sheckley was my good friend, and even my collaborator in the year before his death.

Bob had an infallible way of beating Writer's Block He set himself an absolute minimum production of 5,000 words a day. If he couldn't think of anything else, he told me, he'd write his name 2,500 times. And on those days he *was* blocked, he'd sit down and force himself to start typing. And to quote him: "By the time I'd typed 'Robert Sheckley' 800 or 900 times, a little subconscious editor would kick in and say 'Fuck it, as long as you're stuck here for another 3,300 words, you might as well write a story.'"

According to Bob, it never failed.

* * * *

E. E. "Doc" Smith was the first pro I ever met at a con. Sweet man, very fond of fandom, very accessible to anyone. I always thought his greatest invention (other than the Lens and the Lensmen) was the seasonal Ploorians. Doc's daughter, Verna Trestrail, was a good friend, and I used to see her every year at Midwestcon and Rivercon. She once remarked that she helped her dad from time to time. So I asked how, and she replied that she had invented the Ploorians.

(Verna also invented the planet where Clarissa had to function in the nude. She told me that Doc bought a gorgeous painting of it—and Mrs. Doc took one look at it and consigned it to the attic for the next 25 years.)

* * * *

I met Robert A. Heinlein only a couple of times, at the 1976 and 1977 Worldcons, so I have no personal anecdotes to tell you about him—but Theodore Sturgeon had one. There was a point in the mid-1940s where Sturgeon was played out. He couldn't come up with any saleable stories, his creditors were after him, and he was terminally depressed…and he mentioned it to Heinlein in a letter. A week later he got a letter from Heinlein with 26 story ideas and a $100 bill to tide him over until he started selling again. And, according to Sturgeon, before the decade was over he had written and sold all 26 stories.

* * * *

I never met Fredric Brown. I know he grew up in Cincinnati, where I have lived the past 33 years, but no one here remembers meeting him. And I know he spent a lot of time working in Chicago, where I spent my first 33 years, and I never met anyone there who knew him either. But I do know he had a habit, especially when writing his mysteries (which far outnumbered his science fiction) of getting on a Greyhound bus and riding it for hundreds, sometimes thousands, of miles, until he had his plot worked out to the last detail. Then he'd come home, sit down, and quickly type the book he'd already written in his head while touring the countryside.

* * * *

Phil Klass (who writes as "William Tenn") told this one on a panel I moderated at a Worldcon a few years ago.

He was dating a new girl, and he mentioned it to Ted Sturgeon when they were both living in New York. Sturgeon urged Phil to bring the girl to his apartment for dinner. He and his wife would lay out an impressive spread, and Ted would regale the girl with tales of how talented and important Phil was. Phil happily agreed.

What he didn't know was that Ted and his then-wife were nudists. Phil and the girl walk up to the door of Ted's apartment, Phil knocks, the door opens, and there are Ted and his wife, totally naked. They greet them and start leading them to the dining room.

Phil's girl turns to him and whispers: "You didn't tell me we had to dress for dinner."

* * * *

Speaking of dinners…

At our first Worldcon, Discon I in 1963—I was 21, my still-beautiful child-bride Carol was 20—Randall Garrett invited a bunch of new writers and their spouses out for dinner—his treat. Then, during dessert, he excused himself to say something of vital importance to his agent, who was walking past the restaurant. He left the table—and we never saw him again. The rest of us got stuck with the tab (it was an expensive restaurant, we were broke kids, and Randy himself had the most expensive dish and wine on the menu.)

Move the clock ahead three years. Randy spots Carol and me at Tricon (the 1966 Worldcon in Cleveland) and offers to buy us dinner. We say sure. During dessert Carol excuses herself to go powder her nose, and I remember a phone call I have to make. We meet and walk out, leaving Randy with the tab he had promised to pay (but, according to Bob Silverberg, Bob Tucker, and others I'd spoken to before going out with him, had no intention of paying.)

Move the clock ahead one more year, and we're at NYcon III. Opening night Randy spots me across the room, turns red in the face, and yells: "Resnick, I'm never eating dinner with you again!"

I got an ovation from every pro and fan he'd ever stuck with a dinner check.

* * * *

And let me end with one about a living writer, just to be different—my friend, recent Nebula Grandmaster Robert Silverberg.

When Bob started selling to *Astounding*, he wrote under the name of "Calvin M. Knox." Some years later John Campbell asked him why. He replied that the word on the grapevine was that Campbell didn't want Jewish names on the cover. Campbell's reply: "Did you ever hear of Isaac Asimov?"

Then, as the conversation was drawing to a close and Bob was about to leave, Campbell asked him why of all the pseudonyms in the world he chose Calvin M. Knox. Bob replied that it was the most Christian-sounding name he could think of.

Finally, as he's leaving, Campbell asks what the "M" stands for.

Bob's answer: "Moses."

* * * *

How can you not love this field?

THE GREATEST THINKER OF THEM ALL

Science fiction isn't like any other field. Here we consider it an honor when someone builds on our ideas. Alfred Bester could write *The Demolished Man*, and then Robert Silverberg could write his answer to it in *The Second Trip*, and I could write my answer to Silverberg in "Me and My Shadow," and somebody could fictionally answer me, and nobody cries foul.

It happens all the time. But there is one particular writer whose ideas have been built upon by almost every science fiction writer for three-quarters of a century—and the wild part is that not only don't most fans know his name, but most pros who have used his notions as a springboard for their own stories and novels haven't even read him. His idea have been so thoroughly poached and borrowed and extrapolated from and built upon that writers are now borrowing five and six times removed from the source.

So I think perhaps it's time to tell you a little something about that source, because he science fiction's most remarkable thinker. His name was Olaf Stapledon.

Stapledon was a college professor, a Doctor of Philosophy at the University of Liverpool, and except for reading H. G. Wells, he probably had no idea that the field of science fiction existed. He certainly hadn't seen the pulp magazines, and he didn't know Hugo Gernsback's name for it (and in fact, when he began, Gernsback was still using the original "scientifiction" rather than breaking it into two words.)

Stapledon wasn't an elegant writer. I freely admit that his prose tends to crawl rather than soar—but his ideas soared higher than anyone else's ever had.

His first novel was *Last and First Men*, which follows the human race through eighteen startling evolutions for more than two million years, until our eventual extinction. In one evolution, we're nothing but giant brains. Later we emigrate to Venus, and eventually to Neptune, changing our bodies each time to adapt to our new environments.

Not bad for 1930. It is truly a novel of titanic concepts and sweeping vision—and it is condensed into very little more a page in his masterpiece, *Star Maker*, which is nothing less than the history of this and every other universe ever to exist from the beginning to the end of Time. Brian Aldiss has argued that this is the most important science fiction book ever written; I have shared that opinion from the day I finished the book more than 40 years ago.

It was in *Star Maker* that Stapledon explored the notion of galactic empires. He created endless races, some humanoid, some ichthyoid, some arachnoid, each with its own outlooks and morals and goals. People—well, intelligent beings, anyway—travel between the stars and ultimately even among the galaxies.

But there's more. The stars themselves are sentient, and eventually all the sentient entities in the galaxy—men, aliens, stars, everything—merge into a single Cosmic Mind.

But Stapledon didn't even stop there. He was interested in what *created* that Cosmic Mind, and became the first—and almost the only—to tackle the notion of God (*i.e.*, the Star Maker) in a non-religious way.

It's almost impossible to find a science fiction idea in the pulps of the 1930s and 1940s, or even the digests of the last half century, that does not owe something—usually a major something—to Stapledon. (In fact, when Larry Niven's brilliant *Ringworld* came out and credited Dyson Spheres as its inspiration, I decided that that was the first truly major science fictional concept that did not owe anything to Stapledon. I should have known better. When I read Freman Dyson's autobiography a few years later, I discovered—not surprisingly, in retrospect—that he credited Stapledon with inspiring the notion of the Dyson Sphere.)

Those two novels were quite enough to solidify Stapledon's place in the history of science fiction, but he wrote two others, not as huge in scope or as bold in concept, but sufficiently influential that any writer other than Stapledon would be happy to let his reputation rest on them. One was *Odd John*, the first novel of a mental (rather than a physical) superman; and the other was *Sirius*, about a dog with artificially enhanced intelligence. (I wonder how many books and stories owe a tip of the hat to those two "minor" novels? 500? 1,000? More?)

And now, three-quarters of a century after his two major works appeared, the books are all but forgotten. Ask almost any American science fiction writer if he's heard of Stapledon and he's likely to answer in the affirmative. Ask him if he's read *Star Maker* and the answer will usually be No.

And yet Stapledon's ideas are alive and well. You'll find them in almost every story in almost every issue of *Analog* and *Asimov's* and *Jim Baen's Universe*, and in well over half the science fiction novels you'll find in the bookstores and the libraries.

You might even mosey over to your local library or second-hand bookstore, pick up a copy of *Star Maker* (and perhaps *Last and First Men* as well) and experience our greatest thinker first-hand. Some of the concepts in them will seem like old friends, but others are still capable of blowing you away—which is one of the things that the very best science fiction is supposed to do.

THE SUN WILL COME
UP TOMORROW

There was a (brief) time when they closed the Patent Office because there was nothing left to invent. That was not only before the creation of jet planes, polio vaccine, and computers, but before the telephone and the electric light, believe it or not.

Just goes to show that the future has more surprises than most people think.

There was a time when people thought science fiction was all played out, too. When Apollo XI touched down and Neil Armstrong took his one small step for Man, half the talking heads on TV pointed out that now that we had reached the Moon, science fiction writers had run out of stories.

That was before the height of the New Wave (which, like most of the 1960s, took place more in the 1970s), and before cyberpunk, and before slipstream, and before… Well, you get the picture.

Then Dell killed its science fiction line, and so did Playboy Press, and Pyramid vanished, and Fawcett/Gold Medal were no longer players…but lo and behold, along came DAW and Tor and Baen and a host of smaller presses.

Amazing and *Galaxy* and *Marion Zimmer Bradley's Fantasy Magazine* and half a dozen other magazines died, and that was the end of magazines and short stories. Until you activated your computer and found us, and *Subterranean*, and *Clarkesworld*, and a dozen more e-zines, all paying competitive rates.

Sound familiar—like you've heard or read it all before? Like maybe three paragraphs ago?

Now that Sir Arthur C. Clarke has died, the last of the so-called "Big Three" (Heinlein, Clarke, and Asimov) has gone, and I'm hearing the same pessimism about the future from all the self-appointed experts who are as ignorant of the field as they are of its history.

Just about the time Stanley G. Weinbaum and Robert E. Howard and H. P. Lovecraft passed from sight, along came Robert A. Heinlein and Isaac Asimov and Theodore Sturgeon and A. E. van Vogt and Leigh Brackett. And when some of them went off to war, or out to Hollywood, here came Jack Vance and Ray Bradbury and Arthur C. Clarke. And when some of them went into teaching or Scientology, why, we had Robert Sheckley and Alfred Bester and Cyril Kornbluth in the full flowering of their literary powers. And when some of them deserted us for movies and non-fiction, here came Robert Silverberg and J. G. Ballard and Anne McCaffrey, and when everyone was sure there was no more talent out there, along came Roger Zelazny and Larry Niven and Ursula K. Le Guin…and it's been like that ever since.

I just came back from Worldcon and DragonCon, and I can tell you that there is still a *lot* of new talent that just came through the door or is about to start knocking at it. John Scalzi's only been around three or four years, but he's already got a Campbell, a Hugo, and a bestseller. Tobias S. Buckell has a Campbell nomination and a Nebula nomination. Naomi Novick, another Campbell winner, was a hit from the start, and the start was only three years ago. And there are a handful of (current) unknowns whose work I've seen, here at *Jim Baen's Universe* and elsewhere, who are just making their first sales now, and a number of them are going to be major forces in the field a few years up the road.

Just as there's always a new generation of writers, there's always a new generation of naysayers. The thing to remember is that history is not on their side.

And who knows more about future history than science fiction people?

* * * *

A little sidenote to those of you who nominate for the Hugos. If you're reading this, you're subscribers—and if you're subscribers, I have to assume you like the job Eric and I are doing with *Jim Baen's Universe*.

There are always five nominees in each Hugo category. This year it took 35 nominations to make the ballot for Best Short Fiction Editor.

Eric Flint received 15 nominations. I received 13 nominations. Eric and I as a team received 15 nominations. That's a total of 43, quite enough to make the ballot, which would have been very nice publicity for a relatively young magazine…but officially, they were totals of 15, 15 and 13. Next year you might nominate the pair of us together. Just a gentle suggestion.

WORDS MATTER

Ever hear of Joe Esterhaus?

No reason why you should. He doesn't know that *Jim Baen's Universe* exists. As far as I know, he's never read a word of science fiction.

I know about *him*, though. The reason I know is because he makes over a million dollars a screenplay, and is one of the very few writers, even in an industry that seems to play with Monopoly money, to pull down that kind of fee.

Ever hear of Tom Cruise? Brad Pitt? George Clooney? Harrison Ford? Julia Roberts? Sandra Bullock?

Sure you have. They make ten million or more per film, plus a piece of the gross—and that, of course, has nothing to do with the quality of the film. Film bombs, film makes no sense, film has an IQ that would freeze water (and they've all made their share of them), they get their money anyway.

So what does this have to do with science fiction?

Bear with me while I explain.

Recently Carol and I rented some *Tales of Tomorrow* DVDs from Netflix. That's a show that was run from 1949 to 1951, starting when we were 7 years old. It was in black-and-white, of course, always performed live (and you wouldn't believe how many professional actors from Lee J. Cobb on down muffed their lines), and boasted a series of young actors like Paul Newman who became household names.

About one in every seven episodes was pretty good, always allowing for the minimal budget and live performances by unprepared actors. About one in seven was acceptable. And about five in seven were unwatchable.

Moral: if the story is dumb, an actor, no matter how good he is, can't make it any smarter.

Then we tried *Suspense*, also from 1949. Another nice batch of actors: kids like Newman and Charlton Heston, established stars like Lili Palmer and Boris Karloff.

Not just bad, but embarrassingly snicker-out-loud bad. Even those brilliant actors couldn't save it.

Finally, for her birthday, I got Carol a complete set of bootleg DVDs of the fondly-remembered but never-released 2-year 78-episode run of *Science Fiction Theater* from 1955 and 1956, a time when most purported science fiction movies were actually anti-science and usually ended with lines such as "There are some things man was not meant to know." *Science Fiction Theater* was life a breath of fresh air, because it was clearly of the opinion that there is *nothing* man wasn't meant to know or learn. Each of these shows was introduced by Truman Bradley, in a state-of-the-art lab (circa 1955) that I would kill to play in. He'd show a couple of related cutting-edge experiments, and then explain that the episode you were about to see extrapolated from the experiments he'd just demonstrated. No stars at all. Probably the biggest names were Warren Stevens and John Howard, a couple of journeyman B-movie actors.

And the shows were pretty damned good. Hell, for the time, they were remarkably good.

And they were good for a simple reason: the producer understood that without a good script, all the stars in the world can't turn a sow's ear into a silk purse.

The principle still holds true today. Take a look at the latest Indiana Jones film. Got a huge superstar—Harrison Ford. Got the most powerful director in history—Stephen Spielberg. Got the most successful producer in history—George Lucas. Got a laughably bad script. End result: a laughably bad film.

It was true in 1949, and in 1955, and it's true today: every play and every movie starts with The Word. You ignore the words and you'd better be making a silent film or a ballet, or else you're in deep trouble from the get-go. Writers know that; television and movie executives still haven't figured it out.

Let me close with a wonderful (and true) story:

The great director Frank Capra was giving an interview to a few members of the press back in the 1940s, talking about how he put the famed "Capra Touch" on this scene and that… and finally his screenwriter could stand it no more. He walked over with a ream of blank paper, tossed it on the startled director's desk, and snapped: "Here! Put this Capra touch on *this!*"

A lesson worth remembering.

JOE SMITH

There's a secret author I want to tell you about. You don't know him, but you've bought some of his books. You probably didn't think much of them, but it didn't stop you from going out and buying more.

Editors don't like to talk about him much, because sooner or later they're forced to deal with him, and they don't dare reject him. Writers know about him, but he's got a lot of friends and a lot of clout, so they only talk about him to each other, in private. Critics know all about him, but they're not being paid to review his books—exactly.

So it's up to me to tell you about him.

A little background first: if a writer becomes successful enough, the day will come when he is, in the parlance of the field, "editor-proof."

What does it mean?

Simply this: no editor will dare risk losing that writer by performing his editorial duty thoroughly and properly.

You can write the scene yourself. "Stephen baby, it's a wonderful book, but it drags at the end, so could you tighten it a bit, please—maybe cut 20,000 words? Oh—and lose the brother, who doesn't contribute anything to the story anyway."

And the second scene, which follows immediately, is just as easy to write: "Screw you, fella. I'm taking the book down the street to Editor B, and he's going to take it (and, of course, *me*) without changing a word, and it'll my usual million hardcovers and three million paperbacks, and he's going to get rich, and my new publisher's going to get rich, and of course I'm going to get richer—and you, you poor son of a bitch, when your publisher finds out you let me get away, regardless of the reason, you're going to be on the unemployment line next week."

That's what it means when we say that a particular writer is editor-proof. Every field has a few of them, including science fiction.

Now, writers have as much pride in their work as anyone else, and very, very few of them turn in a piece of hackwork that they *know* is hackwork. They do their best, and everyone in the field will grant them that.

But try as they will, they don't always produce their best work first (or third, or fifth) time out of the typewriter or computer, and that is what editors are for. But as I pointed out, some editors are unable to fulfill their function when dealing with an editor-proof writer. They accept the manuscript, whatever the length, whatever the market, without question, or they lose the writer and probably their jobs.

So now and then, probably a little more often than we'd like, a very improvable book hits the stands, and it sells like crazy, based on the author's name, reputation, and past performances—but it's a turkey. The emperor has no clothes, and sooner or later most of the readers realize they've bought another book by Joe Smith.

Yeah—Joe Smith, Whenever one of these books (or stories) hits the stands, the writers and editors will admit, very softly, when almost no one is listening, that it didn't pass what has come to be known as the Joe Smith Test.

Which is to say, if the very same manuscript showed up on the editor's desk, and the author's name was Joe Smith, instead of Stephen or Dean or Danielle, could it have sold? And the answer is invariably: No. It sells based on the author's reputation and readership, rather than on its minimal quality.

How many books by Joe Smith have *you* bought lately?

LAST IMPRESSIONS

I met a young man at a recent convention. He had submitted a story he thought was wonderful to *Jim Baen's Universe*, and it had been turned down. Never got as far as Eric or me.

Okay, these things happen. Lots. For every would-be writer who can sell a story, there are dozens who never will.

But let me give you a little hint: if *you* don't have faith in your story, why should anyone else—like, for example, an editor? First impressions are important…but it's last impressions that count. I'm not saying that every rejected story is a misunderstood gem, but a story that remains in a desk drawer or a computer file never has a chance of being understood *or* misunderstood.

Ever hear of a novel called *Up the Down Staircase*? It spent a year on the *New York Times* bestseller list, and was a major motion picture starring Sandy Dennis, back in the bygone days when she was a major motion picture actress.

That was a last impression. You know how many times the book was turned down?

88.

You know how it finally sold? The author, Bel Kaufman, showed it to her minister's wife, whose brother happened to be peripherally connected to the publishing industry, and one thing led to another, and suddenly the 88-times-rejected manuscript was the Number One seller in the country. I guess it's lucky that the author didn't burn the damned thing after the 50th or 75th turndown after all.

You think that just happens in other fields?

Every publisher, major and minor, in the science fiction field turned down Frank Herbert's *Dune*. Every one, without exception. You know how it finally sold? Sterling Lanier, who had written some science fiction in the 1950s, was editing at Chilton, a book company that specialized in, so help me, books on motorcycle maintenance. He had hardly any budget to spend on such a flyer, but Herbert had reached the point where he was happy to take hardly any money for it. And the rest is history: a perennial bestseller, with something like 40 million copies sold worldwide, five bestselling sequels by Herbert and a batch more by his son Brian in collaboration with Kevin J. Anderson, two movies already made and a third in pre-production. All because Herbert believed in his book, and despite all those editorial first impressions that it was unsaleable, it was the last impression that counted.

Just one example, you suggest? Not hardly. One of the three or four most prestigious novels since *Dune* has been Joe Haldeman's *The Forever War*: Hugo winner, Nebula winner, bestseller—and, according to Joe, it was turned down by 16 publishers before he sold it.

It doesn't just happen in novels, and it doesn't just reflect poorly upon some editors.

For example, a single brilliant novelette is sometimes enough to make an author's career. That was certainly the case with Tom Godwin's "The Cold Equations," which 55 years after its initial appearance remains the most-discussed novelette on the internet, and was even the basis for a made-for-TV movie. Roger Zelazny became a superstar very early on with the publication of "A Rose for Ecclesiastes." Cyril Kornbluth is remembered (as a solo writer, apart from his collaborations with Fred Pohl) primarily for "The Little Black Bag." A couple of brilliant novellas, Walter M. Miller Jr.'s "A Canticle for Leibowitz" and Orson Scott Card's "Ender's Game" were so stunning and influential that each was expanded into a perennial bestselling novel.

And the same is true of novellas. Harlan Ellison's "A Boy and His Dog" and Thomas M. Disch's "The Brave Little Toaster" were both so well-written and had such universal appeal that they were made into motion pictures.

Speaking of motion pictures, Kurt Vonnegut's *Slaughterhouse-Five* was a major theatrical release with a top-notch cast. They haven't made any movies out of Gene Wolfe's *Book of the New Sun* series or Niven & Pournelle's *The Moat in God's Eye*, but there's no question that these have entered the realm of universally acknowledged Science Fiction Classic.

And you know something? Every single book and story I named in the preceding three paragraphs lost the Hugo. I don't mean that they were overlooked in obscure publications, or they came out so late in the year that no one had time to read them. Every one of them was a Hugo nominee—and not one impressed enough voters at the time to win.

I have to think that any writer would rather have had any of these stories to his credit that the mostly-forgotten tales that beat them at the time.

I was told a long time ago that if I wrote a good story, and it was rejected, I could give up on the editor and/or the market, but I should never give up on the story. I take that to be an axiom, and I need look no farther than the examples I have just offered you to conclude that last impressions beat the hell out of first ones.

LOOKING CLOSE TO HOME

Science fiction tends to take place a long distance away from here, both in time and in space. But it has always been able to take today's problems and explore them in exotic settings that help remove them from the emotional bitterness and even hatred that they engender among those who find themselves on the other side of the issue.

And today, as always, there are some major problems that science fiction should be (and is) tackling in less personal settings.

For example, as I write these words, it is late May of 2009, and while both sides of this particular issue have been arguing it for a couple of years, President Obama and former Vice President Cheney have just drawn clear distinctions between the two positions, and each has argued his case passionately. And the question the American people are being asked to decide is: at what point, if any, are harsh interrogation methods justified? At what point do they become torture? And is torture itself ever justified?

I would guess that every civilized person's first response is to say that no, of course torture is never justified—so why are we having the debate?

Okay. We now have been told by Mr. Cheney that waterboarding revealed the existence of a planned attack on a bank tower in Los Angeles, a plan that was thwarted only because the victim of the waterboarding, who had refused to cooperate with his interrogators for weeks prior to that, gave them all the vital details they needed during his unpleasant experience.

Unjustified?

According to the polls, the American people are split on it. After all, there were a lot of planned attacks. This one might not have come off.

Now let's pretend that my wife works in that building, and would be instantly killed if and when a plane rammed into it.

Still unjustified? Not to me, not when I have that kind of personal stake in it.

So we come to the crux of it: is torture acceptable under rigidly-defined extreme circumstances, like saving the 5,000 Angelinos who might be in that tower at Zero Hour? Or—everyone's favorite example—if it is the only way to find out where a bomb (possibly a nuke) has been hidden before it explodes?

But there's another consideration, too. Everyone will grant that waterboarding and similar methods are harsh methods of interrogation indeed. But *are* they torture?

After all, the terrorist who revealed the information about the tower was perfectly healthy the next day. He suffered no ill effects, and waterboarding him may have saved a few thousand lives. (Of course, it may not have saved them; as President Obama points out, we'll never know what continued gentler methods might have achieved.) But the fact remains that, unlike the torture our soldiers suffered at the hands of the Japanese in World War II, this man emerged none the worse for wear. Indeed, our navy Seals undergo waterboarding routinely to prepare them for it should they fall into enemy hands; no one has ever died or been permanently disabled by it.

Still, many—including our President—feel that it is opposed to the principles embedded in the Constitution. There is an argument, perhaps valid, that using such methods makes us no better than our enemies. And there is another argument that until you *know* there is a hidden bomb set to explode in three hours, you apply all legitimate methods of questioning on the assumption that sooner or later you'll get the answers you need.

I realize there are two sides to the question, and each side is sure it has the morally correct position. Which makes it perfect fodder for science fiction.

You want another one, plucked from today's headlines?

Is a preventive war ever justified? *Must* a moral, ethical nation (like, hopefully, us) wait to be attacked before going to war?

Now, when polled, most people today say the war in Iraq was not justified, because clearly our intelligence was wrong about the weapons of mass destruction. But that's not the example science fiction should pay attention to; it has been proven that no nukes existed in Iraq. Case closed.

But as I write this, the North Koreans tested a nuke in a major underground explosion 36 hours ago, and every watching and listening post says that what they tested was more powerful than the bomb that was dropped at Hiroshima. And between that test and this minute, they've tested a missile that could deliver nuclear warheads.

And they don't like us very much.

So *this* is where science fiction can examine the question from both sides: stories in which we *do* attack an enemy with devastating weapons that has threatened us, and stories where we don't, where we apply diplomacy, economic pressure, or simply hope for the best.

Another?

Look at our southern border. Extrapolate that any way you want: we become an isolated island nation, with walls the length of the Mexican and Canadian border; we become a Spanish-speaking nation that is 85% Hispanic by 2060 A.D.; or we find a happy compromise—and if so, what is it?

Scientific American and its sisters are valid sources for material…but everywhere you look there's material for stories, set in the almost-here-and-now or examining the same problems in the far future, with aliens and robots and what-have-you substituting for waterboarding and North Korea and Hispanics. And this is one editor who thinks these very human problems are more important than how your space-ship can avoid meteors at light speeds.

Politicians can predict the future, usually with great flourish and very little intelligence, but only science fiction can *show* it to you, can lay it out and examine all the consequences.

That's why we remain the most important form of fiction in the entire realm of literature.

WHAT'S IN A NAME?

So here's the situation. Street and Smith, the giant pulp chain, also owns a radio show back in 1929, a mystery anthology show with no continuing characters except the announcer—and the announcer happens to be the one of the most popular characters on the air, a mysterious figure known only as the Shadow.

So someone at Street and Smith decides, just to make sure no one swipes the character, maybe they should put him in a one-shot pulp magazine, so they can prove that he's copyrighted and that they own him.

They hire Walter Gibson, a guy who splits his time between being a magician and a pulpster, and pay him $500 to come up with a novel, which he does in a few weeks' time. No one thinks much will come of it, and Gibson writes it as "Maxwell Grant," possibly so it won't be associated with his real name when he's applying for magic gigs. Street and Smith accepts the manuscript, assigns the cover art, prints it, and that, they think, is that.

But the magazine sells out in near-record time, so they decide to make *The Shadow* a monthly, and Gibson is hired at $500 a novel to start churning them out. This is not bad pay in 1930, because the average American is making about $1,200 a year—and about 25% of the average Americans can't find work.

So "Maxwell Grant" starts grinding out a Shadow novel a month, and Street and Smith publishes it—and suddenly more than a million people are buying each issue, and *The Shadow* is the hottest property they've got.

They can't believe their luck, so they do nothing for a couple of years, and then they decide to go monthly, since the magazine is still selling like hotcakes. They approach Gibson, tell him how much they love him and that they're all one big happy family, and ask if he can turn out two Shadow novels a month. He says yes. Fine, they say; we're in business. Just a minute, says Gibson; you're selling millions of copies, you're making money hand over fist, and surely you can afford to give me a raise to $750 a manuscript.

Suddenly they don't love him quite so much, and maybe he's not really related to their big happy family after all. We're paying $500, they say; take it or leave it.

If you don't give me $750, says Gibson, I'm walking— and I'll take my millions of readers with me.

Street and Smith laughs. (You didn't know heartless corporations could laugh? Now you do.) You can leave, they say—but your audience is staying right here. Next month there will be a new Maxwell Grant and who will know the difference?

It takes Gibson about three seconds to realize that Street and Smith are holding all the cards, and he gives in and keeps writing $500 Shadow novels.

And the gentlemen running Street and Smith decide that they have lucked onto a pretty good policy. It is time to develop another "hero pulp"—which is to say, a pulp magazine with a continuing character—and after speaking with pulpster Lester Dent they hit upon Doc Savage. Only this time it isn't the author who decides to use a pseudonym; it is Street and Smith, who insist upon it, and henceforth all 180+ Doc Savage novels are be written by "Kenneth Robeson," just as the 300+ Shadow novels are written by Maxwell Grant.

And rival publishers are not slow to notice just what Street and Smith is doing to combat inflation (for which read: avoiding paying a fair price to writers). Henceforth, although most of the Spider novels are written by Norvell Page, every one appears under the byline of "Grant Stockbridge."

"Kenneth Robeson" is so popular as the author of Doc Savage that he also writes *The Avenger* series of pulps. The only author of a continuing hero pulp character who doesn't have to put up with this is Edmond Hamilton, who is writing

Captain Future novels for Better Publications, and the only reason why he doesn't have to put up with it is because he is the only science fiction writer working for Better, and no one else there knows how to write this Buck Rogers crap.

Well, the last hero pulp died in the late 1940s, and that was the end of the practice for more than 30 years.

Now move the clock ahead, and wander over to the romance field, where a young woman named Janet Dailey began writing for Harlequin when she was 31 years old, and by the time she was 37 she had sold a truly phenomenal total of 110 million books for them. They loved her, and they thought she loved them...

...and then Silhouette (which is now owned by Harlequin, but was its greatest rival back then) bought Janet and her millions of readers away.

And Harlequin swore this would never happen to them again, that they might lose a writer from time to time, but never the writer's millions of book-buying fans...and finally someone (or maybe someone's grandfather) remembered the hero pulps—and suddenly, if you were a Harlequin writer, you were not allowed to use your real name. If you wanted to sell them, you *had* to use a pseudonym.

Now, the world and the law had changed a little over the years, and Harlequin (and Silhouette, too, after Harlequin bought it) had to concede this much: only the author who first created the pseudonym could use it. If an author left, there wouldn't be a new author writing under that name the next week...but the flip side was that the author couldn't take the pseudonym with her when she left.

That was the situation when my daughter, Laura—an award-winning fantasy writer these days—first broke into print as a romance writer. There was a settlement somewhere in the late 1990s and Harlequin reluctantly allowed authors to be themselves again.

But good ideas never die, they just hibernate from time to time. I would imagine publishers will be using this particular one to protect themselves and shaft writers at least once more during my lifetime.

PROS AND CONS

There was a time—and not so long ago, either—when if you were a fan and you wanted to see your favorite author(s), there was only one place to go: Worldcon, the World Science Fiction Convention.

For the first decade of its existence it was the only game in town, and for the next three decades it was still the 900-pound gorilla in the convention room. But the world changes, and that includes the world of science fiction conventions.

Worldcon's organizers and powers-that-be decided some time back that they didn't want to be bothered by all the "peripheral" fans—the gamers, the comic book fans, the TV fans (unless it was an Approved TV show like *Star Trek* or *Babylon-5*), the anime fans, and so on. So those fans were made to feel somewhat less than welcome, which is to say there was very little attention or programming paid to their special interests—and before long they began looking for other conventions that were more congenial to them.

And they found them.

In quantity.

And suddenly, one day, the Worldcon, which at its all-time largest, the year they showed all the *Star Wars* movies before they were released on tape, never reached 10,000 attendees, and usually numbered from 5,000 to 7,000, found itself dwarfed by conventions that welcomed everybody and programmed for everybody, that were run by competent professionals rather than by hit-or-(usually)-miss volunteer staffs.

And here we are in 2009. ComicCon drew 120,000 attendees. DragonCon drew 50,000. A-Kon, an anime con, drew 17,000.

And Worldcon, the biggie, the one you absolutely couldn't miss? If you believe their inflated figures, just under 4,000; I don't know of anyone who attended and feels there were as many as 3,000.

But whether it was 3,000 or 4,000, that's just a small corner of a room at the ones I mentioned above.

Okay (I hear you say), so they draw a lot of fans. Good for them. But Worldcon's where you go for the writers, right?

Well, yes—but that's not quite as right as it used to be.

We're in a very poor economy, and publishers are being careful how and where they spend their money. And they tend to spend it where there are the most readers. ComicCon drew more science fiction publishers this year than Worldcon, which would have been unthinkable even five years ago. I have been to the last three DragonCons (where Baen Books is always a presence), and the number of publishers and editors has literally tripled in that short time.

Part of this sea change is simply because certain Worldcon movers and shakers decided years ago that they didn't want "peripheral" fans taking up space and demanding programming that catered to their special interests. Another major part is the Worldcon's choice of venues. We can call it "*World*con" all we want, but the fact remains that most of the publishers, most of the writers, and most of the fans are in the United States. When Worldcon was held in other countries perhaps twice a decade, as it was for the last third of the 20th Century, attendance plummeted as expected, but it had little or no effect on subsequent Worldcons' attendance. But Worldcon has gone a little overboard lately: next year's Worldcon (in Australia) will mark the fifth time in eight years that it has been out of the country. Add 2008's Denver Worldcon, which was not very close to anything when gas was $4.50 a gallon, and it's easy to see why fans have chosen other conventions.

And as I pointed out, publishers spend their money where it will do the most good, which is to say: where the potential book buyers are. Even the Worldcon committees should have no problem with that logic—and indeed, while a couple of editors went on their own nickel, this year's Worldcon had no official presence from Eos, Bantam/Spectra, Ballantine/del Rey, Pyr, DAW, Golden Gryphon, Orbit, Subterranean, F&SF, Realms of Fantasy, and a dozen et ceteras.

I think what the Worldcon movers and shakers haven't yet figured out, or possibly don't particularly care about, is that if the publishers stop supporting Worldcon and support other conventions instead, their editors will show up at those other cons.

And like it or not, writers will go where the editors are. This is, after all, a business.

And eventually—and it's clearly happening; all you have to do is look at the attendance figures for the last few Worldcons—the fans will follow the writers.

I hope Worldcon wakes up and smells the coffee. I have been going since 1963, and I'll continue to go as long as Worldcon exists—but I'm a fan as well as a writer. The part of me that writes for a living has already added DragonCon and ComicCon to my regular schedule.

So if you're out to meet your favorite writer(s), before you commit to Worldcon or nothing, start checking the web pages of the rival conventions (and don't forget World Fantasy Con—not huge, but always star-studded.) You just might be pleasantly surprised.

THE CRITICS, LORD LOVE 'EM

The critics are secure in their opinions, and I suppose that's a good thing.

The critics also have very short memories, and I suppose that's what leads them to be so secure in their opinions. In fact, I can think of no other reason.

Our first major crtitic was Damon Knight, whose most important reviews and opinions were collected by Advent Press in three separate editions of *In Search of Wonder*. He took Ray Bradbury to task for all the flaws in his science. Yeah, the same Ray Bradbury who became the only science fiction writer ever to win a Pulitzer Prize, when he was awarded one last year for his lifetime contribution to science fiction.

Never one to pull his punches, Knight also stated that Robert E. Howard and H. P. Lovecraft bored him. Although they both died in the mid-1930s, and Damon was still writing in the 1990s, there's an awful lot of Howard and HPL available today, and almost none of Damon.

The next major critic was James Blish, who knew critics had to answer for faulty judgments and wrote most of his criticism as "William Atheling, Jr.," the best of which were collected in two volumes, *The Issue at Hand* and *More Issues at Hand*. He couldn't stand the fact that Robert Sheckley wrote one funny story after another in the 1950s, in a field that was created to explore serious extrapolations. But 50 years later Sheckley was a Worldcon Guest of Honor, and humorists like Douglas Adams and Sir Terry Pratchett were living on the bestseller list, while almost all of Blish's serious extrapolations were long out of print.

When the New Wave came along, a lot of the critics announced that science fiction had finally come of age, and pronounced hard science dead. Damned good thing no one ever told Vernor Vinge or Greg Bear or Greg Benford or Catherine Asaro or Sir Arthur C. Clarke or that whole crowd.

There was a time when the critics were shocked that science fiction acknowledged that there were two sexes, and that girls were more than just lumpy boys who were there to hold the hero's horse (or spaceship), or to be rescued when they were one grope away from a Fate Worse Than Death. Then along came Philip Jose Farmer, and then Ursula K. Le Guin, and Joanna Russ, and the entire New Wave, and suddenly there wasn't a critic around who hadn't always known that science fiction was the perfect vehicle for examining the differences—and relationships—between the sexes.

If you look at the bookstores today, you'll see that the critics have kept their perfect record intact.

Back about thirty years ago two writers came up with major innovations. The brilliant William Gibson became the partial creator, most popular practitioner, and poster child for cyberpunk, and the critics adored it, pronouncing it to be nothing less than Science Fiction Come of Age (their Pronouncement of Choice).

At the same time Anne Rice decided that far from being ghoulish, blood-sucking, unclean dead things, vampires were actually kind of sexy. Critics laughed and snickered.

Okay, move the clock ahead to December of 2009, and take a look at the results. Gibson has pretty much abandoned cyberpunk, and I'd be surprised if the field is producing three cyberpunk novels a year. But I'd be equally surprised if we were publishing less than one vampire romance (excuse me: "paranormal romance") a day, and it looks like next year there will be almost as many zombie romances as legitimate science fiction novels.

Wherever would we be without the critics?

CHEMO FOR ALGERNON

(Many of you will read this here for the first time: a wonderful writer, Kage Baker, is in the hospital, fighting for her life against brain cancer. I've never run a reprint in this space, but this seemed a proper time for the following, which I wrote a few years ago.)

* * * *

Like most people, I grew up in a household where cancer was considered the deadliest killer of all, and where the word itself was uttered only in hushed whispers. I suspect if we'd been Catholics we'd have crossed ourselves every time we mentioned it.

So when Carol, my wife, was diagnosed with breast cancer in 1999, it looked an awful lot like the end of the world.

Just goes to show how out of touch with science even a science fiction writer can be.

First of all, they didn't have mammograms when I was growing up; they do now. The cancer showed up on a routine mammogram. It was still microscopic. 25 years ago it would have gone undetected until it formed a discernable lump, at which point the very best Carol might have hoped for was a mastectomy, and the likelihood of it killing her was better than 50-50.

But *this* cancer was only two cells wide. Cells, not inches or centimeters.

The first step was to cut it out. It wasn't a mastectomy. It wasn't even a lumpectomy. It was a one-inch incision that removed an area about the size of a golf ball—considerably larger than the affected area. Outpatient surgery. She was home an hour after they finished.

They did some more mammograms, and determined that they'd cut it all out. We thought they were done—and ten years ago they would have been—but they then suggested to Carol that she undergo radiation treatments and start taking the medication tamoxifen citrate. Why, we asked, if the cancer was gone? Because, they explained, the radiation treatments—there would be 33 of them—would catch any stray cancer cells they might have missed, and the tamoxifen (she would take one pill daily for the next five years with absolutely no side effects) would just about guarantee that the cancer would never recur.

Just about? Right. The odds of recurrence were 20% without the radiation and the tamoxifen, and less than 1/2 of 1% with them. Carol can count as well as the next person, and liked 200- to-1 odds better than 4-to-1, so she agreed to the treatments.

That's when our friends decided to warn us off. Her hair will fall out. She'll be vomiting day and night. She'll lose 40 pounds. I'm surprised that they didn't suggest that the enamel on her teeth might melt.

Turns out they were as uninformed as I was. Yes, 20 and 30 years ago radiologists bombarded a cancer patient rather indiscriminately with cobalt, which often did as much harm as the cancer itself...but 20 years in the field of medicine is like 2,000 years in the field of archaeology—ancient history.

They still use cobalt, but they were able to pinpoint the radiation so it hit only the target, nothing else; the trunk of her body was never radiated. The treatments took about a minute each; she'd enter the hospital's radiation lab at 1:00 every afternoon, and be done ten minutes later. She never got sick. She never lost her hair. She never vomited. The only side effect was a slight "sunburn" after about 25 treatments.

In short, the appearance and cure of this dread disease was pretty much of a non-event.

The oncologist seemed resigned to the fact that people didn't know about the enormous steps that have been made in the treatment of cancer. I was sure it was the Number One killer of Americans; I discovered it was Number Four, and moving down the list rapidly.

Early detection is the key, of course, and thanks to the CAT scan and the mammogram they can detect things much earlier than they used to. But it's not just those two remarkable machines. For example, any man over 50 can—and should—get a PSA blood test every year, and they can tell from it whether or not he has (or is likely to soon have) prostate cancer.

The greatest weapon, once cancer is found, is no longer the scalpel, but chemotherapy. Chemo, like radiation, used to make the patient horribly sick on its own. I remember that my mother, who died of cancer 20 years ago, would go into the hospital once a month for her chemo dose; they'd hook her up to a drip overnight and it would run a month's supply into her. She'd be too sick and too weak to stand up for three or four days; then the hospital would release her for another four weeks, and she had to smoke pot the rest of the month to avoid the constant nausea brought on by the chemo.

No longer. Not only has the science of chemotherapy improved to the point where it only attacks the cancerous cells, rather than all suspect and non-suspect cells in a given area, but you no longer need a month's dose all at once. These days you can walk around with a small device discreetly attached to you that will slowly but constantly inject the chemo into you, a drop at a time, around the clock, so you're never sickened and overwhelmed by too powerful a dose. Think back to the dawn of the last century—1900. What could we do about cancer then? Not much. There is a memorable line in John Wayne's last movie, *The Shootist*, when he discovers (in 1899) that he has cancer. He asks James Stewart, the doctor, if he can operate. Stewart sadly shakes his head and replies, "I'd have to gut you like a fish." That, alas, was the state of the art back then.

Now, a century later, if we can find it early enough, we can cure 80% of the cases. (Finding it early enough is the problem. Most people, unbelievable as it seems to me, don't want to hear bad news from their doctor—so if something is wrong, like a small lump, they wait until is it a large lump before reporting it, thereby assuring they it isn't caught early enough.)

Nonetheless, medical science marches on. Are they building a better mousetrap?

Nope. They're building a better mouse.

Honest.

The National Cancer Institute has just funded 19 groups of scientists for what has come to be known as the Mouse Models of Human Cancers Consortium. (Too bad they didn't come up with a name that would lend itself to a snappy acronym.)

And what is this all about?

We've learned enough about genetics and DNA, and enough about cancer, to create a subspecies of mouse that can actually mimic human cancers. Such an animal has never existed before, so almost all meaningful cancer treatments have been tried out on exceptionally small groups of human guinea pigs, and progress, though it seems amazingly fast, has actually been quite slow.

Now, however, we have the ability to reproduce breast cancer, brain tumors, lung cancer, colon cancer, any kind of carcinoma you want, in hundreds of thousands of mice, which will then be subjected to every conceivable type of cure. If you lose a few hundred along the way, it's not like losing a few hundred human patients, so *everything*, no matter how radical, will be tried. By mid-21st century, I would imagine that even highly-developed cancers will be treatable with undreamed-of approaches that make radiation and chemotherapy and drugs such as tamoxifen seem crude and primitive.

Will it work? Absolutely. The University of Cincinnati, one of the 19 groups, has already produced an asthma-resistant breed of mouse that can breathe massive amounts of smog without suffering asthma attacks.

I suppose by the 22nd century this will all be moot, that we'll have found a way to clone our various internal organs so that when you come down with heart disease or lung cancer you simply stop by the lab and trade your diseased organ in ("trade it in" is probably not the right expression, is it?) for the genetically identical heart or lung that's been waiting on ice (no, it won't really be sitting in a meat freezer) for you.

But in the meantime, medical science uses what it has and keeps performing its daily miracles. I think our best hope in the war against cancer is the new species of mouse.

Every new species needs a name. I think we should call these the Algernon Mice.

SO LONG, AND THANKS FOR ALL THE FISH

So here we are, in the final issue of *Jim Baen's Universe*. It's completing its fourth year, I'm completing my third year with it, and we both wish it could have gone on.

But weep not for it. It served its primary purpose, which is to say, it created a market for professional-quality electronic stories that paid professional rates at a time when the short story seemed to be an endangered species.

Back when the internet was just starting to take off, there were dozens of start-up science fiction magazines. Any writer who was around twelve to fifteen years ago can vouch for the fact that we all used to get almost weekly offers from hopeful new e-zines, the gist of which was always: Give us top-qualify stories for free today and we'll make you rich next week (or next month, or next year). Never happened.

Then every wannabee writer started posting their unsaleable stories on the web. There were literally tens of thousands of them, all free, almost all unreadable.

There were a few exceptions. GalaxyOnline.com paid top rates, mostly for non-fiction, but it began running fiction toward the end—and it was gone in less than a year. *Omni Online* paid top rates as well...but the fiction was never a major part of *Omni* in print or in phosphors, and it was gone pretty quickly. *Scifi.com* stuck around awhile, but it was basically a loss leader for the SciFi Channel, and it went the way of all (electronic) flesh.

The first web publisher to actually pay good money and show a profit was the still-extant Fictionwise.com, which went on the assumption that there was so much free dreck on the internet that people would pay actual coin of the realm to read authors of known quality, even reprints—and reprints are what Fictionwise.com provided. They started with just a few science fiction writers—myself, Robert Silverberg, Nancy Kress, James Patrick Kelly, a couple of others—and lo and behold, we were all making surprisingly handsome royalties within half a year. So they began expanding. Before long they'd added Stephen King, Robert A. Heinlein, Dan Brown, Robert Ludlum, and that whole crowd—and these days, I'd guess that half their inventory consists of romance novels.

About halfway through the millennium's first decade it was Jim Baen who decided that it was time to start a legitimate professional science fiction e-magazine, and he got Eric Flint to edit it. It would pay 25 cents a word at the top (compared to 8 cents for the digests), and 8 cents as its absolute bottom rate. It would run about 200,000 words an issue, as opposed to the 90,000 to 100,000 the digests were running. It would do animated covers that were beyond the scope of the digests to match. It would buy at least one first story an issue. It would run full-color illos. It would open Baen's Bar to an ongoing discussion of the magazine, and *JBU's* editors and writers were encouraged to participate. It would charge the same as the digests, but it would also allow more expensive levels of subscription with more perks and benefits to those subscribers who wanted them. It would give readers a viable, legitimate alternative to the digests.

And we did that. We published Greg Benford, Kristine Kathryn Rusch, Eric Flint, Nancy Kress, David Gerrold, me, David Drake, Esther Friesner, Elizabeth Bear, Ben Bova, Barry Malzberg, David Brin, Jay Lake, L. E. Modesitt Jr., Julie Czernida, James P. Hogan, Jack McDevitt, Kevin J. Anderson, Gene Wolfe, and many other stellar writers. We ran the best regular columns we could find. We put two stories on the Hugo ballot.

So what happened?

What happened was that we convinced a bunch of other entrepreneurs to do the same thing. *JBU* was conceived as an alternative to the digests—more names, more art, more pages, all for the same price—and for a year that's exactly what it was.

But then came *Clarkesworld*. And *Subterranean's* outstanding magazine went from paper to phosphors. And Orson Scott Card started a professional e-zine. And suddenly, about the time I joined *JBU* as Eric's co-editor, our primary competition was not *Asimov's* and *Analog* and *F&SF*, which were selling for $4.95 an issue, but half a dozen pro-paying e-zines that charged nothing at all. Take a look at *Subterranean:* the typical issue features Elizabeth Bear, John Scalzi, Joe Lansdale, me, and 3 or 4 other well-known writers...and it's *free*. Try *Clarkesworld*; their recent authors include Robert Reed, Jay Lake, Mary Robinette Kowal, me, Jeffrey Ford, and cetera. And it's *free*.

The business model for *Jim Baen's Universe* was valid when it began, but outmoded within a year of its initial issue. To this day we can compete with the digests...but we can't *sell* an e-zine when so many quality e-zines are available for free.

We'd like to think that we're at least partially responsible for those e-zines. We'd like to think they looked at *JBU* and said, "Hey, we can do that!"

Lest you think I'm exaggerating, here's a simple fact. When *JBU* started up, we were the only e-zine paying what the Science Fiction Writers of America considers a professional rate.

And how many are there today? It's a field in flux, but this list is valid on the day I'm writing this (March 24, 2010):

- *Jim Baen's Universe* (for another week, anyway)
- *Subterranean*
- *Clarkesworld*
- *Orson Scott Card's Intergalactic Medicine Show*
- *Abyss & Apex*
- *Beneath Ceaseless Skies*

- *Cemetery Dance*
- *Brainharvesting*
- *Fantasy Magazine*
- *Flash Fiction Online*
- *Futurismic*
- *Heliotrope*
- *Shock Totem*
- *Strange Horizons*
- *Chizine*
- *Lightspeed*
- *Cobblestone*
- *The Pedestal*

At the same time, there are still just three digests among the print magazines. *Realms of Fantasy,* a full-sized "slick" magazine, died and was just purchased and resurrected by Warren Lapine.

And that's the ballgame as far as magazines that pay what SFWA considers pro rates. *Amazing* came back from the grave for a 4th time and died yet again. The resurrected *Argosy* looked great and expired after 3 issues. *Marion Zimmer Bradley's Fantasy Magazine* fell by the wayside. So did *Aboriginal SF*. So did *Science Fiction Age*.

That's right. There are 22 professional science fiction (and related) magazines. 4 of them are print; 18 of them are electronic.

It looks like the science fiction short story has been saved. I like to think we had a little something to do with it.

PART 2: INTRODUCTIONS TO BOOKS BY FRIENDS

INTRODUCTION TO PART 2

Over the years I have been asked by any number of friends and editors to write introductions to books, mostly but not always collections. These are just a sample, selected because they show you something other than a listing of the contents story by story, but tell you a little something about the writer as well.

INTRODUCTION TO *A THOUSAND DEATHS*

There is a wonderful exchange in one of my favorite films, *They Might Be Giants*, between George C. Scott, who thinks he is Sherlock Holmes, and a Mr. Bagg, whom he has just met:

MR. BAGG: I thought you were dead.
"HOLMES": The Falls at Reichenbach? I know. I came back in the sequel.

* * * *

We used to talk about character actors coming back in the sequels—they'd die in one B movie and there they'd be, back again, two months later—but the above scene was the first time anyone ever actually gave voice to the notion for public consumption.

And then came Sandor Courane.

Actually, the title of this book—*A Thousand Deaths*—is a wild exaggeration. I doubt that Courane has died much more than eight or nine times. Surely less than a dozen.

But they weren't phony deaths. When I was a kid and we had the first television set on our block, back in the late 1940s, my friends and I used to gather around the tube after school and watch the endless Tom Mix serials. At the end of one episode we'd see him and Tony (his horse, for the uninitiated) fall over the side of a mountain and plunge to their deaths, or get run over by a train. Then we'd wait breathlessly for a few days until the next episode, which always started a minute before the last one ended, and we would see that our eyes had betrayed us, that we only *thought* we'd seen Tom and Tony fall to their doom, that Tom had somehow dived to safety in the last nanosecond.

There's none of that sleight of hand for Sandor Courane, no sir. When he dies, he *dies*, and there's no two ways about it. He stops functioning. He stops breathing. He enters what you might call a long-term open-ended state of non-life.

But he still comes back in the sequel.

Most people don't have any trouble coping with reality. Every now and then you get someone like Philip K. Dick, who questions it just about every time out of the box. But no one ever played as many tongue-in-cheek games with it as George Alec Effinger, the sly wit who took such pleasure in constantly killing Courane and bringing him back.

Take, for example, *The Wolves of Memory* and "Fatal Disk Error." In the former, TECT runs the universe and eventually kills Courane. But in the sequel, "Fatal Disk Error," Courane kills TECT, and then we find out that it was really George Alec Effinger who created (and destroyed) them both. And since George was never content merely to put in one or two unique twists when he could come up with more, we also learn that the story was rejected by an editor who was a little too based in reality, so George resurrects TECT just to kill it again.

Or consider "In the Wings." Doubtless at one time or another you've seen or read Ionesco's classic play, *Six Characters in Search of an Author*. This one might just as easily be titled: "Effinger's Stock Characters in Search of a Plot." The entire story takes place in the wings (or perhaps the locker room) of Effinger's mind, where Courane and other regular Effinger characters are waiting impatiently for George's oversexed muse to get him to write Chapter 1 so they can go to work. And of course, Courane is killed again. At least once. (Not to worry. It is impossible to let the cat out of the bag when discussing an Effinger story. If you like the image of cats, it's a hell of a lot more like herding them. Trust me on this.)

Okay (I hear you say), now I know what a Sandor Courane story is: things happen and he dies.

Okay, I answer. Go read "The Wicked Old Witch" and then tell me what a Sandor Courane story is about. This one may be one of the least likely love stories you'll ever read. (Or it may not be a love story at all. George was like that.)

There's one here that I commissioned some years ago, when Disney's Aladdin movie was coming out and I edited an anthology of stories about genies and magic teapots and the like, and of course I invited George to write a story for it. What I got was "Mango Red Goes to War." It's a Courane story, of course, or it wouldn't be here—but it's a lot more than that. For one thing, it's George explaining to me exactly how he's constructing the story, not by phone or e-mail but as part of the story itself. And with all the three-wish stories that filled the book, George's was the most original. (George was like that, too.)

Poor Courane has reality yanked from under him yet again in "From the Desk Of," in which he's a science fiction writer. (George loved to write about science fiction writers. Nothing ever went smoothly for them.) He's a science fiction editor in "The Thing From the Slush," a story I am convinced George wrote after reading one too many Adam-and-Eve endings in some magazine's slush pile.

I won't tell you a thing about "Posterity," except that it ends with a question no one else had ever thought of asking, but a legitimate, even an important, question nonetheless, one that most writers I know would have a difficult time answering. (George could be so amusing that sometimes people didn't recognize the fact that he asked important questions. Lots of 'em.)

In the course of his career, which ended all too soon with his death in 2002, George created three ongoing characters.

Marid Audran was the star of the Budayeen books and stories—*When Gravity Fails, A Fire in the Sun*, and the like—and that is clearly the most important work he ever did.

Maureen Birnbaum was the ongoing star on a new genre of humor that George created, which I call Preppie Science Fiction. She was the funniest of all his creations.

His third character, of course, was Sandor Courane. Not as important as Marid, not as funny as Maureen Birnbaum. But I'll tell you something: the Courane stories are far and away the most creative, the most off-the-wall stories that George or just about anyone else ever put to paper.

Enough introduction. Sit down and read them, and I'll bet Courane's life you agree with me. (After all, what have I—or he—got to lose?)

A LARGE AND REMARKABLE TALENT

I've been waiting a long time for this book.

Hell, *everyone* has been waiting a long time for this book.

The first time I ever encountered the name of Nicholas A. DiChario was when an unsolicited story arrived in my mailbox for an invitation-only anthology I was editing. I probably should have sent it back without looking at it—and if I had, I might well have robbed the science fiction field of one of the most remarkable talents ever to come down the pike. Instead I started reading it (just to see how bad a story I hadn't solicited could be, you understand), and by Page 3 I knew that nothing in the world could keep "The Winterberry" off the Hugo ballot. Yes, it was by an unknown, and yes, anthologies had about a quarter the circulation of the major magazines, and yes, there was no traditional science fiction element in it—and there was still no way it could fail to make the ballot.

I wish I could pick horses the way I pick stories. "The Winterberry" was a Hugo nominee, and a World Fantasy Award nominee, and Nick himself was nominated for the Campbell, which is science fiction's Rookie of the Year Award. And we were off and running. From that day forward, it was almost unthinkable for me to edit an anthology that didn't have a DiChario story in it. And since I didn't edit enough anthologies to get my fill of DiChario stories, I started collaborating with him. When we had sold enough collaborations we gathered them and sold them as a book entitled *Magic Feathers: The Mike and Nick Show*.

Not that Nick needed my collaborative or editorial efforts to shine. He made the Hugo ballot again a few years later, and in between produced one of the three or four best novellas of the decade, a strange and wonderful piece called "Unto the Land of Day-Glo."

In fact, just about *all* of Nick's stories are strange and wonderful. We collaborated on a story for an anthology about kings—and while everyone else was writing about British and French kings, Nick came up with King Kong. It wasn't a funny story, either; that would have been too easy. Instead, it was a sad and sensitive one. For an erotic anthology assignment during the time that *The Joy of Sex* was at the top of the bestseller list, Nick came up with "The Joy of Hats."

We—the reading public, of which I am a small part, and the almost-as-large DiChario fan base, of which I am a small but always-vocal part—kept waiting for Nick to write that first novel and blow us all away. And we waited. And we waited. And we waited.

And while we were waiting, Nick taught some writing courses, and bought a bookstore, and did some other things, none of which we cared much about except that if it made him happy enough or secure enough to finally give us that novel, we were all in favor of it, whatever *it* was.

And then one day came the phone call I'd been waiting for for about a decade. It was Nick. He'd sold his first novel, and would I possibly consider taking a look at *A Small and Remarkable Life*? I explained that if he swore on a stack of Bibles, Torahs and Korans that he would e-mail it to me within 24 hours I probably wouldn't come to upstate New York and rip his computer out of his office and take it home with me. A master at the art of self-preservation, he e-mailed it to me that night.

I had no idea what to expect, but I knew what not to expect: there would be no generic space battles, nothing that one could see in the mindless "sci-fi" films that permeate the landscape, nothing that you could look at and say, "Heinlein (or Asimov, or Bradbury) did it better," or even "Heinlein (or whoever) did it earlier."

I'm not going to tell you much about the book you hold in your hands, because you *are* holding it in your hands, and you've either bought it or are preparing to buy it, and Nick will tell you the story of Tink Puddah a lot better than I ever could.

But I *will* note that, as always, it's a story told in a way only Nick could tell it. Where else does a story begin with the rather lengthy funeral of the protagonist? And where else do you feel you know the protagonist better before you're even introduced to him than you know most heroes halfway through a book?

I don't think there's ever been a true villain in a DiChario story. But the one who fills the structural role of a villain here, which is to say, the man who finds himself in opposition to the hero, is guilty of only one "sin": he wants to save the hero's immortal soul.

A hero who begins the story dead, and a villain who wants to keep the hero from going to hell. That's the kind of spin my pal Nick puts on the ball.

There are a lot more spins in the pages up ahead, but as always with the best writers in any field, be they the Bradburys and Sturgeons of science fiction, the Chandlers of the mystery story, or the Eric Amblers of the international intrigue novel, the characters are always the most important and memorable things you're going to encounter.

By now you've figured out that I'm glad and proud to know Nick DiChario. After reading this novel, I can truthfully say that I would have been just as glad and just as proud to have known Tink Puddah. There are not a lot of characters I can say that about—but if enough of you encourage Nick to write another novel, I'm sure there will be a few more such characters before long.

INTRODUCTION TO *STAR SMASHERS*
OF THE GALAXY RANGERS

Back a little more than four decades ago, when I was a callow young student at the University of Chicago, I had an English professor who arbitrarily declared that there was a Writers' Heaven, and that the man who wrote the words "A rose-red city half as old as Time" was guaranteed admission there (and probably really good tee times at the local golf course) just for having stuck those nine words together in that particular order.

Well, let me tell you—if there is a Humorists' Heaven, Harry Harrison is guaranteed a spot there, and he did it with seven words less that my professor's choice. The words are "Employment Counselors," they need to be read in context, and they're waiting for you up ahead in Chapter 12.

But before you come to them, you've got a *lot* of good old-fashioned star smashing parody to read (and a lot afterward, too). I don't want to single out Doc Smith, since this can be seen as a loving parody of the entire space opera genre, especially as it existed in the pre-Campbell days of science fiction, but in truth it seems like Harry is holding Doc's beloved, if somewhat creaky, *Skylark of Space* up to a funhouse mirror after smearing it with cheddar cheese. (Don't ask; you'll understand soon enough.)

This takes place back in the days when two guys with a monkey wrench, a hammer, a couple of nails, a few bucks, and a high-school science textbook could cobble together a spaceship in their back yard.

And in them thar days, no spaceship took off without a plucky stowaway of the female persuasion, since we knew we were going to encounter a bunch of mad scientists and potential galactic emperors and sex-starved (and somewhat misguided) aliens in the adventures to come, and no one really cared if Chuck or Jerry (you'll meet them in just another page or two) were one grope away from a Fate Worse Than Death, whereas pretty perky Sally...

This is the kind of book that *has* to be done with love, because it would be all too easy to do it with contempt for the kind of science fiction it's having fun with. It's clear that Harry loves the Good Old Days and the Good Old Stuff and wants you to enjoy them too, as filtered through his sense of fun and the ridiculous.

There are a lot of wonderful short science fiction parodies. Some years back I edited a book of them—*Shaggy B.E.M. Stories*—and to this day I couldn't begin to tell you which is the best of them. It depends on your mood and your taste and probably the time of day.

But I will state unequivocally that *Star Smashers of the Galaxy Rangers* is the finest book-length parody of science fiction the field has yet produced.

So enough of me. It's time to join Chuck and Jerry and (*sigh*) pert perky Sally aboard the *Pleasantville Eagle* as they flit across the galaxy, unveil the Loathesome Lortonoi, and learn the Secret of the Salami. It's quite a trip.

INTRODUCTION TO *TARZAN ALIVE*

There are a lot of reasons why *Tarzan Alive* is a remarkable book, not the least of which is its origin.

Back in the late 1960s, one of the major West Coast sex book publishers started a line of high-quality, even literary pornography. It was called Essex House, it paid about twice the going rate, and it attracted some of the better writers of the era. (Yes, I said writers, not pornographers.) One of them was Philip Jose Farmer, who will go down in history as the man who single-handedly broke down the sexual barriers of written science fiction with his classic "The Lovers," after which nothing was ever the same again.

Phil wrote some very well-received books for Essex House (which died as soon as the readers figured out that some subversive editorial staffers were trying to give them literature with their porn). One of them was *A Feast Unknown*, which featured Tarzan (for legal reasons Lord Greystoke became Lord Grandrith) and Doc Savage (who, also to avoid lawsuits, became Doc Caliban). The book was a cult classic upon publication, and is *still* a cult classic in science fiction circles.

I'm sure most of you are aware that almost the moment a book or a movie becomes a hit, it invariably inspires a porn film or porn novel spinoff. But *A Feast Unknown* stood tradition on its head, and became the first and only pornographic novel to give birth to four non-pornographic spinoffs. (Well, four and a quarter, actually.) I find that absolutely remarkable, and of course it's a tribute to the fact that Phil always wrote at the highest level of literary ambition, regardless of category or genre. Whether it was Essex House or one of the great New York publishers, he gave his best every time.

A Feast Unknown was published in 1969. In 1970, Ace Books came out with an Ace Double—remember the old Ace Doubles, bound back-to-back and upside-down?—one half of which featured Lord Grandrith in *Lord of the Trees*, and the other half starred Doc Caliban in *The Mad Goblin*. *Tarzan Alive* came along in 1972, *Doc Savage: His Apocalyptic Life* in 1973, and there was a wonderful novella, kind of an add-on to *Tarzan Alive*, titled "Extracts From the Memoirs of 'Lord Greystoke" in *Mother Was a Lovely Beast*, an anthology Phil also edited in 1974.

Not a bad slew of progeny from one little sex book.

Phil has always found the notion of Tarzan worth playing with. Along with all the above, he also wrote an excellent novel, *Lord Tyger*, about a young man being raised to become a Tarzan type. In fact, Phil has spent a considerable portion of his career resurrecting, reinventing, and examining the heroes of his youth, those whose mighty bodies and awesome weapons graced the covers of the pulp magazines when he was growing up.

The most fascinating and impressive of those heroes has always been Tarzan of the Apes. *Tarzan Alive* is Phil's tribute to him—but because Philip Jose Farmer was never content to take the easy way out, this is far more than a mere recitation of Tarzan's adventures. Anyone with the complete works of Edgar Rice Burroughs and sufficient time on his hands could do that. Only Phil could have invented the Wold Newton family.

Over the years, a number of writers have created consistent and all-encompassing (of their own works) future histories. Robert A. Heinlein was the first to make public the timeline in which he set most of his stories. Isaac Asimov wrote two disparate series during his lifetime—the robot stories and the Foundation stories—but toward the end of his life he managed to put them into one cohesive and reasonably consistent future. I myself have set some 25 of my novels and perhaps 15 shorter stories into a future I created back in 1980.

Kid stuff.

Phil has dwarfed all those efforts with the Wold Newtons. I won't tell you much about it, since he's going to do so in the pages up ahead. I'll simply point out that the rest of us were concerned only with putting our own works into our own future histories. Phil has created a family that encompasses—with histories, timelines, bloodlines, and whatever else it takes—just about every fictional character he admires, from Elizabeth Bennett, Sherlock Holmes, The Scarlet Pimpernel, Leopold Bloom, and Bulldog Drummond to Lord Peter Wimsey, Doc Savage, Nero Wolfe, Tarzan, and the Spider. (Personally, I'd pay good money to believe in that family, and even more to be invited to one of its gatherings.)

It's fascinating stuff, and you don't have to know every member of the family to admire the work that went into it.

So what about Tarzan (I hear you ask)? After all, that's what attracted you to the book in the first place.

Well, rest assured that when you finish *Tarzan Alive*—and it's easy going—you'll know almost as much about Tarzan and his 20+ books worth of adventures as Edgar Rice Burroughs did. Phil postulates that Tarzan is alive, and that he is a member of the Wold Newton family, but he never forgets that it is Edgar Rice Burroughs' Tarzan who initially attracted his—and your—attention, and he does the apeman justice. You'll follow him from his birth in a tiny cabin in Africa to the kingship of the apes of the tribe of Kerchak, from his true love to his momentary infatuations with the High Priestess of the Flaming God and the Mad Queen of the City of Gold, from his battle against the Germans on African soil in World War I to his exploits in the Pacific in World War II. You'll visit the kingdom of the ant men, and the lost land of Pal-ul-Don. You'll follow the exploits of his son, and even briefly meet his grandson.

But because Phil is far better read and better educated than Burroughs (sorry, Edgar), he also gives you insights not only into the adventures and their chronology, but he puts Tarzan's world and deeds into their true historical context. Where critics have said certain things were impossible, Phil quotes from the works of Jane Goodall, Joy Adamson and others to prove that far from impossible, many of the seemingly far-fetched suppositions in the Tarzan books were actually quite likely in view of what we've learned since they were written.

It's a hell of a *tour de force*, half meticulous research, half unbridled imagination.

Which is to say, it's 100% Philip Jose Farmer.

INTRODUCTION TO
DARKNESS FALLING

Jack Williamson has been my friend for just about 40 years.

Believe it or not, he's been science fiction's friend for twice that long. When you speak of the history of science fiction, you're speaking, to some degree, of the history of Jack Williamson. He is a gentle and unassuming man who seems completely unaware that he is truly a giant in our field—but take my word for it: he's one of the tallest. (Or don't take my word. Read the book instead.)

Hugo Gernsback created the publishing category of science fiction with *Amazing Stories* in 1926. One look at it was all Jack needed to know what he wanted to do with his life. His first effort, *The Metal Men*, appeared in the December, 1928 *Amazing*—and we're reprinting it here to show you where he started and just how far he's come.

By 1931 Jack had expanded his markets to include *Wonder Stories*, and we're bringing you "Twelve Hours to Live!" from those bygone days.

For a while it seemed that Jack and his pal Edmond Hamilton were taking turns destroying and saving the galaxy every other month, but Jack's work was never that one-dimensional. To prove it, he began writing for *Weird Tales*. Despite its name, it was publishing the most literate stories in the fantastic field, and Jack was there with "The Wand of Doom" in 1932.

Jack was too much in demand and too prolific to stay within one branch of the field, or even one publisher within a branch, so along with selling to all the science fiction magazines, he not only found time to write for *Weird Tales* but also its rival, *Strange Tales of Mystery and Terror*, where "Wolves of Darkness" appeared in 1932.

Astounding, destined to become the most influential magazine in science fiction history, was just getting its feet wet in 1933. Jack helped it along with "Terror Out of Time."

It was when John Campbell took over the helm of *Astounding* that it became the behemoth we all know about. A number of writers couldn't adjust to Campbell's vision of science fiction, and they fell by the wayside. Needless to say, Jack wasn't one of them. Perhaps his greatest single work of science fiction, clearly his most influential, and probably among the half-dozen most important novellas ever produced in the field, was "With Folded Hands." You'll find it waiting for you—I'm inclined to say "patiently, with folded hands"— in the pages up ahead.

Jack kept moving, changing, and improving with the times. For the most part he stuck to novels, but every now and than he'd lay a short story on a major market, just to prove he hadn't lost the touch, as with "Jamboree," which he produced in 1969 for *Galaxy*.

When Harlan Ellison was assembling *The Last Dangerous Visions*, Jack was an obvious choice—a top-notch and always-innovative science fiction writer who had survived half a dozen evolutions of the field and could be expected to add his might to the New Wave as well. Jack responded with "Previews of Hell." Although the anthology has never been published, we're proud to bring you the story in this collection.

Of all the magazines ever to appear in this field, my personal favorite was John Campbell's short-lived *Unknown*— and of all the stories Jack ever wrote and all the stories *Unknown* ever ran, my favorite is "Darker Than You Think." I can't begin to tell you how thrilled we are to be able to bring you the original magazine version.

I think the highest compliment you can give someone regardless of his profession is that he is not content to rest on his laurels, that he works at improving every day of his life. To me, Jack Williamson is the perfect exemplar of that. "The Metal Man" has its crudities, but it was good enough to sell. The work in the 1930s showed greater craft and more control of his material. The unquestioned classics, "With Folded Hands" and "Darker Than You Think" were produced in the 1940s.

And still he continued to work and to improve. The Jack Williamson who wrote those two novellas probably couldn't have written "Previews of Hell" as skillfully as the Jack Williamson of the early 1970s did.

In 1975 Jack became only the second writer in history to be given the Nebula Grandmaster Award for lifetime achievement by the Science Fiction Writers of America. In 1977 he was the Worldcon Guest of Honor.

A nice way to cap off a career. Now he was free to sit around basking in the sun and sipping cool drinks.

Did he?

If you think so, you don't know Jack Williamson.

Jack won the 1985 Hugo for the Best Non-Fiction Book. He was 77 at the time.

And was that the end of it?

Not a chance.

In 2001, at the ripe young age of 93, Jack beat a stellar field to win the Hugo for Best Novella.

He is not only the universally-acknowledged Dean of Science Fiction, but he's a dean who is never content to rest on his laurels. He is the walking history of science fiction, not because he knows that history (though of course he does), but because he *created* such a large portion of it.

Enough. Start reading the stories and see exactly how he did it.

INTRODUCTION TO *MAD SCIENTIST MEETS CANNIBAL*

Fifteen or twenty years ago there were a number of books published about the field of science fiction, each aimed at enticing the new reader and giving him a road map to the treasures and pitfalls that lay ahead. One of the things almost all those now-forgotten books did was offer comparisons, based on the potential reader's potential tastes. They were filled with statements such as, "If you like Asimov, try Clement," or "If you like Tenn, you'll love Sheckley."

Except when it came to R. A. Lafferty, possessor of the most unique and idiosyncratic voice of his era. In his case, the books all said, in essence, "If you like Lafferty, buy everything of his you can find, because no one else is remotely like him."

In the couple of decades since those books came and went, there's been only one writer like that: multiple Hugo nominee Nick DiChario.

And now, twenty years later, there's another, because *nobody* sees the world quite the way Robert T. Jeschonek does.

This little book gives you five Jeschonek stories, and I hope it starts off with "Dionysus Dying" and "Something Borrowed, Something Doomed," both of them fine stories, both a bit off the beaten track, written with an easy grace and skill, and just the sort of things to lull you into thinking that the rest of the book won't contain the most off-the-wall trio of stories you've read in years, or *will* read for years to come.

Take "Food Chains." I suppose it actually qualifies as a hard science story. It has a sympathetic narrator, a scientific extrapolation, a conflict that must be (and is) solved—and by the end, the wily Mr. Jeschonek not only has the reader accepting cannibalism as a viable and beneficial practice, but has him actually rooting for it. It's a really fascinating mind game he's playing here—but anyone can play mind games; playing them within the context of a well-wrought story is something only the Laffertys and DiCharios and Jeschoneks of the world can do.

And then there's "The Day After They Rounded Up Everyone Who Could Love Unconditionally," a small masterpiece that breaks all the known rules of storytelling and works anyway. It's 750 words. It's told in the present tense. It's episodic, or a montage, or (choose your own term), but what it isn't is a strong continuous narrative flow, which is usually fatal in novels and novellas and is supposed to be nonexistent in short-shorts. He takes a title that could be a bad 1960s folk-rock song, shows you in the first 100 words that whatever you thought it was going to be about you were wrong, and comes up with a kicker at the end that will have you thinking about it not only immediately after you've finished it, but at the oddest times weeks and even months afterward. The late Fredric Brown was the acknowledged master of the short-short, and he wrote more than his share of cute ones, but Brown never attempted anything like this, either thematically or stylistically.

And then there's my favorite, and not just because I grew up reading the moldering old pulp magazines. "Playing Doctor" is an almost-love-story between a mad scientist and her slavishly-devoted sycophantic toady…and only Jeschonek would have had the—I don't know: skill? lunacy? chutzpah?—to tell it in the first person of the toady, *and to make it work.* I don't have a thing for mad scientists (oversexed, scantily-clad Pirate Queens are more to my taste), and I have no idea why the toady admires this one, but by the time you're halfway through you are missing a couple of nuts and a bolt if you don't start rooting for him to win her heart (or whatever passes for it). It is a totally unique, off-that-wall, completely successful almost-love-story, and you don't get any more individualistic than that.

I've never met Robert T. Jeschonek, but I expect that's going to change pretty soon. He'll be at some convention or other that I'm attending. He'll be easy enough to spot. I'll look past all the guys in costumes, all the weirdos with wall-to-wall pupils, all the goshwowboyoboy fans lined up for autographs. Instead, I'll look for a perfectly normal-looking guy who gives the impression that he is happily looking at a world (probably but not necessarily ours) that no one else can see, and when an errant thought crosses his mind and a little wouldn't-that-make-an-interesting-story smile flickers across his face, I'll know I've found him.

INTRODUCTION TO *THE QUEEN OF AIR AND DARKNESS*

So let me tell you about one of science fiction's true Renaissance Men, because Poul Anderson never tooted his own horn, and as a result, while everyone knows he was a popular and prolific writer, most people don't know the truly profound effect he had on the fields of fantasy and science fiction.

Poul had a degree in physics. ("Don't all science fiction writers?" I hear you ask. Actually, you'd be surprised how many of us don't have degrees in anything.)

He was a founding member of SCA, the Society for Creative Anachronists. (He and Randall Garrett boldly chose to defend John Campbell's honor in a joust on the lawn of the Claremont Hotel at the 1968 Worldcon. I must have been somewhere else at the moment, but Robert Silverberg still recalls how quickly the pair of them—Randy a little drunk, Poul a little short-sighted—were pounded into the ground by two of SCA's finest and most experienced swordsmen. Somehow John's honor survived anyway—and so, since they were firing with blank swords or the equivalent, did Poul and Randy.)

He was an early President of SFWA (Science Fiction Writers of America).

He was the Worldcon Guest of Honor in 1959.

He became a Gandalf Grand Master in 1978.

He became a SFWA Grand Master in 1997.

He won 7 Hugo Awards, and is tied for second on the all-time list among writers.

He won 3 Nebula Awards.

He won 4 Prometheus Awards, including a Lifetime Achievement one. (The Prometheus is for libertarian writing, a strain that is common in Poul's work.)

He won a John Campbell Memorial Award in 2000.

He even won a filksinging award, the Pegasus, in 1998, in collaboration with Anne Passavoy.

In my opinion, he wrote the ultimate hard science novel with *Tau Zero*. I know, I know, a lot of people would select Hal Clement's very fine *Mission of Gravity* for that honor, but *Mission of Gravity* is about Mesklinites (fascinating little wormlike critters) and *Tau Zero* is about *people*. And when all is said and done, people are what count.

This collection contains two of Poul's most famous stories: the Hugo-and-Nebula winning "Queen of Air and Darkness" and the Hugo-winning "The Longest Voyage." (So why didn't "The Longest Voyage" win the Nebula too? Easy. It came out in 1960, which is a few years before SFWA was formed, and the Nebula is SFWA's award.)

I recently attended the 2009 Nebula weekend, and got to spend some time with Poul's widow, Karen Anderson. Karen is an author in her own right (her own write?), was Poul's credited collaborator from time to time, and was his uncredited collaborator far more often. I told her that I'd been asked to introduce this collection, and that I hated the thought of just saying what the stories are about, because if you're reading this then it's clear that you're about to read them too. So what I wanted was Karen's reminiscences on exactly how Poul got the ideas for some of them.

(Isn't that what every science fiction writer is always being asked: "Where do you get your crazy ideas?")

So, from the source (Karen) through the middleman (me) to the reader (you):

Ed Emshwiller (who signed his paintings and drawings "Emsh") was the dominant science fiction artist in the 1950s and early 1960s, and one day Poul turned to Karen and said, "Tell me a painting." Karen asked what he meant, and he told her to describe an Emsh cover so he could write a story around it. Which cover did he have in mind, she wanted to know. Oh, not one that existed, answered Poul; just a *typical* Emsh cover, replete with his well-known wit. So Karen described a non-existent Emsh painting that featured a robot sitting in an office, slaving away at a desk and smelling a flower—and Poul sat down and wrote "Critique of Impure Reasoning."

When Poul wrote "Uncleftish Beholding," Karen says he decided to use Germanic-rooted words only. This kind of learned writing was actually named after him, and became known (don't wince) as Ander-Saxon.

Poul and Karen decided to plot a "biter-bit" story together and see just how many twists they could put into one story. It became "Innocent at Large."

Karen suggested that Poul base a story on Marlowe's *Tamerlaine*, perhaps one in which a time traveler gets stuck in ancient Persia and finds himself becoming unwillingly involved in local affairs. Poul took the idea and ran with it; you'll find it up ahead as "Brave to Be a King."

Karen didn't recall the genesis of "The Pirate," but tells me that upon finishing it, Poul claimed that no one under the age of 40 could ever truly understand it.

Poul came up with what he thought was a unique way to transmit a secret code. Karen suggested he borrow the structure of the story from one of their favorites, which almost no one remembered, a story titled "Mr. Glencannon Ignores the War." He did, and it became the very popular "Say It With Flowers."

And of course there's the biggie, "Queen of Air and Darkness." Poul loved the title, which is the title of the second of the four parts of T. H. White's *The Once and Future King*— and then decided to write exactly the kind of story that you would *not* expect from such a title. He got some critical flak for treating it as science fiction rather than fantasy (given its awards, clearly not enough flak to matter), and his lyrics became a very popular filksong at conventions for the next decade.

He was quite a remarkable writer, equally skilled at science fiction, fantasy, folk tale, and myth. Of all his contemporaries, probably only Fritz Leiber displayed such range, and with no disrespect to Fritz, he couldn't write rigorous hard science the way Poul could. Poul could turn out carefully-reasoned science fiction, myth-inspired fantasy, could create characters like Nicholas van Rijn who was good for an entire series of books, and he was a pretty sharp parodist; when I was assembling an anthology of science fiction parodies more than two decades ago I bought a Conan parody from him that remains the funniest sword-and-sorcery parody I've read. And when he wasn't writing, he was starring; he showed up as the hero of a Philip K. Dick novelette, "Waterspider," that I bought for another anthology.

Poul, as I said at the start, was a modest man. I remember a day he spent driving me around Northern California, showing me the scenic highlights, and never once mentioned anything he'd written or anything he was going to write, any awards he'd won or hoped to win. He asked me about my own writing, and did everything he could to put me at ease—because while he was a modest man, he realized at some level that most of us were awed by his talent. Harry Turtledove is prompt to declare his debt to Poul; so are Jerry Pournelle, Greg Bear, Joe Haldeman, and a score of others. That debt may well have been greatest in his Hoka collaborator and close friend, Gordon R. Dickson.

We lost Poul to cancer in 2001, but thanks to NESFA Press we won't soon lose what made him so special to our field. So enough of my writing this introduction and your reading it; there are some wonderful futures and universes up ahead, just waiting for you to discover (or rediscover) them.

INTRODUCTION TO *NANO COMES TO CLIFFORD FALLS*

Her name is Nancy Kress, and I fall a little more in love with her every year.

She writes a little more every year. There is a connection.

As you're about to find out, Nancy Kress is what we in the trade call a writer's writer, which is to say, she is a writer that other writers read, and admire, and study, and try to learn from. And sometimes fall a little bit in love with.

As an editor, I have been buying stories from Nancy for a couple of decades now. She's never turned in a bad one, or a mediocre one; she's never sleepwalked through one; she always turns in her best effort, and her best effort, as you doubtless know, has been good enough to give her a shelf full of Nebulas, Hugos and the like.

(I should add that as an editor, I have also been buying from her protégées for almost as long, and it's always easy to spot a newcomer who's been through Nancy's workshops, because they are better-trained in the basics than any other set of beginners I have ever encountered.)

As a writer I have sold to Nancy (well, okay, it was a reprint, but what the hell, it was a reprint anthology), and I have collaborated with Nancy.

And as a reader I have been enjoying Nancy's work for as long as she's been producing it. I have said on a number of occasions that the late Jack Williamson was the only writer I knew who demonstrably improved with every passing decade. Nancy's got a few decades to go to catch Jack (his work appeared in *nine* of them), but she improves by the decade, by the year, almost by the story. Like I say, a writer's writer.

So what does it mean, being a writer's writer?

For one thing, it means you let the story dictate your approach to it. For example, Nancy knows that horror tends to dissipate the longer it runs, so she held "To Cuddle Amy" to under a thousand words. She knows that humor works best in short, strung-together sequences, so she wrote "Patent Infringement" as a series of letters. She knows that some stories, even if you can summarize the basic plot in three or four sentences, have to be novella length to include all the details that are needed to make them work, so she wrote "Shiva in Shadow" (and put twice as much material into her 20,000 words as I put into *my* 20,000 words in the same anthology). She knows when to tell a story in the first person, when to use humor, how to give the reader necessary information without boring him with interminable info dumps. She's no scientist, but I'm not aware that anyone's ever caught her in a scientific error.

And while she writes science fiction, she understands, as all the very best writers do, that eventually every story is about *people*. Ideas are wonderful, and Nancy's stories abound in them; science is fascinating, and Nancy's stories have their share of it; extrapolations can be shocking and mind-boggling, and Nancy can shock and boggle your mind with the best of them; but when all is said and done, Nancy's stories stick in the mind because she—and you—care about her characters.

And oh, the things she can do with the tropes of science fiction! Take, for example, "Ej-Es." Right now that title will make no sense to you. And (I'm not encouraging this, mind you) if you read the last line first, it seems like gibberish. But read the story, let her work her magic on you, and suddenly the title makes sense and the last line is not only comprehensible but is, in retrospect, the very best last line the story could have (and upon even further consideration, possibly the *only* last line it could have.)

Or try "My Mother, Dancing." A perfect title for a near-perfect story. (She spends a lot of time on her titles. It shows.)

I dare you to read it without an emotional response. Maybe two. Yeah, that's something else: her stories are only *deceptively* simple. There's the complexity of a brilliant mind at work behind and beneath each of them.

And never confuse complexity with inaccessibility. It is very easy to read a Nancy Kress story; the only hard thing is putting it down before you're finished. And then, like a fine meal, it stays with you a bit while you digest it.

A bit? Hell, I'm *still* digesting "Beggars in Spain," her acknowledged classic. I've only read it three times; maybe another four or five and I'll have gotten everything out of it that she put in it.

Okay, reader, you're primed and ready to plunge into this collection, and I guarantee that what lies ahead is more interesting and enriching than anything I have to say about it. (And Nancy, if you're reading this, I hope you understand that the next time I pinch you in the elevator at a convention, at least part of that emotion is directed toward your stories.)

INTRODUCTION TO *RELATIVITY*

Rob Sawyer hit the ground running. One day he hadn't published a word of science fiction, and (it seemed) the next day he was atop the field, turning out one award-caliber novel after another. I was present at Long Beach when he won his first Best Novel Nebula, and I was applauding him at Toronto when he pulled off the unprecedented double of winning the Hugo for one novel and the Seiun (the Japanese Hugo) for a different one.

But you know all that, or you probably wouldn't have picked up the book you now hold in your hands. Anyone can tell you about Rob Sawyer the Superstar Writer; I'd like to tell you about the Rob Sawyer I know—the Superstar Fan and Friend.

If Rob has ever refused a request for anything—an autograph, a word of encouragement or advice, a speech, a non-paying fanzine article, a few moments of his increasingly-valuable time to someone he barely knows—it's not only escaped my notice, but just about everyone else's. I've often said that Robert Bloch is my role model, not as a writer, but as a professional—and especially as a professional who interacts with fans. Rob is simply the Canadian version.

An exceptionally gracious man, when he won his Nebula he thanked me for my help and encouragement—neither of which had anything to do with his success—in his acceptance speech. I still remember turning to Carol with an excrement-eating grin on my face after hearing that and bragging, "I got to hold the hero's horse!"

And a hero he is. He remains to this day the only winner of the Best Novel Hugo to remember to thank not only his editor and publisher, but his American and Canadian distributors. I mean, hell, we'd all be starving to death without our book distributors, but only Rob ever thought to thank them publicly.

I don't remember quite when we first met in person—we already knew each other through the internet—but it must have been at a convention in the 1980s or early 1990s, and we've been friends ever since. It's pretty hard not to be Rob's friend; once you get past being dazzled by his talent, you find yourself equally dazzled by his quick intellect, his wide-ranging knowledge, his humor, and his always good-natured personality.

And I like to think that I had a little something to do with one other bit of dazzling Rob does on occasion—the short story. It's an unhappy fact that if you want to make a living writing short stories in this field and your name isn't Ray or Harlan, you're going to wind up in the poorhouse. So if you have any skill as a novelist, you go where the money is, and if you're as skilled as Rob, you are contracted many books and many years in advance.

But along with novels, I happen to like writing and editing short stories, and I also happen to know that Rob has an incredibly difficult, almost impossible, time saying No to his friends. So over the years I have frequently asked him to contribute stories to anthologies I was editing, and, being Rob, he has yet to turn me down. Or hand in a story that was anything less than stellar in quality. One of them won an award; others were nominated. When Rob says Yes, it's never a half-hearted Yes; he gives it his best.

And some of his best are right here in this volume. I'm proud to say I was responsible for a pair of them—"Immortality" and "Relativity." But there are some other gems that I had nothing to do with (except, like you, to enjoy as a reader), gems like "Come All Ye Faithful" and "On the Surface." And to show his versatility, Rob has also included a dozen how-to-write columns that he's done for *On Spec*—the Canadian equivalent of my "Ask Bwana" columns for *Speculations* (or maybe my stuff is the American equivalent of Rob's)—plus a pair of speeches, and a touching tribute to Judy Merril.

I read somewhere that Rob recently made his 200th television appearance, which must be close to a record for anyone not named Isaac; and I know he's been very active promoting science fiction on radio, too. And when I say promoting, I don't mean just his own work; he always goes out of his way to find competitors and newcomers to praise and promote. As they say, you can't pay back (although I wouldn't mind if he'd loan me $67,084.22 until payday), so you pay forward—and Rob pays those dues about as well and generously as anyone.

And now that I've told you a little about Rob Sawyer and a little about what awaits you in the pages up ahead, let me simply point out that this book can be considered Essence of Sawyer: fiction, non-fiction, how-to pieces, tributes, speeches. If you buy it—and why would you be reading this if you weren't going to buy it?—and Rob is anywhere around, hunt him up and ask him to sign it. I guarantee he'll be happy to. And if he's not around, take it with you to the next convention he'll be attending; you'll not only get a signature, but you'll get a chance to meet a real *mensch* as well.

A *mensch*? You don't know?

Well, it means a lot of things. In the Fandango dialect of western Botswana, it means a tuskless elephant with three testicles and a bad attitude. In Barsoomian, it means The Foul Perpetrator of a Fate Worse Than Death. In ancient Egyptian, it means He Who Does Vile Things To Mummies Under Cover of Night.

But where I come from, it means a man's man and a writer's writer—in other words, Robert J. Sawyer.

INTRODUCTION TO *FANGS AND ANGEL WINGS*

Karen Taylor is a wonderful writer.

Well, now, let me re-word that just a tad. Given that no one can match her at writing stories of erotic horror, maybe I should have said that Karen Taylor gives great tale.

She's been giving us one great tale after another for quite some time now. This is not a flash in the pan, this Taylor. Her novels include *Blood Secrets, Bitter Blood, Blood Ties, Blood of My Blood, The Vampire Vivienne, Resurrection,* and *From the Ruins*. Everyone knows about them.

But not everyone knows she's just as skilled at short fiction, probably because she doesn't write as much of it. In fact, you now hold in your hands her lifetime's production of short fiction, which is almost as much of a tragedy as the fact the she choose to live on the East Coast rather than come to Cincinnati and become an Official Mike Resnick Auxiliary Wife.

I urge you to check these stories out; they're really quite remarkable. And don't take *my* word for it. Look at the record. "Mexican Moon" was a Bram Stoker finalist, and you can't get much better than that.

You can't get much better than Karen, either. Redheaded, vivacious, outgoing, with enough curves to satisfy even the most jaded introduction writer, her constant willingness to think the unthinkable through to its logical conclusion (as John Campbell used to say) has been the hallmark of her work. I assigned her one of the stories in this book, for an anthology of science fiction tales about dinosaurs. As I did so I remarked, jokingly, that having just finished reading a couple of her more erotic novels, I expected nothing less than a sex scene between a human and a dinosaur.

Campbell would have been proud of "Romeo Falling."

But why are you reading Resnick when you could be reading Taylor? Stop standing there thumbing through the pages, take the book up to the cash register, shell out your money, and hurry home to one of the more unique reading experiences you're going to have this year.

INTRODUCTION TO *SHIPS IN THE NIGHT*

So let me tell you a little about my friend Jack McDevitt, and about the wonderful stories that lay waiting for you in the pages up ahead.

Jack submitted the first story he ever wrote to *Twilight Zone Magazine*—and sold it. That immediately put him about two hundred rejection slips behind most of his peers.

It didn't take him long to figure out that you could sell a story a month and qualify for food stamps, so he began writing novels as well. His first effort, *The Hercules Text*, sold to the most prestigious line of science fiction books in history, the Ace Specials, and won him the Locus Award for Best First Novel.

Are you getting the notion that we're talking about a very talented fellow here? Well, strangely enough, not all American editors shared that notion, more fools they, and he had a devil of a time selling "Ships in the Night," the title story of this collection, to any US magazine for the standard $1,500 or so that a novella brings. So his wife Maureen entered it in the UPC contest in Barcelona, where it won the $10,000 first prize. (Jack and I belong to a very small fraternity: we're the only two US writers ever to win that particular contest.) Of course, once word of the prize got out the novella sold here very quickly, as does most of his work.

Jack has been nominated for the Nebula Award six times—four times with novels, and twice with stories that you'll encounter in this collection. He is what we in the trade call a Writer's Writer: he's always readable, he never misses a deadline, he's continually looking to expand his considerable skills, he helps newcomers, and after a quarter century in the science fiction field he's still improving (and as I pointed out, he was pretty damned good to begin with).

He's also a genuinely modest man. I've already praised his writing more in the ten minutes I've been working on this introduction than I've heard him do in all the time I've known him.

I've been waiting a long time for this collection. All of Jack's fans have. His short story production slowed down when he had to make a living with his novels, but the quality never diminished, and now he finally has enough outstanding stories to form the book you hold in your hands.

Let me tell you a little about them.

Leading off is "Nothing Ever Happens in Rock City," an absolute charmer that's no longer than it needs to be (another McDevitt trademark). His fellow writers agreed that it was just the right length, and nominated it for a Nebula.

"The Far Shore" is a far future story, and a hard science story, but what it mostly is is a story about old-time radio (another passion I share with Jack.)

The story behind "Good Intentions," a Nebula finalist, is almost as interesting as the story itself. Jack and *Analog* editor Stanley Schmidt created a science fiction role-play scenario at an Asimov seminar. Then, when the seminar was over, Jack and Stan decided to take it one step farther and not only write the story but add the supposition: what if the seminar had been manipulated? Who would have done so, and for what purpose?

Sooner or later everyone tries a time travel story, and sooner or later the characters discover that time travel is never quite as smooth and easy as they had anticipated. "Time's Arrow" is Jack's addition to the canon.

The "choice" story has come a long way since John Carter of Mars, confronted by two doors, invariably chose the wrong one. Add a century of maturity and sophistication, and the result is "Dead in the Water."

I loved the movie *The Road Warrior*, but it had some pretty silly aspects. Would you like to know what *really* happens in Australia's post-apocalyptic Outback? Read "Windrider" and wonder no longer.

The only thing I'll tell you about "Deus Tex" is that Jack selected it for my forthcoming anthology, *This is My Funniest*.

Jack tells me that "Report From the Rear" was suggested by an experience of H. L. Mencken. I have no problem with that, and neither will you once you read the story.

Time to pause for a moment and point out that while Jack's science is always accurate, the little thumbnail sketches I've given should demonstrate that like all truly fine science fiction writers, his stories are about people, not science.

Science fiction writers have always loved to have their characters explore deserted alien artifacts and discover their secrets. The most famous is probably Sir Arthur C. Clarke's *Rendezvous With Rama*, and I think the late James White did it even better with *All Judgment Fled*. Jack's "Oculus" ranks among the better and more intriguing efforts.

Science fiction writers also love end-of-the-human-race stories, or approach-of-the-end stories, a tradition that stretches from Olaf Stapledon's *Last and First Men* (and even earlier) through Jack Vance's *The Dying Earth* and Gene Wolfe's *Book of the New Sun* tetralogy. And with "Last Contact"—a great title (says the author of *Second Contact* who recently helped vote a retro-Hugo for Murray Leinster's "First Contact")—Jack takes his place among the pantheon of writers who have handled it with exceptional skill.

The Christmas story is an annual challenge for science fiction writers. Most of the magazines love to run a science fictional Christmas story in their December issues—but there are just so many science fictional Christmas stories to be told. Sure enough, Jack found a new and memorable one with "Midnight Clear."

Everybody knows that the very best kind of *Analog* story is strong on science, and even stronger on posing a serious problem and then solving it in a unique but totally fair way. And while Jack specializes in stories about people, he renews his problem-solving credentials with "Blinker."

Always expanding his horizons, Jack took a shot at one of the most popular sub-categories of science fiction, the alternate history story, with "The Tomb"—and still managed to make it a compassionate, human story.

Finally there's his UPC winner, "Ships in the Night," in which a noncorporeal alien visits a hardware store owner in North Dakota (although it's much more complex and multi-layered than that.) There's a bit of Clifford D. Simak's mood and charm here, but it's clearly a McDevitt story—probably the one upon which his reputation would rest if he hadn't already solidified that reputation with a flow of outstanding novels.

Reader, if you haven't encountered these stories before, I envy you—and when you're through with them, it'll be your turn to envy me, because I just bought Jack's latest novella, "The Big Downtown," for an anthology I'm editing titled *Down These Dark Spaceways*. That means I got to read it half a year ahead of everybody else.

Talk about Hog Heaven.

INTRODUCTION TO *THE BEST OF DAVID GERROLD*

So it's come to this. Here I am, in the prime of my advanced state of youth, minding my own business and not bothering anyone, when the order comes down: I must write an introduction for *The Best of David Gerrold*.

What does that entail, I want to know.

Just say a few nice things about him and we'll throw tons of money at you, is the answer.

Well, as I sit here at my keyboard, I can look at the trophy case across the room and see four Hugos lined up on a shelf. That encourages me. They state for all the world to see: "Here is a professional liar of unquestioned ability." When all is said and done, what better qualification does one need to say nice things about David Gerrold?

David and I go back a long way. (Actually, David goes back much farther because I am only 23, no matter what anyone says.) I first became aware of him when I saw "The Trouble With Tribbles" on *Star Trek*. I thought it was a pretty good script, especially for a new kid on the block. A few million Trekkies later agreed with me; it was voted the most popular episode in the history of the series.

The first time I ever encountered David in the flesh was at the 1969 Worldcon in St. Louis. I stopped by the SFWA Suite to meet someone or other, I can't remember the details. David somehow found out that I wasn't a member—*that* detail I remember—and he and Anne McCaffrey, who was the secretary or treasurer or something that gave her authority over lesser beings, found out I had sold a few sf novels and literally would not let me leave until I had signed up and paid my dues. As I write these words I have been a member of the

Science Fiction Writers of America for 34 years, and I am still not sure I have forgiven either of them for that.

I saw David from time to time after that, usually at Worldcons. I remember picking up his novel, *When H.A.R.L.I.E. Was One* when it came out, and deciding that I really hated anyone who was that good that early in his career. It should have won the Hugo for Best Novel; it lost to a far bigger name, but not to a better book. I believed that then; I believe it now.

A few years later David produced another near-classic novel, *The Man Who Folded Himself.* Is it the best time paradox story ever written? I don't know. Heinlein wrote two pretty fair time paradox stories himself: "By His Bootstraps" and "All You Zombies." But I will state without equivocation that it is unquestionably the finest time paradox *novel* ever written.

I kept running into David at conventions. In 1978 we judged the Worldcon masquerade in Phoenix. It was three million degrees that night, give or take a degree, and if you want to know why that particular masquerade had more runthroughs than any other in history, it's because we discovered that the only room in town where the air-conditioning was working full-force was the judges' deliberation room, and we kept going back to it to sit in the cool, drink our lemonades, and exchange market info while one costumer after another fainted from the heat.

That's when I decided he wasn't such a terrible fellow after all.

We stayed in touch, sat on some panels together, chatted on Compuserve and elsewhere, even toyed with collaborating on a round-robin novel…and then came the fatal day back in 1991 when I invited him to contribute a story to *Alternate Presidents*, an anthology I was editing for Tor Books.

So why was it fatal, since nobody died?

Simple: my opinion of David as a brilliant novelist who didn't much dabble in short fiction died. (I should have known better; I loved "With a Finger in My I" when it came out. I probably just forced myself to forget who wrote it.)

Well, the gist of it was that David's story was so good that I had no choice but to invite him back for *Alternate Kennedys*. And then for still more anthologies: *Alternate Outlaws, Dinosaur Fantastic, More Whatdunits, Aladdin: Master of the Lamp, Witch Fantastic, Deals With the Devil, Alternate Warriors, Sherlock Holmes in Orbit, By Any Other Fame*...

Move the clock ahead to 2003 and I'm still inviting him. This year he contributed stories to *Men Writing SF as Women* and to *Stars*, for which I am only 50% responsible since I co-edited it with Janis Ian, so if you don't like his story send half of your hate mail to her.

This is not the easiest guy in the world to work with, this Gerrold. When I got the editing assignment for *Christmas Ghosts*, I asked for stories about the ghosts of Christmas past, present or future. David replied that he would only contribute if he could write about the Ghost of Christmas Sideways. *All right, you cocky son of a bitch*, I thought; *let's call your bluff and see what happens*. (*sigh*) What happened was a brilliant story about the Ghost of Christmas Sideways.

In 1996, at the Worldcon in Los Angeles, Bantam took all of its authors, including David and me, to the La Brea Tar Pits for a banquet. It proved to be fertile ground for David's perverse mind. He wrote a story about why he shoved me—sweet, innocent, lovable me, who wouldn't say boo to a goose—into the tar pits for *Return of the Dinosaurs*.

I've seen him in serious moments as well. When he won the Nebula in 1995 for Best Novelette with "The Martian Child," he gave as moving an acceptance speech as I've ever heard. I won Best Novella and had to follow him; it was as painful as having your story follow "The Martian Child" in a magazine.

He pulled the same trick a few months later at the Worldcon in Scotland. Won the Hugo for Best Novelette. Even shed a tear. (I shed a couple myself; the dirty bastard beat my own novelette for the award.) This time when I won the Hugo for Best Novella and had to get up on stage right after David, I was prepared. I muttered "Thank You" and went right back to my chair.

So if my relationship with David consists mostly of joining a schizoid organization, losing a Hugo to him, and waiting in vain for him to write a story I could reject, what's the real reason I consented to write this introduction?

Easy.

Damned near half the stories in this book wouldn't have been written if I hadn't commissioned them.

I had to do *something* to expiate my guilt.

INTRODUCTION TO *THE GREY PRINCE*

I have a confession to make. Few things in science fiction annoy me more than having to learn a few dozen new words and as many not-quite-human names simply to be able to work my way through a single book. And one of the things that *does* annoy me more is a novel with forty or fifty footnotes (or feetnote, as the late James Blish dubbed them.)

I have another confession to make: I find that I don't mind new names, new words, or footnotes at all when a master like Jack Vance incorporates them into one of his books, such as, for example, *The Grey Prince*.

I first read this novel more than thirty years ago. I wasn't aware of all the controversy it was engendering; I read it simply because I made it my business to read all of Jack's books as they came out. I thought it was pretty typical, which is to say, a fast-paced novel with interesting characters and beautiful word-pictures, crafted by one of our master stylists.

So you can imagine my surprise when I started reading reviews and reader comments to the effect that it was racist, or a right-wing polemic, or both.

(A few years later I would be accused, by an equally small handful of critics, of writing racist and sexist tracts in my "Kirinyaga" stories, which are about the Kikuyu people of East Africa trying to form a Utopian colony on a terraformed planetoid. Oddly enough, at the same time those stories came out, I wrote a science fictional allegory of Kenya's history titled *Paradise*, but although my Kikuyu analogs shared every trait and belief with the Kikuyu of "Kirinyaga," they were alien in shape and had alien names—and not a single one of those critics thought *Paradise* was racist or sexist, which I think says a little more about the critics than about the author or the literature. Jack clearly made his aliens a little *too* human.)

This is a very tricky book, this *Grey Prince*. Not only did it fool some of the knee-jerk critics, but it approaches everything in a very indirect manner. (Well, why *shouldn't* a wordsmith of prodigious talent be subtle?)

For example, the viewpoint character is clearly Schaine Madduc, but she is missing from large parts of the narrative, and a strong case can be made that she is too naïve for her own good.

For example, Jorjol is the title character, the Grey Prince, but he is *not* the viewpoint character, nor in the end is he an especially nice person, though he is surely a motivated one. There are times when you think he's a bit of an ass who just happens to be on the side of Right and Justice, and there are times when you think he is a reasonably decent character who just happens to be dead wrong. There are as many opinions about him as there are characters in the story who know him, which is precisely as it should be (and so rarely is in a work of fiction.)

As for the true subject of the book, it's as difficult to define in a single sentence or paragraph as the Grey Prince himself, though possibly not to the critics who claim this is a right-wing diatribe. They would tell you, when speaking of the Land-barons, that it is evil and immoral to take land from an indigenous people—and they would be right as far as that argument goes. But what Vance points out is that the "indigenous people" weren't born there, any more than the Apaches or Commanches or Maasai or Kikuyu were born on *their* "ancestral land," that they simply took it from someone else just as surely as various people took it from them.

Not so simple when viewed that way (which is to say, Jack Vance's way), is it?

Then there's the charge of racism.

I suppose you could make a case (or at least *I* could) that the book's Nomads are Amerind analogs, that the Erjin slaves are analogs of the Negro race of perhaps two centuries ago, and so on. But again, nothing in *The Grey Prince* is ever quite as simple and clear-cut as it seems. You have a slaveholding culture secure in its moral superiority to the Land-baron culture that "steals" the Nomads' land…while the Land-barons know *they* are the superior culture because they do not keep slaves. If you are a Nomad or an Erjin, you don't think too highly of *either* of them.

And finally there are the Morphotes, the true indigenous race, who have a bone to pick with just about everybody.

I have a feeling that the critics who screamed "right-wing tract" and "racist trash" the loudest not only completely misunderstood the book, but also ignored or never understood the fact that guilt is not eternal, that after a certain number of generations have passed most people no longer feel responsible or guilty for the actions of their distant progenitors, but learn to live with the conditions as they now exist. (Actually, most people don't feel guilty ten minutes later or they wouldn't have done whatever it is that inspires guilt, but that has nothing to do with the point I'm making.)

I think I know which side Jack Vance is on, but he makes sure every side is represented by the arguments a believer would make. There comes a point in Patrick McGoohan's still-popular television series of four decades back, *The Prisoner,* when McGoohan runs for office of the mysterious Village, promising to find out "who are the warders and who are the prisoners." You might make a case that, below the surface sheen of exotic other-world adventure, Vance is concerned here with who are truly the oppressed and who are truly the oppressors. I think it was his temerity in even asking the question that upset that small handful of critics I mentioned earlier. After all, this is supposed to be mindless escapist fiction, or if not mindless, at least it should direct the mind to problems of science.

To which I reply: welcome to the works and worlds of Jack Vance.

INTRODUCTION TO *TIDES FROM THE NEW WORLDS*

The first time I met Tobias Buckell was in the wilds of Michigan, where I was teaching at Clarion, that unique course for embryonic science fiction writers. There were some very bright, very talented people in that class; I think more than half have already broken into print, but Tobias made a very special impression. They all listened, but he *assimilated*. You could just look at his face and say to yourself: Hey, this stuff is getting through to him. He was the youngest member of the class, and by far the hardest-working.

He'd hand in a 6,000-word story, and the class would criticize it, sometimes brutally. And while they were each taking a week or more to hone their 5,000-worders, there Tobias would be the next morning, unshaken and undeterred, with a brand-new story, and it wasn't a one-time phenomenon. Tobias produced a new story every day that I was there—and he had a learning curve you wouldn't believe. I could see a difference in just the week that I was there—and what he produced that week was light-years ahead of the stories he had written to gain admission to the program.

He had an interesting background. He was raised in the Caribbean, and there was a strong flavor of it in some of his stories. He had a work ethic you couldn't help but admire. And he clearly had skill.

We became friends, and when the course was over I told him to keep in touch and let me know how he was doing. Well, by now everyone knows: sale after sale, a continuous trajectory of improvement, and finally a nomination for the Campbell Award, science fiction's Rookie of the Year award.

Along the way I bought some of the stories in this book for anthologies I was editing, and I collaborated with him on another. At the 2001 Worldcon in Philadelphia, I introduced him to an agent I thought would fit him, and sure enough, he soon sold his first novel to Tor Books.

This young man's got a hell of a future ahead of him. But he's also got a very impressive present, so it's probably time for me to stop telling you about it and let you experience it for yourself.

Enjoy. I certainly did.

INTRODUCTION TO *PICASSO'S CAT*

I've known Ron Collins for a long time now, ever since he was knee-high to a brontosaur. (Which means I met him as an adult.)

Ron is, without question, the hardest-working and most disciplined writer I've ever met. A lot of writers (most, in fact) hate writing but love having written. They apply their imaginations not to their stories, but to the avoidance of writing those stories except in situations of extreme financial desperation.

Not Ron. I don't, to this day, know for a fact that he loves the act of writing...but I know that ran or shine, sick or healthy, temporarily rich or temporarily poor, he's there every morning before the sun rises, turning out his day's quota of wordage.

Now, just producing a lot of words, while quite an accomplishment in itself, it relatively meaningless if those words aren't worth reading. That has *never* been Ron's problem.

I know. I've collaborated with him. I commissioned three of the stories in this book, and a bunch more than I'm sure will appear in future books.

Take a look at the stories in this volume. There are no weaklings here. Ron doesn't write weaklings.

"The Disappearance of Josie Andrews" addresses a major contemporary problem in a science fictional way, as the very best science fiction is supposed to do.

Some very fine stories tend to get lost. They appeared in the wrong magazine, or the wrong anthology, and good as they are they somehow miss their audience. One such story is the wonderful "G-Bomb," which I commissioned from Ron for one of my anthologies. I'm delighted to see it get another airing here.

Them there's a trio of stories all set on the same world: "Stealing the Sun," "The Taranth Stone," and "Parchment in Glass." All appeared in *Analog*, never an easy market to crack; and one of them ("The Taranth Stone") was both the cover story and a HOMer Award winner.

The story Ron and I collaborated on went to an anthology titled *Mob Magic*. What I didn't know at time was that I saw his second effort on the subject. He wasn't pleased with his first start, so he set it aside until he could analyze what was wrong with it and how to fix it, a feat he accomplished quite amusingly in "Just Business."

The field of science fiction gives the writer all of time and all of space in which to set his stories, and no theme or style is taboo. The good ones—and Ron is certainly one of them—take advantage of that freedom to write all kinds of stories. Up ahead you'll find "The Test of Time," a dinosaur story; "1 is True," a cyberpunk noir story; and a stunning little thousand-worder, "Picasso's Cat."

Once you buy this book (and I urge you to), try to seek Ron out at a convention and get him to sign it for you. And get him talking while he's doing it. You'll find that he's as friendly, approachable, and brilliant as this collection would lead you to believe.

INTRODUCTION TO *THE TARZAN TWINS*

When I was a kid growing up in the 1950s, only a handful of Tarzan books were available. They were Grosset & Dunlap reprints, and they were marketed for young adults.

In retrospect this seems rather strange, because from the day Edgar Rice Burroughs created him Tarzan had always—with the exception you hold in your hands—been sold to adult magazine and book markets. I suspect it was the subliterate Tarzan of the MGM films, as best (or at least, most often) exemplified by Johnny Weissmuller that led publishers to think anyone that learning-disabled couldn't appeal to adults. (They were probably right. The problem is that Edgar Rice Burroughs' Tarzan bore almost no resemblance to MGM's.)

Anyway, Tarzan was a favorite of adults, selling millions of copies here and abroad during his first 14 years of existence. Then, in 1926, Burroughs got an interesting suggestion from Dr. J. C. Flowers, the president of the firm that had recently acquired the F. F. Voland Company: would he consider writing a Tarzan book aimed specifically at young adult readers? Burroughs hemmed and hawed and dragged his feet, but finally agreed to write a book for Volland called *The Tarzan Twins.*

Flowers was thrilled when he heard the title. He was less thrilled when Burroughs explained that the "twins" were to be cousins, Dick and Doc. Couldn't they be twin brothers, Flowers wanted to know—but Burroughs was adamant.

Then came Flowers' next suggestion: since they're not really twins but cousins, couldn't one of them be a girl? That way Volland would be putting out a book for *all* young adults rather than just young adult males.

Burroughs, whose stories reek of Victorian hang-ups about the sexes, refused again, this time because if the twins were going to have adventures in the wilds of the jungle, they would shortly be reduced to wearing nothing but loincloths, just like Tarzan. He planned to make them 14 years old, the age of his target audience, and since the book would be heavily illustrated, he couldn't have a 14-year-old girl running around in a loincloth and nothing else. (I don't know why not. *I'd* have bought it.)

Flowers kept asking questions and making suggestions, and Burroughs kept ignoring them and reassuring him that the only difference between this book and a regular Tarzan novel would be that "I am simply omitting the love scenes and using two boys about fourteen years of age as the principal characters."

(Oh? You didn't know about the "adult" scenes in other Tarzan books? Well, believe it or not, Tarzan has a fondness for absinthe and cigarettes, and occasionally loses all self-control when in the presence of mad queens or High Priestesses of the Flaming God—which is to say, every sixth book or so, he briefly loses his head and kisses one.)

In early 1927 Burroughs handed in the manuscript, which is about two teenaged cousins who are distantly related to Tarzan. They get lost and are captured by cannibals while on a trip to Tarzan's African estates (yes, "estates"; Burroughs never used the singular for Tarzan's holdings in 40+ years of writing about them. I picture farms and hunting reserves all the hell over the continent.) Flowers realized that there was a lot of adventure, but that Numa and Tantor and all the other animals everyone loved were missing—and so, incidentally, were little things like character development and anything resembling a plot. He and his editor, Margherita Osborne, asked Burroughs to add a quick 5,000 to 7,000 words to correct these omissions. Burroughs, who may or may not have thought of himself as an artist prior to typing "The End" but loved to consider himself a hard-nosed businessman thereafter, refused unless they paid him more money. It was then up to Volland, and Flowers elected to go with the manuscript as it stood, hiring Douglas Grant as the illustrator. Burroughs approved Grant's illos in mid-August, and the book came out on October 10, 1927.

The silence was deafening.

Sure that they must be doing something wrong, that it was impossible for Burroughs to write a Tarzan book that didn't sell zillions of copies, they put out a second edition, this time in a gorgeous box.

The book promptly won an award from the American Society of Graphic Arts, so Flowers knew that any lack of sales wasn't Volland's fault. Burroughs couldn't believe the poor sales either, and tended to blame poor proof reading (unlike most writers, who realize that the galleys are the last point at which you can catch a mistake and avoid looking like an idiot in public, he evidently didn't proof his own galleys).

Well, the book ran through seven editions from Volland. Eventually it earned a few dollars, but not enough to encourage either party to write a planned sequel with a somewhat-less-undressed teenaged girl as a main character.

Burroughs took a final half-hearted whack at the young adult market before turning it over to Hollywood and the comic books when he produced *Tarzan and the Tarzan Twins With Jad-Bal-Ja the Golden Lion,* which was published by Whitman (the publisher of Big Little Books) in March of 1936. It sold for 29 cents, and was at least as much a coloring book as a Tarzan book. Canaveral Press combined the two in a handsome hardcover edition, illustrated by Roy G. Krenkel in 1963.

Though it's seen a few publishers and a few editions (and a few illustrators, though none in Krenkel's class), this has always been the rarest of the Tarzan books. It's interesting to compare Burroughs' notion of a young adult book (this one) to Grosset & Dunlap's notion (*Tarzan of the Apes),* and of course it's always nice to have *any* Burroughs book, even one as atypical as *The Tarzan Twins,* back in print.

MANLY AND JOHN

- "Back to the Beast" (November, 1927 *Weird Tales*)
- "Disc-Men of Jupiter" (Sept. 1931 *Wonder Stories*)
- Warrior of Two Worlds" (Summer 1944 *Planet Stories*)
- "Giants From Eternity" (July 1939 *Startling Stories*)
- "Dream-Dust From Mars" (February 1938 *Thrilling Wonder Stories*)
- "Rocket of Metal Men" (Dec. 1940 *Astonishing Stories*)
- "Venus Enslaved" (Summer 1944 *Planet Stories*)

* * * *

Interesting line-up. Blood-'n-guts space opera that typified the second quarter of the 20th Century. Every major magazine is there. Well, except for John Campbell's *Astounding*, and Manly Wade Wellman sold to Campbell too.

It's hardly the kind of list that implies that the author was one of science fiction's few authentic, legitimate artists…but he was. In ways, Wellman must have felt, back when he was starting out, like a caveman who wants to paint in oils or write a piano concerto: there was simply no outlet for things like the Silver John stories when he broke in, or for many years thereafter. And until there was, he wrote science fiction and mysteries and Westerns and anything else that he could place in the voracious penny-a-word pulps. He even borrowed Edmond Hamilton's Captain Future long enough to write *The Solar Invasion*. Along the way he also wrote as Gabriel Barclay (8 stories), Gans T. Field (35 stories), Hampton Wells, Levi Crow, M. W. Wellman, and Will Garth (26 stories).

The first great fantasy magazine of the century (at least, if you will consider *Weird Tales* to be a horror magazine) was John Campbell's *Unknown,* but it wasn't a market for the Silver John stories. First, it dealt in urban fantasy, which was not what Wellman wanted to tell, and second, it was killed three years after its birth by the World War II paper shortage, and except for one issue in 1948, was never resurrected.

Wellman had to wait for *The Magazine of Fantasy and Science Fiction*, which began just before the century's midpoint, to find a home for his fabulous tales of Appalachia, and his singular protagonist, the unforgettable Silver John.

To say that Wellman lived in a literary family is an understatement: his brother, his wife, and his son were all writers too (and good ones). He gave an early hint of what he could do when he found a magazine market that would give him free rein. It was *Ellery Queen's Mystery Magazine*, and he won the very first Ellery Queen Award for Best Mystery Story in 1946. There was a pretty good field that year; the runner-up was William Faulkner (who, it is said, never quite got over losing to a refugee from the despised pulps.) Then, just to prove it wasn't a fluke, Wellman won an Edgar (which was then known as the Mystery Writers of America Award) in 1955, and was nominated for a Pulitzer Prize in 1956, but that didn't raise any eyebrows because he'd already been writing the Silver John stories for a few years.

Wellman was born in Angola in 1903. His family returned to America when he was six, and he soon developed an abiding love of the Appalachian area—which didn't stop him from getting degrees from Wichita and Columbia. He sold his first story, listed above, in 1927, and went full-time freelance in 1930, moving to New York to be nearer his markets. Soon after the end of World War II he moved to North Carolina, where he taught at the University of North Carolina in Chapel Hill, and where he would spend the remainder of his life. He also built a cabin close to his very best source material atop Yandro Mountain in the Smokey Mountains; it was named for the monster-covered mountain you'll encounter in "The Desrick on Yandro."

We've had a lot of science fiction and (especially) fantasy that was rooted in Hindu mythology, and Greek mythology, and Roman mythology, and you-name-it mythology, but until Silver John hit the scene we'd never had any stories rooted in the folklore and mythology of Appalachia—and it was a mythology that played to every one of Wellman's many strengths.

First there was the music. Wellman loved the folk songs, hymns and ballads of those Southern mountains. He knew them inside-out, knew the men who kept the musical traditions alive, and used many of those songs in his stories, as well as adding some of his own. Silver John is also known as John the Balladeer, for he travels the mountains with his silver-stringed guitar, keeping alive the music and traditions just as his creator did, singing for his supper as Wellman wrote for his own. Many of the songs that appear in the stories can still be heard today, recorded by such notables as the Weavers, the Dixie Ramblers, the Bitterroot Mountain Bluegrass Band, and others.

But there's a lot more to the stories than just the music. For one thing, there are the creatures drawn from the local folklore, creatures like the Behinder (which is never seen, and always hides behind its victims), the Bammat, and the gardinal, creatures you won't find anywhere except the mountains that Wellman loved so deeply. Most writers follow H. P. Lovecraft's lead and explain, in frightened whispers, that their creatures are hideous but indescribable. Not Wellman—or Silver John, if you prefer. The Flat is a carpet with an attitude, the Skim is a cross between a discus and a frisbee, and so on. Lovecraft's monsters were very New England-ish; Wellman's are rustic and almost familiar.

And then there's religion. It's a very real, very intimate part of the mountain people Wellman wrote about, and it's a very real part of the stories as well. Parts of the Bible are literal truth in the Silver John stories, and no, it's not the author preaching; it's the author using every aspect of mountain life and belief to dramatic advantage—and it's Silver John drawing the strength from that religion to face up to the devil in his many manifestations.

Let's not overlook the language, either. A lot of science fiction and fantasy writers make up languages out of whole cloth—and it shows. Some try for foreign dialects by mimicking bad character actors doing the same thing on television. Not Wellman. He had an ear for the dialect of the mountain people, and every single line rings true for it.

Finally there's Silver John himself, the narrator of these tales, the character who has secured Wellman's place in our field's history. Humble, honest, curious, a Korean War veteran, a musician, a singer, a folklorist, a wanderer, a collector of some songs and myths and a creator of others.

I first encountered Silver John in what remains my favorite of his adventures, "Vandy, Vandy." I immediately set out to find more stories of this remarkable traveler, and in quick order I found (and loved) "One Other," "Call Me From the Valley," and "The Derrick on Yandro."

It was 1963 when Arkham House brought out *Who Fears the Devil?*, a collection the first eleven Silver John stories. I was 21, a new husband and newer father, and I couldn't afford it...but I bought it anyway. There were two characters I was bound and determined to collect in any and all forms in which they appeared, and Silver John was one of them. (C. L. Moore's Northwest Smith was the other. Not a bad daily double.)

The stories were entertaining, familiar in a racial-memory sort of way, and educational (most Americans thought that the Kingston Trio and the Limelighters were doing true-quill folk music back then)...but they were also comforting and uplifting. Silver John has a healthy respect for the devil, but he doesn't fear him, because he's got the twin shields of innocence and right (in a religious sense) to protect him. It makes for some very interesting confrontations, never quite terrifying, never ever pedestrian, just stories than somehow feel exactly *right*.

Ballantine brought out *Who Fears the Devil?* in a mass market paperback, Wellman kept writing Silver John stories, and eventually Baen Books brought out a much larger collection, *John the Balladeer*. Wellman wasn't content to keep Silver John confined to short stories. If you like this collection (and the smart money says you'll love it), you can also look for Silver John in five novels: *The Old Gods Waken*, *After Dark*, *The Lost and the Lurking*, *The Hanging Stones*, and *The Voice of the Mountain*.

And now that I've praised the stories and touted you onto the novels, let me tout you *off* something. Hollywood made a film out of the Silver John stories, done with Hollywood's usual taste and respect for the material. It is called *The Legend of Hillbilly John*, and the change from Silver John to Hillbilly John pretty much says it all.

Anyway, there are some brilliant and evocative stories waiting up ahead for you. There's the one that got it all started ("O Ugly Bird!"), the last story Wellman ever wrote ("Where Did She Wander?"), a couple that have never appeared in any Silver John collection ("Frogfather" and "Sin's Doorway"), and some that it is not an exaggeration to say have already become classics.

A suggestion: dip into the collection, read one or two a night rather than going through it all in one sitting. Make it last. Let Silver John get to know you as you get to know him. Chances are you won't meet many more admirable characters in your life—or more interesting ones either.

INTRODUCTION TO THE 2012 EDITION OF *A GUIDE TO BARSOOM*

I came into science fiction fandom through the Burroughs door about half a century ago, and John F. Roy was my guide and my dear friend for many years. (Not many people know, or remember, that he was a Royal Canadian Mountie when he wasn't being the preeminent Edgar Rice Burroughs scholar of our time. He looked really heroic in his red jacket and Dudley Do-Right hat, sitting atop his horse.)

Burroughs created Barsoom with "Under the Moons of Mars," literally a century ago, but it took another 64 years before the field produced someone competent enough to create the book you are now reading. And given the popularity of Barsoom, it *needed* to be created. Burroughs created a reasonably consistent world over the span of 10+ novels, including a language (or at least a number of words that were used with some degree of consistency), a history, a background, customs, weapons, scientific innovations and scientific shortcomings, and a few resident races. It took someone with John's thoroughness and dedication to codify it all, as he does in the pages up ahead.

And another need for this book is that there are some areas in which Burroughs wasn't *that* consistent. Ask anyone who's ever tried to create a map of Barsoom about that (and believe me, back in the 1960s, a *lot* of us took a crack at it, with no two maps coming out the same.)

John shared his expertise with Burroughs fans through a seemingly endless series of scholarly articles in the leading Burroughs fanzines of the time, primarily Camille Cazedessus's *ERB-dom*, which to this day remains the only Burroughs zine ever to win a Hugo. He had no interest in writing sequels, as so many others did. He was a scholar, and all of his considerable talent was channeled into that pursuit.

How high was the field's regard for his expertise? Back in 1964 I wrote a 28,000-word sequel to *Llana of Gathol* (with ERB, Inc.'s authorization, of course). There was a stipulation: it couldn't be printed until John vetted it for stylistic and factual consistency, and gave it his approval, which he did after I made the changes he stipulated.

I have many wonderful memories of John and his lovely and loving wife Ev. Ev wasn't much interested in Burroughs, science fiction, or conventions, but she encouraged John to pursue his interest, always accompanied him, and usually spent her days touring and sightseeing in whatever city the convention happened to be, then joining him for dinner and the evening parties. I remember one Worldcon, the 1966 Tricon, where I stayed up so late each night that I slept right through the alarm every morning, and I expressed the fear that I'd do it again on getaway day, and that Carol (who had been unable to wake me and get me moving in much less than half an hour) and I would miss our train home. So at 6:00 AM the phone rings, I groggily pick it up, and John begins reciting the silliest damned Burroughesque nonsense rhyme I'd ever heard…and in a couple of minutes I was laughing so hard that I stayed awake the rest of the morning and we caught our train.

He was a good and decent man. The Burroughs field doubtless misses its finest scholar, but nowhere near as much as I miss my wonderful Canadian friend. I cherish my first edition of this book, with John's inscription and the wonderful Neal MacDonald illustrations, but not as much as I cherish my memories of John himself.

A RE-INTRODUCTION TO *THE PROCEEDINGS: CHICON III*

A lot was happening back in 1962.

JFK was playing nuclear chicken with Nikita Khruschev. We swapped Russian spy Rudolf Abel for American spy Francis Gary Powers. John Glenn became the first American to orbit the Earth. A bit more locally, the White Sox, which had won their first pennant in 40 years in 1959, were in the 3rd years of another 40-year drought. (Well, 46 years, but even so it looks pretty good next to the Cubs.) Mayor Daley the First was entering his second decade as Boss.

And Chicago fandom hosted ChiCon III, the 20th Worldcon, at the Pick-Congress Hotel.

Worldcons were a bit different back then. Oh, they still had a Guest of Honor (usually just one, who was usually—but not always—a writer), and they had speeches, and they had a masquerade of sorts, and they gave out Hugos, but they were *small* compared to today. Chicon III had well under a thousand paid members, and I suspect that there were less than 500 warm bodies on the premises.

What did that mean?

The main thing it meant was that everyone could fit into the program room(s), so they had single-track programming. Only one thing was going on at a time, so the attendees never had to miss an item.

Compare that to the schedule from Chicon 6 in 2000. Here's the choices you were confronted by at the not-wildly-busy hour of 4:00 PM Friday, when half the con was getting ready to go out to dinner:

Grand Ballroom A: *It Came From Outer Space.* The NASA Space Product Development Program.

Grand Ballroom B: *Critics' View of the Recent Crop of Science Fiction Movies.* Panel with Bob Blackwood, Paul Barnett, Randy Dannenfelser, Matthew Springer, John Flynn.

Grand Ballroom C-D: *Volcanos and Ice.* The Last Days of the Gallileo Spacecraft, A Bill Higgens slide show.

Regency A: *Military Issues.* Elizabeth Moon, John Laprise, Joseph T. Major, Charles Walther, Jim Groat.

Regency B: *The James Tiptree Award Auction.*

Regency C: *Creation of a Publishing House.* Jim Baen, Tom Doherty, Toni Weisskopf, Lois McMaster Bujold, Mark Shepherd.

Gold Coast Room: *21st Century Fanhistorians.* Joe Siclari, Filthy Pierre, Moshe Feder, Keith Stokes, Dick Smith.

Buckingham Room: *Should the Vote be Earned, a la* Starship Troopers? Audience panel.

Picasso Room: *'50's-'70's Vintage.* Using clothes from the 1950s through the 1970s for costuming.

Columbian Room: *Ancient and Medieval Economic Systems (And How to Use Them in Your Work).* Greg Costikyan, John Fast, Mike Moscoe, S.M. Stirling.

Haymarket Room: *How to Make a Million Dollars Publishing a Fanzine.* Charles Brown, Ed Bryant, Gary K. Wolfe, Mark R. Kelly.

Addams Room: *Is the Science Fiction Book Club Still Necessary in a World of Online Booksellers?* Steve Miller, Andrew Wheeler, Alice Bentley, Therese Littleton.

Fishbowl Room: *Book to Costume to Paint.* Bob Eggleton, Joy Day.

State Room: *Little Answers to Big Problems.* Wil McCarthy, Larry Ahearn, John G. Cramer, Howard Davidson.

Regent Room: *ASFA and the Chesleys.* Panelists discuss the art awards. Teresa Patterson, Mel White, etc.

Crystal Room: *Presentation of the Prometheus Awards.*

Ambassador Room: *The Future of the Human Form.* Lee Martindale, Edwin Strickland, etc.

Embassy Room: *Comics Underground.* Len Wein, etc.

Childrens': *Children's Belly Dancing.*
Childrens': *Children's Live Action Role Playing.*
Childrens': *Land Before Time Workshop.* Hal Clement.
Kaffeeklatsch: Kevin J. Anderson.
Kaffeeklatsch: Linda Dunn.
Kaffeeklatsch: April Lee.
Reading: M. Shayne Bell.
Reading: Carol Berg.
Reading: Mary Marshall.
Reading: Sue Blom.
Tour of Fan History Exhibit: Mike Resnick.
Autographing: Nancy Kress.
Autographing: Jerry Oltion.
Autographing: Karen Haber.
Autographing: Edward Rosick.
Autographing: Orson Scott Card.

And of course the round-the-clock movies were proceeding on schedule, and you could always browse the Dealer's Room or the Art Show or the special exhibits.

There were some interesting items—but no matter how hard you tried, you were going to miss about 95% of them, and that's if you attended something every hour from 9:00 AM until midnight.

As this book will show, there's something to be said for the Worldcons of my youth. With only a few hundred attendees, you stayed in just one hotel (there were seven in Denver and ten in Montreal in 2008 and 2009), and you got to meet everyone you wanted to meet. There were none of the legendary "secret pro parties," because there weren't enough fans to bother hiding from—and besides, back in 1962, about three-quarters of the pros had come from fandom. (What did Frederik Pohl, Cyril Kornbluth, Damon Knight, Robert Silverberg, Marion Zimmer Bradley, Ray Bradbury, Harlan Ellison, and dozens of others have in common besides writing science fiction for a living? Answer: Each of them had published a fanzine before—and sometimes after—turning pro.

And artists like Hannes Bok and Jack Gaughan illustrated them.)

The other advantage was that, if you wanted, you could see every single item. No panel was in competition with any other. There was no programming against the Guest of Honor speech or the Hugos or the masquerade. It really was one big family, which is what attracted so many of us—possibly, given that Chicon 6 schedule, *too* many of us—to Worldcons in the first place.

I didn't go to ChiCon III. My first was Discon I, a year later. I lived in Chicago, and even though I was as dead broke as most 20-year-olds, I was a 25-cent El (well, El and subway) ride from the hotel, and membership was dirt cheap. But a future Campbell winner named Laura chose the latter half of August to get herself born, so we had to travel all the way to Washington, D.C. the next year to finally meet Chicago fandom.

Speaking of Chicago fandom, it kept busy—and not just hosting the Worldcon. A number of area fans, led by Earl Kemp and George Price, had formed Advent:Publishers, and they were putting out some remarkable books. Basically, if you read everything they published, which came to maybe a couple of books a year, you'd read 90% of the important books to come out about science fiction and fandom for a decade in each direction from ChiCon III. They published Robert Bloch's delightful *The Eighth Stage of Fandom,* Damon Knight's *In Search of Wonder,* James Blish's *The Issue at Hand* and its two sequels, the Panshins' *SF in Dimension* and *Heinlein in Dimension,* a number of others, all of them fine books, and because they didn't believe in "instant rarities" some are still available all these years later. And along with all that they did something else, something in addition to the highly-praised criticism and "sercon" books, that no one else had ever attempted, and it worked so well that they did it again the next year as well.

What did they do? They tape-recorded every word of ChiCon III, and after they finished transcribing it, and Earl finished editing it, and they added photos by Jay Kay Klein, Dean Grennell, Richard Hickey, Jean Grant (and some unused *Life Magazine* photos as well), and George Price finished producing it, they brought out the first edition of the book you hold in your hands: *The Proceedings: ChiCon III*.

There were giants present at that convention. Most of them have passed from the scene—they weren't young men and women half a century ago—but they were there, they were approachable, and they were willing to perform, to autograph, to participate in every way asked of them. The Guest of Honor was Theodore Sturgeon, who had broken into print less than 25 years earlier. So had some of his fellow panelists, like Leigh Brackett, Poul Anderson, Fritz Leiber, Frank M. Robinson, Marion Zimmer Bradley, Hal Clement, Poul Anderson, Fred Saberhagen, and a surprise last-minute arrival, Robert A. Heinlein, who showed up long enough to pick up a Hugo for *Stranger in the Strange Land*. Quite a few of the "old pros" were there too, including Jack Williamson, Clifford D. Simak, Edmond Hamilton, and E.E. "Doc" Smith (who attended the masquerade dressed as C.L. Moore's hero, Northwest Smith). Since the convention was in Chicago, home at the time of *Playboy*, Hefner and the crew were there too.

And as you read through this book, you'll see another advantage of the Worldcons of old: since they didn't have fifteen or twenty things going on at once, they didn't have to split up their major writers so that every simultaneous panel would have one. At 3:00 PM Saturday, you'll read a panel that boasted Jack Williamson, Anthony Boucher, Fritz Leiber, Judith Merril, and Theodore Cogswell, with Robert Bloch—who later gave an hilarious speech—tossing up a question from the audience.

24 hours later, at 3:00 PM on Sunday, you had a panel featuring Katherne MacLean, Frederik Pohl, Theodore Sturgeon,

Lloyd Biggle, Philip Jose Farmer, Donald A. Wollheim, Avram Davidson, Algis J. Budrys, and Charles Beaumont.

I put it to you that while some of the participants of Chi-con 7 will be future generations' giants, you just won't see that many of them on a panel all at the same time. (Nor was ChiCon III devoid of fannish giants, as evidenced by the photos of Sam Moskowitz, Bob Tucker, and Forry Ackerman.)

And it wasn't just the panels that make this book fascinating reading. Consider Theodore Sturgeon's Guest of Honor speech, with a never-before-told story about Heinlein that's as memorable as they come.

The photos also give you a flavor of what it was like, too—what they wore and how they looked. We were a big happy family back then, and we're a bigger, happier family now. It's always good to know where we came from, to remember our roots—and since we're writers and readers, it's even better to re-read them.

Okay, enough history from me. Turn the page and start re-living it yourself. Welcome to ChiCon III!

INTRO TO *THUNDER IN THE VOID*

I am probably C. L. Moore's biggest fan. I love just about everything she's written. When my sense of wonder needs a shot of adrenaline, I just read a "Northwest Smith" story and I'm fine twenty minutes later.

I have never quite forgiven her for not marrying me, though to be fair she married Henry Kuttner in 1940, two years before I was born. And here I am writing an introduction for a collection by my rival for Catherine's affections. (It was a long-distance rivalry; I only met her once, in 1972, long after he was dead.) So years ago I figured, well, if she wasn't willing to wait for me, maybe I ought to find out a little something about this Kuttner guy. And I've been studying him and begrudgingly admiring him ever since.

Henry Kuttner was a highly-skilled and incredibly prolific writer. Before the dust had cleared over his career, he'd created, alone or with Catherine, the Baldy stories, the Gallegher stories, *Fury*, "Mimsy Were the Borogoves," and a host of other classics and semi-classics.

But long before he began writing for John Campbell and all the other top markets of his day, he had a priority: he had to eat.

Now, there has always been a field in American fiction where, if you were fast and facile and willing to occasionally hide behind pseudonyms, you could make a living while honing your skills. Back when I was just starting to push nouns up against verbs, that field was known as the "adult" field (it's been called worse). A lot of science fiction writers, such as Robert Silverberg, Barry Malzberg, and I paid our dues there, as did mystery writers such as Donald E. Westlake and Lawrence Block.

Now, before there *was* an adult field, you learned to write and paid your dues in the bottom-end pulps. While Robert

A. Heinlein and Raymond Chandler were making a living at the very top of the field, someone had to fill those half-cent a word bottom dwellers. He had to be energetic. He had to know pacing. He had to be wildly prolific. And, since readers were paying for this stuff, he had to be good.

In short, he had to be Henry Kuttner.

And that's what we have here: a collection of tales published in secondary markets back when being Henry Kuttner was nothing to write home about.

There are a couple of stories up ahead that first introduced me to Kuttner's early work (as opposed to the more famous stuff he made his reputation with). Move the clock back to November, 1960. I'm an eighteen-year-old kid, a sophomore at the University of Chicago, and I'm in a local bookstore— and when no one's looking, I pick a copy of *Playboy* out of the rack and start thumbing through it, hunting for photos of pneumatic naked ladies. And suddenly I am the center of attention, because I am laughing my head off, looking at a bunch of hilarious parody covers of science fiction pulp magazines by *Mad* and *Little Annie Fanny* artist Will Elder.

I buy the magazine, and it remains to this day (March 31, 2011, if anyone cares) the only copy of *Playboy* I have ever kept, indeed one of the very few I have ever bought. The reason I kept it is that Elder's covers illustrated an even funnier article, titled "Girls for the Slime God," by William Knoles, which was a nostalgic look back at the days of the salacious science fiction pulps, when every cover showed some variation of a B.E.M. (that's Bug-Eyed Monster, for the uninitiated) ripping the clothes off a gorgeous Space Girl. It's difficult to say what the B.E.M. would have done next, since the physiologies didn't often match up, but young and lustful readers didn't really think that far ahead.

Now, one of the interesting this about the article was, as Knoles pointed out, that while all the covers promised salacious doings on the insides, only one magazine delivered them, and that was the short-lived *Marvel Science Stories*.

The lead novels in the first two issues were "Avengers of Space" and "The Time Trap," both by (you guessed it) Henry Kuttner, and both awaiting you in this collection.

Knoles ran a few excerpts to prove his point, especially from "Avengers of Space," where plucky girl reporter Lorna Rand indulges in this compulsive urge to keep putting her clothes back on, even though they have a half-life of about two pages before being shredded by either "a teratological baroque spawned by no sane world" or by the hero of the piece, Captain Shawn.

A year or two later I stopped by a second-hand shop specializing in pulps of all types, and bought *Marvel Science Stories* #1 and #2, just to see if Knoles had played fair with his excerpts. (They were a dollar apiece then; you'd be lucky to get the pair for $75.00 today.)

Well, Lorna spent more time naked than clothed, but beyond that "Avengers of Space" was a fast-paced space opera which, without the nudity, could just as easily have appeared in *Planet Stories* or *Super Science Stories* or the like, where indeed a number of the stories in this book did appear.

(A coda to this tale. I was married then, and Carol found the stories as delightful as I did. So much so that at the 1979 NasFic—the North American Science Fiction Convention, which is held whenever Worldcon goes overseas—she created an "Avengers of Space" costume for us and two friends, and it won Best in Show at the masquerade, thank you Henry Kuttner.)

(Come to think of it, there's a second coda. Back in 1997, I edited an anthology containing the two Kuttner novellas, a third story he'd written for the same market as "James Hall," got the rights to run the Knoles article, got permission to run Isaac Asimov's funny fictional response to the *Playboy* article titled "Playboy for the Slime God," ran a new intro and a new afterword by myself and Barry Malzberg, and titled the book *Girls for the Slime God*. If you try abebooks.com or book-finder.com, you might still be able to find a copy.)

I mentioned those two stories first only because they're the ones I'm most intimately (you should pardon the expression) acquainted with, but they're far from the only reason for you buying this book or me telling you a little about its author and its contents.

Kuttner got his start in *Weird Tales* with "The Graveyard Rats" back in 1936. Now, *Weird* was hardly one of the truly debased pulps—in point of fact it was the primary home to H. P. Lovecraft, Robert E. Howard, Clarke Ashton Smith, and a couple of new kids on the block, Robert Bloch and (*sigh*) C. L. Moore. But *Weird* paid late if at all, and little or less, and that was the economic level Kuttner was at in 1937, when he wrote and sold "Raider of the Spaceways."

Then, in the order of this book at least, came the two *Marvel* novellas, with the exquisite Lorna and the equally unclad and luscious Barbara of "The Time Trap." Next we come to "The Lifestone," and by now Kuttner was grinding them out so fast he had to use pseudonyms just to stop people from thinking that there was so many stories by "Henry Kuttner" that it had to be a house name. This tale sold to Fred Pohl's *Astonishing Stories*, and probably paid enough to buy a cup of coffee, circa 2011, but not the cheese Danish that should go with it.

"Monsters of the Atom" was a sideways move, because it went not to a science fiction magazine (with a title like that, yet!) but to *Super Detective*. An interesting side note is that despite the fact that it is clearly science fiction, it's missing from most Kuttner bibliographies, which of course tend to center on his science fiction until the final days of his career, when he and Catherine turned to mysteries. Anyway, while he was grinding out these endless pulp stories, he was also honing his craft. (I was going to say "learning" his craft, but he knew his craft from the beginning.) Consider his opening sentence: "The game wasn't on the level." Six words, but it sets the scene and drags the reader to the next sentence, which is what pulp writing was all about.

"Red Gem of Mercury," also under his own name, went to Fred Pohl again, this time at *Super Science Stories*. Again, check the brief opening line; Henry was getting awfully good at this pulp stuff.

He hit Pohl again (Fred always knew a good thing when he saw one, and his later magazines picked up a bunch of Hugos to prove it), this time with "The Crystal Circe" for *Astonishing Stories*. By now he'd already written the classic "A Gnome There Was" for the major market, *Unknown*; next time out he and Catherine would produce "The Twonky," a semi-classic; and those excursions into quality showed up in his grind-it-out pulp stories as well. By the middle of 1942, he and L. Ron Hubbard were in a class by themselves for the ability to churn out dozens of readable, saleable pages every day.

And in between all the pulp adventures, Kuttner kept turning out stories that have been endlessly reprinted for the 1940s to the present day. Within a year of "War-Gods of the Void" he'd written his first Gallegher story, as well as "Mimsy Were The Borogoves."

Not that there was anything with "War-Gods," which appeared in *Planet Stories* (which would later run most of Ray Bradbury's *Martian Chronicles,* when Ray didn't put in enough science to hit the majors, difficult as that is to believe at this late date).

The title story of this collection, "Thunder in the Void," does not appear to be a sequel or continuation of "War-Gods of the Void," and indeed it appeared in a rival magazine, Pohl's *Astonishing* again. This time, instead of a one-sentence grabber to open it, Kuttner chose to look back from a future we had not yet experienced, though he used icons we all know. It was an approach he'd use a few more times, always effectively, over the years.

"We Guard the Black Planet," which seems to have lost an exclamation point during its many reprintings, appeared in *Super Science*. When Sam Moskowitz included it in *Modern*

Masterpieces of Science Fiction he held it up as an example of fast-paced adventurous science fiction, which it was; and also as an example of what was considered modern science fiction circa 1942, which, a few years after Asimov, Heinlein and Sturgeon had made their debuts, I suspect it was not.

Kuttner was back in *Astonishing* with "Soldiers of Space," a nice, fast-paced story told in the first person, which was a lot less common back in the early 1940s than it is now. And perhaps I should point out that many of these stories use approaches, concepts, methodologies that were little used back then, and which, once he was comfortable with them, would show up in the classics and near-classics he created in collaboration with Catherine, especially under their favorite pseudonyms of "Lewis Padgett" and "Lawrence O'Donnell."

Plagues, androids, "gods," an ancient city, a depressed hero, a hot lady scientist, blood-sucking vampire plants, even a sexy ghost. "Crypt-City of the Deathless Ones" sounds like a cross between mainstream fiction and Robert E. Howard, or perhaps a low-budget action/adventure/horror movie, but it is none of them: it is pure Henry Kuttner at the peak of his pulp powers. The story sold to *Planet*, but it could have appeared in *Weird, Astonishing, Super Science, Amazing,* possibly even *Unknown*, just about anywhere except *Astounding*.

He hit *Planet Stories* again with "The Eyes of Thar," an understated (for that magazine) space opera set on Mars. Though he still had to feed himself, Kuttner was rapidly moving away from being the pulpster who could put this sure-fire opening with that tried-and-true plot, add this mildly different hero and that somewhat unusual villain, mix them together and spill them out in an always-satisfying story. At the same time he was writing "The Eyes of Thar" he was turning out "The Children's Hour" and "When the Bough Breaks," and was preparing to write the oft-dramatized (and occasionally swiped) "What You Need" plus the unsurpassed "Vintage Season."

And then we come to the last story in the collection, "Carry Me Home," written under the pseudonym of "C. H. Liddell" a few years after the others in this book, still not bearing the Padgett or O'Donnell names, but clearly the work of a mature team that had served their time in the pulps, learned their lessons, and were writing mainstream fiction in science fiction settings for magazines like *Planet* simply because the true market for such things, *Saturday Evening Post* or perhaps *Colliers*, didn't even know Henry and Catherine existed.

And by this point, they were simply too good for the pulps, and they moved almost entirely to the digests, where Horace Gold's *Galaxy* and Anthony Boucher's *F&SF* were busy proving that John Campbell's *Astounding* was not the only, or even the best-paying, game in town.

Kuttner died young, in 1958, at the age of 42. In the handful of years he lived after "Carry Me Home" he produced, with Catherine, such stories as "A Cross of Centuries," "The Ego Machine," "Home There's No Returning," "Two-Handed Engine," and "Or Else."

How good was he? Here's Barry Malzberg's take on it:

"What Ray Bradbury wanted desperately in the early 1940s was to sell to Campbell, become an *Astounding* and *Unknown* mainstay. He didn't make it. If he had succeeded in his goal, if he had had what he wanted…he would have been Henry Kuttner."

Clearly there were lesser talents and worse careers to aspire to.

I persist in thinking Moore was the deeper of the two, the more emotional, the more comfortable with a non-sexual eroticism that colored so many of her and their stories. Kuttner was unquestionably the master plotter, a chameleon who could ape Lovecraft with his earliest efforts, Howard with his "Elak of Atlantis" series, Thorne Smith with "The Misguided Halo," any pulp adventure writer who ever lived…and after he'd served his apprenticeship he could bring forth any style and any approach a particular story required.

I think it's entirely possible that, had Moore written "Vintage Season" (which is far more hers than his) on her own, it would still have been a powerful story, but might not have been the absolutely brilliant classic it has become. "Private Eye" may have been her concept, but it took his decades of experience at plotting to pull it off. She had a lot to do with *Fury*, but it was the forcefulness of his plot and prose that moved it into high gear.

She was brilliant from the start. He was not only very good, but he made her better.

Okay, Catherine—you could have done a lot worse. I finally forgive you for not waiting for me.

AFTERWORD TO *SIMULACRON-3*

Daniel F. Galouye was a remarkable writer, a man both behind and ahead of his time. He could write pulp adventures with the best of them, though the time for pulp adventures had pretty much come to an end. (Okay, a temporary end; they're still with us, they're just using modern technology.)

But he was also a visionary, dealing—as you can see in this book—with something that, while popular today, almost all other writers would ignore during his lifetime (which ended all too soon in 1976, at the age of 56.)

Dan was born in New Orleans, graduated from Louisiana State University, and then worked as a journalist until he enlisted in the Navy during World War II as an instructor and test pilot. He crashed, was not often in good health thereafter, and retired early, at 47.

His injuries/disabilities didn't stop him from writing some of the best science fiction around. He wrote for almost all the major digests of the day—*Galaxy*, *Amazing*, *F&SF*, *If*, *Fantastic*—and began developing a reputation as a dependable, professional author. But nothing he had done up to 1961 prepared the public for his debut novel, *Dark Universe*.

Dark Universe was a classic the day it was published, and remains one to this day. The only reason that it hasn't been turned into a blockbuster movie is because if the adaptation bore any resemblance to the novel, you'd be watching a totally black screen for the first forty minutes.

The book was written during the depths of the Cold War, when every week brought a new threat of nuclear conflict, and the affluent all created bomb shelters to hide in when the nukes began dropping. Dan took a good hard look at the notion that the deeper underground you went, the safer you would be. He postulated an incident that seemed dead certain to lead to a nuclear Armageddon, and had entire segments of the population go deep under the surface in an almost endless series of natural and artificial caves and shelters.

And at the last minute sanity prevailed, there was no war, and everyone returned to the surface of the planet. Except for one group that never got word of it, and spent the next few generations far beneath the surface of the planet, living in total darkness.

How would such a society evolve? How would they find their way around their dark universe? How would their social mores change? And most fascinating of all, when someone finally stumbles across them, how would they react to a noise-less sound that hurts the eyes—light?

How good a book was it? Well, it was a Hugo nominee, which is something that almost no first novels achieve. But it was more than that. Here's a story I have only told to a few people, but it is absolutely true.

I met Dan at the 1968 Worldcon in Berkeley, California. We'd corresponded some, but the only time we ever met in person was at the convention hotel, the Claremont, which has become known in fannish legend as the Transylvania Hilton. We had a meal together, and during the course of it, while discussing *Dark Universe*, he mentioned that he had actually voted for Robert A. Heinlein's worldwide bestseller, *Stranger in a Strange Land*. What I later found out was that *Stranger* had beat *Dark Universe* by *two* votes, and if Dan had voted for his own novel—which would be one vote less for Heinlein and one more for himself—his debut novel would have tied for the Hugo with one of the most popular novels of the decade.

He followed *Dark Universe* with *Lords of the Psychon* in 1963. It had only one thing in common with *Dark Universe* (and with a lot of other science fiction of the time): the threat of nuclear devastation. Only this time the bombs *did* drop, and the remnants of the United States armed forces have to deal with some sphere-shaped aliens who move in, operating not unlike galactic scavengers. A fine and wildly creative science fiction adventure, dealing with optics, energy fields, the annual "Horror Day," and all-but-incomprehensible aliens—but as good as it was, it was something that could have been done by Henry Kuttner or Philip Jose Farmer or many of the field's better writers.

Then, as people were wondering if he was a journeyman writer who had one great science fiction novel within him, or a brilliant writer who just wanted to have some fun writing an up-to-date science fiction adventure with his second book, he answered all the questions with the novel you hold in your hands: *Simulacron—3* (which appeared in England as *Counterfeit World*). It's been around for almost half a century, and it's been made into a television play and a movie, so people who know the book tend to take it for granted, That's a mistake, for *Simulacron-3* was dealing with the stuff of "cyberpunk" two decades before William Gibson's brilliant *Neuromancer* officially began the cyberpunk movement.

Most of the novel takes place inside a computer. Possibly all of it does. Because Galouye poses a large problem and implies an even larger one: if you somehow, through luck or brilliance, figure out that you are a computer simulation, an artificial being composed of 0's and 1's, created to respond to various stimuli like a human being for purposes of study, and you find that out, and you even find a way to get from that world to this one…how do you know *this* one isn't a computer simulation as well?

There's more to it than that, of course, but that use of the computer, before anyone knew anything about computers except that a computer that filled three rooms and was called Univac could occasionally make correct election predictions based on sparse returns, was many years ahead of its time.

Though Dan has left us, the novel refuses to die. It was turned into a German teleplay titled *Welt am Draht* in 1973, and then became a movie, *The Thirteenth Floor*, in 1999. A lot of readers and critics have suggested that *The Matrix* and its sequels owe a lot to *Simulacron-3* as well.

Dan continued to work, though his health was failing. He produced *A Scourge of Screamers* (British title: *Lost Perception*) in 1968, and a final novel, *The Infinite Man*, what we call a "fix-up"—a novel pieced together from previously published stories—in 1973. Along the way, he had two collections of stories: *The Last Leap* in 1964, and *Project Barrier* in 1968.

He's been gone for more than a third of a century, and he produced only five novels and a handful of stories, but because two of those novels are classics there has always been a perceptive publisher—Bantam Books, Gollancz, Gregg Press, and now Arc Manor—happy to bring them to a new generation of readers.

There is an award named the Cordwainer Smith Rediscovery Award, given out annually at Readercon. There are four judges, and they vote to give it to a deceased writer whose work should be "rediscovered" by today's science fiction readers. In 2007, the four judges—each of us performing the task for the first time—were Gordon van Gelder (editor/publisher of *F&SF*), Martin H. Greenberg (anthologist with more than 2,000 titles to his credit), Barry N. Malzberg (Campbell Memorial winner, and multiple Hugo and Nebula nominee), and myself.

Daniel F. Galouye was our unanimous choice.

PART 3: INTRODUCTIONS TO MY ANTHOLOGIES

INTRODUCTION TO PART 3

As with the previous section, I frequently write introductions to my anthologies and collections. Here's a sampling of them. I think it would appear too self-serving to include intros from my collections, so these are all from various anthologies I have edited (or, in two cases, co-edited).

INTRODUCTION TO *DOWN THESE DARK SPACEWAYS*

They used to say it couldn't be done, that no one could blend the mystery story with the science fiction story, that if you played fair with the reader the key to the puzzle would hinge on some obscure scientific fact that no one not conversant with science fiction could possibly spot, and that if it *didn't* turn on that type of clue, then why make it science fiction at all?

It was just over half a century ago that two brilliant and totally dissimilar science fiction mystery novels—Alfred Bester's *The Demolished Man* and Isaac Asimov's *The Caves of Steel*—buried that theory once and for all.

There has always been a lot of cross-pollenization between the two fields. Some of science fiction's finest practitioners—Fredric Brown, Jack Vance, Henry Kuttner, Isaac Asimov, Leigh Brackett, Wilson Tucker, and others—also wrote mysteries, and one of mystery's current superstars, Walter Mosley, recently tried his hand at science fiction.

Though I make the bulk of my living in science fiction, I enjoy both fields, and have even sold an occasional mystery. I have to confess that I'm not especially thrilled with some of the current trends in mysteries; these days there are times when I think the best way to sell a mystery novel is to make your detective a cat who doubles as a gourmet chef. (To be fair, there are some current trends in science fiction that are not exactly to my taste either.)

Despite the plethora of truly wonderful science fiction writers past and present, I persist in thinking that the single finest writer to come out of the pulp magazines in *any* category was Raymond Chandler, and that he and Dashiell Hammett did the mystery story an enormous service by giving murder back to the people who are good at it. Instead of wealthy amateur sleuths solving ingenious locked-room mysteries in English mansions, Hammett and Chandler's detectives followed their clues and their prey, as the saying goes, "down these dark alleys."

I decided that it might be interesting to use what is known as the *Black Mask* school of writing as a jumping-off point for a sextet of science fiction novellas. These would not be slavish imitations of Hammett and Chandler and James T. Cain and Ross MacDonald, but they *would* be stories that were clearly in that tradition, rather than the classic British mysteries or today's "cozy" mysteries. There would be no Sherlocks or Wimseys or Poirots here; instead there would be the descendants of those fallen angels who stalked the dark alleys, who understood going in that the odds were against them, who were not surprised when their enemies lied to them and their friends deserted them, who knew that the rewards would never measure up to the risks but took those risks anyway. In short, these stories would extrapolate from the dark alleys of the mid-20th Century and take us "down these dark spaceways" instead.

I met an enthusiastic reception when I proposed the book to the Science Fiction Book Club. The next step was to find five more writers (there was no way I was going to edit this without asking myself for a submission), and I decided to go after some of science fiction's best.

It turned out not to be a very difficult task at all. As their stories make clear, every contributor shares my love for both categories. Hugo and Nebula winner Robert J. Sawyer takes a term that didn't even exist twenty years ago and tells the tale of the only detective on Mars in "Identity Theft." Hugo and Campbell nominee Robert Reed revisits some of his characters aboard a huge and fascinating ship that will be familiar to his legions of readers in "Camouflage." Nebula winner and Hugo nominee Catherine Asaro also brings back some of her characters and embroils them in "The City of Cries." Hugo and Nebula nominee and Campbell Memorial winner Jack McDevitt gives us a female detective and takes us to "The Big Downtown." Hugo and Nebula winner David Gerrold was the only one to set his story on near-present-day Planet Earth, but when you find yourself "In the Quake Zone" it's *time*quakes he's talking about. Your editor is a Hugo and Nebula winner, and presents some of the problems that arise when a private eye finds himself doubling as a "Guardian Angel."

Today nobody denies that you can write a good science fictional mystery story. Our hope is that after you finish this book you'll find yourself thinking that it ought to be done more often.

INTRODUCTION TO *ALIEN CRIMES*

Two years ago I edited *Down These Dark Spaceways*, an anthology of six hard-boiled science fiction detective novellas, for the Science Fiction Book Club. It was pretty well received: Robert J. Sawyer's novella was nominated for a Hugo and a Nebula, Catherine Asaro's was nominated for a couple of awards, others appeared in various Best-of-the-Year anthologies.

So last year I approached the Book Club and suggested we do another. They agreed, with the stipulation that *this* book of alien crimes not contain any hard-boiled mysteries, that we show that the infinitely-adaptable field of science fiction is able to encompass *all* kinds of mysteries. After all, Alfred Bester's *The Demolished Man* and Isaac Asimov's *The Caves of Steel*, the two archetypal science fictional mysteries, weren't hard-boiled novels.

Hence, *Alien Crimes*. Once again I chose some of the very best writers in field and put the challenge to them: give me a science fiction mystery, make it novella length, play fair with the reader, and this time let's have no genuflecting to the Hammett/Chandler school of writing. In due time they delivered their stories, and I think you'll find the broad range of approaches and subject matter as interesting as the mysteries themselves. Hugo winner and bestseller Harry Turtledove examines the odor of crime in "Hoxbomb," I bring back my *Down These Dark Spaceways* detective Jake Masters, but this time he's working for the police and trying to solve "A Locked-Planet Mystery," Hugo winner and Edgar nominee Kristine Kathryn Rusch demonstrates that things are not always with they seem in "End of the World," Hugo nominee and Clarke winner Pat Cadigan gives us an interesting lady investigator with a unique problem to solve in "Nothing Personal," Nebula winner Gregory Benford seems to be telling a contemporary mystery in "Dark Heaven," and then proves that appearances can be deceiving; and finally, in Womb of Every World," Nebula winner Walter Jon Williams brings you a story that…well, whatever you think it is, it's almost certainly not.

I think, like its predecessor, this book proves that science fiction can always bring something fresh and new to other forms of fiction—especially the mystery story.

INTRODUCTION TO *MEN WRITING SCIENCE FICTION AS WOMEN*

In a recent novel of mine called *The Outpost*, one of the characters asks a somewhat-larger-than-life hero: "What's the most dangerous race you ever came across?"

"Women," says the hero.

"I mean an alien race," explains the questioner.

"So do I," answers the hero.

That's the gist of it. If women have trouble understanding men, and they do, men have even more trouble understanding women. It's as if the God of Science Fiction, who has a truly caustic sense of humor, took two races that would forever be alien to each other, dressed them up as human beings, and turned them loose on Planet Earth.

Science fiction, in its early days, was aimed primarily at adolescent boys, so almost all the heroes were men. Women were there to hold the hero's spaceship, get captured by the villain and threatened with a Fate Worse Than Death, or to flash a malicious smile (while flashing other even more enticing things) and attempt to seduce or at least distract the hero while the Bad Guys were off doing evil deeds.

It was exceptionally rare for the main character of a science fiction or fantasy story to be a female. C. L. Moore created Jirel of Joiry, but she could be forgiven since she was a female writer. Arthur K. Barnes invented Gerry Carlyle, perhaps the least believable interplanetary female big game hunter of all time. It remained for the big guns to do a somewhat better job of it—Isaac Asimov with his robotics expert, Susan Calvin, and Robert A. Heinlein with Podkayne, Friday, and a handful of others, none of whom quite rang true.

No male science fiction writer ever attempted a major novel written in the first person of a woman. Heinlein, always willing to try something new, came close with *I Will Fear No Evil*, but that was a first-person story of a man who had taken over ownership (possession? residence?) of a woman's body. It remained for Ian Fleming, who was almost a science fiction writer, to pull it off, rather lamely but at least courageously, with the James Bond thriller, *The Spy Who Loved Me*.

And, since science fiction is, at least partly or occasionally, about truly understanding alien viewpoints (and how *we* must appear to aliens), we challenged a number of the best male writers around to write science fiction stories not just *about* women but *as* women.

There were only two rules: first, the story had to be in the first person of a woman, and second, if changing her from Victoria to Victor didn't invalidate the story we didn't want it.

Welcome to some truly alien worlds.

INTRODUCTION TO *WOMEN WRITING SCIENCE FICTION AS MEN*

When we speak of the "opposite sex," most women will be happy to tell you that sexes can't get much more opposite than men.

And yet, at least partially due to the demands of the market place in the early days of science fiction, when all the heroes were men and the primary audience was adolescent boys, women have been writing about men since the field began.

(Yes, since it began. Mary Shelly's creation, Victor von Frankenstein, was a man—and his monster was, if not a man, at least a male monster.)

Back in the early 1930s C. L. Moore gave us Northwest Smith, one of my all-time favorites. Leigh Brackett followed in the 1940s with Eric John Stark. The most popular science fiction hero of the new millennium is almost certainly Lois MacMaster Bujold's Miles Vorkosigan. In between Northwest and Miles, hundreds of female writers have given us hundreds of male heroes and viewpoint characters.

But there is a difference between writing *about* a male and writing *as* a male.

It's a lot easier to describe a man's actions and reactions than to take us inside his head and convince us you *are* that man—and it's doubly difficult to do so if you're a woman to begin with.

So, since we hate to make things easy for science fiction writers, and since we had confidence that the ladies who practice the art were up to the challenge, we put forth the proposition to a handful of the best: write us a science fiction or fantasy story, not about a man's actions, not using him as a main character, but *as* a man.

There were only two rules: first, each story had to be told in the first person of a man, and second, if changing the narrator from Victor to Victoria didn't invalidate the story we didn't want it.

As usual, they did not disappoint.

INTRODUCTION TO *I, ALIEN*

Science fiction loves aliens. We've had cute aliens, frightening aliens, brilliant aliens, stupid aliens, friendly aliens, hate-filled aliens, lustful aliens, aliens who think and sound just like us, and aliens whom we will never begin to understand.

The true alien is a cipher that doesn't serve much use in science fiction. If he exists—excuse me: if *it* exists—it probably breathes methane, excretes bricks, smells colors, reproduces by budding, and has totally different concepts (if it has any at all) of love, hate, fear, and pain.

So very early on science fiction writers learned to use aliens as metaphors for various aspects of the human condition—as a funhouse mirror they could hold up to humanity to examine whatever happens to be pleasing or annoying the writer that particular day.

The history of science fiction is filled with aliens, many of whom became more popular than the humans from the same stories. You can go all the way back to Tars Tarkas in the Martian stories of Edgar Rice Burroughs; the whole crew of Second Stage Lensmen in Doc Smith's Lensman saga; Tweel in Stanley G. Weinbaum's "A Martian Odyssey"; and on through memorable and beloved aliens created by Eric Frank Russell, Roger Zelazny, Vonda McIntyre, and dozens of others, right up to Chewbacca in the Star Wars saga.

Every science fiction writer has created aliens at one time or another. Even Isaac Asimov, who populated his robotic and Foundation futures with nothing but humans, eventually got around to it in *The Gods Themselves*. And certainly every writer in this book has created aliens in previous stories.

But this time we asked them to do something different. Remember that I said aliens were incomprehensible? Well, not any more—because each author was asked to write a story in the first person of an alien. The aliens in these stories are not just the main characters; they're the narrators.

Last year I edited *Men Writing Science Fiction as Women* and *Women Writing Science Fiction as Men* for DAW Books. Those were nice imaginative stretches, but nothing compared to the stretching the authors in this book were asked to do.

And, being science fiction writers, they succeeded in ways that surprised even the editor.

INTRODUCTION TO *SPACE CADETS*

Hell, yes, I remember Tom Corbett and those beautiful far-flung shores of outer space.

It'll be difficult for most people reading this book to imagine, but there was a time before television. Fortunately it didn't last too long; five billion years and out.

My family had the first TV set on our block, on the South Side of Chicago, We got it in 1948 when I was 6 years old, and I can still remember every damned family in our apartment building crowding into our living room to watch the Indians play the Braves in the 1948 World Series—on a 7-inch black-and-white set that weighed about 300 pounds and cost almost as much as my father's car.

By 1950 everyone had TV sets, which is just as well, because Tom Corbett hit the airwaves in 1950 and I wasn't about to share him with anyone. I lived and died with the crew of the *Polaris*. I was heroic like Tom, nasty and backbiting (but eventually a Good Guy when the chips were down) like Roger Manning, and I was certainly more alien than Astro the Venusian. (He looked like a math teacher with a crew cut. Let's face it: *everyone* was more alien than Astro.) I didn't identify with Captain Strong at all. I mean, the man was almost 35, practically in the grave.

Well, I grew up. I discovered Sheckley and Bester and Kuttner and Moore and Heinlein, and eventually I began writing science fiction myself—but I never forgot Tom and the cadets aboard the good ship *Polaris*.

And then one day I got an e-mail from the LACon IV Committee: Frankie Thomas—*Tom Corbett himself!*—was going to be the Media Guest of Honor at the 2006 Worldcon, and would I be interested in editing a book of space cadet stories in honor of that event?

Would I? Is the Pope Catholic? Do bears perform their ablutions in the woods?

So I began inviting some of the best writers in the field. And you know what? Anyone remotely my age remembered old Tom and the gang as fondly as I did, and those who were younger resented the fact that they *hadn't* seen the show and had to settle for the books and comic strips, which seem to have been imprinted on the inside of their eyelids, given the facts and figures they could rattle off on a second's notice.

Initially I figured this was going to be a labor of love. Now I know better: it's 22 labors of love.

Thanks, Tom and Frankie, for inspiring it.

INTRODUCTION TO *BUG-EYED MONSTERS AND BIMBOS*

(2011 Edition)

This is the first anthology I ever edited. I was the Toastmaster at Nolacon II, the 1988 Worldcon, and the committee asked me if I'd be willing to edit an anthology on any topic that appealed to me. I've always loved humor, so I agreed if I could put together a book of science fiction parodies.

I titled it *Shaggy B.E.M. Stories* (in science fiction parlance, a B.E.M. is a Bug-Eyed Monster). I scoured the professional magazines, but also the fanzines, and finally came up with some 30 stories, some by superstars like Asimov and Clarke, some by relatively unknown fans.

I turned in the manuscript, and they went to press...but none of them had ever been involved in publishing, and they didn't know that they were supposed to return the galleys to the editor and the authors for proof-reading, so the final version had about 200 typos in it. (And even so, it was *still* a damned funny book.)

Shaggy B.E.M. Stories was a limited edition, and about 75% of the print run sold out the weekend of the convention. Finally, after a dozen years or so, I decided it was time to bring it out again, and I sold it to Byron Preiss, who promptly re-titled it *Dirty Rotten Aliens*. Money changed hands, I paid all the writers a second time—and then Byron was killed in a tragic accident, and the book never came out.

Move the clock ahead another decade, and I thought I'd try again. And now you hold in your hands the second edition, proudly wearing yet its third title, this time *Bug-Eyed Monsters and Bimbos*.

And you know what?

Whatever they call it, it's still a totally delightful collection of some of the best parodies of science fiction every written. Enjoy.

INTRODUCTION TO *THIS IS MY FUNNIEST*

Science fiction writers like to laugh.

Maybe it's because so much science fiction is dystopian—after all, by definition, no one can create more than one Utopia—but whatever the reason, the fact remains that no field of fiction has as long and rich a track record of publishing humorous stories as science fiction. I don't think there's ever been a magazine or anthology editor who would refuse to buy a good story simply because it was funny, and sooner or later just about every practitioner take a shot (or five, or thirty) at writing a humorous story.

We have a long and respected tradition of it. Back in the earlies, we had Stanton A. Coblentz, who at least thought he was funny, and Edgar Rice Burroughs, who was never subtle but often funny (usually on purpose). Move the calendar ahead and we had Fredric Brown, Henry Kuttner, Eric Frank Russell, and Fritz Leiber, none of them writing humor exclusively (or even predominantly), but each writing enough to make a reputation as a humorist (or, more accurately, as a humorist *too*.)

Then, starting at the halfway mark of the century, the humor and the humorists started coming fast and thick—Robert Sheckley, William Tenn, Harry Harrison, and their contemporaries. Then came John Sladek and George Alec Effinger and *their* contemporaries. Even Isaac Asimov got in on the act with his books of limericks and *The Sensuous Dirty Old Man*. These days we've got Connie Willis and Esther Friesner, and we've got some humorists like Douglas Adams and Terry Pratchett who live on the bestseller lists. The next generation has already made its appearance in the person of young Tom Gerencer.

The most frustrating part of editing this book was explaining to the dozen or so writers who asked for input that the title was *This is My Funniest* and not *Mike Resnick Thinks This is My Funniest*. More than once I had to forcibly restrain myself from asking for *my* favorite rather than *their* favorite. (I did break down once and tell the late Bob Sheckley which one I hoped he'd choose. To his credit, he stuck with the one he liked best.)

So here they are, a broad cross-section of our very finest writers, some whom are known for their humor, and some whose appearance here will surprise you (until you read their stories and then wonder why the hell they don't do it more often.)

Enjoy. And maybe even giggle here and there.

INTRODUCTION TO *THIS IS MY FUNNIEST 2*

We always knew that science fiction writers like to laugh. That's why we assembled *This is My Funniest*.

Well, now we know something else: science fiction readers like to laugh, too. As a rule, science fiction anthologies, even those with all original stories, sell about a third as well as novels, often even less than that. But *This is My Funniest*, a reprint anthology, outsold every science fiction novel in BenBella's catalog in less than half a year.

So what could we do but bring you *This is My Funniest 2*?

Don't look for the same writers (with one curmudgeonly exception). They already gave you *their* funniest. But we've got a new batch, just as prestigious, who are happy to share their most hilarious pieces with you. We've got Worldcon Guests of Honor like Gene Wolfe, Greg Bear, and Gregory Benford; *New York Times* bestsellers like Kevin J. Anderson, Mercedes Lackey, Ron Goulart, Larry Niven, and Eric Flint; Hugo and Nebula winners like Michael Bishop, Terry Bisson, Frank M. Robinson, and Jack Dann; and that's not even half the line-up.

You'll get satires, parodies, mock scientific essays, and just out-and-out funny stories, in and out of dialect. We've got novelettes, short stories, and short-shorts. We've got men, we've got women, and we've got at least two writers I suspect of being aliens.

Mostly, what we have is continuing proof that for all the dire predictions and tales of warning they produce, science fiction writers love to laugh. One of the very nice things about this field is that every editor who has ever worked in it has been willing to buy a well-written humorous story, and sooner or later just about every writer who works in the field has gotten around to producing one (or six, or 53).

Probably it wouldn't hurt to thank Glenn Yeffeth, the publisher of BenBella, for having the guts to okay the first book at all, and the second book so quickly. If he someday decides to green-light *This is My Funniest* numbers 3 through 8, I can promise you one thing: we're not going to run out of authors, and as these first two volumes show, as long as we don't run out of authors we're not going to run out of funny stories.

So why are you still reading this with a straight face? Turn the pages and start chuckling.

INTRODUCTION TO *NEW VOICES IN SCIENCE FICTION*

People always worry about where the next generation is coming from.

Babe Ruth retired, and suddenly baseball was blessed with Joe DiMaggio, Ted Williams and Stan Musial. Secretariat retired, and we got Seattle Slew, Affirmed, and Ruffian. Richard Rodgers passed away, and suddenly we had Stephen Sondheim, Harvey Schmidt and Cy Coleman.

It's the same in fantasy and science fiction. Stanley G. Weinbaum and Robert E. Howard and H. P. Lovecraft all died within a couple of years, and suddenly we had Robert A. Heinlein, Isaac Asimov, and Theodore Sturgeon. Another slight dip, and we were visited by Robert Silverberg, Harlan Ellison, and Brian Aldiss. Another lull, and it was Roger Zelazny, Samuel Delany and Ursula K. Le Guin to the rescue.

It never fails. There is always a next generation, and it is always filled with talent. The most satisfying thing is to spot it early on and watch it grow and mature. So when SFWA (the Science Fiction Writers of America) asked me to edit an original anthology of stories by our newest faces, our coming stars, I was only too happy to oblige. It's pretty easy to look at the field today and say that Joe Haldeman and Connie Willis and Nancy Kress are wonderful writers; the trick was to spot that talent after they'd only been writing a year or two, and the satisfaction was to watch that talent grow and develop.

So how (I hear you ask) do you find these future superstars before anyone knows they're going to be superstars?

Well, a safe place to start looking is with the Campbell Award, which goes to the Best New Writer every year, and which has a shortlist of five or six nominees per year. That's where I found Michael A. Burstein, Susan R. Matthews, Kage

Baker, James Van Pelt, Julie E. Czernada, Cory Doctorow, Shane Tourtelette, and Tobias S. Buckell.

Even better places are the Nebula and Hugo Awards, where Kage Baker and Michael A. Burstein had been nominated.

Then there are the bookstores, where Kay Kenyon, Susan R. Matthews, and Kage Baker have each produced multiple novels and have a growing following of devoted readers.

There's Clarion, that special school for embryonic science fiction writers. The year I taught I encountered the stories of Tom Gerencer, Hillary Moon Murphy, Tobias S. Buckell, David Kirtley, and Mark Stafford. (In fact, I workshopped the Kirtley and Stafford stories at Clarion.)

Since I've edited many other anthologies, sometimes the writer is one who has sold to me before, like Adrienne Gormley, Barbara J. Galler-Smith, Robyn Herrington, or superstar singer Janis Ian.

Sometimes it's a newcomer that established writers have recommended to me, like Lisa Mantchev or Charlie Stross.

Sometimes it's just a confluence of fortuitous circumstances, as when I judged the James White Memorial Story Contest, found that winner David D. Levine was a newcomer, and bought the story after it was the unanimous choice of the judging panel. (When I bought it it hadn't appeared in America or in any professional publication, but then Dave Hartwell asked permission to run it in his Best of the Year anthology... and how could I tell a new writer that I wouldn't permit his story to appear there? So, after the fact, it has become the one unoriginal story in this original anthology.)

And sometimes it's just a newcomer who has heard of the book and asked to be considered for it, like Paul Crilley of South Africa.

Will they all be successful? Of course not. But my guess is that, fifteen or twenty years from now, when the historians of the field name the ten best writers to break in within three years, either direction, of the millennium, you'll find at least half of them in this book.

INTRODUCTION TO *THE WORLDCON GUEST OF HONOR SPEECHES*

by Mike Resnick & Joe Siclari

In our opinion—and it's shared by most people in the science fiction field—there is no higher honor than being named Guest of Honor at a Worldcon (the informal name for a World Science Fiction Convention). It is the acknowledgement of a lifetime's excellence (and is it definitely not an over-the-hill award; four writers and an editor have been Guest of Honor twice, and one of them—Robert A. Heinlein, of course—three times.)

The only thing the Worldcon requires of the Guest of Honor is that he or she give a speech. These used to be formal affairs, given during the Hugo banquet—and even before the creation of the Hugo, the Guest of Honor speech was a highlight of the convention.

It occurred to your editors that it wouldn't be too long before almost all those wonderful speeches were lost to posterity. Only Heinlein's speeches ever came out from a major publisher, and only three of the Worldcons ever printed Proceedings that included transcripts of their Guest of Honor speeches. And we're well past our 60th Worldcon.

So we started wondering if it was possible to hunt up enough of the speeches to fill a book. We began by looking in small, obscure, long-out-of-print fanzines, because it was traditional for the Guest of Honor to write out his speech, read it at the convention, and then turn it over to a fanzine. And we found quite a few that way, including the first two, from 1939 and 1940. Many of them had fallen into the public domain; where they hadn't, we moved heaven and earth to get permission to reprint them.

But as conventions—and life—became less formal, a lot of writers chose to wing it, to speak extemporaneously. Some were tape recorded, a very few were videotaped, many weren't recorded at all. We hunted up all the recordings we could find, had them transcribed, and then ran them past the speakers for their approval.

When the dust had cleared, we'd found more than 30 Guest of Honor speeches. They're not all here. In three cases, we could not get responses—favorable or otherwise—from either the Guests or their agents, despite the fact that the speeches had been printed in fanzines. In other cases, we were still trying to hunt down tape recordings and exceptionally rare fanzines when our deadline arrived. We *think* there are enough speeches still extant that with a few years of digging, and a few permissions we couldn't get in time for this book, we can produce a companion volume, perhaps not quite as thick, but historically important nonetheless—as we believe *this* volume to be. After all, these are our most accomplished writers and editors, and many of them gave their speeches to very small audiences, more than half of which have passed on or at least lost touch with the science fiction field. (Check the record: only one of the first nine Worldcons drew more than 200 people—and not everyone made it to the speeches.) We think it was vitally important to assemble this book before even more of the speeches were impossible to obtain: this is a record of what these titans had to say on the day that they stood, alone and unchallenged, at the very apex of the field.

We want to thank Steven Silver and ISFIC Press for realizing this book's importance and offering to publish it with the certain knowledge that no one is going to get rich off it. And of course we want to thank all those who did the transcriptions: Bonnie Jones, John McCoy, Anne Murphy, Isabel Schecter, Elaine Silver, Steven Silver, Edie Stern, and the Science Fiction Oral History Association (sfoha.org).

And finally, we want to thank the Guests of Honor for being exactly what they were and are: the people who made—and continue to make—this the field we love.

INTRODUCTION TO *THE DRAGON DONE IT*

by **Eric Flint & Mike Resnick**

It was simply a fortunate confluence of events. Mike had just edited a pair of science fiction mystery anthologies—*Down These Dark Spaceways* and *Alien Crimes*—for the Science Fiction Book Club. Not too long ago Eric had edited a massive collection of Randall Garrett's beloved Lord Darcy stories, the first edition in history that puts all the stories together.

In short, both of us were thinking along the same lines: science fiction, fantasy, mystery. And it occurred to us that, to the best of our knowledge, no one has yet put together an anthology of fantasy detective stories, as opposed to science fiction mysteries. It seemed hard to believe; since there are certainly enough examples out there, going back at least to the works of Poe and to the hinted-at but never-written Sherlock Holmes tale of "The Giant Rat of Sumatra." So we got together, approached Jim Baen with the idea, and got a contract—one of the very last he issued before his untimely death.

Probably the two most famous fantasy sleuths are Lord Darcy, and Seabury Quinn's Jules de Grandin, who appeared in 121 stories in the old *Weird Tales* magazine. We were very familiar with the Darcy stories, but hadn't read the Quinn stories in decades. So Eric read half of them and Mike read the other half, and we came to the unhappy conclusion that they're a little too dated and a little too clumsily written.

Having anchored the volume with one of the best Lord Darcy stories, we went a-hunting—and came up with stories by such superstars as Neil Gaiman, Harry Turtledove, Gene

Wolfe, and David Drake. We resurrected a story by William Hope Hodgson, recent winner of the Cordwainer Smith Rediscovery Award, which was as old as the Jules de Grandin stories but read a lot better. Agatha Christie proved long ago that the detective story is not the private property of male writers, and we picked up fine stories from Esther Friesner, Tanya Huff, and Laura Resnick, then rounded out the book with another seven stories.

We then looked at what we had. We felt they were a fine batch of stories but that perhaps something was missing. Since we each had written our own series of fantasy detective tales over the years, we decided to make this an even more unique collection by writing brand-new novelettes featuring our detectives, and start and finish the book with those two brand-new stories.

So Mike wrote a new John Justin Mallory story, which is now the sixth novelette to go along with the original Mallory novel, *Stalking the Unicorn*. Those have been published in *The Magazine of Fantasy and Science Fiction* and *Black Gate Magazine*, and the anthologies *Newer York*, *A Christmas Bestiary*, and *Masters of Fantasy*. He's still negotiating the contract as we write these words, but he will be writing at least two more Mallory novels in the very near future. Eric and Dave Freer wrote a new novelette in the Heirs of Alexandria fantasy series they're doing with Mercedes Lackey. (*Shadow of the Lion, A Mankind Witch, This Rough Magic, Much Fall of Blood*—with at least three more novels coming.)

We hope you enjoy the anthology. We think the most interesting thing about it is that, given the rules of each magical venue, the authors play as fair with the reader as Dashiell Hammett or Rex Stout ever did. Which is harder than you think in a universe filled with witches, goblins, and dragons.

PART 4: INTERVIEWS

INTRODUCTION TO PART 4

I seem to get interviewed more often every year, and as often as not the interviewer is from another country. Here's a sampling that isn't too repetitious, a pitfall you have to constantly avoid in interviews.

GERMAN INTERVIEW

Thank you for taking the time for this interview. How did you come up with this crazy world in which Mallory finds himself?

Back in the mid-1980s, there were so many not-very-good fantasy novels on the stands that someone, I think it may have been Bob Silverberg, came up with a pejorative term for them: "elf-and-unicorn trilogies." And when I decided, after maybe 15 science fiction novels in a row, that it was time to write a fantasy, I thought it would be interesting to write one that had an elf and a unicorn and wasn't like any of those truly dreadful and totally generic elf-and-unicorn books.

I set it in New York simply because more readers are familiar with the landmarks of Manhattan than any other American city, so they would be quick to see the changes on familiar settings that I use during the series to show that this isn't quite the Manhattan you know—the Vampire State Building instead of the Empire State Building; Greenwitch Village rather than Greenwich Village; Madison Round Garden instead of Madison Square Garden; and so on.

The mystery case is very complex. How did you manage not to loose focus?

It comes from being a professional writer who, even in 1987, had sold more than 10 million words. There's no secret to it: you plot out the book before you begin, you work out all the complications, and then you write it.

How did you come up with the ideas to write more than one novel about Mallory?

I thought Mallory was retired after *Stalking the Unicorn*. I seriously had no intention of writing another—I was contracted about five or six books ahead, all of them science fiction rather than fantasy.

Then, two or three years later, Lawrence Watt-Evans was editing an anthology of stories called *Newer York*. Some potential contributor asked him if she could do a fantasy story rather than science fiction, and he replied if it was as good as *Stalking the Unicorn* he'd take it. Flattery gets you everywhere with me, so I wrote him a Mallory novelette, "Post Time in Pink."

Then Martin H. Greenberg asked me for a Mallory story for *A Christmas Bestiary* ("The Blue- Nosed Reindeer"), Kristine Kathryn Rusch commissioned one for *F&SF* ("Cark Shark"), Bill Fawcett asked for one for *Masters of Fantasy* ("The Amorous Broom"), *Black Gate Magazine* commissioned one ("The Chinese Sandman"), an editor over in England, wanted one for *The Solaris Book of New Fantasy* ("Shell Game"), and I sold one to myself for *The Dragon Done It*, an anthology I co-edited with Eric Flint ("The Long and Short of It.")

Those last two were done just a few years ago, when I started writing the Starship series for Pyr, and my editor there, Lou Anders, read them and asked me if he could reprint *Stalking the Unicorn* and if I was willing to write some more Mallory novels. I said yes—I truly enjoy writing them—and in the next two years I gave him *Stalking the Vampire* and *Stalking the Dragon*.

I got too busy to write any more Mallory novels for awhile, but those seven stories (well, 6 novelettes and a short story) were just a few thousand words away from being enough to fill a collection. I needed a "Stalking" title anyway, so this winter I wrote "Stalking the Zombie," which has never appeared anywhere, but will be the lead story of the Mallory collection, *Stalking the Zombie*, that will be coming out just before Worldcon this summer. Sorry for giving you such a long answer.

In the original version the cover art for "Stalking the Unicorn" (Jäger des Verlorenen Einhorns) has been done by Boris Vallejo, a master of arts who has been a favorite of mine since ages. What did you think when you saw the cover for the first time?

I liked the cover by Boris, but I have to say that the Pyr reprint from 2008, by Dan Dos Santos, has become one of my two or three favorite covers (and that includes well over 100 science fiction and fantasy novels, collections, and anthologies.)

You're a writer with dozens of published texts and novels. What do you do for leisure?

A reporter once asked Pablo Picasso what he did for a hobby. He replied: "I paint." And the reporter said that no, that's what he did for a living; what did he do to relax? And Picasso said: "I paint." Me, I write.

Which novel was the most fun for you to write?

I've written some bestsellers, and I believe *Kirinyaga* probably has more awards than any other science fiction book in history—but my favorite, the one I most enjoyed writing, was *The Outpost*. Never heard of it? (*sigh*) Almost no one has. Go figure.

Currently you're editing an anthology "The Worlds of Edgar Rice Burroughs". I've been a big fan of his works since I first read his novels. How did you feel about including your novella "The Forgotten Sea of Mars"?

I have mixed emotions. I was 21 when I wrote it (I'll be 70 in early March), and it was purposely written in the style of Edgar Rice Burroughs rather than Mike Resnick. But Burroughs fans seemed to love it when it was published, and I've seen copies selling for as much as $300 on eBay and in dealer's rooms, so it seemed like a good time to bring it back in print at a more reasonable price. And if you don't like it, please remember that I'm 48 years better now.

Your project of "Mike's Writer Children" is absolutely fabulous and exciting. How did you come up with that idea?

I had just sold reprints of the first three Lucifer Jones books (he's my favorite character) to Arc Manor, a relatively new press that I hadn't worked with before, and Shahid Mahmud, the publisher, asked me if I had any idea for a new line of books, something no one else was doing. I remembered that Maureen McHugh invented the term "Mike's Writer Children" to describe the 20 or 25 beginners I've kind of "adopted" and helped along the way—collaborating with them, buying stories from them when I've edited anthologies, introducing them to editors and agents at conventions—and it occurred to me that I couldn't be the only writer who did this. So I suggested what has become the Stellar Guild line, a series of team-ups where an established star writes a novella, and then a protégé of the star's own choosing writes a novelette set in the same universe, and they share cover credit.

A lot of people told me: "Oh, you'll never get the biggest names in the field to write a novella, not at the rates"—above average, but not huge—"that you're paying." Yet every single one I've approached, once I explained the line and that they could chose the newer writer, has agreed, The first two books, by Kevin J. Anderson and Mercedes Lackey (and their protégés) are out, and we've got Robert Silverberg, Harry Turtledove, Eric Flint and me under contract. Come back in 6 months and I'll bet we have from 6 to 10 more stars signed up. Like they say, by the time you're in a position to pay back in this field, you can't, since everyone who helped you is rich or dead or both, so you pay forward. The Stellar Guild line just makes it creative and easy to do so.

Your newest novels in English are somewhat Steampunk. What do you think is the appeal of that genre that so many authors now dive into it?

I'll be totally honest, I have very little interest in steampunk. What I had always wanted to do was write a novel about Doc Holliday and Johnny Ringo, who were the only two college-educated gunslingers in the Wild West. So when Lou Anders asked for a "Weird Western," with both magic and steampunk, I figured, well, I'm in my late 60s and I still haven't written that book, so it's probably a choice between doing it as a part-steampunk part-fantasy novel or never getting around to it at all. I wrote it as *The Buntline Special*, it was very well received, I wrote a sequel that just came out in December titled *The Doctor and the Kid*, and I just signed for two more: *The Doctor and the Rough Rider* (which will feature my two favorite historical characters, Teddy Roosevelt and Doc Holliday), and *The Doctor and the Dinosaurs* (which will take place during the "bone wars" between the warring American paleontologists, Edward Drinker Cope and Othniel Charles Marsh).

What project would you like to do most? Which ideas are still in your head that simply have to see light?

Well, I have to write another book and a half about Lucifer Jones, until I get him thrown off every continent on Earth. (I say "book and a half" because his adventures are appearing in just about every issue of Subterranean's online magazine, and half of what will become the 5th Lucifer book have already appeared. For the record, the first four are *Adventures, Exploits, Encounters*, and *Hazards*. The fifth will be *Voyages*.

Somewhere I have two more Santiago books outlined, if I can ever fit them into my schedule. I have notes on eight or ten others, and of course I've got about seventy or eighty short stories waiting to be told. And that's just in this field. I did a mystery novel a few years ago, I really enjoyed it, and I think I'll be doing a sequel to it pretty soon, maybe this summer. And there's always more. I think I have 11 books coming out in 2012, and I expect to keep writing up to the day I die (and maybe even a bit beyond that.)

Thank you and I am looking forward to the next installments of Mallory's adventures "Mallory und die Nacht der Toten" (Stalking the Vampire), already out, and "Mallory und der Taschendrache" (Stalking the Dragon), coming out in July 2012.

BULGARIAN INTERVIEW

Mr. Resnick, the first thing that made an impression on me was your extraordinary kindness and eagerness to talk to a complete stranger and to grant me an interview even without knowing who I am... But afterwards I learnt that you don't always accept interviews. Now I am wondering what actually made you do it? Is it an intuition... or what?

I don't remember ever refusing an interview, with this exception: if it's an interview concerning a subject about which I know nothing (and there are many), I respectfully decline.

Being a former editor of men's magazines, can you explain why such magazines often print science fiction stories?

I haven't looked at a men's magazine in 30 years, and I don't know the current economics—but back when I was editing them, the men's magazines paid far more than the science fiction magazines, and writers have bills to pay. Back in the 1960s and early 1970s, *Playboy* was paying $5,000 a story and other men's magazines were paying from $300 to $1,000, while the science fiction magazines were still paying about 3 cents a word.

A recently dead science fiction author was J.G. Ballard, who in his novel The Day of Creation *wrote about hunger-stricken Africa, and a more or less insane emergency-aid worker's dreams of helping Africa out of it's misery. You have traveled a lot in Africa, so how is your point of view to this problem?*

There's a lot wrong with Africa: hunger, disease, poverty, continent-wide corruption of such a magnitude that most people can't conceive of it. There are two schools of thought: one is that we must do everything we can to help them (which thus far has not worked). The other is that if you feed, for example, a million starving Sudanese, then after the next drought you'll have to feel three million starving Sudanese and it's better to turn your back on the continent and let it solve it's own problems in a uniquely African way (which seems at least as heartless as it is practical). I don't think there's any easy solution, or we'd have found it by now.

Back in the 1950s, during Kenya's Mau Mau rebellion, Robert Ruark wrote an international bestseller titled *Something of Value*. The title was taken from a statement that when you take away a people's culture, you must replace it with something of value. I think it's pretty clear that we destroyed most of the African cultures, but we have yet to replace them with anything of value to Africans.

What is your attitude about awards? Do they mean anything, or are they mere expressions of populism ... or cheating?

Since I am the all-time leading award winner (according to *Locus*) for short fiction, and 4th on the list when you add in novels, I think I can be forgiven for thinking awards are meaningful. I know that awards make it much easier to sell the books and stories to other countries, and to the movies, and in truth they make it a little easier to sell whatever I'm writing next.

Now, does a Hugo (or other award) mean my story was the best of the year? Not necessarily. It just means a particular cross-section of voters thought so.

As far as I know, you are very interested in fables and legends. Would you tell me more about this interest of yours?

Probably it comes from watching a lot of cowboy movies and reading (or listening to) a lot of fairy tales when I was a kid. The late R. A. Lafferty once wrote (in his novella *Space Chanty*): "Will there be a mythology of the future, they used to ask, after all has become science? Will high deeds be told in epic, or only in computer code?" The day I read that sentence I knew I wanted to spend at least part of my career creating those future myths.

I am a moderator of the Bulgarian online club Vampires (we are interested in arts, history and mythology). One of your books is named Stalking the Vampire. *I admit that unfortunately I haven't read it... so I can only base my next question on the presumption that you are interested in the same issue? Would you, please, tell me details about this book?*

I think the title may have misled you. In 1987 I wrote an urban fantasy set in an alternate New York, a New York filled with goblins and leprechauns and similar creatures, titled *Stalking the Unicorn*. It featured the adventures of a detective who found himself in this alternate New York, and it was actually a very funny book. In 2008 Pyr, one of my regular publishers, asked me to resurrect John Justin Mallory (the detective), who had appeared in 7 novelettes but no novels since 1987, and I wrote *Stalking the Vampire*. The vampire himself is quite a dangerous killer, but again, the book is funny. In 2009 I wrote a third novel in the series, *Stalking the Dragon*, which just came out in August. I'm not through with the series, but I'm going to put it aside for a couple of years to write other things I want to do.

You wrote some Battlestar Galactica, Tomb Raider, *and* The Widowmaker *series. How does it feel to work for television?*

I *hated* writing *Battlestar: Galactica*. It was 1980, the show had already been cancelled, and the writer who had novelized the first few books was in a bad situation: his wife had cancer, and the publisher was demanding a fast delivery. Since I wasn't doing anything important that month I said I'd do it. To this day I've never seen the series, and hope to go to my grave without knowing what a Cylon it. The script was just dreadful. I wrote the book in 4 days, and a week later I couldn't have told you what was in it.

I wrote *Lara Croft: Tomb Raider* in 2003; I owed del Rey a book from a previous contract, and this was the one they insisted on. Again, to this day I have not played the game or seen the movie, but unlike *Battlestar* this was a lot of fun. I was told that the current game ended with her buried in the rubble of a temple in Edfu, Egypt (I've been there), and the next game began with her showing up, alone and disillusioned, in Paris (where I've also been). All I had to do was get her—in an adventurous way—from one to the other. So her adventures took her all across Africa, into the Seychelles, and finally to Paris...and it became the Slightly Fictionalized Mike Resnick Travel Diary, because she went all the places I've been. If she enjoys a meal I'm recommending that restaurant; if they try to poison her, I'm saying to stay away from it. Same thing with hotels and safari camps: if she spends a peaceful night, I'm recommending it; if someone shoots at her or puts a poisonous snake in her bed, I'm suggesting that you find a different place to stay when touring Africa.

The Widowmaker is my own creation. I've done 4 novels—*The Widowmaker* (1996), *The Widowmaker Reborn* (1997), *The Widowmaker Unleashed* (1998), all of which were *Locus* bestsellers, and *A Gathering of Widowmakers* (2005), which wasn't (but unlike the first three, it was a hardcover and never had an inexpensive paperback edition). The series has been optioned by Jupiter 9 projects, and the last time I heard about it they were trying to sell it as an animated TV series, but so far nothing has come of it.

If I am capable of counting, you should have edited... 32 anthologies? Right? Why so much? Do you like this job and why? It is something different that writing after all...

Actually, I've edited over 40. Why so many? Because I enjoy it, and primarily because it lets me buy from new writers. This is a very difficult field for newcomers. If you're trying to sell to, say, *Asimov's*, you're competing against maybe 1,200 submissions a month for one of six or seven spots in the magazine. Not only that, but you can't just be as good as Connie Willis or Michael Swanwick or Nancy Kress or me; you have to be *better*, because we've established fan followings who will buy the magazine solely because they see our names on the cover. That's a difficult situation for any newcomer… but when I edit an anthology, I might buy 20 or 25 stories. I'll need ten or fifteen "Names" for the cover and the sales staff, but that still lets me buy five or ten stories from newcomers and less-well-known authors. (Why do I care? Because this field has been so good to me that I feel an obligation "pay forward" and help the next generation enjoy what I've enjoyed.)

Most successful writers were rather unsuccessful for a beginning. They strived for many years, living in the shadows. What is your story, and weren't you angry before you were finally recognized?

I sold my first article when I was 15, my first short story (not science fiction) at 17, and my first novel (also not science fiction) at 20. I knew I was good enough to sell, and I also knew I wasn't good enough or mature enough to write good science fiction (a fact I proved with 3 novels in the late 1960s; I stayed away from the field for 11 years to give people time to forget them). I learned my craft and earned a handsome living writing under pseudonyms in the "adult" field until 1976. We had been breeding and exhibiting collies with considerable success, I couldn't face another year of grinding out 20 or 30 "adult" novels, and I didn't think the kind of science fiction I wanted to write would sell very well, so we bought the second-largest luxury boarding and grooming kennel in America. By 1980 the kennel was doing very well, we had a staff of 21, and I went back to writing science fiction…and when the science fiction out-earned the kennel five years in a row (1988-1993), we sold the kennel, and writing has been our sole source of income ever since.

I've never been bitter. I've never been angry. All I ever wanted to do was write science fiction, and I feel like the luckiest guy in the world that I've been able to so successfully for most of my adult life.

You are a legend in the SF world. I am sure that you receive numerous queries for help from aspiring writers. Doesn't it burden you? And what's your advice to them?

No, I've never considered it a burden. I always try to make time to answer their questions. My main advice is that writers *write* and people who will not become successful writers merely *talk* about writing.

During the 1990s, when I was doing most of my anthology editing, I bought more first stories that *Asimov's*, *Analog* and *F&SF* combined, and my proudest achievement as an editor is not that I commissioned a bunch of Hugo nominees and a winner (which I did), but that eight of "my" discoveries were nominated for the Campbell Award (which goes to the best new writer), and one of them—my daughter—won it.

Over the years I've also collaborated with a number of new writers, mostly to help them get in print before they get discouraged and give up their dreams of becoming science fiction writers. I wrote so many with one of them, Nick Di-Chario, that we actually had a hardcover collection published containing our eleven stories. These days I'm collaborating a lot with another brilliant newcomer, Lezli Robyn from Australia; we sold 4 stories in 2009, and have 6 more assigned for 2010, and I expect we'll be doing at least one novel in the next year.

So no, talking to and working with newcomers doesn't bother me at all. I was a newcomer once, too, and I remember what it was like.

What does make you feel happy and relaxed in your everyday life? Your readers don't know too much about the "human being" Mike Resnick, I think... or am I mistaken? Do you like revealing yourself?

I write so much—more than 130 science fiction novels, anthologies and collections, and more than 230 stories, just since 1980—that my entire life seems to revolve around writing. What makes me happy is when, at the end of the day, I read what I've written and it is pretty much what I hoped it would be when I sat down to work.

Beyond that, I enjoy the musical theatre, horse racing, traveling, reading (though since I went blind in one eye 5 years ago I read less; I have to save that vision for writing)… and I spend a lot of time interacting, in person and online, with my friends, almost all of whom are science fiction fans or professionals.

The last time we chatted you told me you were in a hurry to take your wife out for a lunch. You seem to be a happy person. What's your recipe for a happy life with the beloved?

Do what you enjoy, be happy with your own successes and never be bitter over someone else's, and live each day as if it may be your last, because one day you'll right.

CZECH INTERVIEW WITH MARTIN SUST

Where was born your love for Africa?

When I was 9 or 10 years old, I came across two books by an American who'd been one of the earliest professional hunters in Africa. His name was Alexander Lake, and the books were *Killers in Africa* and *Hunter's Choice*. Despite the titles they weren't endless stories about killing big game. One had to do with filling a zoo's orders for 60 apes by getting them drunk. Another tells you how to prepare and cook that animal you've just shot for the pot. Relatively few of his reminiscences have to do with actually shooting anything. He loved Africa, and that love was transmitted to the reader. From the day I discovered his books, I've shared his fascination with Africa. I've read hundreds of other books on the subject, but Lake was the impetus that got me to take six (non-hunting) safaris, and write maybe ten science fiction novels and twenty science fiction stories about Africa or African analogs. (Half a century after first reading him, I brought Alexander Lake back into print in *The Resnick Library of African Adventure*, a series I edited for Alexander Books.)

What do you mean about the success about the Kirinyaga stories? Before them you was known only as novelist and now you are one of most awarded short stories authors.

I was never very interested in short stories until the late 1980s. I thought you needed 75,000 words to say something Important (note the capital "I"). Then I wrote "Kirinyaga" and realized that I was wrong, that I could do meaningful work at shorter lengths. That was 5 Hugos, 34 Hugo nominations, and about 250 stories ago.

Where isn't much more english or american science fiction about African continent, for example Ian McDonald's Chaga saga, but it's only one of a few exceptions. Where is the reason of that ovelooking of that continent?

I can't speak for the British, but most Americans don't know much about Africa, and I think the major reason is that we've never had any African colonies. The only time we've ever had a major presence was in North Africa in World War II, when we were busy fighting Rommel and not learning about the continent. And until the advent jet passenger planes, it was a *long* trip. Robert Ruark's memoir of his first safari, *Horn of the Hunter*, points out that it took five days to fly from New York to Nairobi.

Why do you return to Kirinyaga stories in Kilimanjaro novella? That novella is like the whole Kirinyaga saga in one story about the new African tribe and it works.

One of my American publishers, Bill Schafer of Subterranean Press, a very good personal friend as well as a publisher, kept nagging me to write something more about Kirinyaga. I kept explaining that the story was done, that there was nothing left to say. During one such conversation I mentioned—again—that Kirinyaga's story was complete, and that if I *had* to write something, it would be about another Utopian colony that hoped to learn from Kirinyaga's mistakes. That night he deposited the money for a novella in my PayPal account and told me that now that I'd been paid I owed him the story. So I sat down and wrote "Kilimanjaro." (He's done this twice more to me, for the African novellas "Shaka II" and "Six Blind Men and an Alien." About once a year he decides he wants a new African novella, pays me in advance, and makes me feel so guilty about taking his money that I write it.)

What is the most important thing for short story writer? Do you have some simple advice for beginners?

He has to remember that in a short story, there are no digressions; he has to make every word count. He can't spend too much time drawing the reader into the story, and he can't linger very long after the end of it. The other thing is that he does not have to moderate his ambition; in the hands of a good writer a short story can be every bit as powerful as a 100,000-word novel.

The best advice I have is that writers *write*, and would-be writers who are never going to be successful *talk* about writing.

The other advice is to never do an editor's job for him, by which I mean, never be afraid to send a story to an editor because you've seen examples of his taste and you think he won't like it. Maybe he won't—but let *him* reject it. Don't *you* reject it for him by not submitting it.

What was your biggest experience or adventure from your African tours? You can pick one or two, if it is necessary...

We were charged by a rather angry elephant in Botswana (she stopped about six or seven meters away from us), and by a rhino in Tanzania's Ngorongoro Crater (he put a large dent in the door of the Land Rover). In Zimbabwe we had to chase a pretty big snake out of our tent.

And I remember the graveyard in Nairobi. Just reading the headstones would give anyone stories to tell: "Killed by a lion," "Killed by the Maasai," "Died from Cholera," "Killed by a leopard," "Killed by a Nandi spear." I spent 2 or 3 hours there one day with my video camera, just capturing those brief and tragic stories.

You like the fables or legends and many of your stories are told in that manner. Why are you attracted in this type of the story?

I suppose as a young boy I grew up with fables and legends of the American frontier—true ones like the Gunfight at the O.K. Corral, and the saga of Billy the Kid, and the Battle of the Little Big Horn. And also fables like Paul Bunyon and his blue ox Babe, and Johnny Appleseed, and similar tales. They stirred my imagination and sense of wonder, and I suppose they encouraged me to try to stir others' as well.

If we imagine various types of Utopias on Earth orbit, on which of them will you move from our planet?

The easy answer would be one with gorgeous naked women and no men. But the truth is that my Utopia is very much like a World Science Fiction Convention, filled with friends of a lifetime, books everywhere, parties (by which I mean animated discussions) all night long, and people with whom I share a number of interests. So I guess I visit my Utopia for a week almost every year.

PHIL ATHENS INTERVIEWS
MIKE RESNICK

As part of the process of writing *The Guide to Writing Fantasy & Science Fiction,* I interviewed a few key players in the SF/fantasy community. Their wisdom and generosity is liberally sprinkled throughout the book, but I couldn't use every word—and wanted to do some follow-ups. This is an expanded interview with science fiction and fantasy author Mike Resnick, presented with my sincere thanks for all his help.

Mike Resnick, according to *Locus* magazine, is the all-time leading award winner, living or dead, for speculative short fiction. A 53-year veteran of the professional writing game, Mike sold his first article in 1957 and his first book five years later. His first published SF novel was 1967's *The Goddess of Ganymede*, which also happens to be the first of his books I actually read. He's also been an active SF/fantasy fan since 1962. His daughter, Laura Resnick, is herself an accomplished author of fantasy and romance novels, including *The Purifying Fire,* which I had a small hand in publishing for Wizards of the Coast.

The first question was one I asked everyone who completed an interview for *The Guide to Writing Fantasy & Science Fiction:*

Athans: *Please define "fantasy" in 25 words or less.*

Resnick: Fantasy is fiction that purposely and knowingly breaks one or more of the known laws governing the universe.

Athans: *Please define "science fiction" in 25 words or less.*

Resnick: Science fiction is concerned with an alternative past, an altered present, or an imagined future and obeys the known laws governing the universe.

Athans: *What advice can you give an aspiring fantasy author on how to approach action scenes? Is there such a thing as too much action?*

Resnick: I'd tell him to study the particular market he's considering, and put in a little more or a little less action than the competition—not so much or so little that it doesn't fit the format—to make his story stand out a bit.

Yes, you can have too much of *anything*. Look at the movie *Van Helsing*. One supernatural creature can be fascinating and/or terrifying; hundreds of them are simply boring. As for action scenes, you have to make them subjective. Getting hit or cut *hurts*, and hero or not, if your character doesn't feel pain, there's no reason why your reader should feel apprehension.

Athans: *How do you approach the creation of monsters and/or aliens? When do you know you've created something worthy of exploring in greater detail?*

Resnick: First, they have to fulfill the needs of the story. Second, I try to create monsters or aliens that are not quite what the reader is expecting. Mainly, I try to keep them from ever being considered generic.

I try to make my non-sentient life forms fit the ecology in which they have evolved. As for aliens, they have to *be* alien; they can't just be men and women in funny costumes.

Athans: *Is there one magic ingredient that makes a character a hero?*

Resnick: No. But there is one thing that makes him a boring hero: no flaws.

You start by making him as real (as opposed to heroic) within the context of the plot and setting. And you try to remember that if your Protagonist, a word I much prefer to Hero, doesn't have doubts and fears and misgivings to overcome, it's a lot less heroic to face an enemy of any type or proportion.

Athans: *Care to offer examples from your own work?*

Resnick: Sure. The Forever Kid (*Soothsayer*) has lived too long and *wants* to die in battle. Wilson Cole (the five Starship books) is incapable of following a stupid order, even though he knows that *not* following it will cost him his command. Thaddeus Flint (the four Galactic Midway books) has no loyalties and no empathy. And so on.

Athans: *Do you look to history for inspiration in creating future or fantasy political systems, nations, or leaders? Are there other sources for inspiration for SF or fantasy political structures?*

Resnick: Of course there are other sources, and the more unusual and the less-used the better. I won the Prix Tour Eiffel [and at the time he was the only American, the only English-language writer to win it] for my novel *The Dark Lady*, told in the first person of an alien whose entire society was extrapolated from the matriarchy and herd instincts of the African elephant. Which is to say: source material is *everywhere*, and if you don't just look where everyone else is looking you're more likely to create something unique and memorable.

Athans: *Any advice on avoiding clichés?*

Resnick: Yeah: avoid 'em. Seriously, read your story aloud, even if you're the only one in the room. You'll spot clichés and awkwardnesses that get past you when you're proofreading and editing on paper or screen.

Athans: *How do you approach research and note-taking? Do you establish a set of "rules" for your setting?*

Resnick: If it's science fiction, the universe has already established the rules and I try not to break them. If it's fantasy, I decide what few rules I plan to break, and then figure out what the consequences are. If it's all in a contemporary fantasy New York, as my three recent novels for Pyr are, I can keep track of it all in my head; if it's a world that's invented from the ground up, then I make and keep as many notes as I need.

Athans: *What's more difficult, getting your first book published, or maintaining a career after that debut?*

Resnick: Selling the fourth book is always more difficult than selling the first. You sell your first on promise; you sell your fourth on your track record, and your publisher probably hasn't poured any promotional money into your first few.

Athans: *You've written at least one tie-in novel—what was the most difficult part of playing in someone else's playground?*

Resnick: In the case of *Battlestar: Galactica* (this was the 1980 version, not the current one): Keeping a straight face. That was close to the silliest, stupidest teleplay I've ever seen. I did a Lara Croft book in 2003, but that required almost no research; I had to get her across Africa (where I've been many times) from the end of one game to the beginning of the next, with no other continuing characters.

Athans: *If it's possible that anyone reading this hasn't yet read any of your work, where should they start? I know that could be like asking which of your children you like best, but assume they'll read and love them all eventually, and get them started!*

Resnick: The best selling of them, by far, is *Santiago*. The most honored and awarded by far is *Kirinyaga*. The author's favorite, and I don't think anyone agrees with me, is *The Outpost*.

Athans: *We'll consider it an assignment to read all three! And we'll keep and eye out for* Blasphemy, *from Golden Gryphon;* The Buntline Special, *from Pyr; and* The Business of Science Fiction, *with Barry Malzberg, from MacFarland, all coming this year!*

FACEBOOK INTERVIEW

You are generally considered the most decorated writer of short speculative fiction. In your opinion, what is the key to a successful short story?

If you just count Hugos, Connie Willis and a couple of others are ahead of me. The *Locus* list, which you are quoting, counts not just Hugos but all major awards from all over the world.

In answer to your question, I think when all is said and done, a story must make an emotional impact on the reader. It must *move* him—to laughter, to tears, to fear, to sympathy, to anger, to *something*. If it makes him think, so much the better, and the author has written a better story for it—but if it doesn't make him *feel*, then it fails as a story, even as it may succeed as a polemic or a technological crossword puzzle in prose form.

You often write about Africa and, in particular, the problems caused by colonialism. What do you see as the biggest current challenges facing that continent? And is there an attitude or misperception toward colonialism that you would you most like to change through your writing?

The biggest problem right now is a continent-wide corruption on a scale unimaginable to those who haven't been there (and no, tourists have *not* been to the real Africa). Robert Ruark wrote an international bestselling novel about the Mau Mau back in the 1950s titled *Sonething of Value*. The meaning of the title is that if you are going to take away a people's culture, you had better replace it with something of value or you've got a big problem on your hands. 50 years after Ruark, we still haven't replaced it with anything of value to Africans, and we have 40+ separate and distinct big sub-Saharan problems on our hands.

You have said that your Lucifer Jones novels are particular favorites of yours. Is this true, and if so, is there a specific reason?

I prefer writing humor to anything else, though of course my reputation is based on my serious work. And of all the humor I've written, which comes to maybe a dozen books and 90 or more stories in this field, what I most enjoy writing are the Lucifer Jones stories. They're parodies of every bad B-movie and trite pulp magazine I read when I was growing up, and the language is a delightful cross between the purple prose of *Trader Horn* and the fractured English of *Pogo Possum*. Some of the story and chapter titles will give you a broad hint: "The Island of Annoyed Souls," "The Clubfoot of Notre Dame," "A Jaguar Never Changes Its Stripes," "The Best Little Tabernacle in Nairobi," and so on. They're just a pure delight to write.

You are the executive editor of Jim Baen's Universe, which is closing as of April 2010. The closing has been handled masterfully, but it still seems a sad thing for the industry as a whole. Is there anything you'd like to say about that? And, as a corollary, from your perspective, what are the happiest and unhappiest current trends in speculative fiction publishing.

Jim Baen's Universe had a fine business model when Jim conceived it and started it, but that statement was invalid before the magazine was a year old. (I joined it in its second year.) The notion was to pay the major writers a quarter a word, three times the top rate of the digests, and to run a couple of hundred thousand words an issue—and against the competition that existed when the magazine debuted, against *Asimov's*, *F&SF* and *Analog*, it made sense to pay those rates, put together that many words, have sparking, *moving* covers by a top artist like Don Mattingly, and charge $30 a year for a basic 6-issue subscription. After all, when you compared values, we were giving you more big names and more words than the digests for the same price.

But as it turned out, after we'd been in business for about a year, we were no longer in competition with the digests. We were in competition with Subterranean Magazine (which was running people like John Scalzi, Lucius Shepard, Elizabeth Bear, Joe Lansdale and myself in just about every issue), and Clarkesworld (which ran stories by Tobias S. Buckell, myself in collaboration with Lezli Robyn, and similar), and a dozen other e-zines that were paying pro rates and were *free*.

How do you compete with that? Suddenly a bunch of e-zines were almost matching our firepower (and in the case of Subterranean, totally matching it) and not charging a penny. Suddenly that $5.00 an issue didn't look like such a bargain.

We had other problems. *Asimov's* came back from a near-death experience thanks to selling a few thousand issues a month via Kindle and Fictionwise/Barnes/the "Nook." But Baen Books felt that our going to Kindle or Fictionwise would abrogate our distribution agreement with Simon & Schuster, so that was a potential lifeline that was denied us.

Weep us no tears. We announced the ending far enough in advance so that no subscriber would be left with paid-for-but-unreceived issues, no writer would deliver a commissioned story only to be told that the magazine was full and/or couldn't pay for it, and no serial would be cut off in the middle. We showed the way, and when I took a quick count tonight, there are, excluding *Jim Baen's Universe*, 18 magazines paying pro rates, and 14 of them are e-zines.

I know you write primarily in Science Fiction, but do you have any favorite fantasy writers? Any writers of short fantasy fiction for our fans at fantasy http://www.facebook.com/l/2e79e;literature. com to watch for?

I'm no stranger to writing fantasy, or to appreciating it. Among the classics, I most admire T. H. White's *The Once and Future King*, which I find far superior to Tolkien or C. S.

Lewis. I'm also a fan of *Orlando Furioso*. I believe that *Unknown*, with stories as diverse as Sturgeon's "Yesterday Was Monday," Williamson's *Darker Than You Think*, Heinlein's "Magic, Inc." and Leiber's Gray Mouser stories, was far and away the greatest fantasy magazine of all time. More recently, I loved Lisa Goldstein's *The Red Magician*, Jonathan Carroll's *The Land of Laughs*, Arthur Byron Cover's *Autumn Angels*, and of course you could do a lot worse than Ray Bradbury's *Dandelion Wine* and *Something Wicked This Way Comes*. Oh, and let's not forget Jack Vance's *The Dying Earth*. And while I have no interest in or admiration for paranormal romances] there is nothing wrong with the source: Bram Stoker's still-brilliant *Dracula*.

STELLAR GUILD SERIES QUESTIONS FOR MIKE RESNICK:

You've edited numerous books over the years, so at this point could probably have your choice of just about any series to edit that you wished—what was it that particularly excited you about, and piqued your interest in, The Stellar Guild Series?

As I explain in the intro that precedes each of the first few books, over the years I have help quite a few new writers—I've taught them, collaborated with them, bought from them for my anthologies, introduced them to editors and agents, 8 or 9 have made the Campbell ballot…and Maureen McHugh calls them "Mike's Writer Children." And when Shahid and I put our heads together to come up with a unique new series, it occurred to me that I couldn't be the only guy with "Writer Children." The reason I have them—and that so many of us do—is because by the time you're well-enough established in this field to pay back, you can't. Everyone who helped you is dead or rich or both, so you pay forward. And I just had a feeling that our major writers would be as enthused about the notion of teaming up with one of their protégés, actually sharing the cover with him or her, as I have been over the years. And it turns out I was right.

What challenges does editing The Stellar Guild Series present to you that a traditional book, or short story anthology, does not, and how have you worked to overcome those challenges?

There are far less challenges than you would think. You don't see seamless continuity, because this isn't a novel; it's a novella and a novelette, set in the same universe, but not necessary directly sequential. I don't have to worry much about the quality. The stars have proven they have it, over and over again; and they want their protégés to shine, so they're even more demanding if them—in a gentle way—than I am.

What is the most meaningful part of this project to you, and why?

As I said, it's the change to pay forward, to take a couple of years off the apprenticeship of talented newcomers. You share cover credit, and a book, with Harry Turtledove or Mercedes Lackey or any of our other stars, that's got to do your embryonic career more good than selling to half a dozen magazines and anthologies, where your story and your name are just one of many. There's also the unspoken brag: "Hey, of all the beginners in the world, he chose *me*!"

What guidelines do you give the writers as they start upon the project?

These are bestsellers and multiple award winners, so all I do it give them the basic guidelines: we want 30,000 to 35,000 words from the star, and 15,000 from the protégé, whose story can be a prequel, a sequel, or a companion piece, but has to be sent in the same universe as the novella. I enourage the protégés to confer with the stars, not with me, about what they'll be writing, since they're doing it in the stars' universes.

How are the writer pairings decided upon, and what role do you play in choosing or 'okaying' those pairings?

That choice is left solely up to the stars. If they should choose someone who I think is too far advanced in his career—these are beginners, but not unpublished beginners—I'll step in, explain that, and suggest they choose a different one. Or if a star asks me to suggest a talented newcomer who I think would match up well I'm happy to do so…but for the most part, they know who they want to work with.

So often, when a collaboration takes place between a newer writer and an established author, the "newbie" does a lot of the work and the established name takes much of the credit. Here it's much different: while the established writer definitely is the name the "sells" the book, the up-and-coming author also gets to shine on his/her own terms. How does that help the newer writer? What potential is there for harm?

As I said, this should take a couple of years off any new writers' apprenticeship. An average sale for a Kevin Anderson or an Eric Flint book is probably six to ten times what a good sale for a beginner comes to. And I can guarantee that if, for example, Bob Silverberg's name is on the cover, it'll get ten times the reviews that a newcomer's first or second book is likely to get. Which is the purpose behind the line: to introduce the next generation, and ease their path just a bit.

So far, of the two books I have seen, there have been more-or-less traditional sequel/prequel stories. Yet there are many other options (different viewpoints of the same set of events, distinct yet somehow related events in the same world, etc.). Are there plans for different approaches to telling the stories in the future, and if so, what can you share with SCI FI readers?

Yes, there are. I won't speak for any other works in progress—there's a difference between being told what they'll be, and actually seeing the finish product—but I know that one I'm doing with my own protégé, Lezli Robyn, will not be one of your sequel/prequel things. I plan to tell one of my bigger-than-life tall tales, and she plans to tell the truth about what really happened, and why the author (me) would lie about it.

Along with Anderson and Lackey, I also understand that Eric Flint and Harry Turtledove are on the docket for future editions. What can you tell SCI FI readers about their stories, who they will be working with, etc.?

Eric hasn't chosen his protégé yet. I actually suggested a couple for Harry—he has three brilliant and beautiful daughters, two of whom have won major writing contests—and he'll be doing his Stellar Guild book with his daughter Rachel. (I also told him that after my daughter, Laura, won the Campbell Award back in 1993, my stud fee tripled. Who knows? That may have been the deciding factor. ☺)

Is there anything else about The Stellar Guild Series, or anything else you are working on, that I have not asked that you would like SCI FI readers to know?

No it's still in its infancy. But I'll tell you what I'm most proud of. Every one of these stars iis busy as hell. Most of them are contracted two and three years ahead. When I approached them, I got as far as saying I wanted a novella and that we were paying an above-average-but-not-Wall-Street rate, and each of them began to regretfully say No. Then I came to the part about their choosing and working with a protégé, and every last one of them immediately said Yes—which is exactly what I love about this field. We may compete for the same markets and the same awards, but we are the most generous group of writers you'll find anywhere on this Earth.

PART 5: ARTICLES

INTRODUCTION TO PART 5

These are articles I've written and sold since *Resnick at Large*. They different from the articles in *Once a Fan...* and *...Always a Fan* (all from this same publisher) in that they were written for professional markets.

EFFICIENCIES ON THE DARK CONTINENT,

or, *Darwin Was Wrong*

by Mike Resnick and Ralph Roberts

For *You Did What?*

Africa is a big continent, so big that we can't confine this chapter to a single story or example. Bear with us.

Inefficiency is nothing new to Africa. That said, the fact remains that the Dark Continent is constantly finding new and better ways to be inefficient.

ONE OF OUR NAVIES IS MISSING

The most recent incident occurred in the fall of 2002, when an African nation lost its navy. Okay, it was a navy of just one ship, but still…

"The situation is absolutely under control," Transport Minister Ephraem Magagula assured the Swaziland parliament in Mbabane, according to the *Johannesburg Star*. "Our nation's navy is perfectly safe. We just don't know where it is, that's all." The navy in question was the landlocked country's only ship, the *Swazimar*. That's right—a navy of one ship. ship. (Well, let's be reasonable. Just how many naval vessels does a tiny landlocked country need anyway?)

Explained Magagula: "We believe it is at sea somewhere. We did send a team of men to look for it, but there was a problem with drink and they failed to find it, and so, technically, yes, it's temporarily lost. But I categorically reject all suggestions of incompetence on the part of this government.

The *Swazimar* is a big ship painted in the sort of nice bright colors you can see at night. Mark my words, it will turn up. The right honorable gentleman opposite is a very naughty man, and he will laugh on the other side of his face when my ship comes in."

When last we heard, Swaziland was still looking for its navy.

THE PUSSYCAT OF SOUTHERN AFRICA

While we're on the subject of Swaziland, let's consider young King Mswati II—one of the few absolute monarchs left anywhere in the world.

King Mswati is the marrying kind. He recently took his tenth wife, a 17-year-old schoolgirl. Of course, Mswati has quite a way to go to match his daddy, old King Sobhuza II, who died in 1986. (Sobhuza had 60 wives and made sure he could keep them by abolishing the constitution and all representative forms of government in Swaziland.)

Mswati realized that marrying so many women in this day and age might not sit well with his subjects, so he issued a degree that gave him total censorship over all the media in his country, on the not-unreasonable assumption that you can't get mad if you don't know what's going on.

Then, since he had so many wives to transport on state visits to the far reaches of his country (which happens to be considerably smaller than Florida), Mswati contracted to buy a $50 million private jet while his nation of a million people is short on food and living on a per capita average of less than a dollar a day.

Or, as Mel Brooks says, "It's good to be the king!"

(And it's getting better. He just got engaged again.)

So how does the Studmuffin of Swaziland stack up against some of the recent African heads of state?

IT'S THE ECONOMY, STUPID

Well, the champ is the late Joseph Mobutu (who changed his name to Mobutu Sese Seku), dictator (in Africa the term is President-For-Life) of Zaire. Mobuto came to power at the height of the cold war, put his loyalty up for auction, and was purchased by the West. Over the years the United States and its allies gave Zaire $10 billion in aid. At the time of his death, Mobuto's Swiss bank accounts and European real estate holdings were estimated to be worth more than $9 billion.

Another African leader who won't be going hungry soon is Daniel arap Moi, President of Kenya from 1977 until 2003. He'd been a schoolteacher before Jomo Kenyatta tapped him as his vice president, and he succeeded to the presidency shortly thereafter. With no savings, and on the minimal salary paid to Kenya's president, Moi managed to acquire the ownership of every Mobil gas station in Kenya (renamed Kobil gas stations), every Mercedes taxi in Nairobi and Mombasa, the entire Air Kenya fleet of DC-3 airplanes, and a few hundred thousand acres of prime farmland in Kenya's White Highlands. The only conclusion: he must have brown-bagged a *lot* of lunches.

But never let it be said that every African dictator takes it all with him. When the Emperor Bokassa was being deposed in the Central African Republic, a mere handful of years after the French donated some $25 million to his Ascendancy Ceremony, one of his last imperial acts was to stop by the nation's treasury and set it afire.

INVESTING IN AFRICAN REAL ESTATE

King Mswati uses his absolute rule for self-indulgence. Nothing unusual about that; being the top dog has always been a great way to get girls…literally, in his case.

But Uganda's Idi Amin, who just died in exile in Saudi Arabia, was a cat of a different stripe.

Being a total dictator, self-indulgent, and evil to boot, can start to wear on the old nerves. You need a holiday retreat of some sort. Old Idi had his—23-acre Mukusu Island on beautiful Lake Victoria. There Idi whiled away many a pleasant afternoon indulging in his hobby of torturing a wide variety of victims and feeding them to the crocodiles.

Today, over twenty years after the end of Idi Amin's genocidal dictatorship, this island still bears the scars of his lazy afternoons there. You might stop by it sometime: a great little fixer-upper, with cattle prods, chains, and crocodiles included. (Idi called it Paradise Island—perhaps because of the many people he and the crocs dispatched to Paradise while he was there.)

Amin had some other little problems in the area of civilized behavior. It's said on good authority that he ate at least one of his infant sons. He declared that Adolf Hitler was his hero and erected a statue of him in the capital city of Kampala. Math was never his strong suit, and he simply never understood why he couldn't just print more money when he needed it. So print it he did—and there came a day when a loaf of bread cost in excess of a million Ugandan shillings.

He remained convinced (deluded is probably a more accurate word) that his people wanted him back, and he left his Saudi reservation a few years ago, certain they were ready to roll out a red, if not bloodstained, carpet for him. He got as far as the Zaire-Uganda border when he was recognized and refused entry.

THERE WERE PROBLEMS BEFORE IDI

Ruling Uganda stupidly didn't begin with Idi Amin, who took over in 1969. A few years earlier, the country was having a problem with tsetse flies.

Now, the tsetse fly tends to live on herbivores, usually wild ones—but if you bring enough cattle into an area, the tsetse isn't all that selective, and will just as happily live, breed and dine on domestic cattle. The problem is, wild game has a built-in immunity to the tsetse fly, and domestic animals don't.

Now, in any reasonable society, if your cattle were infested with tsetse flies, you'd spray heavily with DDT or something similar, and of course you'd begin dipping your livestock regularly.

But this was Uganda. Let us, they reasoned, get rid of the wildlife, and then the tsetse flies will have nowhere to go.

So they declared an unlimited open season on their game. Hunters came from all over. It's estimated that half a million animals were killed.

The result?

Well, some of the wounded game animals ran a thousand miles before dying, thus introducing their tsetse flies to areas that had never known them before. As for the bulk of the tsetse population, it moved lock, stock and barrel to the domestic livestock without losing a beat.

SPORTS MEDICINE

Being slow to pay your witch doctor is just about as stupid as living any place that Idi Amin would call Paradise Island. But a government minister in the Ivory Coast did just that. (Well, let's be fair. Maybe his Blue Cross didn't cover it.)

It seems that more than a decade after the Ivory Coast's soccer team managed its only African Nations Cup win, the local witch doctors were finally paid. Why? Because they are convinced they helped win the trophy by means of their professional services.

Back in 1992 the Minister of Sport decided to provide the national team with a bit of an edge and hired the witch doctors as spiritual consultants. Named the Elephants, the team managed a narrow win during a penalty shootout in Senegal.

Fine so far—but then the sports minister kinda sorta forgot to pay the bill. The witch doctors, who live in the village of

Akradio, took this oversight rather poorly. They immediately put a hex on the team. And their magic worked again—no wins for the next ten years!

Finally bowing to pressure from disappointed fans, the Minister, one Moise Lida Kouassi, decided it was time to pay up. He offered humble apologies, a bottle of liquor, and two thousand dollars to the witch doctors.

There will be two signs by which we'll know if Kouassi's capitulation worked: the first will be that the Elephants win again; the second will be that his head doesn't fall off. The current odds are 6-to-5, pick 'em.

THE MOST RECENT COLONIAL WAR

Most people you talk to (except for Minister Kouassi of the Ivory Coast, who any moment now may find himself missing a head to talk with) will tell you that the age of colonialism is over, that all of Africa is independent now.

Not so. One of the oldest European colonial powers, Spain, still has several African possessions. In fact, you may recall a recent news article which reported that five Moroccan soldiers captured a small rock of an island claimed by Spain. The next day, nine Spanish troops recaptured it, thus ending the latest colonial war in Africa.

Obviously, armies have downsized since a force of 60 Tanzanian soldiers overthrew the government of the Seychelles back in 1977.

AFRICAN MATH

"I have promised to keep his identity confidential," Jack Maxim, a spokesman for the Sandton Sun Hotel in Johannesburg, told the *Cape Times*, "but I can confirm that he is no longer in our employment.

"We asked him to clean the lifts and he spent four days on the job. When I asked him why, he replied: 'Well, there are forty of them, two on each floor, and sometimes some of them aren't there.' Eventually we realized that he thought each floor had a different lift, and he'd cleaned the same two twelve times. We had to let him go. I understand he is now working for GE."

With that kind of math being exported to GE, heaven help our next generation of space shuttles.

SO YOU'RE UNHAPPY WITH THE WAY WE RUN OUR AIRPORTS?

We'll admit that some of the cases we've discussed will stretch your credulity. Not this one. This one will throw it right out the window. Of an airplane. That isn't going anywhere. In Kenya.

"What's all the fuss about?" Weseka Sambu demanded at a hastily-convened news conference at the Jomo Kenyatta International Airport in Nairobi. "A technical hitch like this could have happened anywhere in the world. You people are not patriots. You just want to cause trouble."

So what was Sambu's problem?

He is a spokesman for Kenya Airways, and he was explaining why a flight that was to originate in Kisumu, stop in Nairobi, and then continue on to Berlin, Germany just a tad behind schedule.

It all began when 42 passengers boarded the plane, ready to fly to Nairobi, when the pilot noticed that one of the tires had gone flat.

That could happen anywhere. But what came next could only happen in Africa.

First problem: Kenya Airways didn't have a spare tire at Kisumu.

Second problem: the airport's nitrogen canister was empty, so they decided to take the tire to a local gas station for repairs.

Third problem: someone had stolen the jack and they couldn't get the wheel off—so they tried to inflate the tire with a bicycle pump.

Fourth problem: the bicycle pump didn't work, so the pilot climbed out of the plane and tried to blow into the valve with his mouth.

Fifth problem: the pilot passed out from his efforts—and the tire remained flat. For all we know, it's still flat as we write these words.

"When I announced that the flight had to be abandoned," said Sambu, "one of the passengers, a Mr. Mutu, suddenly struck me about the face with a life-jacket whistle and said we were a national disgrace. I told him he was being ridiculous and that there would be another flight in a fortnight. And in the meantime, he would be able to enjoy the scenery around Kisumu, albeit at his own expense."

Okay, now tell us how much you resent the security lines at your local airport.

PROJECTS

The Italians spent $300 million building roads in Somalia. What's peculiar about that? At the time, it came to more than $200,000 per vehicle.

In 1990, Lilongwe, the capital city of Malawi, had a state of the art television broadcast tower. What's unusual about that? Except for the Capital Hotel in Lilongwe, the Mount Soche hotel in Blantyre, and the various palaces of President-For-Life Hastings Banda, there were less than 50 television sets in the country.

President Omar Bongo of Gabon talked the French into spending more than half a billion dollars building the most ambitious railroad on the continent. It required some 50 bridges, made with the finest hardwood, each spanning enormous canyons, but eventually it was done. What's unusual about that? Gabon's only export, the only thing they would ship to the coast aboard their state-of-the-art train, was hard-wood; they used it all up building the railroad.

Remember our old pal, the deposed Emperor Bokassa? Everything was going well for him until he decided to build a factory that made uniforms for the local schoolchildren. And since it was his idea, and he was the Emperor, of course he owned it. What's unusual about that? Well, the average outfit cost $100, and the average family earned about $150 a year, so they were understandably reluctant to purchase the out-fits. Then Bokassa passed a law—when you're the Emperor passing laws is pretty easy—making it mandatory that all schoolchildren wore his company's outfits. That's when the students, most of them not yet adolescents, marched on the capital in protest. And *that's* when Bokassa decided they were an irritant and ordered them shot. And that was the beginning of the end for Bokassa.

The Ivory Coast's late President-For-Life Houphouet-Boigny, ruling a country that was saddled with one of Africa's biggest per-capita debts, built a huge cathedral in the capital of Abidjan. He was so pleased with it that, while rescheduling the country's debt payments, he decided to build the world's biggest church, and not in Abidjan, but in the little village of Yamoussoukro.

The structure, which was designed to dwarf St. Peter's basilica in Rome, was about halfway up when it was finally shown off to foreign journalists in 1987. An American writer asked if it might be considered folly to build the world's big-gest church in the middle of the African bush, especially when so many of the people were hungry. The guide, who had been well-schooled by the 150 Frenchmen who were getting rich off the project, replied, "Don't you think there were starving and homeless people when the cornerstone was laid for Notre Dame?" End of discussion.

ECOLOGY, AFRICAN STYLE

The Nile perch sometimes grows to 300 pounds, and inhabits Lake Turkana in northern Kenya. Why not, reasoned the government, capture some young ones and put them into Lake Tanganyika, the largest fresh-water lake on the continent, and let them breed? Think of how much protein we can pull out of the lake in a few years to feed our hungry masses.

The Nile perch proceeded to eat almost everything else in the lake. They themselves made slow, easy targets for the thousands of crocodiles. It'll be years before the last of them is dead and the lake's balance is restored.

The same geniuses put beautiful, flowering water hyacinths into Kenya's Lake Naivasha. Why not? They were lovely, and the hippos liked eating them.

But they multiplied a *lot* faster than the lake's hippos, and on any given day 40% to 50% of the lake's surface is covered by the things.

You can go too far the other direction. Botswana has done such a splendid job of protecting its elephant population—and word went out on the elephant grapevine, because elephants who were being decimated by poachers in Angola, Zimbabwe and Zambia migrated there—that suddenly what Botswana has is a lot of starving elephants. The Chobe National Park, which can reasonably support about 18,000 to 22,000, currently has 60,000 and the number is growing as the food supply is vanishing. But because Botswana is a signatory to the CITES agreement—a total continent-wide ban on ivory, created because other countries couldn't control their poachers—they cannot even cull their own herds and use the proceeds from the ivory to relocate some of the hungrier survivors.

SEE? IT'S NOT JUST MUGABE

It's generally considered that, after two decades in office, President Robert Mugabe of Zimbabwe has lost his sanity. It took him less than three years to bankrupt the country, turn a healthy populace into an army of starving beggars, and generally make himself a pariah among civilized leaders.

So why didn't the people rise up and throw him out of office?

Well, there are many reasons, including his death squads, but one reason no one has suggested to date is that it's harder to tell a Zimbabwe madman than you think.

Consider this item from a Bulawayo newspaper:

"While transporting mental patients from Harare to Bulawayo, the bus driver stopped at a roadside *shebeen* (beer hall) for a few beers. When he got back to his vehicle, he found it empty, with the 20 patients nowhere to be seen. Realizing the trouble he was in if the truth were uncovered, he halted his vehicle at the next bus stop and offered lifts to those in the queue. Letting 20 people board the bus, he then shut the doors and drove straight to the Bulawayo Mental Hospital, where he hastily handed over his 'charges,' warning the nurses that they were particularly excitable.

"Excitable was an understatement. Staff removed the furious passengers; it was three days later that suspicions were roused by the consistency of stories from the 20. As for the real patients: nothing more has been heard of them and they have apparently blended comfortably back into Zimbabwean society..."

WHAT'S NEXT?

It's hard to say. But for every Shaka Zulu, who began with a village the size of a football field and wound up with an empire three times the size of France, there's an Idi Amin, who began with a country like Uganda and wound up confined in a small house thousands of miles away. For every Albert Schweitzer who devotes his life to truth, there's a South African president who tells the press that AIDS is a capitalist myth. For every Jomo Kenyatta who outlaws hunting, there's likely to be a game department officer with a unique way of eradicating tsetse flies.

But they do keep things interesting, don't they?

THE WONDERFUL ICE CREAM SUIT

For *Cinema Futura*

This is the story of five losers who, for one magical night, become winners. It's really as simple as that—which is, of course, not very simple at all.

"The Wonderful Ice Cream Suit" has had quite a long history. Ray Bradbury wrote it and sold it to *The Saturday Evening Post* in 1957. It became a half-hour production in a television anthology series in 1958. It then became a stage play, and after that, a stage musical. And finally, in 1998, came the movie. Bradbury has been quoted as saying "It's the best film I've ever made." I've enjoyed *Something Wicked This Way Comes* and *Moby Dick* and some of his others, but I have no argument with that conclusion.

So: the five losers. Gomez (Joe Montegna) is a con man whose schemes work so badly that he's dead broke and constantly being locked out of his apartment by his landlord. Dominguez (Esai Morales) is a wandering guitarist who can attract neither listeners nor women. Villanazul (Gregory Sierra) is a soapbox orator who couldn't draw flies at a watermelon party. Martinez (Clifton Collins Jr., billed for some strange reason as Clifton Gonzales Gonzales) is young, unemployed, and in love with a girl who lives next door and doesn't know he's alive. And Vamenos (Edward James Olmos) is a bum who hasn't shaved in years, hasn't washed in decades (he claims he's allergic to water), and is, as the Supreme Court might say, without a single redeeming social value.

What do these five losers have in common? Only their height, weight and measurements. They live in the impoverished barrios of East Los Angeles, and in a cheap men's clothing store (run by Sid Caesar and Howard Morris in a pair of delightful cameos) there is a white suit which represents all their hopes and dreams to them. And it costs $100, which none of them has (or probably has ever had)—but when they each toss $20 into the kitty, suddenly they can buy the miraculous ice cream suit that they know will transform their lives.

And, strangely enough, it does. They decide that on the first night they own it, each will wear it for one hour. Dominguez is the first. He goes out with his guitar, and women can't keep away from him. Next it's Villanazul, and he draws a huge worshipful crowd. Martinez has a smaller dream, but it comes true anyway: the girl next door finally notices him. Gomez plans to abscond with the suit and take a bus to El Paso, but instead the suit absconds with his greed, and he returns, chastened and humbled, to his companions. Olmos gets to do a wild comic turn as Vamenos: he must be shaved and bathed before being allowed in the suit, and then saved when he abandons common sense in favor of booze, juicy tacos, an even juicier 300-pound girlfriend, and her murderous boyfriend.

Doesn't sound like it should be my favorite fantasy film, does it? But then, I haven't mentioned that Stuart Gordon, whose work I have loved since he directed all three episodes of *Warp* in a small neighborhood theater in Chicago almost 40 years ago, directed this film with love and style. You come to *care* for these five losers, and you find beauty everywhere in their poverty-stricken lives and neighborhood. The score by Mader, ranging from a Mariachi band to a sad, sweet solo guitar, is exquisite, and some Disney exec is burning in hell right now for not releasing a CD of it. The credits are the finest sand animation I've ever seen.

The movie was made for direct-to-video release. It's a pity, because a few million more people should have had the opportunity to fall in love with it—but because it went directly to video they didn't feel the need to pad it out. It is 77 minutes long, exactly the proper length for this magical story.

The star, of course, isn't Gordon or Mader or one of the actors, brilliant as they were. It's Ray Bradbury. I have loved his work since I was a kid, which was a *long* time ago. I knew that he was a master of sentiment, and of terror, and of the evocation of childhood, and of wonder—but until I saw this movie, I never knew that he (or anyone) could produce such out-and-out totally unselfconscious *charm*. You are captivated a minute or two into the film, and you never want it to end, though it ends at exactly the right moment on exactly the right line.

Is it a fantasy film? After all, there's not a single incident that you can point to and say, "See? *That's* fantasy." To which I reply, 50 years ago Damon Knight and James Blish were excoriating *The Martian Chronicles* because the science was so wrong it clearly didn't qualify as science fiction. To which millions upon millions of readers replied with their money and their devotion, saying, in essence: "When it's this good, who cares?" Which is my precise answer to the question of whether or not it's a fantasy film in the strictest definition of the term. When it's this good, who cares?

There is a point, after a wild scene in which Olmos, using the white jacket as a cape, is nailed and thrown through the air by a bull (well, a car that sports a bull's horns as a hood ornament). The suit is miraculously undamaged, and as he is being carted off to the hospital after breaking his leg and almost destroying the suit, he asks, plaintively, "Can I still be in the gang?" And the other four losers, all transformed by their experiences in the suit, agree that of course he can.

You know what? After seeing the movie, I want to be in the gang too.

FLAVORS OF FRED

For *Gateways*

Fred Pohl was editing *Astonishing* a year before I was born. He was a giant in the field by the time I started reading science fiction. He won a shelf of Hugos for editing, and another shelf for writing.

I've probably read 80% of the words he's written, which is one hell of a lot, and I subscribed *Galaxy* and *If*, and I read most of the Bantam books he edited, plus those early Star anthologies. But when I think of Fred, those aren't the memories that pop to mind first.

I think of Fred, and I instantly smell cigarette smoke. I was a heavy smoker when we were both hitting a lot of Midwestern conventions, so was he, and we seemed to always find ourselves in each other's company, sneaking out of some boring banquet for a smoke, sitting in splendid and befogged isolation in the smoking suite, or otherwise polluting the convention.

I also remember a Windycon where there was a Fred Pohl Roast, and the committee asked me to be the roastmaster because no one else would say anything nasty/funny about him. I poured through his wonderful autobiography, *The Way the Future Was*, and found a most interesting fact hidden away in the middle of it. Once, when (like so many writers) Fred needed a little salaried income, he took a job at a racetrack as the guy who irritates the winning horse's genitalia with an electric prod to get urine samples for the track vet. I built an entire routine about how after years of causing the same reaction in editors and readers, he'd finally found his calling. Just before the roast a couple of panelists insisted I couldn't say those things about an icon, but I did—and no one laughed louder that Fred.

When our mutual friend Algis Budrys died, it was Fred who contacted me and suggested we put together a collection of his very best works before they were forgotten—but only on the condition that we take, at most, an absolutely minimal fee, and that the bulk of the advance and all of the royalties go to Ajay's widow. I accepted instantly. Why? Partially because Ajay was a friend...but my main reason was that after well over half a century of reading him, and smoking with him, and appearing on panels with him, and roasting him, I was finally offered the opportunity to work with one of my heroes. Health considerations have slowed the project down, but it'll still come to fruition one of these days.

Everyone knows what a fine writer and editor Fred is, but he also has some accomplishments that have gone relatively unheralded. For example: a lot of writers have found one teammate and turned out a series of fine collaborations. L. Sprague de Camp and Fletcher Pratt come to mind, or Henry Kuttner and C. L. Moore, or Larry Niven and Jerry Pournelle. But no one's ever been part of two long-lived, stellar, wildly successful teams—except Fred, who did it with Cyril Korn-bluth, and then, just to prove it wasn't a fluke, did it all over again with Jack Williamson.

He also wrote the single best article on self-promotion to appear in the past fifty years: "The Science Fiction Profes-sional," which appeared in Reginald Bretnor's *The Craft of Science Fiction* back in 1976, and so impressed me that when I collected seven years of my "how-to" columns from *Specu-lations* in book form, I titled it *The Science Fiction Profes-sional*. (Holster that lawsuit, Fred; the statute of limitations ran out in 2007.)

Science fiction doesn't have many renaissance men, no matter how much we like to believe we do. Fred's been an authentic one for damned near three-quarters of a century, and has improved his art with almost every passing decade. We're not going to see too many men like that, and I'm proud to have known him.

I HAVE SEEN THE FUTURE— AND IT AIN'T GOT A LOT OF DEAD TREES IN IT

For *Nebula Award Showcase 2008*

Let me start by saying that I love books and magazines. I like the heft and feel of them. I grew up with the printed page. I can't remember ever having a house where most of the wall space wasn't covered by overflowing bookshelves. I don't especially like reading my science fiction off the computer screen.

But as a science fiction writer—and one who has to pay the bills with his science fiction—it's my job to look ahead and see what's coming, and whether I like it or not makes no difference. It is not a matter of Good or Bad, but rather of True or False. And the truth is that we're not going to be pulping as many forests in the future.

Twenty years ago, when the Internet was just taking off, just about every established science fiction writer was approached by start-up publishers. The pitch was always the same: give me something for free today and I'll make you rich tomorrow (or maybe next week, or possibly in 17 years, or conceivably in…) Every one of them went belly-up.

Then *Omni Online*, which certainly had deep pockets (or at least could borrow from *Penthouse's*) came along, and suddenly we had a paying market. It lasted long enough for Ellen Datlow to become the very first to win a Hugo for editing an electronic publication. But it didn't last a lot longer than that.

Then we had GalaxyOnline.com of sainted memory. My God, we writers loved it! Half a buck a word (if you wrote the minimum. It was a set amount.) But it was a loss leader for a film and TV company that never made any films or TV shows, and it was gone within a year.

Then there was *scifi.com*, which paid more than double the going rate of the digests, and lasted long enough to win Ellen Datlow another Hugo for editing another electronic magazine…but it, too, bit the dust.

So what's with the title to this article (I hear you ask)? All these places had high hopes and high pay rates, and they all wound up in publishing's graveyard.

What can I tell you? The first few settlers who tried to reach the West Coast didn't make it either.

But they paved the way for those who came after them.

The first success story came from an unlikely source: Fictionwise.com, which publishes only reprints. They started out in 2000 with a small handful of science fiction writers—Robert Silverberg, Nancy Kress, James Patrick Kelly, myself, just a few others. And they paid twice as much for a short fiction reprint as the average anthology paid. And we all thought: wow, how long as this been going on? It's like stealing!

And we never thought of it again—until later that same year, when the royalty checks went out, and we realized that, hey, there are thousands of people out there who, when confronted by trillions of free words of drivel on the Internet, prefer to pay for *reprints* by known authors.

That was only eight years ago. These days Fictionwise. com has literally thousands of authors, including such heavyweights as Dan Brown, Stephen King, Robert Ludlum, Isaac Asimov, Robert A. Heinlein, and that whole crowd.

They proved you could sell literally billions of words of electronic reprints, many (in fact, in the beginning, *most*) of them science fiction. So it was only a matter of time before a major science fiction publisher took a look at the direction the world was heading and decided it was time to go electronic. As I write these words, the pioneer is Baen Books with *Jim Baen's Universe*, but I'm sure by the time you read this (maybe a year from now) others will have joined the parade.

And I wouldn't be surprised to see some of the major houses start publishing novel-length science fiction online as well.

Will they have any trouble getting writers?

Not a chance. The online magazines can pay three and four times what the print magazines can pay, and the book publishers can easily offer 30-40% royalties, rather than the 10-12% most hardcovers pay and the 8-10% that usually goes to paperbacks.

How can this be?

Easy.

Let's take a print magazine. It sells, let us hypothesize, for $5.00, give or take a nickel.

What does it cost to get that magazine in your hands?

Well, first of all, the publisher has to buy the stories.

There's an office, which means an overhead.

There's paper for the magazines to be printed on.

There are color separations for the covers.

There is the cost of printing tens of thousands (formerly a couple of hundred thousand) of copies of the magazine.

There are shipping costs. The subscribers don't drive to the printing plant to pick their copies up. Neither do the distributors. Neither do the stores.

There are the distribution costs, both for the national and local distributors. They're good guys, but they don't place the magazines in the stores for free.

There are the stores themselves. If they sell a $5.00 magazine, most of them are going to want $1.75 or thereabouts for their trouble.

There are warehouse costs for those magazines that are neither sold nor pulped.

And a month later, every copy has vanished from the newsstands and bookstores, to be replaced by the next month's issue, and the publisher will never make another cent on that out-of-date issue.

Now let's take a look at how these expenses effect an electronic magazine.

There is no office expense and no overhead, because the editors work out of their houses.

There are no paper expenses, because the magazine doesn't appear on paper.

There are no color separations, because they simply post the artwork right on the screen.

There are no printing expenses, because the magazine is not printed.

There are no shipping costs, because the magazine is not shipped.

There are no national or local distribution costs, because they are not distributed. They're right there online, and they don't have to pay anyone to put the magazine in your physical proximity.

There is no cut for the bookstores, because the magazine is not sold in bookstores. Or newsstands. Or supermarkets. It's online. You pay the price, you get the magazine, and there are no middle men. (You might think about that. When you pay $5.00 for a digest magazine, the publisher might wind up with about $1.85 of it—and that'll be his average *only* if he sells the entire print run, which never happens, or even comes close to happening these days. You pay $5.00 for an electronic magazine, and the publisher *gets* $5.00.)

There are no warehouse costs, because the magazine exists in electronic phosphors, not paper pages. They'll post the next issue in another month or two, but this one won't be through earning money, because it will always be available for anyone who wants it.

Do you begin to see where the print magazines are at a bit of a disadvantage?

Now it should be clear to you why electronic publishers can outbid the print publishers for the writers they want. The print magazines are paying authors, overhead, color separations, paper, printing, shipping, national distributors, local distributors, bookstores, and warehouses.

And the electronic publishers? They're paying…authors. Period.

So of course they can triple or quadruple what the print magazines pay. (I assume we don't have to go over the whole thing again with books. Just cut to the last sentence: So of course they can triple or quadruple the hardcover and paperback royalty rates.)

Ah, but is there an audience out there in the vast electronic wilderness? After all, buying *The Da Vinci Code* or *The Shining* or *The Foundation Trilogy* from Fictionwise.com is one thing, but will computer users go for *new* science fiction? (The obvious answer is: certainly they will. An electronic story has already won the Nebula, and another one was just nominated for a Hugo the same week I am writing this. But those are voters, not masses of buyers, and you want numbers, right?)

Okay—numbers you want, numbers we got.

I'm a luddite, especially in a forward-looking community like science fiction writers and fans. Last summer I didn't even know what the word "podcast" meant. Then the young man who runs a website called *Escape Pod*, one of many such sites, bought reprint rights to some of my stories. I didn't give it another thought until he mentioned, a few months later, that the story of mine he had run most recently had received 22,000 hits in its first month online.

22,000 hits? The issue of the science fiction magazine it had appeared in had only sold 18,500 copies. More people *heard* my story online (or on their iPods) than *read* it.

I was sure it had to be an aberration. So when my next story, which was *not* a traditional science fiction story, but had been sold to a young adult anthology, came out, I waited two weeks and then asked how it was doing.

14,000 hits. In two weeks. For *me*. Not for Kevin Anderson or Anne McCaffrey or Robert Jordan or someone else who lives on the bestseller list.

That's when I knew beyond any doubt that the world was changing, that the readers are still out there in quantity, but they're not necessarily browsing the bookstores or the news-stands any more.

No sea change ever happens smoothly, especially not in as hidebound, old-fashioned and unimaginative a business as publishing. Some of the start-ups that look good today may be dead by the time you read this. But if so, others will take their place. There are 37 holes in the dike, and traditional publishers have only ten (figurative) fingers.

Like I said, I still love the feel of a book, the smell of an old pulp, the pleasure I get just from browsing a bookstore.

But I also can see the future coming at full speed, and I don't think anything's going to stop it. Certainly not me. I may not *like* reading electronic pages, but I'm editing an electronic prozine, and I'm selling to every podcaster I can find, and more than 200 of my books and stories have been sold as electronic reprints.

I'm not happy with electronic publishing. I probably never will be. But I'd be a hell of a lot less happy if I was left behind.

SCIENCE FICTION IN THE 1990S

Waiting for Godot...or maybe Nosferatu

For *Nebula Awards Showcase*, 2010

The science fiction field seemed to have no boundaries in the 1990s. Six figure advances no longer made headlines; seven figure advances were not unheard-of; there were even some eight-figure advances, this in a field where more than half the acknowledged classics had been written for two cents a word or less.

There was a time when science fiction movies were solely for the true believers. They were made up of guys in robot suits, scientists' beautiful daughters who couldn't get work in "A" movies, and painfully clumsy and obvious special effects. No more. By the end of the decade, more than a dozen of the top twenty all-time box office grossers were science fiction or related films, and mighty few A-list directors and stars didn't take a shot at one (or more).

There was a time—a lot of people don't remember it, and the younger ones usually don't believe it—when Star Trek was a dismal flop, when it hung out near the bottom of the Nielson ratings for the entire three years of its existence before the network, which had given in to Bjo Trimble's Save Trek campaign once, elected not to do so again. Move the calendar ahead, and counting animation there were over one hundred science fiction shows on television in the 1990s.

Things looked pretty rosy. The Old Wave/New Wave wars were over, the general public was discovering that we weren't all just writing that crazy Buck Rogers stuff, there were viable publishers everywhere you looked, and there was a constant influx of new, talented writers.

If you looked closely enough, there were some problems too. At the three-quarter mark of the century, there were something like seventeen New York houses with science fiction lines. We published more books in 1999 than 1975, far more....but there were only eight houses with science fiction lines (and in another decade there would be only six. That's not a lot of editorial taste to spread around.) The anthology market was incredibly healthy at the beginning of the decade, less so at the end. The magazines had been selling very well in 1990; by 1999 each had lost more than half its circulation, and a new title, *Science Fiction Age*, which was actually the bestselling of them all a year or two into its existence, was gone by the end of the decade.

There were a number of truly fine novels in the 1990s, but I don't believe any had the immediate classic status of predecessors such as *The Forever War*, *Dune*, *The Left Hand of Darkness*, *Neuromancer,* or *Ender's Game*. Still, there were some wonderful and popular novels, among them Lois McMaster Bujold's *Barrayar* and *The Vor Game*, Connie Willis's *Doomsday Book*, Nancy Kress's *Beggars in Spain* (an expansion of a now-classic novella), and the truly unique and important trilogy of *Red Mars*, *Green Mars,* and *Blue Mars* by Kim Stanley Robinson, each of which won a Hugo or a Nebula.

Speaking of awards, the decade was dominated by Connie Willis, who won 7 Nebulas and Hugos, and by 1999 was the all-time leader in both categories. Others to win three or more Hugos and Nebulas combined during the decade include Lois McMaster Bujold (4), Kim Stanley Robinson (3), Nancy Kress (3), Joe Haldeman (5), and your humble undersigned (4). Major work was also done by Robert J. Sawyer, Michael Swanwick, Greg Bear, Vernor Vinge, David Brin, Kristine Kathryn Rusch, James Morrow, Allen Steele, Ursula K. Le Guin, Harry Turtledove, Maureen McHugh, William Gibson, Neal Stephenson, and many others.

Among the editors, Gardner Dozois won 9 of the 10 Hugos given during the decade (there is no Nebula for editing), and Kristine Kathryn Rusch won the other. Among artists (where there is also no Nebula), Bob Eggleton walked away with 5 Hugos, while Michael Whelan and Don Maitz won 2 apiece, and Jim Burns picked up the remaining one.

We also had our share of very talented newcomers break into science fiction during the 1990s, including Kage Baker, Ted Chiang, Tobias S. Buckell, Michael Burstein, Nalo Hopkinson, Cory Doctorow, Kay Kenyon, Susan R. Matthews, Laura Resnick, Ellen Klages, Mary Doria Russell, Nicholas A. DiChario, Michelle Sagara West, Julie Czerneda, and many more.

We also lost our share of writers: gone were Isaac Asimov, Fritz Leiber, Roger Zelazny, Lester del Rey, Marion Zimmer Bradley, James White, Walter M. Miller Jr., Avram Davidson, John Brunner (who became the first writer or fan to die at a Worldcon), Bob Shaw, Judith Merril, Jo Clayton, Frank Belknap Long, Ed Emshwiller, Jack Finney, and more.

A number of our authors appeared regularly on the various bestseller lists: Robert Jordan, Anne McCaffrey, Terry Goodkind, Stephen Donaldson, Sir Arthur C. Clarke, Sir Terry Pratchett, Kevin J. Anderson (alone and in collaboration with Brian Herbert), Timothy Zahn, David Weber, and more. Dean Koontz, who used to write halves of Ace Doubles for $1,500 a shot, joined Stephen King as the two writers of the fantastic who belong to that tiny community of authors whose manuscripts command eight figure advances.

It was no longer difficult to get funding, or stars, or star directors, for science fiction movies. CGI has made it possible to put anything you can imagine on the screen, which we all thought would be a boon to the cinema…but I have come to the conclusion that it may be the very worst thing to happen to science fiction movies, because they can now throw so many mind-blowing images at you that more and more often the images are taking the place of plot and characterization.

This is not to say the audiences weren't pleased, and weren't willing to shell out multiples of $100 million at the box office. 1990's *Jurassic Park* took in a billion dollars by the time the DVDs were through selling. (It also asked you to believe that a hungry T. Rex cannot spot you from six inches away if you don't move.) The sequel, *The Lost World*, another megahit, suggests that a Tyrannosaur can catch an elevated train, but cannot catch a bunch of panicky tourists fleeing on foot in a straight line. *Armageddon*, which became Disney's top live-action grosser until Johnny Depp visited the Caribbean, asked you to believe that some not-very-bright wildcatters could become astronauts easier than highly-trained physically-fit astronauts could be taught to find and extract oil. *Starship Troopers* poured money into the production, but would have been better titled "Ken and Barbie Go to War." The long-awaited fourth *Star Wars* movie (or first, if you're into fictional chronology) was in profit before a single foot of film was shot, which was all for the best. *Terminator 2* and *The Matrix* had their moments, and the latter sported a stunning cyberpunk look, but I think at decade's end the two most artistically successful science fiction films were two of the least demanding and ambitious (which may well explain why), *Men in Black* and *Galaxy Quest,* a pair of delightful comedies.

(I have been discussing theatrical releases here. Actually, the best fantastic film of the decade was *The Wonderful Ice Cream Suit*, scripted by Ray Bradbury from his own story. It had charm, grace, poignancy and beauty in abundance—so of course it was released directly to video.)

I gave up on television in the early 1980s, and have not watched a single network series since then, so I asked a number of fans from my Listserv to suggest the best of the 1990s television shows, and it is their consensus that the following were the best of the lot: *Babylon 5, The X Files, Highlander, Star Trek: Deep Space 9, Star Trek: Voyager, Buffy the*

Vampire Slayer, Lois and Clark, Sliders, Xena, Third Rock from the Sun, and *Stargate SG1.*

As the decade drew to a close, no one was quite sure what was coming next. But with the advantage of hindsight, it's not too difficult to see that there were two major innovations between the end of the New Wave as a movement, and the beginning of the new millennium: William Gibson became the creator and the finest exemplar of cyberpunk; and Anne Rice decided that vampires, which had hitherto been unclean dead things that sucked away your lifesblood, were sexy.

The critics loved cyberpunk and snickered at vampire romances. Which is one more reason why we don't pay much attention to the critics. I doubt that there are three cyberpunk novels a year these days; I also doubt that there are less than ten vampire romances a week, and a lot of them live on the bestseller list. It's a billion dollar industry, and more and more science fiction publishers are starting to yield to the pressure.

I don't think anybody in the 1990s saw it coming. So much for science fiction's vaunted talent for prognostication.

THE CHILLY EQUATIONS

For *SFWA Bulletin*

I want to tell you about a story I read more than half a century ago, and just re-read this afternoon. I think you may find it kind of interesting.

There's a spaceship. It's a prototype, and its mission is such that it has to be totally stripped down. Its fuel has been measured to the ounce and/or the gram. The weight factor is so vital that not a single extraneous thing can be permitted onboard—not even so much as an extra sandwich or a hairbrush.

The mission is not going to be a long one. Every factor and every possibility has been carefully calibrated. There can be no errors, nor are any anticipated.

The ship takes off, and it isn't long before the pilot realizes that something is very wrong: it's using much too much fuel. It's only a few hours into the flight and the mission is seriously endangered.

The engines are checked for malfunctions. They're working perfectly. The fuel tanks are checked for leaks. They're airtight. The exterior is checked for damage by meteors or space debris. Its structural integrity has not been compromised.

The pilot goes down the list of possible causes, and finally he finds that the ship is carrying extra weight, maybe 120 pounds' worth. It's a stowaway, a beautiful girl—and an ugly problem. If he can't find 120 pounds' worth of things to jettison in one hell of a hurry, the mission—and quite possibly the ship itself—is doomed...but the ship had been stripped down to its essentials. There is absolutely nothing to jettison.

Except the girl.

With her onboard, nothing survives. Without her, the cold equations suggest that the mission will just barely succeed, but only if her weight is removed *quickly*.

And, amidst tears and regrets, the innocent stowaway is jettisoned into space.

The end.

Sound familiar?

Well, it probably should—*if* you were reading EC's *Weird Science #13* back in the summer of 1952. It was titled "A Weighty Decision," with Wally Wood supplying his usual fine artwork.

It wasn't identical to Tom Godwin's "The Cold Equations." There were three crew members (and none of them, after ten months of training, could perform either of the others' jobs, so none of them could be jettisoned). The ship wasn't delivering desperately-needed medicine. And the girl wasn't somebody's kid sister, but the pilot's fiancée.

But the thing that made the story go, the thing it hinged upon, the thing that made it memorable, was the cold equation that cost an innocent and lovely young girl her life.

"The Cold Equations" is probably the most-discussed science fiction story ever written, even more so than Heinlein's *Starship Troopers*. Not a day goes by that you can't find people talking about it on the internet, 56 years after it first appeared. It was a special story, no question about it.

But it wasn't the first to tell that special story. I suppose one could claim that Godwin wrote it without ever seeing the comic book, and quite possibly he did; I have no knowledge of that. But I would argue with anyone who says he wrote it *before* the comic book came out. The comic had a May-June, 1952 cover date, and the *Astounding* with Godwin's story had an August, 1954 cover date. Add in lag times, and does anyone seriously think John Campbell sat on that story for between 2 and 2 ½ years? (Yes, I know Godwin said Campbell put him through some rewrites, but surely not two years, or even six months, worth of them.)

Well, hell, people have only been discussing and arguing "The Cold Equations" for 56 years. Maybe this'll give 'em another year's grist for their mills.

TERRORISTS CAN'T HOLD A CANDLE TO BUREAUCRATS

For *You Did What?*

On September 11, 2001, terrorists rammed their stolen jet-liners into the World Trade Center, killing 3,000 people and changing the world forever.

They were amateurs.

Let's turn the clock back 101 years and 3 days, and move the locale from Manhattan to Galveston, Texas.

The United States government had a relatively new agency: the U.S. Weather Bureau. The same one you get on your cable TV, or that your local newscast quotes when telling you to wear your raincoat or your galoshes. *That* Weather Bureau.

It was a new science, forecasting the weather. Oh, people had been *predicting* the weather for centuries. See a hairy caterpillar in October? Bad winter coming. Did the June bugs show up in late April? Long dry summer on tap. You know the routine.

But now, in 1900, weather forecasting was finally recognized as a *science*. They used instruments. They studied the barometer. They contacted outposts in all directions to track storms. They were the newest of the new, these weather forecasters.

And they protected their turf.

We'll get back to them in a minute, but first let me tell you a little bit about Galveston, because these days it's dwarfed in its own home state by Dallas and Houston and San Antonio—but back then, in 1900, it ranked behind only Houston as the major city of Texas. Not only that, but in the entire country it was second only to New York City as an entry point for immigrants. In fact, it was nicknamed the "Western Ellis Island."

How big was it? Well, the population was always in flux due to immigration, but the best estimate was 30,000, give or take. The climate was pleasant, the land was lovely, property was inexpensive, and though it was on the water everyone knew it was safe from typhoons and hurricanes and the like. And if they didn't know, the Weather Bureau was only too happy to tell them so.

The shining light of the Galveston Weather Bureau was a gentleman named Isaac Cline. He was their superstar. Cline was quoted as saying that it was "an absurd delusion" for anyone to think Galveston could possibly ever suffer serious damage from a hurricane.

He based this conclusion on two erroneous beliefs: first, that any high surf or storm tide would flow over Galveston into the bay behind it and then into the Texas prairie, doing no lasting damage at all; and second, because of the shallow slope of the Gulf coastline, the incoming surf would be broken up and made much less dangerous.

Cline was so sure of this that he ridiculed the notion of building a sea wall to withstand storms, and because he was, for all practical purposes, the voice of the United States government on this particular subject, the wall was never built.

Now, the Weather Bureau was still in its infancy, but the people manning the Galveston division were pretty confident in their skills. Certainly more confident then they were of the skills of the Cubans they had defeated just two years earlier when Teddy Roosevelt led his Rough Riders up San Juan Hill. The Cuban weathermen *meant* well, decided the Galveston Weather Bureau, but after all, they were just illiterate peasants, right?

So when, on September 7, 1900, Cuba began reporting that the biggest storm anyone had ever seen was heading right toward Galveston, the Weather Bureau was so sure they were totally mistaken and panicking needlessly that they refused to make the Cubans' warnings public.

After all, everyone *knew* that Galveston couldn't suffer serious damage from a storm. Either it would turn away before reaching shore, or it would pass right over and blow itself out somewhere over the vast Texas prairie.

But by the morning of September 8, it became apparent to Cline and his co-workers that the storm *wasn't* going to turn away and miss Galveston. In fact, it was apparent to everyone in the city. All they had to do was look to the south and east and see what was approaching.

Should they evacuate the city, they wanted to know.

Certainly not, Cline and the Weather Bureau assured them. This is Galveston, not some shanty town that's likely to get blown away by a strong wind. Our houses are well built, we're sitting right on the slope of the Gulf coastline, and haven't you ever seen a thunderstorm before?

So the people—most of them, anyway—trusted their government bureaucrats and stayed put.

At least until the water became knee-high, and then waist-high, and then neck-high. Pretty soon those who hadn't fled the town were perched on their roofs.

And pretty soon after that there weren't any roofs, because the houses began collapsing, and boats capsized, and bodies—infants and the elderly at first, then men and women in their primes—began floating down the streets, through the windows, over the vanished roofs.

And still the storm continued.

At one point a train from Beaumont entered the town, but halted well short of the station. The passengers wanted to leave and find some high ground, or at least some roof-tops, for safety. The conductors, hearing the reassurances of the Weather Bureau, urged the passengers to remain where they were. After all, this was a *train*, a massive thing of steel. Surely no storm can harm it or wash it away, and you don't have to take *our* word for it; just ask the Weather Bureau.

Ten passengers looked out the window, said, in essence, "Bullshit!," and waded and swam through the rampaging water to try to find some safe haven. 85 passengers believed the bureaucrats of the Weather Bureau and stayed with the train.

By the next morning, all 85 were dead.

I should add that this wasn't entirely the fault of Cline and his Galveston bureaucrats. They were in contact with a branch of the Bureau in the West Indies, which was anxious to show up the Cubans—their recent enemies—and to prove that these Spanish peons were pressing the panic button needlessly.

Of course, back in Galveston, by the time it became clear that, if anything, the Cubans were *underestimating* the danger, no one could find the panic button. It was hidden under tons of water.

So did help rush in, as Americans have always helped their own and others?

Nope.

You see, Cline was in control of the forecasting, but his immediate superior, Willis Moore, was in control of the whole damned Galveston Bureau, and Moore was more concerned with Galveston's—and his Bureau's—image than with saving citizens that he had convinced himself weren't really in all that much danger to begin with. So a call for help never went out.

The city's newspapers colluded with the Bureau, and downplayed the story. In fact, an unpublished editorial in the *Galveston Tribune* the morning after the storm hit assured the public that there was very little danger from the storm, and "no possibility of serious loss of life."

Why (I hear you ask) was it unpublished?

Because the press floated out to sea before the issue could be printed.

All the phone and telegraph wires were dead by 4:00 PM, and Galveston was effectively cut off from the rest of the world. By 7:00 PM the winds were over 120 miles an hour, and some were as high as 200 mph before midnight. Contact wasn't re-established with Galveston for another 28 hours, until 11:30 PM on September 9. In the interim, the closest any train had been able to approach the city was 6 miles. Anything beyond that was too dangerous.

When it was over, it was estimated that Galveston had lost between 3,000 and 4,000 houses and buildings.

It was always going to lose them. The people were something else again. If the bureaucrats of the Weather Bureau had simply told the truth, had shared the information they'd been sent from Cuba, had not been so pig-headed in their certainty that no storm could ever damage Galveston...

No one knows exactly how many people died in New York on September 11, 2001. The best estimate is 3,000, out of a population of more than seven million. That comes to four ten-thousandths of one percent.

No one knows exactly how many people died in Galveston on September 8 and 9, 1900. The best estimate is 10,000, out of a population of about 30,000. That comes to 33 percent.

Terrorists can't hold a candle to bureaucrats.

ME AND LUCIFER

Lucifer Jones was born one evening back in the late 1970s. I was trading videotapes with a number of other people—stores hadn't started renting them yet, and this was the only way to increase your collection at anything above a snail's pace—and one of my correspondents asked for a copy of H. Rider Haggard's African adventure classic *She*, with Ursula Andress, which happened to be playing on Cincinnati television.

I looked in my *Maltin Guide* and found that *She* ran 117 minutes. Now, this was back in the dear dead days when everyone knew that Beta was a better format than VHS, and it just so happened that the longest Beta tape in existence at the time was two hours. So I realized that I couldn't just put the tape on and record the movie, commercials and all, because the tape wasn't long enough. Therefore, like a good correspondent/trader, I sat down, controls in hand, to dub the movie (which I had never seen before) and edit out the commercials as they showed up.

About fifteen minutes into the film Carol entered the video room, absolutely certain from my peals of wild laughter that I was watching a Marx Brothers festival that I had neglected to tell her about. Wrong. I was simply watching one of the more inept films ever made.

And after it was over, I got to thinking: if they could be that funny by accident, what if somebody took those same tried- and-true pulp themes and tried to be funny on purpose?

So I went to my typewriter—this was back in the precomputer days—and wrote down the most oft-abused African stories that one was likely to find in old pulp magazines and B movies: the elephants' graveyard, Tarzan, lost races, mummies, white goddesses, slave-trading, what-have-you. When

I got up to twelve, I figured I had enough for a book…but I needed a unifying factor.

Enter Lucifer Jones.

Africa today isn't so much a dark and mysterious continent as it is an impoverished and hungry one, so I decided to set the book back in the 1920s, when things were wilder and most of the romantic legends of the pulps and B movies hadn't been thoroughly disproved.

Who was the most likely kind of character to roam to all points of Africa's compass? A missionary.

What was funny about a missionary? Nothing. So Lucifer became a con man who presented himself as a missionary. (As he is fond of explaining it, his religion is "a little something me and God whipped up betwixt ourselves of a Sunday afternoon.")

Now, the stories themselves were easy enough to plot: just take a traditional pulp tale and stand it on its ear. But anyone could do that: I decided to add a little texture by having Lucifer narrate the book in the first person, and to make his language a cross between the almost-poetry of *Trader Horn* and the totally fractured English of *Pogo Possum*, and in truth I think there is more humor embedded in the language than in the plots. (And as the series extended to more books, his language became a little more fractured too.)

Lucifer, bless him, isn't the brightest bulb in the lamp. Upon seeing Lord Carnavon's caravan bringing the contents of King Tut's 3,000-year-old-tomb to Cairo, only he could ask, "Just settling the estate now, are they?"

Because this was a labor of love, I also started putting in a bunch of references that would be clear only to a tiny segment of the audience. For example, in *Adventures* Tarzan is Lord Bloomstoke, the name Edgar Rice Burroughs originally chose for him before changing it to Lord Greystoke. Every character in Casablanca is named after a car, in honor of Claude Rains (Lt. Renault) and Sydney Greenstreet (Signore Ferrari) from the movie *Casablanca*. A number of the details were historically accurate: Bousbir really *was* the biggest whorehouse in the world in 1925, there really *was* a nude painting of Nellie Willoughby hanging over the Long Bar in the New Stanley Hotel in the 1920s, the Mangbetu really *were* cannibals, and so on.

Then, since I had leaned rather heavily on the pulps for my plotlines, I started borrowing characters from the B movies: The Rodent is a thinly-disguised Peter Lorre, Major Dobbins is Sydney Greenstreet, the Dutchman is Walter Slezak, and so on; every one of my favorite 1940s scoundrels made it from the screen to the page.

Finally, I needed a con man who was even better at his job than Lucifer, lest the book end too soon, and so I came up with Erich von Horst, who makes very few appearances—everyone else in a Lucifer Jones book keeps showing up time and again in the oddest places—but lays a number of economic time bombs across the continent that Lucifer keeps encountering at the least opportune moments. In fact, halfway through the fifth book (where I am as I write this), von Horst has made more appearances than any other character.

The most fun I ever had in my life was the two months that I sat at the typewriter working on *Adventures*. I've done books of more lasting import, and I've created characters of far more depth and complexity, but during that period I fell, hopelessly and eternally, in love with Lucifer Jones.

I sat on it until I was well-established at Signet, which was publishing all my science fiction novels at the time. They didn't quite know what to do with it, so they sat on it for a couple of years and finally released it in 1985, labeling it Science Fiction, which it most decidedly is not, and implying on the cover that the Honorable Right Reverend Doctor Lucifer Jones was just another adventurous version of Doctor Indiana Jones, which he most certainly is not.

The book came out, did all right but never really found its audience, and vanished a year or two later. A few mainstream newspapers found it—one New York reviewer called it the greatest parody of the adventure novel ever written—but for the most part it didn't make any waves.

I had plotted out five more Lucifer Jones books, one on each continent (each, like *Adventures*, would end with the various national governments acting in concert to kick him off that particular land mass). *Exploits* takes place in Asia from 1926 to 1931, and includes an Insidious Oriental Dentist, a Chinese detective with too many sons, a hidden kingdom where no one grows old, an abominable snowman, a seductive criminal known as The Scorpion Lady, and the like. *Encounters* takes place in Europe from 1931 to 1934, and boasts vampires, werewolves, the theft of the Crown Jewels, the discovery of Atlantis, the Clubfoot of Notre Dame, and similar. *Hazards* takes place in South America from 1934 to 1938, amid all its lost cities, tropical jungles, and strange religious rites. *Voyages* has Lucifer island-hop from South America to Australia, finding lost treasures, a giant ape, naked goddesses along the way, and he also gets to explain why it's not really his fault that the Japanese bombed Pearl Harbor. And finally there will be *Intrigues*, set in Australia and Antarctica, at the end of which he will have been barred from every land mass in the world.

I had it all planned out when I finished *Adventures*—except that Signet decided they didn't want anything but true-blue science fiction, and at the time I had no other publishers. Over the next few years I moved over to Tor and Ace, and while I still longed to get back to Lucifer Jones, I was turning out serious, prestigious, award-winning stuff at all lengths, and it never occurred to me to ask if anyone was interested in him. In point of fact, I thought I was the only person who even remembered Lucifer Jones.

Until 1991, when Brian Thomsen of Warners asked me to write a book for him. I explained that I would love to—Brian and I had been friends for years, and I'd always wanted to work with him—but I was under contract to both Tor and

Ace, and between them they held options for all my science fiction.

"But I'm free to sell Lucifer Jones," I added, half expecting him to ask who the hell Lucifer Jones *was*.

"I *loved Adventures*!" exclaimed Brian, and we were in business.

Warners decreed that for the price they were paying me—I was considerably more valuable then when I'd written *Adventures* they needed considerably more than a dozen of Lucifer's adventures. So I wrote *Exploits* and *Encounters*, handed them in, and called it *The Chronicles of Lucifer Jones*.

And that was it for eleven years. Then Bill Schafer of Subterranean Press asked for me to resurrect Lucifer, and he's been running him in almost every issue of *Subterranean Magazine*. When I'd finished a dozen South American episodes, he collected them as *Hazards*, and as I write these words I've done seven of the episodes for *Voyages*.

I've received more acclaim for other things I've written. I've won five Hugos, and I have more than one hundred trophies, scrolls, certificates and the like in my trophy room. And if someone told me I could keep them or keep writing Lucifer Jones stories but not both, I'd kiss them all good-bye without a second thought.

Lucifer remains my favorite of all my characters. I love him, and I hope after reading this book you will too.

HOPE FOR THE COLOR-BLIND

For *Black Gate*

Three of my five favorite films—*The Maltese Falcon*, *Casablanca*, and *Mask of Dimitrios*—have one thing in common: they're in glorious black-and-white.

The American Film Institute polled its members in 1998 and again in 2007. The poll topper for the best film ever made, both times, was *Citizen Kane*. And yes, it's in black-and-white.

The other day mystery writer/editor Ed Gorman and I were discussing some of our favorite films over on Facebook, and of course many of them were black-and-white. Irish science fiction editor John Kenny joined the discussion, and told us that his kids won't watch any black-and-white film. A number of other parents had the same complaint. It reminded me of an incident about a decade ago, when I was teaching at Clarion, and David Barr Kirtley handed in a story titled "The Black Bird," about 90% metaphor and 100% brilliant. (I later bought it for an anthology I was editing.) We had a class of 19. Since he was the writer David's opinion didn't count, but the total was that two of the students loved the story and 16—the 16 youngest—didn't. It occurred to me to ask for a show of hands: how many of them had actually seen *The Maltese Falcon*? Two hands went up—the two who liked the story. I asked the other 16 why they hadn't watched this classic, which is on somewhere almost every week. The answer, from all of them: it was in black-and-white.

So before these brilliant films, and the opportunity to watch them, get swallowed up by history, I thought I'd point out some excellent fantasies, as well-made (or better) than any $70 million full-color travesty playing in the theaters today. Here they are, in no particular order:

Portrait of Jennie (1948). This is adapted from Robert Nathan's novel, which managed to stay in print for three-quarters of a century. Joseph Cotton is a struggling painter; he has skills and technique, but there's simply no soul, no *feeling*, in his paintings. One night he is wandering through the park and runs into a little girl, maybe seven or eight years old, named Jennie. They talk, and he is charmed by her (in a non-pedophile way). A few nights later he runs into her again—only now she's maybe eleven. And every few nights he meets her, and each time she's older, trying (as she explains) to catch up to him. He is captivated, and begins painting her portrait. Jennie, who is played by Jennifer Jones in one of her better performances, tells him details of her life, and he realizes that she was a little girl maybe 30 years ago. Gradually, as she changes from a girl to a young woman, he falls in love with her, and the portrait finally begins showing the one quality that was missing in his previous paintings. He tries to learn more about her, and discovers that she died about a quarter century ago in a boating accident. He rushes to the scene of the accident, not sure this all hasn't been a dream, and arrives just too late to save her—but his feelings for her translate into the painting that makes his reputation, the "Portrait of Jennie."

* * * *

Miracle on 34ᵗʰ Street (1947). A charming fantasy in which one of those bell-ringing Santas you see on every street corner and store front in December turns out to be the *real* Santa. Edmond Gwenn plays Santa, a very *very* young Natalie Wood plays a girl who believes in him, and the film's a delight from the beginning right through the trial where the government can't prove he *isn't* Santa, and the Post Office settles the issue once and for all.

* * * *

The Canterville Ghost (1944). Charles Laughton plays Sir Simon de Canterville, a 17th Century nobleman who flees to his castle to avoid a duel to the death. As a punishment for his cowardice, his father seals him in the room where he is hiding, and curses him to spend all eternity as a ghost, unable to rest in his grave until a descendant performs an act of heroism. Move the clock ahead past three centuries of cowards, and we come to the latest descendant, Cuffy Williams, a cowardly U.S. soldier played by Robert Young. It takes a 6-year-old noblewoman, Margaret O'Brien, to bring matters to a happy solution.

* * * *

The Ghost and Mrs. Muir (1947). A young widow, played by Gene Tierney, inherits a seaside cottage that is haunted by the ghost of a roguish sea captain, played by Rex Harrison. When her sources of income dry up, it's Harrison to the rescue, dictating his obscenity-laced and salacious memoir to her. She manages to sell the manuscript, begins to make a living in publishing, and the romance between Mrs. Muir and the ghost continues to grow. Finally, an old lady, she breathes her last—and suddenly there is the ghost, waiting for her, and hand-in-hand they go out through the front door and wander off together into the mist.

* * * *

The Devil and Daniel Webster (1941) From Stephen Vincent Benet's Pulitzer winner, and re-released as *All That Money Can Buy*. Jabez Stone, a local farmer, has two kinds of luck: bad and worse. In desperation, he sells his soul to Mr. Scratch (the devil, played by Walter Huston) to keep his farm, then realizes what he's done and gets the best lawyer in the country, Daniel Webster (played by Edward Arnold), to plead his case to keep his soul before a jury consisting of corpses and ghosts who are all in Satan's thrall. Undeterred, Webster goes to work, and in the climax delivers such a brilliant and passionate oration that even the dead, soulless jury votes in favor of his client.

* * * *

Death Takes a Holiday (1934)y. A real oldie, and it still moves people. Frederic March plays Death, who can't understand why people fear him so, and he comes to Earth in human form to find out. And he falls in love. And no one dies, not even the thousands of people who are in utter agony and *should* die. And eventually he must make a choice: stay with the woman he loves, or leave her and go back to work so that people can die once again.

* * * *

Topper (1937). Taken from the bestseller by the fantastic humorist (or humorous fantasist) Thorne Smith, this is the story of George and Marion Kirby (Cary Grant and Constance Bennett), who drive recklessly once too often and die in a crash. Since they have lived a totally useless life, consisting mostly of drinking, carousing, and partying, they find themselves not in heaven or hell, but in limbo. To ascend to the higher level, they must do a good deed, and they decide to help their friend, Cosmo Topper (Roland Young). Problems ensue when Marion falls for Topper, George gets jealous and vengeful, Topper's wife is not amused, and the story goes from one outrageous scene to another before it's finally resolved.

* * * *

I Married a Witch (1942). Another fantasy/comedy taken from a Thorne Smith novel, this time *The Passionate Witch*, which was completed by Norman Matson when Smith died suddenly while writing it. This one stars Frederic March as a candidate for governor and Veronica Lake as a resurrected witch who falls in love with him, helps him with the governorship, and undergoes numerous changes from witch to woman to ghost and back again before there's a satisfactory conclusion.

* * * *

Topper Returns (1938) is the third Topper movie (the less-than-inspired *Topper Takes a Trip* was the second). It once again features Roland Young and Billie Burke as Cosmo Topper, but this time there is no George and Marion Kirby (the married ghosts), but rather a murder victim, Joan Blondell, who wants to solve her own murder in time to prevent her friend Carol Landis from being murdered. And if that sounds too serious, remember that these are Thorne Smith's characters.

* * * *

Lost Horizon (1937). Directed by Frank Capra, this story of a lost land of eternal youth stars Ronald Coleman and Jane Wyatt, and if you don't know story, what are you doing reading *Black Gate*? (But just in case: an airplane is hijacked and lands in the Himalayas, and is taken to Shangri-La, an idyllic valley where everyone lives in peace and no one ever grows old. Coleman's hijacking turns out not to have been an accident or a crime; the High Lama is finally dying of old age after hundreds of years and has chosen Coleman as his successor. Circumstances lead Coleman to leave with his brother and a woman from the village, who soon ages and dies once beyond Shangri-La's border. They are rescued by a search team that's looking for them, but Coleman soon eludes them and after seemingly endless searching, sees Shangri-La in the distance and heads for it.

* * * *

The Picture of Dorian Gray (1945). Taken from the Oscar Wilde story, this stars Hurd Hatfield as Dorian Gray, a handsome young man who is totally corrupt. He has his portrait painted, and as his sins and debaucheries continue, his face remains unmarked, but the portrait, which he hides in the attic, becomes uglier and uglier. Eventually a shred of conscience convinces him to stab the portrait with a knife, and as the portrait is destroyed, he himself dies, as the two were somehow linked. Nice supporting cast of Angela Lansbury, George Sanders, Peter Lawford, and Donna Reed.

* * * *

The Bishop's Wife (1947). A charming fantasy, in which an Anglican bishop (David Niven), who has ignored family and friends in the attempt to plan and build an elaborate new cathedral, has reached a dead end, and prays for guidance—and lo and behold, here comes Dudley (Cary Grant), an angel sent to help him. Dudley instantly charms everyone else in Niven's household—his maid, his daughter, even his wife—but Niven is no closer to getting his cathedral, and very soon it appears that Niven's wife (Loretta Young) is falling for Dudley. Finally Niven lies and tells Dudley that funding and designs for the building have arrived, his prays were answered, and Dudley can go away. Dudley doesn't quite believe it, and Niven realizes that he's probably lost his wife without having gained his cathedral. When he admits that his wife means more to him than the cathedral, Dudley reappears to tell him that his prayer has been answered. No, not that he'll get his cathedral, but that he realizes what's important in life. "But I asked for a cathedral," says Niven. "No," says Dudley, "you asked for guidance." And now he has it.

* * * *

The Seventh Seal (1957). Not all black-and-white fantasies have to be made before 1950, and not all have to come from the United States. This 1957 Swedish classic by Ingmar Bergman takes place during the Black Plague, and features the most famous chess game ever filmed, between a knight (Max von Sydow) and Death, with the knight's soul as the stakes. The film ends with a very solemn and very memorable dance of death.

* * * *

Dracula (1931). So okay, *Dracula* is an antique. It creaks. It's overwritten and overacted and underachieved. But it has the definitive Dracula of the first three-quarters of a century of filmmaking, as portrayed by Bela Lugosi. It wasn't until Frank Langella's version that the image of Dracula changed, and people realized he could be articulate, speak without an accent, and be sexually appealing to women of all ages. Prior to that, every performance in every vampire film owed something to Bela.

* * * *

King Kong (1933). I know some people consider King Kong a science fiction film rather than a fantasy, but they are people who never heard of the square-cube law, and haven't figured out what all these multi-ton carnivorous dinosaurs found to eat on that tiny island. It's a fantasy through-and-through, and it ends with one of the half-dozen classic lines in film history, right up there with "Frankly, my dear, I don't give a damn," and "Louie, I think this is the beginning of a beautiful friendship." "It was beauty killed the beast" takes a back seat to none of them. Yeah, the special effects were a little shaky, but I've yet to hear anyone call either of the remakes a classic.

* * * *

It's a Wonderful Life (1946). This Frank Capra film is probably (and by far) the most-watched black-and-white fantasy in history. George Bailey, after a life of doing good deeds for others, is dead broke and has all kinds of problems, and decides to end it all. His bumbling guardian angel beseeches him not to. George mutters that he wishes he'd never been born. The angel shows him with the lives of all the people he's helped, all the people who love him, would be like if indeed he never had been born. Totally moved, George pleads for his life back, rushes home to the town and family he loves, and finds that they—and life—are repaying him on this Christmas Eve.

* * * *

There are many more, of course. I haven't even touched on the black-and-white fantasy musicals, which include *One Touch of Venus* (a riff on Thorne Smith's *The Night Life of the Gods* with music by Kurt Weill); *I Married an Angel* (a wry, almost cynical Rodgers and Hart show); *Cabin in the Sky* (a delightful all-black musical); and more.

So the next time your kid says "Humphrey who?" or "Whoever heard of someone spelling her name 'Bette'?" buy or rent him one of these black-and-white fantasies and show him what he's been missing. And if you're under 35 or 40, take a look yourself.

Who knows? You may discover a whole new interest.

THE MAU MAU REBELLION

For Bill Fawcett's *How to Lose a War*

It must have looked so easy.

They surveyed the situation and probably said to each other: "There are six million of us, and only a few hundred of them. We know the territory and they don't. We are an army and they are farmers. How can we lose?"

They found out.

* * * *

It began with the land, as it almost always does in agricultural societies. The finest farmland in Kenya is the area in the vicinity of Mount Kenya and the Aberdares Mountains. The Kikuyu, Kenya's dominant tribe, had been living there for as long as anyone could remember.

Then Kenya became a British colony. The farther we get from the era of colonization, the more difficult it is to understand why any European country felt it had the right to colonize (*i.e.*, dominate and economically plunder) an African, South America or Asian country, appropriate the land, and impose their laws and religion on the populace, but no one gave it a second thought prior to the last few decades of the 20th Century. Indeed, Sir Winston Churchill, considered a pillar of fair play and democracy, did nothing to harm his reputation by giving a famous speech in which he declared "I will not preside over the dissolution of His Majesty's empire." Which is to say, "I won't return control of their land, their government, and their economies to the people who live in the countries we have appropriated."

Clearly, this is not an attitude designed to win friends and influence people in the lands you have colonized, and sure enough, by the early 1930s most Kenyans, and especially the Kikuyu, were starting to get uppity notions of freedom. The British didn't help much. They appropriated most of the Kikuyu homeland, which became known as the "White Highlands," a term that told one and all who could own farmland there and who, by omission, could not. The colonizers imposed a hut tax, a tax on each dwelling, which could only be paid in British currency—and the only way to get British currency was to work on now-British land for British farmers. By 1948, the ever-expanding White Highlands constituted more than eighty percent of the Kikuyu homeland, and employed more than one hundred and twenty thousand Kikuyu, who had no other way to raise the money required for the hut tax than to work on land they had previously owned and for which they had never been compensated. A huge number of Kikuyu opted to move to Nairobi, doubling its population during the decade of the 1940s, and turning almost all of it except the area of tourist hotels and restaurants into an enormous slum.

A few Kikuyu decided that there must be some means of gaining redress, and led by Harry Thuku they formed the Kenyan African Union. No one paid it much attention. There were hardly any members, they had no means of reaching the bulk of the people, they were not allowed to carry arms or even spears, and if this let them blow a little steam off, why, it probably eased the tensions.

Except that more than a few people listened, and one of them was a brilliant and charismatic man named Jomo Kenyatta. He had gone to Europe to school, and he understood not only how colonialism worked but also how to organize a political party. He proceeded to do this all during the 1940s. The British would ignore him for awhile, then ban whatever party or group he was forming.

But discontent kept spreading. Kenyatta may have been the impetus, but it soon reached far beyond his control. The Kikuyu formed secret societies, administered terrible oaths to each other, murdered those who would not take those oaths, and brought swift death to those who took but ignored their oaths (one of which had to do with killing any Kikuyu who *didn't* take the oath). They paralyzed Nairobi for nine days with a general strike that was broken only by a massive display of British force. The leaders, of course, were arrested and imprisoned.

Kenyatta and his less radical followers sought political change without threatening violence. It was an exercise in futility. Kenyatta wanted twelve black Kenyans added to the Legislative Council that ran Kenya. Instead, the British Colonial Secretary reorganized the government as follows: the handful of white settlers got fourteen representatives, the hundred thousand Asians got six, the twenty-five thousand Arabs got one. And the six million black Kenyans? They got five, all named not by themselves but by the white government.

Radicals tried to wrest control of the Kenyan African Union from Kenyatta, but he outmaneuvered them, still hoping for a political solution. He was the public face of Kenyan unrest—but a bunch of private faces got tired of waiting, and started killing Kikuyu who were loyal to the British.

By 1952 the movement had a name—Mau Mau—and a purpose: to drive the British back to Britain. They torched some houses, mutilated some farm animals, and killed some more black loyalists. The British were sure

Kenyatta was the movement's leader, and they brought him to trial on what proved to be trumped-up charges. You are the leader of this subversive group that calls itself the Mau Mau, accused the British. I do not even know what "Mau Mau" means, was his honest reply. The British gave him a seven-year prison sentence to think about what it meant. He was put into a small cell in Kapenguria in the arid Northern Frontier District, a place that had no rail or phone communication with the rest of Kenya, and that, thought the British, was that. A State of Emergency had been declared the day Kenyatta was arrested, eight thousand Kikuyu were arrested within the next month, and when Kenyatta (who would later become Kenya's first president) was found guilty it was assumed the danger was over.

Memo from the Kikuyu to their colonizers: Welcome to the real world. The first European was killed three weeks after Kenyatta was incarcerated.

* * * *

The problem, of course, was that only Kenyatta really understood what his people were up against.

For example: if you are fighting a war, you want to win the hearts of the people, to gain support for your cause. If you find someone is undecided as to which side is right, you talk to him and convince him that you are fighting for the right.

But the Mau Mau never tried to convince anyone to join them. What they did was *terrorize* people into joining. If you spoke out against the Mau Mau, if you mentioned that you were content working for the British, you were as likely to be speared to death or hacked to death with *pangas* in broad daylight as to be ignored. If you converted, it was not because of the arguments of the Mau Mau, but rather the knowledge of the consequences if you *didn't* convert.

So while they had a country of six million, most of whom had no use for the British and wanted to be free, a huge majority was terrified of them. The populace may not have loved the British, but they weren't afraid of them either.

* * * *

The next thing you want is a brilliant field commander, a Douglas MacArthur or a Tommy Franks, especially when you are outnumbered and outgunned.

What they got were a bunch of countries.

Let me explain that. Most of the Mau Mau generals were as uneducated as their followers. They wanted names that would impress the rank and file, and being uneducated they were unaware of names like Alexander and Caesar and Napoleon. So what you got was General China, and General Tanganyika, and a bunch of General some-other-countries. It's doubtful than any of them except General Tanganyika could find their namesake on a map. In fact, it is doubtful than many of them could even read a map, which does make it difficult to plan a campaign.

They felt safe in the mountains, so they set up headquarters there. The problem is that it meant climbing down the mountain every time they engaged in a military action—and it also meant, once it was known where they were hiding, that all the British had to do was station men at the base of the mountains to cut the Mau Mau supply lines.

The one general who kept his own name was Dedan Kimathi, and he led the British a merry chase through the

Aberdares mountain range for a couple of years. He used the mountainous terrain to stay hidden, but when you're hiding on a relatively unpopulated mountain, you're not presenting much of a military threat until you come down off it—and of course the British were waiting for him at the base of the mountain.

* * * *

Speaking of unpopulated mountains, let's talk about the battlefield terrain for a moment.

Where was the enemy?

Most of them were in Nairobi, Mombasa, and other cities. Once the British realized that they were up against a military operation, no matter how poorly organized, they fortified the cities and the Mau Mau never made any successful forays against them.

In the course of four years the Mau Mau actually killed very few colonists. Farm fields tended to be flat and out in the open, and everyone was on the alert. Most farmers kept guns, dogs, and loyal Kikuyu on hand to hold off any attacks.

So who *did* the Mau Mau attack?

With the white settlers and the cities too well-protected, they went after the loyalist Kikuyu. They mutilated them, they chopped them to ribbons, they killed them wherever they found them—and then they wondered why they had so much trouble recruiting soldiers to their cause.

* * * *

When it became obvious that they didn't have the sheer force of arms to win, they decided to try something a little different. They would attack with such savagery, such brutality, such barbarism, that the British, being a weak and civilized race, would be convinced that they no recourse in the face of such horrible things but to go home.

Well, they convinced the British, all right: they convinced them that they couldn't leave the colonists to face such hideous attacks.

They convinced someone else, too: a tabloid columnist, who spent most of his adult life hanging out in fancy New York nightclubs, reporting on the comings and goings of local celebrities, a rival to Walter Winchell. His name was Robert Ruark, and all his life he'd wanted to take a safari. So he took one in the late 1940s, loved it, and started going back every year—and began to see what the Mau Mau were capable of. So he gave up being a gossip columnist and sat down and wrote the one of the bestselling novels of the decade: *Something of Value*. It was the story of the Mau Mau, told from the twin viewpoints of a second-generation white colonist to whom Kenya is the only home he's ever known, and a Mau Mau terrorist. The hideous blood oaths, the animal and human mutilations, the utter callousness of the Mau Mau campaign were all presented in vivid detail in the novel.

It is said the Mau Mau assumed America, which had overthrown the yoke of British colonialism 175 years earlier, would rush to the Kikuyu's side, or at least send them money and weapons. The only conclusion one can draw is that none of the Mau Mau leaders ever read Ruark's novel, or understood the effect it had on a few million Americans who had no other knowledge of Kenya.

It had an effect on one Englishman, too. When they rushed the film (starring Rock Hudson and Sidney Poitier) into production, there was a brief introduction by Sir Winston Churchill, explaining to each of the millions of moviegoers that the Mau Mau depicted in the film were real, and if anything more dangerous than Ruark made them seem.

So much for foreign aid.

* * * *

Okay, if you can't outmaneuver them and you can't out-recruit them, then the next best thing is to outgun them.

The colonists all had firearms. Most had powerful rifles. Once the British military showed up, they had assault weapons, all-terrain vehicles (which certainly didn't hurt when hunting the Mau Mau at 10,000 to 15,000 feet of altitude on Mount Kenya and in the Aberdares), they even had airplanes. (Bombs dropped from the planes into heavy cover on the mountains killed a lot of Mau Mau. They also killed a lot of elephant, rhino and buffalo, and more than their fair share of smaller animals too.)

What did the Mau Mau have to combat this?

Well, they stockpiled weapons for a year before the uprising, and when it began they possessed 460 precision-made firearms, spread over a country somewhat larger than the state of Ohio. They mostly came armed with spears, *kibokos* (a whip that cuts to the bone, made from treating and stretching the private parts of a male rhino), *simis* (short swords), and *pangas*, which were actually farm tools but which functioned as machetes for the Mau Mau.

They realized that they were outgunned, so they established a couple of secret "factories" where they created more guns. Problem is, most of them exploded when fired, and accounted for ten times as many Mau Mau deaths and injuries as British.

* * * *

Okay, so you're trying to infiltrate the enemy's society (in this case the enemy being anyone who hasn't taken the Mau Mau oath), not only to find out what the British are planning, but also to hide from the British army. After all, if they find you walking around Mount Kenya with a spear and a *panga*, they pretty much know who and what they're dealing with.

The trick, of course, is not to let your men be caught or arrested, because once they're incarcerated, there's no telling who might collaborate with the enemy, and what they might say.

So how did the Mau Mau fare in this respect?

Let me give you some figures.

On October 30, 1952 the British arrested 500 suspected Mau Mau.

On November 25, 1952 they arrested another 2,000.

On April 17, 1953 the British rounded up and arrested another 1,000.

It gets worse.

On April 24, 1954 the British arrested 40,000 suspected Mau Mau and sympathizers.

By October, 1955 some 70,000 suspected Mau Mau and sympathizers had been incarcerated, and huge camps had to be built to hold them.

Were they all Mau Mau?

Of course not.

Were enough of them Mau Mau that the British were able to get the intelligence they needed about the leadership and the military movements?

Absolutely.

So much for keeping your men out of enemy hands.

* * * *

Well, what else is left?

One of the things most Americans were surprised to learn during World War II was that despite George Patton's aggression, despite the number of battles he fought and won, his men suffered very few casualties compared to those under other leaders. The man was a brilliant general, and he took care of his troops.

You'd have to say if you're outmanned, outgunned, and outmaneuvered, the very best thing you can do is preserve what you have in the way of manpower and not waste the lives of your troops.

How did the Mau Mau fare under the leadership of General China, General Tanganyika, *et al*?

When the dust cleared at the end of hostilities in 1956, more than a thousand Mau Mau had been hung by the British military. It's estimated that over 50,000 Kikuyu were killed. Probably 15,000 or so were Mau Mau, another 15,000 were loyalists killed *by* the Mau Mau, and the rest just got in the way.

And how much damage did this army which shocked Churchill, angered Ruark, and terrified the British and Americans, inflict on the enemy?

Less that one hundred white colonists were killed during the four years of the Emergency.

* * * *

So let's consider it one more time: how do you lose a war?

- You go up against an enemy with superior firepower
- You fail to protect your supply lines
- You fail to rally the people to your side
- You fail to protect your troops
- You choose uneducated, inadequate military leaders

- You lose the propaganda war
- You are under-financed

If you ever wanted to write a text book on all the myriad ways to lose a war, you could do a lot worse than study the Mau Mau rebellion.

WINGS O'BANNON RIDES AGAIN

If there's one kind of book I like as much as science fiction, it's the hardboiled private eye novel, especially as practiced by Raymond Chandler, Dashiell Hammett, and Ross MacDonald.

While I was writing my series of tongue-in-cheek fantasy detective stories featuring John Justin Mallory (*Stalking the Unicorn*, *Stalking the Vampire*, *Stalking the Dragon,* and half a dozen novelettes), I had presented Mallory with legitimate (if fantastic) problems to solve, and I couldn't descend into parody, much as I would have loved to.

But each of the novels has a number of appendices, fictional bits and pieces related but peripheral to the main story, and about a third of the way through 2008's *Stalking the Vampire* I saw a way to do my parody after all. Mallory is always, through plot machinations, attracting well-meaning but not very helpful sidekicks, and in this case it was a dragon named Nathan Botts who wrote hardboiled mysteries on the side under the pseudonym of "Scaly Jim Chandler."

As the novel proceeds, Nathan—whose fictional hero is Wings O'Bannon, and whose last O'Bannon book sold 651 copies worldwide—is constantly taking notes on Mallory's methodology, and just as constantly explaining the difference between O'Bannon and the disappointing (to him) Mallory. O'Bannon beds a gorgeous woman every chapter, never asks for information when he can beat it out of a bad guy, and, like Mickey Spillane's Mike Hammer, has an oversexed secretary named Velma. (Mallory has a 63-year-old gun-toting partner named Winnifred).

Eventually the dragon starts writing *his* version of the adventure they're on, also titling it *Stalking the Vampire*, and when Mallory's adventure was over, I decided to display the start of Botts' version in one of the appendices, which the illustrious Mr. Lillian is now letting me share with you.

Stalking the Vampire
by Scaly Jim Chandler

(excerpt)

She was prime stuff. She had long blonde hair, cool blue eyes, curves in places where most broads didn't even have places, and only the floor stopped her legs from going on forever. I looked at that full heaving neckline, and figured if she heaved it just a little harder I could catch it without getting up from my chair.

"You were recommended to me, Mr. O'Bannon," she said.

"Was it Fifi?" I asked. "Fatima? Bubbles? Mitzie?"

"Malcolm Burke," she said.

"Oh," I replied. "So it's business."

"I'm in desperate trouble, Mr. O'Bannon!"

"Call me Wings," I replied.

"I'm being blackmailed, Mr. O'Bannon!"

"Wings," I said.

"All right—Wings," she said. "You've got to help me."

"What seems to be the problem?" I asked.

"It's so humiliating."

"Yeah, it usually is," I said. "You want a hit from the office bottle?"

She shook her head. "I am Mrs. Wilbur Carlisle..." she began.

"Are we talking about *the* Wilbur Carlisle?" I asked. "The eccentric reclusive millionaire?"

"Yes." Then: "Well, no, actually. He's a billionaire."

I frowned. "Isn't he something like 75 years old?"

"98," she corrected me.

"If we add your 38-22-36 all together, he's still got you beat by a couple of years."

"Wilbur and I are very much in love," she assured me.

"He's probably mistaking you for your great-grandmother," I suggested.

"Are you going to help me or insult me?" she demanded.

"I thought I was insulting your husband," I said. "But let's get down to business. I get seventy-five a day plus expenses."

"Agreed."

"Velma—that's my secretary—is on her lunch break," I told her. "I'll have her draw up a contract when she gets back."

She pulled a handful of C-notes from her purse and held them out to me. "Will this be enough, Mr. O'Bannon?"

"Wings," I said, taking the cash and sticking it in a vest pocket. "Yeah, it'll do fine. Now suppose you tell me about your problem."

"We were at a high society party," she said. "Do you know the Cuthbertson-Smythes?"

"How many of them are there?" I asked.

"Just two."

"All right," I said, "fill me in. All my experience has been in low society."

"We were all drinking and laughing and having a fine time," she said. "And then…well, I guess I must have drunk more than I thought, because I can't remember another thing."

"Sounds like someone slipped you a Mickey Finn," I said.

"Is that his name?"

"Whose name?" I asked.

"I guess I'd better explain. You see, I woke up in a strange hotel room—and there was a dead man on the floor. His throat had been slit from ear to ear. Is *he* Mickey Finn?"

"Probably not," I said. "And someone's blackmailing you, threatening to expose you as a murderess?"

She shook her head. "He was a nobody. Wilbur could have bought the police off in a minute, if anyone even cared who killed him."

"I can believe it, Mrs. Carlyle."

"My name is Moira," she said.

"If you don't mind sharing a hotel room with a stiff, I fail to see what your problem is, Moira."

"That was yesterday." She reached into her purse. "Today I received *this* in the mail." She pulled out a plain manila envelope, but didn't offer it to me.

"I get plain manila envelopes in the mail all the time," I said. "Usually girlie magazines, sometimes bills."

"This contains some very humiliating photographs of me with a man I've never seen before," she said. "If Wilbur saw them…"

"He'd throw you out?" I suggested.

She shook her head. "He'd get so excited he might keel over with a heart attack."

"Let's have 'em," I said, reaching my hand out.

"I'm too embarrassed to show them to you."

"I've got to know what they are before I can do anything about it."

She walked around the desk. "I'm ashamed to show you the pictures. I'd rather just show you what I did."

"That's less embarrassing than the photos?" I asked.

"My hair was a mess," she explained, slipping out of her clothes.

She was a Moira, all right, with an emphasis on the "Moi." I slid my hand down her back, over the lush smooth curve of her hips, and

[censored]

"Oh!" she moaned. "Don't stop!"

[censored]

"Oh God God God!" she breathed.

[censored, next three pages of manuscript burned, octogenarian proofreader hospitalized]

"Okay, Moira," I said, fixing my tie. "I'll be in touch."

"Again?" she said hopefully.

"By phone," I said.

She looked like someone had run over her pet chimera with a car—probably a Mercedes convertible with gull-wing doors, or maybe a Lambroghini, given the circles she traveled in—and undulated out of the office.

"Can I come in now?" Velma's sultry voice came through the side door.

"Why not?" I said. "Have you been there long?"

"Long enough to be jealous," she said, slinking into the room.

"You could have joined us," I said.

"You have a filthy mind, Wings," she chided me.

"Yeah, but I clean under my fingernails," I shot back.

"So is she your new client?" she asked.

"Yeah, looks like it."

"What's her problem?"

"I'll show you," I said, reaching out for her. Her blouse came away in my hand.

"Velcro," she said. "It was getting expensive, replacing all the clothes you're always ripping off me."

"And some people still think I didn't hire you for you brains," I said as I grabbed her and pulled her to me.

An hour later we began getting dressed again.

"Wow!" said Velma, her face still flushed. "That's some problem!"

"That's why she came to me," I said. "She's being black-mailed."

"Blackmail is an ugly word," said Velma with a shudder that would have had most men baying the moon.

"So is *myxophyceae*," I said. "But *myxophyceae's* not against the law except in Albania."

The phone rang and I picked it up. For a moment all I could hear was the sound of heavy breathing.

"It's for you," I said, offering the receiver to Velma.

"No, it's for you, Shamus!" said a voice at the other end of the phone. "It took me a minute to catch my breath. I had to beat an old lady to the phone booth."

"Why don't you get a cell phone?" I said.

"You gonna listen or you gonna criticize?"

"Who am I talking to?" I asked.

"Don't worry about that now," said the voice. "I got an important message for you."

"If it's that important, use Western Union and stop keeping little old ladies from calling their grandkids."

"Listen to me and listen good, Shamus!" said the voice. "We're gonna be watching your every move. Don't take the Carlisle case or you're a dead man."

"Carlisle who?" I asked innocently.

"You know," said the voice. "She's the dame who…" It took him half an hour to finish describing what was going on in the photos, by which time I was breathing as hard as he was, and he was drooling so much that he finally shorted out his phone.

"Who was it, Wings?" asked Velma, who was sitting at her desk reading a gossip magazine.

"Just another death threat," I said with a shrug.

"That's your ninth this week," she noted.

"Yeah," I said. "Business has been slow." Then I did some serious thinking. "Listen, Angel," I told her, "I've got to start working on the Carlisle case before she asks for her retainer back, and I don't need any interference from a bunch of hired gunsels, so I think we're going to outsmart them."

"How?" she asked, wide-eyed with wonder.

"I've got an extra suit in the closet," I said. "I want you to get into it, wear my hat, and go for a nice long walk in the park. They'll think it's me, they won't shoot as long as you're not following leads for Mrs. Carlisle, and that'll leave me free to operate."

"It'll never work, Wings," said Velma.

"Why not?"

"Because I'm a 44-D," she said, taking a deep breath and thrusting back her shoulders.

"No problem," I said. "My chest is 44 normal and 46 expanded."

"Gee!" she said with a smile. "Maybe it'll work after all."

"Right," I said. "Anyone approaches you, just grunt, lower your voice, and talk about baseball. They'll never spot the difference."

"You're a genius, Wings," she said admiringly.

"Hey, thinking is my business," I said. "Getting shot at all the time is just for exercise."

It took her about five minutes to change into my suit, and then she left by the front door. I waited another ten minutes, then cut out the back way.

I knew that my first order of business was to find out who had taken the photos. There weren't more than six, maybe seven thousand professional pornographers in town, plus another twelve thousand talented amateurs, which mean I had my work cut out for me, hitting porn studio after porn studio, beating time with all the naked oversexed girls until the photographers had time to speak to me. Still, it *might* prove distracting; there were probably as many as twenty of the girls I'd never met before.

Then I started doing the math, and realized I'd never hit all the pornographers before I ran through my retainer, so even though it wasn't going to be as much fun, I decided that the easiest way to get the job done was go have a chat with Blind Benny, who works the ritziest part of town, tin cup in hand.

It took me about twenty minutes to get there, and it wasn't long before I heard Blind Benny begging for alms while adding saying that he'd also settle for any bill that had Ben Franklin's or Andy Jackson's likeness on it.

"Hi, Benny," I said, walking up to him and giving Buster, his guide dog, a friendly pat on the head.

"Hiya, Wings," he said, studying me through his dark glasses. "You're looking well."

"Yeah," I replied. "I haven't had a shoot-out in a week. How are things with you?"

"Just trying to get used to this new dog," said Blind Benny.

"Isn't that Buster?"

"Nah. I sold Buster to some guy who needed him for an art film."

"I thought you loved that dog," I said.

"Loving dogs is another union," said Blind Benny. "I *liked* him. Still, this guy paid through the nose for him. I guess he planned to make a killing off that rich Carlisle broad, and—"

"*Moira* Carlisle?" I interrupted.

"Unless there are two knockouts married to billionaires named Carlisle," said Blind Benny.

"Where can I find him?"

"Carlisle? Penthouse of the Diamond Tower."

"No, the guy who bought your dog."

"It's kind of complicated," said Blind Benny, pulling a pen and a sheet of paper out of his pocket. "I'd better draw you a map."

"He won't be using it," said a voice from behind me.

I spun around and found myself facing two tough-looking gunsels.

"I never saw a tail," I said, surprised.

"We didn't follow you," said the taller of the two.

"Then what are you doing here?"

"We took a cab," he said. "Everyone knows that whenever you need information you come to Blind Benny."

"Right," said the shorter one. "You think we don't read your books?"

"You do?" I said, surprised.

"Everyone does," said the shorter one. He pulled a copy of *The Bloody Corpse Cries Foul* and walked up to me. "Would you autograph it?"

"Sure," I said, reaching for a pen.

"Could you say 'To Vinnie, the one man I was always afeared of'?"

"You got to excuse my partner," said the taller gunsel. "He ain't never got past third grade. It's 'the one man I was always ascared of.'"

"I *liked* third grade," said Vinnie defensively.

I scribbled an inscription and handed it back to him.

"I can't read your signature," said Vinnie, peering at it.

"That's okay," I told him. "I didn't write it anyway. I thought everyone knew that Scaly Jim Chandler writes them."

"*That's* why it's so good!" exclaimed the taller gunsel.

"I really appreciate this, Wings," said Vinnie. "It almost makes me sorry about what I got to do next."

He slugged me in the belly, and as I doubled over he cracked me over the head with a club I hadn't even seen in his hand.

I spat blood. It tasted salty. The salt invigorated me, and I caught Vinnie with a roundhouse left, but before I could follow up his partner had sapped me from behind with a blackjack. I started seeing images of Velma with her clothes on, so I knew they'd done me some serious damage. I came up swinging, catching Vinnie with a right to the jaw and Blind Benny with a left to the solar plexus.

"What the hell are you hitting *me* for?" he demanded.

"When I have time for aimed shots, you'll be the first to know," I grated through torn lips.

The blackjack caught me on the side of the head again, and as I fell to the ground Vinnie and his partner began covering my unprotected body with kicks that would have done a soccer player proud. Time after time one foot or another would crunch into my face. I felt the cartilage in my nose give way, and I heard the sharp *crack!* as my jaw broke.

Finally Vinnie pulled out a pistol and aimed it at me.

"You can't say you wasn't warned, Shamus," he said, pulling the trigger. Five shots buried themselves deep in my liver and spleen.

That did it. Before I'd merely been annoyed. Now I was *mad*.

THE DEAN

He is the unquestioned Dean of Science Fiction. He doesn't just *know* the history of the field; he is the living history of science fiction.

He's Jack Williamson, of course.

When Hugo Gernsback created the first science fiction magazine, *Amazing Stories*, back in 1926, he filled it by reprinting H. G. Wells, Jules Verne, and Edgar Rice Burroughs. But sooner or later he had to have new material if the magazine was to survive, and this Williamson kid was just the ticket. Jack's "The Metal Man" appeared in the December, 1928 issue, and his career was off and running. 77 years later it hasn't appreciably slowed down.

Jack was there when Gernsback lost control of *Amazing* and started all the Wonders—*Wonder Stories*, *Air Wonder Stories*, and *Science Wonder Stories*. He was there when the much-loved but destitute *Weird Tales* finally got a budget. He was there for *Startling Stories* and *Thrilling Wonder Stories* and *Marvel Science Stories* and *Future* and all the other pulps. And he was there as a mainstay of the two major magazines that truly shaped the field, *Astounding* and *Unknown*.

When the book publishers finally discovered us, Jack was there with novels for Fantasy Press and Gnome Press. When New York decided we weren't an overnight sensation (it only took them a quarter of a century to come to that conclusion), Jack sold to Simon & Schuster and Doubleday. When the mass market paperback companies began building their lines, Jack was there, selling to Ace and Avon and Lancer and Berkley and all the rest.

Jack's career pre-dates the Hugo Awards by 25 years, but that didn't stop him from winning them. The original version of the book you are holding in your hands won a Hugo for

Best Related (*i.e.*, non-fiction) Book, and at the ripe young age of 93 Jack won a Hugo for Best Novella.

Jack pre-dates the Science Fiction Writers of America (which he served with distinction as its President) by 37 years—but that didn't stop him from being given SFWA's Grandmaster award, the second writer (behind Robert A. Heinlein) ever to receive the lifetime commendation.

Not a paltry list of accomplishments, you'll have to admit. And the reason I'm dwelling on them, rather than on the remarkable man who achieved them, is because you're about to meet him in the pages up again, and he present himself more honestly and forthrightly than anyone else can. A lot of science fiction writers have written their autobiographies, which are usually just expanded versions of "…and then I wrote… and then I sold…"

Maybe that's why Jack's was the first to win a Hugo Award. It is a true autobiography, and when you're finished you'll know at least as much about this fascinating and beloved man as you do about his bibliography.

BLOOD AND CIRCUSES: THE UGANDA-TANZANIA WAR

For Bill Fawcett's *How to Lose a War*

He was a clown with a difference—when he wasn't busy amusing the press, he killed some 300,000 of his own people and invaded a neighboring country. Even the war had aspects of a circus.

He was Idi Amin, of course. As a young man he had enlisted in the Kenyan army, and had actually become its heavyweight boxing champion. When he returned to his native Uganda, he rose rapidly in the military, and when he could rise no higher, he overthrew Dr. Milton Obote, who was no Lincoln-in-the-making, and became President in 1971.

Obote fled next door to Tanzania, where the President of that nation, Julius Nyerere, gave him sanctuary—and when Amin decided it was easier to kill off his political opposition than win them over to his side with compelling arguments, Nyerere also offered sanctuary to some 20,000 Ugandans who were fleeing for their lives.

All this took place during the first two years of Amin's reign.

Amin, for reasons a lot of us have yet to comprehend, was the darling of the Western press—at least for awhile. But in bits and pieces, Uganda's darker secrets began coming out. He turned government buildings into mass torture chambers. He began committing genocide on any Ugandans who were not from his own tribe. He erected a statue of Adolf Hitler in the middle of the capital city of Kampala, declaring the Fuehrer to be his hero. Though Uganda's economy was pretty much run by, and dependant upon, Indians, Amin kicked them all out of the country. Then, when the economy tanked and inflation skyrocketed, he invited them back—only to kick them out (and appropriate their property and their businesses) a second time. He couldn't afford to feed his army, so he allowed them to poach their meals in the game parks. It's said he even practiced cannibalism on his own infant (or unborn; the accounts differ) son.

He was just a real sweetie.

It took him seven years to bankrupt the country, kill off a sizeable portion of its population, get rid of every Indian, get rid of every technocrat, and go a few billion dollars into debt. Then, just to be on the safe side, he converted to Islam in case he ever had to leave in a hurry; according to the tenets of the religion, no other Moslem could turn him away or fail to offer him sanctuary.

As you may have guessed, not every Ugandan was thrilled with the situation. In 1978, the Malire Mechanized Regiment mutinied, and others followed suit. Then the crack Simba Battalion joined them. They actually mounted an attack on the Presidential lodge in Kampala, but Amin escaped by helicopter.

Amin then sent those troops that were still loyal to him after the mutineers. Many mutineers were killed; the survivors fled across the border into Tanzania, where Julius Nyerere was still providing sanctuary for Milton Obote and 20,000 others.

Amin's subjects were getting restless as the decade drew to a close. It was okay to kill a few rivals, but Big Daddy (the Western press's nickname for him) had carried things too far. At the rate he was going, pretty soon he'd be the only Ugandan left alive. They also weren't thrilled with the fact that it now took twenty million Ugandan shillings to purchase what you could buy with fifteen shillings before Amin took over. Streets, buildings, everything was in disrepair, though Amin lived in obscene luxury.

It has become traditional that no African leader ever criticizes another. It makes sense: most of them are corrupt dictators who attained their offices through murder, revolution or rigged elections, and if Dictator A criticizes Dictator B, why, he leaves himself open to similar criticism, and honest criticism is not what any African dictator wants.

There were only two leaders in all of Africa who constantly spoke out against Amin, and not surprisingly, they were the two who weren't dictators. One was Sir Seretse Khama of Botswana, who was secure in his British knighthood and the fact that he was almost two thousand miles from Uganda. The other was Julius Nyerere, known to his people as Mwalimu—"the teacher"—and he was Amin's next-door neighbor.

So when Amin concluded that the Simba Battalion and the others might start giving his troops and his citizenry too many bothersome ideas about freedom, or at least about replacing him with another dictator, he decided to divert attention by following the few escapees of the rebellion into Tanzania.

That began one of the most futile wars ever waged on the African continent.

Now, on Amin's behalf, there were extenuating circumstances: he was barely literate, and had apprenticed as a boxer, a cannibal, and a genocidal maniac. Along the way, he had totally overlooked his education as a field general.

The first thing he did was annex seven hundred square miles of an area known as the Kagera Salient. The second thing he did was blow up the only bridge across the Kagera River, which certainly slowed any advance Nyerere's army might make, but didn't do a lot for any Ugandan troops who were forced to retreat.

And forced to retreat they were. Nyerere was able to put together a 40,000-man army on the spot: soldiers, policemen, national service, whatever. Within a month the non-dictator had rallied enough of his countrymen to expand the army to 100,000.

Amin took one look at what was facing him across the border, realized his army had never been tested in combat—killing children, old women, and unarmed men didn't really count—and decided he needed some help. So he contacted fellow Islamic dictator Muammar Qadhafi of Libya, who sent a couple of thousand well-trained heavily-armed troops.

Should have made a difference, right?

Well, the Libyan troops get on the front lines, ready to duke it out with the Tanzanians, and what does Amin's army do?

As the Libyans move south to face Nyerere's soldiers, Amin's army starts looting and raping its way north, stealing the Libyans trucks to hold all their plunder. In the process, they managed to spread the HIV virus, which was previously confined to southwest Uganda, throughout the whole country.

Nyerere's army was supported by 20,000 Ugandan exiles, and picked up more every day as they defeated the small handful of Libyans and marched toward Kampala. Suddenly there were other armies as well. There was one commanded by General Tito Okello, who would followed Amin and the restored Obote as Uganda's third consecutive incompetent dictator. And there was Yoweri Museveni, Uganda's president for the past couple of decades, who eventually threw Okello out of office by leading what was literally a children's army, the adults all having been slaughtered during the previous three administrations.

But that was in the future. Amin took a look at the situation, and saw the handwriting on the wall: his own retreating army was doing more damage to Uganda that the conquering army would do, Qadhafi had been burned once and wasn't about to send any more troops, and no other dictator would come to his aid. What was he to do? How was he to save his ass?

Finally he came up with a solution that could have occurred to no one else.

He called a press conference. You probably wouldn't believe it if I didn't give you an exact quote:

"I am keeping fit so that I can challenge President Nyerere in the boxing ring and fight it out there, rather than having the soldiers lose their lives on the field of battle." He suggested that Mohammed Ali would be the perfect referee, and since he, Amin, was a former boxing champ and outweighed the 57-year-old Nyerere by at least one hundred pounds, he would fight with one arm tied behind his back and his legs shackled with weights.

(I feel compelled to tell you that I am not making this up.)

The press loved it. No one took it seriously, least of all Nyerere. After all, he *was* a small, thin man with no athletic experience—and more to the point, it wasn't *his* soldiers that were dying.

His men marched on Kampala in April of 1979 and Amin fled to Libya. Ever the opportunist, he began plotting to overthrow Qadhafi, who gently urged him to find another sanctuary or die, and he wound up his life in exile at a luxurious estate in Jiddah, Saudi Arabia.

He took one brief vacation from Arabia during his later years. Convinced that his people would welcome him back after the equally bloody and inept reigns of Obote and Okello, he got as far as the Ugandan border, dead certain that he would be made President again by acclamation. President Museveni refused to allow him to cross the border, no one came to his defense, and, totally disillusioned, he went back to live out his life in Arabia.

What can an historian learn about the Uganda-Tanzania War?

- After invading your enemy over a river, don't burn your bridges behind you (to coin a phrase).

- Don't pay your soldiers with worthless money.

- Never give poorly-trained and untested troops access to vehicles while a battle is going on.

- Sometimes converting to a new religion isn't enough.

- Don't challenge skinny little intellectual wimps to boxing matches—or if you do, make sure that the outcome of the war doesn't depend on their being dumb enough to agree.

Uganda is a wonderful, beautiful country. It's said that if you spit a peach pit out of the window of your car and come back a month later, there will be a peach tree growing there. Most of the hippos, elephants, buffalo, and gazelles have come back from the army's butchery, and so, finally, have the people—no thanks to Big Daddy. History still hasn't decided if he was Africa's bloodiest madman or the continent's most idiotic clown.

Me, I vote for both.

AMERICAN SCIENCE FICTION IN 2009

For *Science Fiction World* (China)

There have been a number of major changes in American science fiction. There was a time when almost every New York mass market publisher had a science fiction line or imprint; today it's limited to about half a dozen houses: Tor, Baen, Ace and Roc (both owned by the same company and edited by the same woman), DAW, Eos, and Ballantine/del Rey and Bantam/Spectra (which are owned by the same German conglomerate and seem to be in the process of merging.)

However, as the New York market have become less numerous, a number of viable "medium presses"—different from the traditional "small press" in that they pay a living wage—have appeared, including Pyr, Subterranean, Golden Gryphon, Night Shades, Tachyon, and a few others.

The world of the short story has changed even more radically. The three "major" digest magazines still exist: *Asimov's*, *Analog,* and *Fantasy & Science Fiction*, and a recently deceased magazine, *Realms of Fantasy* has been resurrected. But that's still only four printed magazines. The change has come on the internet, where there are 15 electronic magazines paying what SFWA (Science Fiction Writers of America) considers a professional word rate—and three of them, *Jim Baen's Universe, Subterranean Magazine*, and *Clarkesworld*, pay more than any of the printed magazines and are attracting more major writers every day.

But as the world continues to change, so does the field of science fiction. Podcasting has become very popular. I know that I had a Hugo-winning short story, "Travels With My Cats," in an issue of *Asimov's* back in 2005, and that issue sold only about 18,000 copies. I then re-sold the story to Escape Pod, a podcast web page, where it was heard by 54,000 people in its first month—and it's still available four years later, whereas the issue of *Asimov's* was off the stands and could not be found after a month.

Books are now being sold to audio producers, both as CDs and as downloads, and that market is expanding enormously. Amazon.com just paid $300 million for Audible.com, a producer of audio books for download, so it seems safe to surmise that it's a viable market for the foreseeable future.

A small start-up company called Fictionwise.com began in 2000 A.D., buying reprint rights to novels and short stories, buying nothing original—and recently sold its 100 billionth word.

The latest innovation is creating digital copies of books exclusively for mobile media—iphones and other cell phones.

So as I said, the market is growing by leaps and bounds, even in a poor economy.

Movies have helped, of course. I think of the 20 top-earning motion pictures in American history, 15 of them are science fiction or related (*i.e.*, fantasy, horror, etc.) And that prepares each new generation of kids and young adults to go out and buy science fiction and fantasy books and magazines.

Of course, J. K. Rowling's *Harry Potter* books have helped as well, selling an average of 25 million hardcovers each. And lately there is a popular trend of which I disapprove, but which does bring more readers to the field, and that is the vampire (or paranormal) romance.

There are approximately 200 science fiction conventions a year in America, some incredibly large (over 100,000 attendees), some incredibly small (under 100 attendees). The Worldcon still gives out the coveted Hugo Awards, and usually draws from 4,000 to 8,000 attendees.

Locus, the acknowledged newspaper of the science fiction field, keeps an annual tally of award winners. Here is where they stand in 2009:

Tallying all awards *and* polls for short fiction, Mike Resnick leads, adding to his awards tally 6 *Science Fiction Chronicle* poll wins, 5 *Asimov's SF* readers' poll wins, and 1 win each from Hayakawa and Locus magazine polls.

TOTAL WINS

32	Mike Resnick
30	Harlan Ellison
29	Connie Willis
24	Ursula K. Le Guin
23	Greg Egan
21	George R. R. Martin
20	Lucius Shepard
19	Ted Chiang
17	John Varley
15	Neil Gaiman
14	Nancy Kress
13	Robert J. Sawyer, Robert Silverberg, Michael Swanwick, James Tiptree, Jr.
12	Stephen Baxter
11	Poul Anderson, Joe Haldeman, no award, Kristine Kathryn Rusch, Dan Simmons
10	Terry Bisson, Kelly Link, Allen Steele

* * * *

Tallying all awards for short fiction, Mike Resnick leads. Like Robert J. Sawyer he was a favorite of HOMer voters (9 wins for short fiction); he's also done well with Hugo Awards voters (5), and has also won two Ignotus awards, and once each the UPC and Nebula awards.

Total Wins

19	Mike Resnick
18	Connie Willis
15	Harlan Ellison

13	Ted Chiang
12	Ursula K. Le Guin
11	George R. R. Martin, no award, Robert J. Sawyer
10	Poul Anderson
9	Terry Dowling, Fritz Leiber, Robert Silverberg, Roger Zelazny
8	Greg Egan, Joe Haldeman, Nancy Kress, Lucius Shepard, James Tiptree, Jr., John Varley
7	Greg Bear, Neil Gaiman, Margo Lanagan, Kelly Link, Dan Simmons, Michael Swanwick

* * * *

This table shows cumulative tallies for fiction writing—nominations and wins for novels, short fiction, poetry, single-author collections, (though not screenplays), and for achievement awards for lifetime or new writing—for all awards and polls compiled in this Index.

Total Wins

53	Ursula K. Le Guin
46	Connie Willis
43	Harlan Ellison
36	Mike Resnick
34	Neil Gaiman, George R. R. Martin
33	Dan Simmons
32	Greg Egan
31	Robert J. Sawyer
29	Orson Scott Card, Joe Haldeman, Stephen King, Lucius Shepard
27	Robert Silverberg
26	John Varley
23	Poul Anderson, Gene Wolfe
22	Fritz Leiber, no award
21	Isaac Asimov, Ted Chiang, Larry Niven
20	Stephen Baxter
19	Lois McMaster Bujold, Ramsey Campbell, Arthur C. Clarke, Kim Stanley Robinson
18	Bruce Boston, David Brin, Robert A. Heinlein
17	Greg Bear, Terry Dowling, Frederik Pohl
16	Ray Bradbury, Peter Straub, Michael Swanwick, Vernor Vinge, Sean Williams, Roger Zelazny
15	Nancy Kress, James Tiptree, Jr.

14	China Miéville, Tim Powers
13	Anne McCaffrey, Michael Moorcock, J. K. Rowling, Kristine Kathryn Rusch, Jack Williamson
12	Brian W. Aldiss, Michael Bishop, Christopher Priest, Geoff Ryman
11	Catherine Asaro, Michael F. Flynn, Kelly Link, Garth Nix, Andre Norton, Allen Steele, Neal Stephenson, J. R. R. Tolkien, Kate Wilhelm, Robert Charles Wilson
10	Clive Barker, Terry Bisson, Samuel R. Delany, Elizabeth Hand, Joe Hill, James Patrick Kelly, Margo Lanagan, Richard Matheson, Ian McDonald, Terry Pratchett, Spider Robinson, Clifford D. Simak, Bruce Sterling, Jack Vance, Jane Yolen

* * * *

Total Nominations

In sum, the field is still viable, still producing important and enjoyable novels and short stories (and the art seems to get better every year). If books are selling a little less, part of it is doubtless due to the economy—but the other part is due to all the new platforms: audio, podcasting, digital distribution, and all the other things that science fiction has been predicting and preparing us for.

WESTERN STEAM

For *Steamed!*

I had sold more than 60 science fiction novels and 250 short stories, but I had never written any steampunk when Lou Anders, my editor at Pyr, asked me to do a Weird Western with steampunk overtones back in late 2009.

All my adult life I had wanted to write a novel about Doc Holliday and Johnny Ringo, bitter rivals who happened to be the only two college-educated gunslingers in the West (Ringo majored in the classics, Holliday minored in them), and while this wasn't quite the novel I'd had in mind, I couldn't pass up the chance to write about them in *The Buntline Special.*

But of course, nothing about Holliday and Ringo was the least bit steampunkish. (By the way, I'm using the word "steampunk" because that's the accepted term. I don't think I agree with it, since any punk who shows up in a Resnick story dies young and unmourned.)

So I needed a justification to insert the steampunk elements, and since this was a Weird Western, as much fantasy as science fiction, I came up with the premise that the United States as a nation stops at the Mississippi River in 1881, its western expansion halted by the magical power of the Indian medicine men.

Who would the United States government turn to in order to come up with some methodology to combat the magic? Given the dates of his major breakthroughs, it had to be Thomas Alva Edison.

So I moved Edison out to Tombstone, Arizona in 1880 at government expense. Then I asked myself: what would Tombstone look like after he'd been there for awhile?

Well, for one thing, the streets would be illuminated by electric lights as night. So would the houses, the saloons, the dance halls, and just about everything else. But what else would Tom—he'd never be called "Thomas" in a town like Tombstone—do?

Well, for one thing, most of my principals lived by their weapons. Historically Ned Buntline commissioned the Colt Company to make the Buntline Special—but with a genius like Edison out there, why wouldn't he go to Tom instead? After all, a Colt pistol, even with the 12-inch barrel Buntline ordered, just fires bullets. But what could an electrical genius design in the way of a hand weapon?

Then there would be primitive (by our standards) but wildly advanced (for 1880) security systems. Step on a porch that was properly wired and a cowboy or gunman would set off alarm. And Tom did a lot of work with photography in the 1870s, so he'd probably add a hidden camera or two that would be activated by an electrical impulse caused when an unwanted visitor put his weight on a hidden wire.

The days of Billy the Kid or Doc Holliday being broken out of jail by their confederates would be relegated to works of fiction. Tom would rig an electric charge into the metal bars of the jail. Try to free your criminal cohort and you'd still have one hand left to sign your name.

Because this was a work of imaginative fiction, I felt I could get just a little far-fetched and esoteric, having Tom design some very lifelike and functional prosthetic limbs, since many arm and leg wounds required amputation at that time—and eventually he designs some fully functional robot-ic prostitutes, which lead to some moral (but non-electronic) dilemmas.

He'd have to team up with someone who could construct a horseless stagecoach to his specifications, but Tom certainly was enough of an electrical genius to create a motor to power one once it was built.

More? There'd be electrified wires around a corral to give cattle or horses a mild shock if they tried to get out. (I had the same thing when my daughter had a horse while she was growing up. One little jolt and he learned instantly.)

Because this was a novel about Doc Holliday and Johnny Ringo, I never got into the wonders Tom could bring to the frontier kitchen of the 1880s, but there's no question that he would have revolutionized it. The photograph was a *fait accompli*, and so was the phonograph, so there was no need to expand upon them. Ditto his very early work with the fluroscope.

Because steampunk seems to require a lot of brass to appeal to its readership, I had Tom form a partnership with Ned Buntline, who historically was just a self-promoting dime novel writer and publicist, but in this universe has created a form of super-hardened and impenetrable brass, and brought many of Tom's creations off the drawing board and into actual physical being. And having changed Buntline's occupation, I had Tom design lightweight body armor for Doc and the Earps before the Gunfight at the O.K. Corral, which Ned then created.

Nothing except the robots was extrapolated that wasn't at least theoretically possible, given the amazing Mr. Edison's historical accomplishments, and it gave a very different and steampunkish flavor to a town that has lived a lot longer in fact and in legend than any of the participants could have imagined.

MY FAVORITE FRED POHL BOOK

With Jim Frenkel's kind permission, I'm going to tell you about my favorite Fred Pohl book, which is neither a solo novel nor one of the collaborations with Cyril Kornbluth. Nope, my favorite—and I re-read it every few years—is *The Way The Future Was*, and covers Fred's life up to 1978, which is why it is fortunate that the subtitle is "A Memoir" and not "An Autobiography."

It is, of course, an extremely readable book, as all of his books are. But more to the point, it is an *important* book, for in truth only Fred and Damon Knight have written about the Futurians in depth, and it's important to know who they were and what they were like, because except for John Campbell's stable, they *were* science fiction. That bunch of kids and young men, most of them social maladroits, did more to shape science fiction and fandom than other group.

Who were they? Just some youngsters who wanted to take over the field, and except for Don Wollheim and Isaac Asimov and Cyril Kornbluth and Robert A. W. Lowndes and Judith Merril and James Blish and Virginia Kidd and Damon Knight and of course Frederik Pohl, why, most of them never amounted to all that much as science fiction writers and editors.

Fred was the multi-talented one. Wollheim and Lowndes scribbled a few stories, but they were primarily editors. Asimov and Kornbluth and Blish were primarily writers. Merril was a writer and an anthologist. Kidd was a writer and an agent. Knight was a writer and an anthologist. As for Fred, he was and is an award-winning writer, an award-winning magazine editor, the editor of the first-ever series of original anthologies, and yes, even an agent.

So we see not only the inner workings of the Futurians, but the inner workings of the entire science fiction field through

Fred's experience as a writer, pulp editor, a digest editor, a collaborator with such diverse writers as Kornbluth and Jack Williamson, and a book editor. (And, when times got hard and he needed a little steady income, as the guy with the electric prod who "encourages" the winning racehorse to donate a urine specimen to make sure he's dope-free.)

And finally, totally secure as both a writer and editor, Fred explains how he developed his 4-pages-a-day practice, which he kept up for years, at home, on the road, everywhere. It doesn't seem like much, just four pages, but with no days off, that's a trio of 100,000-word novels and ten short stories every year.

It's through his eyes that we see the science fiction field evolve, from a quarter-of-a-cent a word hobby to the point where dozens of writers could actually make a living at it. There's a lot of humor in this volume, and a lot of history, and, because he is an honest man, what you'll mostly find is a lot of truth.

If you want to see how we got from where we were to where we are, told with wit and insight, this is the book for you. (And when I had to emcee a Fred Pohl Roast some years back, this book was all the source material I needed. Like I say: funny and honest.)

PHOSPHORESCENCE AND BEYOND

For *SFWA Handbook*

Back in the 1920s and 1930s, if you wrote science fiction and your name wasn't Wells or Burroughs, you wrote exclusively for the magazines.

By the 1950s there was a growing book market, and by sometime in the 1970s the dominant form of science fiction had probably become the novel rather than the short story. And that's the way things stood until the late 1990s: novelist or story writer, you sold to books and magazines, and that was the ball game.

But a lot can happen in a decade, and all those things science fiction had been predicting for years starting coming to pass.

By the late 1990s writers were being solicited by start-up electronic publishers, usually with a proposal that translated as "Give me your story (or book) for free today, and I'll make you rich tomorrow (or next week, or next year)." Not a lot of established writers were enamoured of such proposals, not a lot contributed their work, and not a lot of those early e-publications lasted out their initial year.

There were a few with special circumstances, of course. *Omni*, with *Penthouse's* millions behind it, went online and paid exceptionally generous (for this field) rates...but *Omni* also folded its tent in a few years. Another well-funded e-zine was *sci-fi.com*, also a handsome payer (and still around, though without any fiction in it), but it was essentially a loss leader for the wealthy Sci-Fi Channel, and hence another exception.

The first major success that did not rely upon other publications or venues for money or expertise was, strangely, not a publisher of new fiction at all, but rather a reprint house:

Fictionwise.com. They began with a small coterie of science fiction writers—Robert Silverberg, Nancy Kress, James Patrick Kelly, myself, a few others—and when they offered double the going rate for reprint fiction we felt like thieves in the night. We took the money and ran—but we slowed down precipitously after three months, when the first of their quarterly royalty reports was issued, and despite the front money we'd received most of us had earned royalties (and those stories have continued earning royalties—from 30% to 40%—for *years*.)

Why? The best bet is that there was so much free junk on the internet at the time that people were willing to pay for known commodities. Nine years later Fictionwise.com is still around, they're up to around four thousand authors now (including Stephen King, Tom Clancy, Dan Brown, and that whole crowd), and they've sold something like 100 billion words. Even some of the printzines saw the handwriting on the wall and have begun selling digital versions to Fictionwise.com and Kindle.

It still took awhile for the more competent entrepreneurs to move over to the internet and make a go of it, but eventually they did, and things began looking up, especially for short story writers. One by one the magazines had been dying—*Science Fiction Age, Marion Zimmer Bradley's Fantasy Magazine, Aboriginal SF*, the resurrected *Amazing*, the resurrected *Argosy*, others, and suddenly we were down to just the three traditional digests: *Asimov's, Analog* and *Fantasy & Science Fiction*. Even after Warren Lapine bought *Realms of Fantasy* and brought it back from the dead, there were only four magazines in print.

As much as the book field has changed, the world of the short story has changed even more radically in the intenet age. There are still only four printed magazines. The change has come on the internet, where there are 15 electronic magazines paying what SFWA (Science Fiction Writers of America) considers a professional word rate—and three of them, *Jim*

Baen's Universe, Subterranean Magazine, and *Clarkesworld*, pay more than any of the printed magazines and are attracting more major writers every day. *Jim Baen's Universe*, for its first three years, was paying 25 cents a word at the top, and its rock-bottom beginner's rate was a dime a word, still more than the top rate of tie digests. *Clarkesworld* pays a dime a word, and *Subterranean* pays at least that.

So who are the others? I'm reluctant to list them, since in the natural evolution of thing four or five may be dead by the time you read this (as will *Jim Baen's Universe*; more about that in a moment), but if they die, you can be sure an equal or greater number will take their place. So, as of Thanksgiving, 2009, these are the e-zines that are paying a nickel a word or more: *Subterranean, Clarkesworld, Jim Baen's Universe, Cosmos (Australian), Abyss & Apex, Beneath Ceaseless Skies, Brainharvesting, Cemetery Dance, Fantasy Magazine, Heliotrope, Flash Fiction Online, Futurismic, Orson Scott Card's Intergalactic Medicine Show, Shock Totem, Strange Horizons* and the newest entry, *Lightspeed*. Most keep all or almost all their stories from previous issues available, and since the standard e-contract calls for a one-year electronic exclusive (and allows the writer to sell reprints to print magazines and anthologies from the get-go), there is a plethora of stories available on the e-zines' sites, and it's growing almost weekly.

One of the problems facing the magazines is that the business model keeps changing. I know a little something about the model for closing-up-shop-in-April-of-2010 *Jim Baen's Universe*, because I co-edited it starting with its second year. And it was a hell of a magazine: it paid the top rates, it was running 200,000 words an issue, every story was illustrated, it was buying at least one first story an issue—and none of that mattered enough to keep the magazine in profit, because it was conceived as a rival to the digests—*those* were our competition, or so we thought, and all we had to do was pay more and print more words—and it turns out that the model was doomed from the first issue.

Why? Because we charged $30.00 a year for a six-issue subscription. A price just about equal to the digests, offering more words, more names, more everything…

…and for a couple of issues we did pretty well. We were the only e-zine paying pro rates. But then one day, after a year or so, we looked around, and there was *Subterranean* running John Scalzi and Joe Lansdale and Elizabeth Bear and myself in just about every issue, and it was *free*. There was *Clarkesworld*, with nowhere near as many words or stories, but paying more than the printzines, and *they* were free. And so was damned near every other professional-level e-zine. We had some money behind us, and we had a lot of talent in each issue, but the handwriting was on the wall: we simply couldn't charge $5.00 an issue when our competition—our *real* competition, the other e-zines—was giving it away for free.

As for other problems: I don't think *Jim Baen's Universe* or any e-zine has yet fully realized that we're in the electronic age. We don't *have* to run traditional art; we can have art that *moves*, as our first two covers did, or art that simulates three dimensions, art that actually *speaks* to the reader. We don't need to run print interviews, not in this era of podcasts and webcams; why not be face-to-face with your columnist or editor/ We didn't make sufficient (or in most cases, *any*) use of chat rooms and all the other methods of becoming interactive with our readership. (We will, of course; it's only a matter of time.

Anyway, we put out a hell of a magazine. The contents were right…but because of the phenomenal speed of change in the field, the business model was wrong.

I think the model for the immediate future will be for the better e-zines to pay *more* per word than the printzines—after all, they have no printing, shipping, or distribution expenses, most have just about no overhead, and they don't give bookstores a cut of the cover price. But the other half of the model is that they will charge nothing for reading it on their web page. The revenue will have to come from a sponsor, from ads (maybe trailers from upcoming movies, which they can do and the print media can't), from making P.O.D. copies and CD copies on demand and selling them piecemeal, and ultimately from the digital readers that have recently emerged.

Asimov's, for instance, found itself a little gold mine in the Kindle, a move that kicked them back into profitability. *Jim Baen's Universe* couldn't do that, because it was felt it would abrogate Baen Books' distribution agreement with Simon & Schuster, but you can bet that every future e-zine will make sure they can sell to Kindle, and the Sony Reader, and the Nook, and whatever other digital readers come along.

Now, while all this was going on, other people learned to use the internet too. Back in early 2006, luddite that I am, I did not even know the meaning of the word "podcast." Then one of the many podcast operations, *Escape Pod*, bought podcast rights to the five 2006 short story Hugo nominees, including mine. I didn't think much of it until a French producer, a man who understood English but couldn't get the magazine my story had appeared in, contacted me and offered me 75 times as much for a French television option as the $100.00 fee I'd received for the podcast rights. You can be sure *that* made me an instant podcast fan, and I began urging some of my friends to seek out podcasters as well.

(Two months later I sold a Hugo-winning story to a podcast. The magazine in which it had appeared had sold less than 17,000 copies, and it's reasonable to assume a few thousand buyers didn't read my story. After a couple of months I asked the podcaster how many people had listened to it. The answer: 54,000 thus far—and that was three years ago. Today you can only find the magazine in a few second-hand stores... but you can still go to the web page and order up the story, which strikes me as an excellent way to reach thousands of new fans who hadn't previously encountered my work, some of whom will eventually part with their money for my books.

And while we're on the subject, when they *do* buy my books, they don't have to just buy the hardcovers or the paperbacks. They don't even have to buy digital copies for the Kindle, or the Sony Reader, or the Nook. Walk into any bookstore, and the one section that gets bigger every month is the audio book section. And as I write this, the 900-pound gorilla in the audio field doesn't even make and distribute CDs for bookstores. It's Audible.com, it's been paying four figures per reprint novel, it bought a couple of hundred science fiction titles in 2009 and plans to buy even more in 2010, and all it sells are downloads through your computer. (Is it viable? Amazon.com thinks so; they bought it for $300 million last year, and have not expressed any regrets to date.)

So okay, there's audio CDs and audio downloads and podcasts and e-zines and e-reprints. We have to be nearing the end of it, right?

Nope. We're just *starting* to realize the potential of the digital age. The latest innovation—four companies are fighting it out as of this minute, so I can't really predict who will be around next year (but you can bet the farm that *someone* will be)—the latest innovation, as I say, is electronic delivery of digital books and stories to mobile media: i-phones and the like, not just here but in multiple languages and multiple continents. The ones duking it out for market share are worldwide organizations, so if you or your agent have been shut out of a certain country when trying to sell your foreign rights, here's another way to get in and establish a readership.

And you can bet that science fiction writers will evolve with the field. For a long time it was felt that if your story wasn't in one of the top three digests, or one of the two or three big-money anthologies of the year, you had no chance for the awards. That's no longer the case. The Nebula has already gone to electronic stories, and the Best Editor Hugo has gone to an editor of electronic stories. I don't believe an e-story has won the Hugo yet, but it's only a matter of time; I know I've had two e-stories nominated out of *Jim Baen's Universe*, and as more readers realize how many top writers are being bought away by the e-zines, I would anticipate a sea change in the voting patterns.

Me, I'm a dinosaur. My family bought the first television set on our block when I was 6 years old, so all this innovation is a little frightening—but I'm a dinosaur who is at least trying to evolve, and I think it is more of a necessity than a choice. I suspect the day is not too far off when a journeyman writer will make more money from media and platforms that didn't exist a generation ago than he will from the printed page.

Good thing? Bad thing? Actually, what it is is a science fiction thing.

MAKING IT

For *Writers of the Future*, Vol. 27

Writers of the Future has been turning out writers—by which I mean successful, bestselling, award-winning writers—for over a quarter of a century now. They've done it long enough and frequently enough that there's no longer any doubt that this program is not a fluke, that they really do know how to pick and train talent.

So let's examine it from the other side. Yes, they know their stuff. They build writers. But can they build *you* into one?

That leads to a plethora of questions. How do you make it as a writer? Do you start with short stories and build a reputation (and *can* you build one in these days of only a tiny handful of print magazines)? Do you start in an easier field (and *is* there any easy field)? Do you begin with novels? Non-fiction? Do you attend workshops and conventions, and start networking with other writers, or are they wastes of that rarest of a writer's commodities: time?

My answer isn't likely to thrill anyone, because what I'm going to do is quote Rudyard Kipling: There are nine and sixty ways, of constructing tribal lays, and each and every one of them is right.

Well, I'll qualify it to this extent: every approach is right for those who have proved it is right for them.

Eric Flint, a Writers of the Future winner, didn't start writing until his late 40s. Within two years he was living on the bestseller list, where you can still find him. Kevin J. Anderson, a long-time lecturer and judge at Writers of the Future, made the bestseller list originally by writing some outstanding *Star Wars* books, but he took that enormous audience with him and has been a bestseller ever since. Patrick Rothfuss won the contest, and found himself on the Hugo ballot and the best-seller list half a dozen years later with *The Name of the Wind*. Tim Powers and I, lecturers and judges here, don't live on the bestseller list—but we were the 2011 and 2012 Worldcon Guests of Honor.

People and careers differ. I sold my first article at the age of 15, my first story at 17, my first novel at 20. I had all the mechanical skills, but I lacked the maturity and ambition to apply myself and write anything award-worthy or even memorable, and it was another 18 years and a couple of hundred forgettable books written under pseudonyms before I moved over to science fiction and wrote anything of value, anything I was anxious to sign my name to. That was a few bestsellers and more than 100 awards and nominations ago, which just shows that we don't all develop at the same pace or in the same way.

And that holds for the Writers of the Future winners and finalists too. Look down the list at Nina Kiriki Hoffman, and Nick DiChario, and Dave Wolverton, and Karen Joy Fowler, and Robert Reed, and Jay Lake, and Tobias S. Buckell, and Stephen Baxter, and Amy Sterling Casil, and K. D. Wentworth, and R. Garcia y Robertson, and Dean Wesley Smith, and all the others. Each got to where he or she is by a different route, some faster than others.

But they have certain things in common. We all do.

First, there's a love of writing. A lot of writers hate writing and love having written. Not the ones who make it. They love words, they love pushing nouns up against verbs and seeing the results, they love creating their very own worlds and then inviting you into them.

Second, there's the constant study of the field. There are certain categories of fiction that require almost no preparation. Others, like the detective story, ask you to create a hero, and then run him through his paces book after book after book. Not science fiction. With all time and space at the author's disposal, about the only thing he *can't* do is tell the same story over and over. He can experiment, he can innovate, he can and must create; what he cannot do is repeat, not only himself but what has gone before, which is why he must be well-read in the field and stay abreast of what's going on.

Third, there's talent, and the ability to get the reader emotionally involved with the characters and the stories. The successful author must make the reader (I'll write it in caps so no one can miss it) FEEL, must make him love or hate or fear or laugh, or, in short, *react*. If he makes him think, as our progenitors Hugo Gernsback (creator of the field) and John Campell (the first great editor) believed was science fiction's mission, so much the better and the author has written a better story for it. But if the readerr can't respond emotionally, then the author has written a fictionalized polemic or scientific crossword puzzle.

And there's one more essential quality, which I will define as a fire in the belly, by which I mean an unwillingness to get discouraged or accept rejection. (A beginner asked me recently if I still get rejected. The answer was yes, every year or two it still happens. She then asked me my reaction. I said it hadn't changed in half a century. It was, spoken so softly only I can hear it: "To hell with you, fella [or Lady]. I'm taking it to you competitor, he'll buy it, and when it wins the Hugo or the Nebula or sells to Hollywood I'll get richer and more famous, so will my editor, and you, pal, are going to be standing on the unemployment line when word gets out.")

Has it ever happened? I did win an award with a rejected story some years back. I don't think anyone ever got fired for rejecting me. But the point is that you—like every writer I named—have to believe in yourself more than you believe in an editor whose tastes and priorities are different. (By the same token, never look at a story and say, "Oh, there's no sense sending this one to Editor A. It's just not his kind of story." Maybe it isn't, but it's not your function to do his job for him. Let *him* decide whether or not to buy it—and remember: he can't buy what he never sees.)

Is there more?

Sure. In this business, there's always more.

I mentioned networking before. The writer with the hunger in the belly gets involved in that early on. He exchanges market information with his peers—and most anthologies are by invitation only, which means he finds out who the editors are and makes sure they know who *he* is. He learns of new markets, and in this day of the internet, they change almost weekly. True, there are only four print magazines, where in 1954 there were 56…but as I write these words (and it's likely to change by the weekend) there are 18 electronic science fiction magazines paying what SFWA—the Science Fiction Writers of America—considers to be a professional rate. And if you don't network, you don't learn about them. You network to find out which conventions you should go to, which ones have the editors you want to meet and the writers you want to befriend.

From the outside it may seem like the publishing world is imploding, as bookstore chains are in big trouble, and publishers are losing more writers every month to the internet, where they have discovered that 70% is a nicer royalty rate than 6% or 10%. But from the inside, there have rarely been so many opportunities. There's traditional publishing, of course. And there are more small and medium presses every year, a handful of which pay rates comparable to the New York houses. And there's self-publishing on the web, And there's pocasting. And there's suddenly tons of money to be made in audio sales. And as quickly as the writer learns what he has to know about all these outlets, of course there will be more. And there'll be improvements and innovations on what we have right now: e-books with animated covers and background music and hypertext, video podcasts, and more.

Who will take advantage of all these opportunities? The same writers who have those four traits I mentioned before: a love of writing, a passionate interest in the field, talent, and (perhaps most important, as I've seen many talented beginners just fade away) that blazing fire in the belly.

The Writers of the Future contestants in this book have all had ample opportunity to get down on themselves, to give up and walk away. Not one of them has quit. Every one of them loves writing, constantly studies the field they're writing in, has enough talent to appear in this book, and has that fire in the belly that all but guarantees this is far from the last you're going to hear from each of them.